COAL BLACK LIES

Appalachian Novels

Mercy's Rain

Liar's Winter

Coal Black Lies

"Masterfully written, evocative and atmospheric, *Coal Black Lies* is a story of pain, love, hope salvaged from grief, and the triumph of redemption. Filled with main characters as human, hurting, and hopeful as the rest of us, read it for the story and come away inspired."

—Tosca Lee, *New York Times* best-selling author

"Whew! I highly recommend that you make sure you can read this in one sitting. There's so much I loved about this book, from precious Aughtie to the heroes who fought for those who couldn't fight for themselves. This story is a beautiful example of how God can use ordinary people to do the extraordinary. Looking forward to the next book."

—Lynette Eason, best-selling and award-winning author

"I've never been to Appalachia, but Sproles makes the impoverished coal miners come alive in this third (and best) of her Appalachian novels. It's a story about greed, murder, and revenge. It's also the story of a mentally challenged child who brings forgiveness and grace into all the lives on Barton Mountain. Each time I read Sproles, I think, This is how Christian fiction ought to read."

—Cecil Murphey, best-selling author, coauthor, or ghostwriter of 140 books

"Breathtaking. Heart stopping. Soul searching. Redemptive. *Coal Black Lies* draws you in from the opening line and doesn't let go, even when you've reached the stunning conclusion. I'll be thinking about this story for years. Cindy Sproles transported me not only into a different culture but into transformative reflection on my own life story. This is simply a masterpiece."

—Lori Stanley Roeleveld, speaker, coach, and award-winning author of *Graceful Influence*

"The dialogue. Whoa. Cindy Sproles had me at 'No, it ain't bad . . . It's just a sign you've moved on. You ain't stagnant in your heart.' *Coal Black Lies* isn't just a story, it's an experience, a pull-up-a-chair, sit-awhile, and take-a-listen experience. Every page turn reveals another gut-level layer of life in the Appalachians. Unexpected loss. Unexpected discoveries. Unexpected deception. And hope . . . always hope. Make room on your shelf—this is a keeper."

—Linda Goldfarb, award-winning author, podcaster, and actress

"To be asked to endorse *Coal Black Lies* was a true honor. I've read other books by Cindy Sproles and have been touched and often changed by the words she's penned. Her stories have depths that make you think, and the pages of *Coal Black Lies* are no exception. Keep tissues nearby, and be prepared to be challenged—you've been warned!"

—Tammy Karasek, speaker and author of *Launch That Book*

An Appalachian Novel

COAL BLACK LIES

CINDY K. SPROLES

Coal Black Lies: An Appalachian Novel

Published by Kregel Publications, a division of Kregel Inc., 2450 Oak Industrial Dr. NE, Grand Rapids, MI 49505. www .kregel.com.

Cindy K. Sproles is represented by and *Coal Black Lies* is published in association with The Steve Laube Agency, LLC www .stevelaube.com.

Scripture quotations are from the King James Version.

Library of Congress Cataloging-in-Publication Data
Name: Sproles, Cindy, author.
Title: Coal black lies : an Appalachian novel / Cindy K. Sproles.
Description: Grand Rapids, MI: Kregel Publications, 2024.
Identifiers: LCCN 2024004504 (print) | LCCN 2024004505 (ebook)
Subjects: LCGFT: Christian fiction. | Novels.
Classification: LCC PS3619.P775 C63 2024 (print) | LCC PS3619.P775 (ebook) | DDC 813/.6—dc23/eng/20240207
LC record available at https://lccn.loc.gov/2024004504
LC ebook record available at https://lccn.loc.gov/2024004505

ISBN 978-0-8254-4823-2, print
ISBN 978-0-8254-7125-4, epub
ISBN 978-0-8254-7124-7, Kindle

Printed in the United States of America
24 25 26 27 28 29 30 31 32 33 / 5 4 3 2 1

Dedicated to Chase Smothers, Casey Eckert, and Kaitlyn Moffitt. Three who know the sting of disabilities, as well as the victories.

Them little lies we tell ourself come on us right quick. They don't waste no time catchin' up to us either, and the consequence ain't the least bit afraid to rain down over us. We all lie. Try to cover 'em, and worst yet, pay the price for conjuring them.

—Joshua Morgan

One

Barton Mountain, Kentucky, 1899

I stood rubbing the cool gun barrel over the stubble on my jaw. The metal slipped over my skin like the turn of a well-oiled wheel. An early summer breeze snagged the barn door and whammed it against the outside wall of the barn. It was another harsh reminder of the slam of the coffin door over our girl. I pondered how Raney'd feel if she knew what I was planning. *She'd be better off. She's a strong woman. Good Lord knows she's stronger than me. I'm just Joshua Morgan, the man who killed his daughter.*

I loved Raney enough to put her outa my misery. She didn't deserve a guilty husband.

I pushed my back against the splintered slats of the barn. The early morning sun seeped through the cracks and drew shadows of bars on the ground. That's how I felt—jailed by the memories. Raney'd be hurt. Naw, once the shock wore off, she'd be madder than a hound that missed the coon, but Raney . . . she'd be fine. Summer was here. The early rye was up. She'd manage.

The hammer of my gun clicked into place. My hand quivered. A coward could never pull the trigger. This was more than I could take. The last five years had dragged past, and I'd tried to put my daughter's death behind me with all my soul. Then watching Manny and Hettie bury their girl was the final straw. Another youngin. Barton's scrip wouldn't pay a doctor in Cumberland. Another innocent child died at the hands of the Bartons. Another murder thanks to the stronghold of the Bartons' power, control, and greed.

No matter. The memory still haunted me like the cold whisper of the wind seeping through the barn slats. Slats I shoulda fixed long ago . . .

I dropped the gun to my side. Once a coward, always a coward. I didn't have it in me to pull the trigger.

Our Anna'd been just a child. Too young for the hand of death to swoop in and steal her away. Still, after five years I walked the path every week to visit my girl's grave—like that'd bring her back. Like she even cared. *Dust from whence she came and dust she shall return.*

My mind went back to a few weeks ago when Raney and me made our way to Anna's grave. A chill run down my spine every time I see her tombstone. It was enough to grieve with my guilt, but watching Raney grieve all those years had doubled the pain.

"Joshua, tears don't fall no more. Is that bad?" Raney had asked as she pulled a handful of grass from around the stone marker.

I'd eyed my wife as she scratched away the ivy from our girl's tombstone. She pulled a fist of flowers to her nose and took in the sweet scent of lavender. I guessed she'd forgiven me, but things was never the same betwixt us after Anna died. Before, Raney'd always talked things over with me, but after Anna died, she pulled away from me, quit talkin'. She walked alone around the farm lookin' to be in deep thought instead of doin' her chores. It was like she was as dead as our Anna.

"No, it ain't bad," I said, surprised she'd asked. "It's just a sign you've moved on. You ain't stagnant in your heart."

I guess I'd hoped Raney had moved on, or at least the best I could see from her. Movin' on didn't mean there wasn't no sadness though. And I suspect it didn't really mean lettin' go either. Neither of us could loosen our grip on Anna's soul.

I reckon there'll always be a hole burrowed out in our hearts, but it wasn't the grief eating me alive. It was the guilt, and I couldn't take it no more. It was like a fresh burn—stinging and stinging. Never easing, no matter how hard I blew at the burn.

I blinked away the tears. Had her death really been my fault? I wasn't sure anymore.

Nobody leaves the coal mines. Nobody. The Company Store owns you. They pay you in a worthless scrip, work you until you can't stand, and toss you out to die when you get the cough. And a worthless pay meant a body had to keep going to the Company Store and asking for money against their pay just so you could buy the necessities your family needed. Worst yet, owing the store meant a man couldn't ever quit his job 'cause that scrip weren't no good anywhere but the Company Store. The Bartons had you over a barrel, and you worked until you paid the debt. If your debt ain't paid . . . well, they come after you and take what little you do have. My debt was owed, and I was looking for a way out from under it—sooner than later.

When the Barton boys had stormed off the mountain and tore across the lower field, they didn't care what or who was in the path.

Them horses sounded like thunder comin' through the valley. Raney had looked up from the porch and squalled, "Anna!"

I took out from the barn to get our girl outa the way. She was pickin' daisies on the lower side by the rye field. My feet felt like they had big rocks tied to them. The harder I tried to run, the heavier the rocks grew. I couldn't reach her before them. They plowed over her like a clod of dirt in the cornfield.

There wasn't time to scream before she'd twisted up under those horse hooves and spit out broken and busted.

I slung my head from side to side tryin' to shake the memory. There wasn't no getting rid of the ghosts in my mind, and the memories was killin' me—sucking the life outa me. Pullin' the trigger surely wouldn't be so hard. Put an end to the agony. Another child's death, my friend's youngin, thanks to the Bartons, made the weight too much to bear. "I'm sorry, Raney. Sorry, Anna. I'm sorry. I'm a coward and a failure." I was sorry it had happened. Sorry I'd caused it, and even more—I was a pathetic excuse for a man.

I brushed the barrel over my lips and slipped it into my mouth. The taste of singed metal drew my mouth tight. Like I'd bit into a raw persimmon. I leaned one hand against the barn door to keep my knees from bucklin'. My finger rubbed across the rough edge of the doorframe, and a coin dropped at my feet. Anna's coin. The penny we'd placed there so long ago.

I recalled when my little girl and me had talked. "Papa, you remember the day Reverend Posey give me that penny? You 'member?"

"I remember." I pushed her long blond curls away from her cheek. Anna took my hand, pried open my fist, and laid that coin in my palm.

"It's our good luck charm. You keep it safe." She kissed the bristly whiskers that lined my jaw. "Keep it safe, Papa. That way you will always remember there is hope."

"There is always hope, ain't there?" I kissed her head. "I'll put it right here on the barn doorframe. Snug as a bug in a rug."

I'd slipped the coin onto the flat edge of the doorframe years earlier. And there it had stayed. Outa sight and safe—until now. A chill climbed my spine. The gun slipped from my mouth. I dropped to my knees, scooped the penny into my hand, and then tossed the gun into the hay. Takin' my life only meant a temporary fix. I'd still have to face my Maker. Then what?

Sobs poured from my soul. And then I coulda swore I heard her whisper.

There's always hope, Papa.

I twisted that coin between my fingers and pulled it to my chest. It's funny how a body's memories can twist reality. I ain't never believed in ghosts. I still don't, but something made that coin drop at my feet. And just in the nick of time. Be it the ghost of my child or the hand of the good Lord. I supposed that my dead daughter saved my life—even when I couldn't save hers.

"Hate will eat you from the inside out." That's what my momma used to tell me. Lord bless her soul. She did her best to teach me the good Lord's will was not always what we wanted. Momma ground in the love of the Lord, but right now, I was findin' loving Him hard. Hate teetered on the edge of every belief I knew. My blame was aimed upward.

I shook the hay from my trousers, and my knees went to shaking. I didn't know what scared me most—the coin falling at my feet or the fact I'd gained the courage to put that gun in my mouth. It took more guts to pull the trigger than I could muster and even more guts to keep on living. I was ashamed the thought of taking my own life had even crossed my mind. Still, the lies I spoke to myself about me I believed.

I hated Barton, and I hated the guilt that followed me. I reckon the two mixed together was a potion for disaster. The coin pressed tight in my palm. Opening my fist, I stared at the piece of money. *How'd this penny show up now? Divine intervention? An angel? A ghost?* I'd bumped that doorframe with tools more times than I could count—yet it had never dropped. Till today. Now. Right at this minute, a broken man was saved. Funny at the twists of life.

I dropped the coin at my side. It sank into the fine dirt of the barn floor. Memories the money held took my breath, and I knew I had a choice to make. Pick up the penny and cherish the fact my girl saved my life, or let the cobwebs cover it and go on livin' like a dead man. This way of life was too much. Too hard. Too . . . sad. My girl was a joy. Would she want this for me? For her mother?

I drew a circle in the dirt around the coin. I couldn't make my fingers grasp ahold and pick it up. Leave it lay and drown in self-pity or take hold and move ahead? *Make a decision.* Grasping it between my forefinger and thumb, I blew away the dust. I held it up and eyed the coin, then rubbed it on my shirtsleeve.

"Anna, I'm sorry. Can you forgive me?" I rolled it between my fingers. It come to me that the memory of that day had halted my livin'. Truth be known, it did the same for Raney. The few times she'd said anything about it, she'd tried to make me feel better, saying that Anna's death was an accident. But I knew better. I could see it in my wife's eyes. Her pain. How she only tolerated the sight of me. The blame showed in her stare. I knew in my heart she hated me to some extent.

How could she not? It was my fault our youngin was dead. I'd been the one to challenge the Bartons to a fight I couldn't win. After a good amount of time had passed, I'd hoped that Raney would come around. I used to love wakin' up in the morning to hear her singin' some sweet song. Raney hummed like I whistled—without even thinking about it. The music left Raney's soul when Anna died, and her mouth grew parched and tight. She rarely spoke unless she had to, and she'd smile from time to time. But when she turned away, the smile left, and her face returned to pinched and painful. Raney never recovered, and I could never give her another child—the one thing she lived to have.

I wanted my life back. I wanted my wife back, and I wanted my daughter. If a body could have a wish, I'd wish that day away.

All me and Raney had done was bury the pain. Instead of us grieving together, we hid the pain deep to protect each other. It was senseless because we still wallowed in the sadness—only alone. When you suffer alone, things fall apart. You draw away from one another, and that's what we'd done. We'd grown apart instead of looking to each other for comfort.

I slid the coin between my fingers. The longer I held it in my hand, the more determined I was to make a change.

"It ends today, Anna. I'm gonna do my best to let this guilt go."

There was something freein' about making a decision. And I chose to live.

Two

I'd pondered putting that gun in my mouth for weeks. Momma used to say regret is an ugly bedfellow, and I couldn't remember the times I'd quoted that remark to others. Still, she was right. I regretted every thought of puttin' an end to things, but that was all I could do—ponder. Until today. I was reminded of that coin every time I walked past the barn door. It was a good thing work around the barn never seemed to end. I stayed busy.

The leather tack needed to be oiled, so I took down a half-empty lard can from the shelf and commenced to grease it up. I caught a brief sound in the breeze—the cry of a child. I cocked my head. There it was again—that sound. I couldn't figure out if it was an echo in the wind or if I really heard something. Either way I'd heard the sound off and on for several days. Flippin' the leather reins over my shoulder, I wiped my hands clean of the lard and leaned out the barn. Listened. Nothin' but rye swaying back and forth in the breeze and the crow's caw. I shook my head. It was nothin'. My hat caught in the morning breeze and flew toward the rye field. I chased it a bit before I snagged and planted it back on my head. Maybe what I heard was the wind singin' around the barn. It would whine through the cracks in the slats when the wind caught it just so. I shook my head. It wouldn't surprise me if I was losin' what little sense I had left.

Makin' my way back into the barn, I laid them reins down on the wooden table and wrapped the rag tight around my index finger. I dipped it in the lard and then rubbed the greasy mess into the leather. It wasn't something I enjoyed doing, but a necessity on the farm to keep the tack soft and workable for the horses. Leather was too expensive to let it dry and crack, so I spent a few hours at the mindless task.

"La laa maa ma." The sound caught my ear again. This time, for the first time, it sounded like the faint voice of a child. Anna had weighed heavy on my mind all week, and I pushed the sounds off as my mind playing tricks on me. I heard the voice of a youngin, but I didn't see a thing. Should I mention this to Raney? She was already frail. She'd probably think I was going stark raving mad. Still, I was thinking of our child. Grievin' her. Try as I might to let go, I was still holding on to the guilt that took her.

The breeze puffed through the barn, grabbing ahold of the rye stalks on the ground. It twisted them into a circle before carrying them out of the barn and into the field. I walked to the barn door again and gazed out over the rye to the place we'd buried our baby. A little head bobbed over the edge of Anna's gravestone, and my heart stopped. I did a double take. My knees grew weak. I didn't believe in ghosts, but I saw a girl. Clear as a bell.

"Anna?" I whispered. I wasn't sure I wanted to leave the barn. That'd mean I believed what my eyes showed me, and I know there ain't no such thing as ghosts. Though I'd heard tales from the miners about seein' dead workers roaming the mine shafts, it was just hooey. That's what it was. Still, I couldn't stop my feet or my curiosity. My heart went to racin', and as I started through the barn door, I snatched my shotgun and cocked it just in case something went awry.

I walked to the edge of the barn and surveyed the fields. Nothing. A deer stood in the brush just at the edge of a stand of trees. Shoving the butt of my shotgun under my arm, I dug into my pocket for the small leather tobacco pouch. Unlacing it, I squeezed two fingers into the bag and pulled out a pinch of tobacco. I never much liked the taste of the mix, but George Hogan ground up teaberry leaves and added them into his mix. It give a bitter leaf a tender, sweet taste. My lip pooched to one side, and my mouth filled with saliva. I spit, and when I looked up, a form floated in the distance. Ghostly-like. Moving up and down along the tree line. My eyes had to be playing tricks on me.

A child. Dirty. Half-dressed. My rifle slid from under my arm. It was pure luck it didn't fire when it hit the ground. I balled my fists and rubbed both eyes. My mind had just gone by the wayside. *This ain't real. It ain't.* When I opened my eyes, she was gone. She couldn't vanish that quickly. Then, sure as shootin', there was that little head again. Her hair knotted and hanging strung around her face and shoulders. The tail of her nightshirt tossed in the breeze. Her hand climbed up her face and shoved the strands of hair to one side.

I fell against the barn, unsure if what I saw was real. I longed to see my girl. Wanted to hold her on my lap and bounce her just to hear her giggle, but this was about more than I could take.

I squinted hard and focused on the headstone across the field. I was sure I could see movement. Of course I saw movement. I saw her swipe her hair. This was me trying to convince myself what I saw was real. She popped up like a rabbit outa its hole. That did it. I picked up my gun and leaned it against the barn, then snagged an apple outa the barrel by the trough. Maybe she'd take an apple as a lure if it *was* a child. If it wasn't, then I'd eat the apple. She had to be hungry. If she was real, I'd been seeing her off and on for days. If she wasn't, I was losin' my mind.

I eased through the waist-high rye, pushing a path across the field. Fear took hold of me, and I shook. What if this was an angel? Or worse, what if I was truly losing my mind?

It was like a tease—that child's head come up and over Anna's gravestone again. This time I acted on what I saw.

The child climbed onto the tombstone and dangled her bare feet. I stopped. Waited. Scaring her was the last thing I wanted to do. *Where did this youngin come from? Is she alone?* I eased up right slow. She could have been a child from the camps, makin' her way down to play in the field of daisies where my own girl had died. But I got a good look at her, and something wasn't right. I inched closer for a better look. Her face showed she wasn't right. I stopped just short of her.

I pulled my knife from the sheath in my boot and ran it around the apple, scoring it so it would split in half.

Easin' up real slow, I extended my hand with the apple. "Hey there, little girl."

She cocked her head. A sideways grin come across her face, and her hand went up. Her short, pudgy fingers spread open, and her palm twisted back and forth on her wrist as she waved. She seemed right sweet. Innocent. And oddly content.

I curled my finger toward her and motioned her to me. She eyed me and slipped one foot over the stone, straddling it. *Don't you bolt and run.*

"Easy does it. It's alright."

She froze and covered her face like she thought I couldn't see her behind them dirty hands.

"It's alright, little one." I slipped up to her and squatted down. "I ain't gonna hurt you. My name is Joshua. Joshua Morgan." I tapped my chest gently with one finger, then stretched my hand toward her. "You got a name?"

She stared, never saying a word.

She had no other clothes, no shoes, just one sock balled up in her left hand, her nightshirt, and her bloomers. I reckon she was about six or so. Coulda been a hair older. The girl had dirt caked along her upper lip like old man Thompson's mustache. I moved like I was stalkin' a squirrel. I spit my chaw on the ground, cut a slice of apple, and eased it into my mouth, then cut another piece. The sweetish-sour taste of the green apple mixed with the leftover amber juice stung my jaws and made my mouth water. I felt like Eve in the Good Book, tempting the child with the fruit.

"You hungry? You like apple?"

The girl reached toward my hand, snatched the slice, and then leaned back.

I reckon since she took the apple, I knew for sure. She was real.

"What's you got all over your face?"

She swiped her arm across her cheek.

I reached the apple slice toward her. "Want another bite?"

I'd heard her in the distance. Thought I'd got a glimpse. Convinced myself I was nuttier than one of Raney's fruitcakes, but now . . . here she was. Skin on bone—real. But where'd she come from? None of my neighbors, short of Manny's boys, had youngins within a two-mile stretch.

The girl snatched the slice of apple from my hand and giggled.

The slap of Raney's broom against a rug echoed across the field as she hung it to beat out the dirt. Turning, I waved my arms in the air to get her attention without scaring the youngin. I jumped up a couple of times and waved harder, and when I looked behind me, the child had hopped off the headstone and was doin' the same thing.

"You mockin' me?" I smiled at the girl. She reached her hand and wiggled her fingers. A grunt seeped from her lips as she pointed at the apple.

"You want another slice?"

Her head bobbed up and down, and I sliced her another piece. I knelt and cut the rest of the apple into pieces. She scooped them from my palm and then sat down, sinking deep into the waist-high grass.

"Where's your momma? You ain't surely here by yourself?" I walked behind Anna's tombstone and into the edge of the woods. "Anybody with you?" *Where on earth was her momma?* Makin' decisions hadn't been my strong suit up until I decided to live. That was a good decision, but now, right in front of me, stood another to be made—leave the youngin on her own, or help her. There'd be consequences to both.

THREE

"YOU STAY HERE, and let me see if I can find your momma." I wagged my finger at her from the stand of trees. "Don't move. I'm goin' a little deeper in the woods—see if I can find your momma."

The child sat leaning against Anna's tombstone, crunching on the apple. I searched a good distance, fighting thorns in a thicket several hundred feet away. I couldn't go too far for fear that the youngin would disappear again. There was nothing. Nothing at all. Surely to goodness this little one hadn't wandered from the coal camps. That was a good three miles up the mountain.

A shot rang out in the woods. I took out in a run to see if someone was shootin' at the girl or me. I rounded some bushes and stumbled over a man in the grass. "Manny? What in tarnation are you doin' laid out in the grass? Are you hurt? You been shot?"

"I'm fine," Manny grumbled. He lay propped on his elbows, rifle resting on his shoulder and pointed toward the foot of the mountain. A buck darted toward the bush.

"I didn't expect you out so soon after losin' little Mary," I said.

"That *was* our supper. I reckon somebody spooked the animal right as I took my shot," Manny snapped. "And just cause my youngin died don't mean I stop feedin' my family. I got a wife and two other children to tend. I didn't think you'd mind if I inched over on your woods to hunt. So much for our supper."

"You scared the devil outa me," I said.

Manny stood and dusted the dirt from his clothes. "Sorry. What brings you out here? I'm surprised to see you down this far, knowin' Anna's grave and all being here."

I raised my hand and shushed him. “I don’t usually.” I pointed in the direction of Anna’s headstone. “Through the woods, just a ways back. I saw a youngin over there.” I headed toward where I’d seen the girl. Manny slipped his gun over his shoulder and followed. The girl was gone.

“She was right here!” I said.

I ran to the front of the grave, only to find bits of apple peel. “At least I know she was real. A ghost don’t leave apple peels,” I muttered under my breath. This youngin could vanish faster than a coyote on a rabbit’s rear.

Manny eyed me. “There ain’t no girl, Joshua.” He patted my shoulder. “I think I see our Mary from time to time. Guess when you lose a youngin, you never really lose sight of them. It’ll be alright.” He bumped me gently. “Y’all come see us,” Manny mumbled, and he walked back into the woods toward his homestead. I stood motionless. *She was just there.*

Every step I took huntin’ that youngin, I asked myself if I was crazier than a fritter. How could I lose a child that quick? But when the summer breeze caught the rye and pressed its fluffy head downward, there she was. Teetering from side to side and heading toward the house. *Lordy mercy—Raney!*

I ain’t rightly sure why I broke into a run. Reckon it was memories I was runnin’ from. Maybe it was a tinge of guilt. Fear someone might think I’d took a child when I hadn’t. But I run past that child, hollering at Raney. I glanced over my shoulder to see if she was following me, but what I saw was a mess about to happen.

I ran hard toward the house. I needed to warn Raney, not let her be took back. She had pulled the rug she’d been beatin’ off the clothesline and was wrestlin’ it to the porch. She’d think I’d lost my ever-loving mind.

I had no intention to get in somebody else’s business, but the circumstance forced my hand. That little youngin, poor as dirt, had twisted at my heart. She didn’t look right, and she didn’t talk neither. The youngin cooed and grunted. Still, she had to belong to someone—she was someone else’s business.

Raney looked up from her rug and shaded her eyes with her hand. I come running, waving at her and shoutin’ for her to come quick. I didn’t find a soul with that youngin. Course I couldn’t just pick her up and drag her home, but the minute she saw Raney across the field, her arms had reached out, and I guessed she decided that was where she needed to be. I reckoned I was about to stomp into a hot pile of somebody else's business and splatter it like manure. But helping that little girl was the right thing to do.

"Raney! Raney, honey." My voice broke as I tore across that field. I was in no real shape to run. Bad lungs—a result of working the mines. Nevertheless, I took out across the field as hard as I could go. I'd run a good distance when I looked over my shoulder, and that girl was right behind me. "Raney," I shouted. A cough raised from my chest as I spit out the words. "Raney!"

Raney met me, takin' hold of my shoulders to help me balance. I stretched my arm and pointed behind me. There come that ragamuffin of a youngin. She carried a slice of apple in one hand and a grin like a cat that had just eat the bird.

Raney stood starin' at the child coming across the field. "Anna?" she whispered.

"No, it ain't Anna. I thought the same thing as you. A ghost of our girl, but I think this youngin has been out by the grave for days." I coughed, trying to catch a breath.

"Days? Why didn't you say something?"

"I . . . I . . . I thought I was seein' things. She'd be there one second and gone before I could get to her. I . . ." I stopped, and the child run past me.

Raney knelt to the ground, and the youngin stretched out her arms, wrapping them tight around Raney's neck. She pulled the child onto her hip and stood.

"Lordy mercy. She's a mess. Look at her." Her legs stretched to Raney's knees.

The girl tightened her arms around Raney's neck and never made a peep. It was like she knew we had good hearts. Her dirty fingers looped together under Raney's hair.

I stood speechless as the girl hung on Raney like a baby possum to its momma. I shrugged and searched for the words to explain.

"I kept hearin' something out in the field. I . . . I . . . thought she was a ghost. One minute she was there. The next she was gone." I rubbed my face with my handkerchief. "I thought I was losing my mind. You know how Anna weighs on my mind, and I . . ." My mouth run faster than my legs had coming across the field. "The child finally come out where I could see she was real and not in my mind."

Tears welled in Raney's eyes, and her arms inched tighter around the little girl. She buried her face in the child's shoulder and hugged her, rockin' back and forth.

"Lord have mercy. Joshua Morgan, who is she?"

"Child needs help." I tore up on the porch and went to pacin'.

"Where did you get her from?" Raney asked.

"I didn't *get* her! Let's be clear about that. She was out at Anna's . . ." I couldn't bring myself to say *grave*. "Down in the lower field," I snapped. "I told you. I thought I was seein' things. One second she was there, the next not, and I didn't bring her home. When she saw you beating that rug, she headed this way. She saw you across the field. I tried to get here first to warn you. The youngin needs help." I huffed.

Raney eyed the ground, ponderin' what I'd said. After a minute, she nodded her approval. The girl's thick legs dangled against Raney's thigh. She propped the little one on the table and swiped her stringy hair to one side.

"You believe what I'm telling you, don't you?"

Raney pressed her hand against my cheek, something she'd not done in ages. A tender touch at that. She smiled an old familiar smile. It was like seeing the sun rise after days of rain. At times, Raney was that different.

"I believe you. And I'm sorry for accusing you. I know better," she said.

I took in a breath and sighed. "Child is nasty."

"No clothes worth a penny." Raney loosened the girl's hand that held a dirty sock.

For a minute I drifted off, thinkin' of Anna's penny—the one that saved me.

"Have mercy." Raney spit on the tail of her skirt and wiped around the child's mouth. "Is that coal dust or dirt?" Raney pressed open the girl's lips and looked at her gums. On the mountain even the dirt held a black color from the coal.

"Joshua, this baby looks like she's been eatin' coal dust. I reckon that'd make her sicker than a dog. She must be starving to death."

"She didn't have no trouble eatin' that apple I gave her."

I was never know'd for my smarts, but I did work the mines on the mountain for the better part of ten years. I know what the black dust does to your lungs. I know how it is to open my lunch pail and eat with the coat of dust that hangs in the air.

I know the taste and how it dries your mouth and makes your tongue feel thick and your lips draw tight. And if this here youngin was wallowing in coal dust, there was only one place she could have come from—Barton's mining camp.

"Draw me a pail of water. Pour it in the pot over the fire, and don't bring that water in until it's tempered. It oughta be warm to the touch. And use your elbow to test it." Raney barked orders like a general. She stood that youngin on the outside table and gave her the once-over. She's a good momma . . . always was. Still was. For a short time, a remnant of the old Raney returned. I reckon mothering ain't something a woman forgets. It's part of them. Their little ones might grow up and marry. They might die like our Anna. But being a momma ain't something a woman just up and forgets.

Seeing her dote over that little girl brought back memories—sweet memories. They overtook the horrible ones. I was happy to obey every command just to see her back. My wife . . . I thought I'd lost her too.

I stoked the fire outside under the laundry pot and heated water while Raney grabbed a big washin' bucket from the porch and stood the girl in it. She soaked a rag from the wash pail and pressed one finger against that youngin's jaw, forcing her clenched mouth to open.

"She's so nasty. We need to try and rinse her out here. That warm water ready?" Raney dipped a rag in the bucket a second time and tried to wash a layer of soot off the child.

"Joshua, she's a purty little thing. I believe she's got a red tint to her hair. I'll need that lye soap to cut the soot."

I poured up a pan of warm water from the heatin' pot.

Raney carried the youngin into the cabin and readied her to bathe. "It'll take two or three washings to get her clean now that we got her rinsed. Keep heating water."

That's when we really took notice that this girl was one of them "sick children." You hear about 'em. Eyes shaped like almonds, forehead wide, mouth small, round face, thick tongue. Chubby and odd little fingers, pudgy legs and feet. Not right bright. She was the kind folks kept locked up outa sight. The ones they was either afraid of or ashamed of.

Raney didn't have to say a word. It was obvious the child was abandoned. It was up to us to make things right.

"Can she talk?" Raney asked.

The youngin sat on the edge of the table, legs danglin'. Raney rolled the lye soap in her rag and rubbed it hard against the girl's legs to scrub the soot.

"Don't reckon I can tell yet. She ain't uttered a word. Just hummed and ate every bite of apple I gave her."

"Get me one of your shirts off the line." Raney stood the girl in her big laundry tub and poured water over the child's head, soaking her, clothes and all.

Beads of water stood on her eyelashes like the dew waiting to fall from trees. Soot streamed in streaks down her skin.

"If I can just get this youngin wet, then we can use the warm water to scrub the soot."

I offered them some privacy whilst Raney stripped her naked. I could hear them wet, nasty clothes make a peelin' sound as Raney pulled them away from the girl's tender skin. I walked to the clothesline and pulled down a shirt. Only had three. Wasn't much choice, but I was happy to give one to the youngin. It was certainly more than what she had.

I didn't know that girl from Adam, but there was something familiar about her. Something special. I tossed the shirt over my shoulder and picked up a pot holder Raney kept by the firepit. I rolled up my sleeve and touched my elbow to the steeping water. Perfect.

"More water's ready, Raney." The muscle in my arm ached as I lugged the cast-iron pot of water onto the porch. Just as I reached the door, I heard Raney singing.

The music had returned.

FOUR

"YES, JESUS LOVES me. Yes, Jesus loves me. The Bible tells me so."

I sucked in a deep breath as memories of Anna flooded back. The taste of that gun barrel that drawed my mouth tight resurrected. I reckon the good Lord has His reasons for takin' a life, especially a child, but I ain't good with that. The thoughts of me even considering taking my own life made my stomach turn. I thought I'd vomit.

I carried that heavy pot of water until my legs turned to mush, and I let the pot thud to the porch.

Raney pulled open the door. "Haul that water in here so I can scrub this youngin's dress. Two pots of water and her nightshirt is still stained with soot." Raney hesitated, then smiled.

"I heard you singin'," I said.

"Reckon you did. It's been a long time since I've sung that song." A slight smile tipped the edge of Raney's lips.

"Purt near made me cry." Anna's coin had saved me, and this child had saved Raney. I fingered the coin in my pocket. My last tie to my girl. Right now, I needed this constant reminder—like a momma encouragin' her baby. I reckon that was what that penny was to me. Encouragement.

Raney touched my cheek. "Bring that pot of water in here before it chills."

The hound come from under the porch, his lip raised, and a deep growl rumbled out of him. I picked up the pot of water. Old Mater wasn't good for much outside of letting me know there was something afoot. "What's your problem, dog? Hush up." I carried the pot into the cabin and headed back outside. Something had the hound riled.

The dog hunkered down, placing one leg slowly in front of the other. He had my attention.

"What's you hear, dawg?" Mater's growl grew louder, then turned to a howl and a bark. I heard hooves just before Mater took off around the house.

"Raney, someone's here. Stay in the house. Keep that youngin quiet." I closed the door and walked the length of the porch. Mater was out of sight, but his bark echoed across the field. The old hound was always better at hiding and barking, instead of standing down on whatever approached.

"Joshua Morgan." A voice boomed from the path.

I knew the voice. Wouldn't never forget it. Thomas Barton. My daughter's murderer. Trouble had come knocking.

"What brings you off the mountain, Barton? I've paid my bill. I don't owe the Company Store nothing. Good sense oughta tell you that you ain't welcome here." I stepped off the porch.

"Lordy, lordy. I ain't lookin' to collect. Reckon you're right. You're paid." He stopped his steed in front of me. "I'm not lookin' for a welcome either. I'm just huntin' a child . . . about six or so. Wondered if you mighta seen one?" Barton pushed his hat back on his head.

He didn't say girl. Maybe it was a different child.

Surely the girl didn't have a tie to Thomas Barton. Anger from the past burned like hot peppers in my mouth. Not just anger but hate. Here I was making a choice that was none of my business. I'd already stomped once in somebody else's mess, might as well stomp again—splatter a little more manure and keep my mouth shut about the youngin. I didn't aim to make this easy for Barton. This child was obviously mistreated. Should she be his, it was as good a time as any to drive in a knife and twist.

"Girl or boy?" I asked. I needed to know if it was the girl. I scrubbed my finger across the two-day stubble on my chin. "I mighta seen a child. Might notta—leastways not since that child you took of mine. Or the one of Manny's. Remember her? Scrip won't pay a doctor in Cumberland."

Barton pulled his hat from his head and rested it on his saddle horn. A snide smile come over him as he pondered on his words.

It wasn't a lie, or at least not a full lie. I'd said "mighta" or "might notta." I never was much of a liar. It ain't my nature. But sometimes a body has to lie to protect those who can't protect theirselves. I reckon I could get good at it if I was forced, but I could tell Barton wasn't convinced by my answer. Truth was, I wasn't convinced either. That's the thing about choosing not to tell the truth. The false words roll off your tongue like they're warm butter. They might even be a little tasty, causing us to dab on a few more truths. Thing is, one butter-coated word leads to another, and then we start to believe they taste right good. It's the lie we tell ourselves to justify the means. Since this youngin was days in the woods and not a soul around, I didn't see a need in givin' her up until I was sure she was safe from the perils she might face. And there was obviously something goin' on.

Barton looked me over and leaned across the withers of his horse. "Sure you ain't seen her?"

Her. There it was. He'd let it slip, and that was what I was looking to hear. This child meant something to him. I drew back and spit. I shook my head and started toward the porch. A drop of amber juice trickled down my chin. I wiped my face against my shoulder.

"Joshua?"

I stopped before I went into the house and looked back.

"You sure?" he asked.

I spit again, then dug my toe into the slobber and drilled it into the ground. I stepped onto the porch, smacked the heel of my boots against the step, and headed to the door.

"I ain't sure about nothin', Barton. Now, get on outa here. Ain't no need for you to bother me and Raney."

I opened the door and stepped in. It clicked closed behind me. "Raney," I whispered, "keep the child quiet." She grabbed the youngin and slipped into the space by the fireplace and behind the door. I tossed Raney another apple from a bowl. "Give her this and keep her quiet."

"Sometimes a body has to protect others from harm," Raney whispered.

I knew what she was aimin' at. Both of us telling a lie—letting on like we didn't know anything about this youngin.

"What if this is his child?" she asked.

"Thomas Barton! A father? Thomas ain't the fatherly type."

I gritted my teeth while Raney gave the girl the fruit to keep her quiet.

Raney pointed her finger and whispered, "Keep this child safe." Her eyes said it all.

Here was my chance to make a wrong a right. I took in a deep breath and straightened the chair by the door.

Thomas's boots clicked along the porch as he walked a circle around the house, nosin' about, before I lifted my rifle off its perch then raised the wooden latch on the door and shoved it open with my knee. The bottom of the door squalled against the floor. There stood Barton.

"Don't you think it's time you stopped snooping around my house? Get on outa here. My debt is paid. I don't owe you nothin'." I shoved him back with the butt of my rifle.

Thomas grabbed the door facing, shoving his foot in enough to keep it from closing. He leaned to peer inside the cabin. "How is Miss Raney these days?"

"Still mournin' her loss, thanks to you." This time I turned the barrel of the rifle toward him, tapping his chest. I pulled back the hammer. It clicked into place. Barton took a step back, and his hands went up. I shoved him away from the door. "Now might be a good time to step back."

He eyed inside the door. Raney and the girl hid in the corner behind it. "You'll let me know if you find her, now, won't you?" Barton eased his hand onto the rifle barrel and moved it to one side.

"Ain't none of my business." I motioned him further back. "Get on outa here. I got nothing you and your black gold ain't already bought."

Thomas backed down the steps and took the reins of his horse. He fit his foot into his stirrup and threw his leg across the saddle, which groaned with his weight. When he settled onto the horse, it snorted, took two steps back, and reared.

"Barton? Is it your child?" I asked.

He turned toward me and said nothing. Just smiled and then nudged his mount.

"You know, Thomas, there's one thing for certain. The devil hisself owns Barton Mountain," I shouted.

"Don't let me find out you're lyin'. Hear me?" Barton just threw his hand up as he turned his horse and headed toward the mountain.

Or what, Barton? You'll kill my daughter?

It was true that the Bartons lived by the notion of what's theirs is theirs and what's yours is theirs. Something was up. Something shameful, and I'd got myself into a mess I was most likely not getting out of. It was strange enough that it forced a right ordinary, honest man to lie, but stranger that a man like Barton was involved.

I sent a gesture his way that would have made my momma slap me. I didn't take well to threats. Didn't take to it when I worked in the Bartons' mines. Wasn't gonna take it now. I pulled my dip bag from my trousers and pinched some tobacco.

I'd been a round or three with Thomas Barton's family. Fought my way from under the tyrant. Life ain't been easy since. So when that threat echoed across my porch, I made one more choice I'd have to live with.

I lifted my gun from my side, peered through the sight, and pulled the hammer back. It clicked into place. My nostrils widened as I sucked in a deep breath and remembered the daughter I'd once had. The one taken from us by Barton.

I homed in on the back of that man's head, and a flood of memories rushed over me. I remembered Anna's pretty long blond hair bouncin' as she run across the field. I saw them men coming after me in a rush on their horses. Not one of them . . . not one offered to stop. They had to see my Anna—but they never slowed them horses.

My finger tightened on the trigger. My eye twitched as I took aim at Barton. I steadied my arm—memories of how Barton's horse blistered over the top of my girl.

A hand grasped hold of my shoulder. "Line it up good. Don't miss." I glanced to the side. Manny stood next to me.

I focused again. And fired.

The shotgun let off a round of buckshot. I've never been a murderer. Even when it comes down to putting a round in Barton, I couldn't do it. Once again a coward. I never know'd of a soul that's ever died from buckshot, but I'd known a few who'd suffered its unpleasant sting. As much as I wanted to fill his backside full, it wasn't in me. I shot the dirt next to his horse.

"Dang it, Joshua. You could have put him outa both our miseries." Manny turned and stomped off the porch. "There's a side of venison I killed yesterday by the porch." He stormed away.

Barton's horse bolted and squalled, tossing him backward into the dirt. I heard the air blow out of his chest when he landed. Thomas pushed hisself along the ground, rubbing his back in the dirt to miss the slapping hooves and cussing like nobody's brother.

"What the . . ." He crawled to his feet.

I slid my fingers through the lever, swung the rifle toward my feet, and backed up, setting it firm in my palm. Cocked. Primed. Ready. Barton stood facing me from the hill. *Not today.* I wanted to be sure the taste of revenge was sweet, not bitter. Today it would be bitter.

"I told you once to get on outa here. I mean what I say," I shouted.

"You was crazy when you worked the mines, and you're still crazy," Thomas shouted as he stomped toward his horse.

"They said that about my momma too. Guess it runs in the family."

"You'll regret today, Joshua. I'll make you regret it. I want the girl, and if you got her . . ."

"If I was to have her, I reckon she's just fine till things is sorted out. If I *was* to have her, that is!"

I stuck my finger in my jaw and scraped out the chaw of tobacco. What sorta man *lets* a helpless youngin get out in the wild? 'Specially one like her—sick and all.

I stepped toward the door. The thought bit at me. Anna had been in the field. Alone. *What sorta man . . .* The words echoed in my mind. Was I no better than Barton?

Regret is a nasty bedfellow. It takes hold of a man, rips and tears at the soul until it bleeds you to death. I shook my head. Tried to shake the memory, make it go away.

Raney stepped onto the porch next to me, and I gave her a hug. I glanced to the end of the porch at the venison Manny had left. "Let's clean that up."

Five

After three days of Raney's scrubbing, that youngin's skin now glowed pink. "She is right purty, ain't she?" Raney sat the girl on the stool and dried her. She brushed her fingers through the wet, tangled hair. "We ain't had no trouble out of the Bartons since you paid the debt. Now you've stirred up a hornet's nest smartin' off to Thomas, and you shot buckshot at him!"

"I ain't had no trouble because they know I'm their path to that vein of emerald."

"Joshua, there ain't no vein. You found one rock of emerald," Raney said.

That emerald stone was one moment in time when I weaved a story to guarantee my family's safety. Up on Noland's Ridge, about a mile from Bartons' mines, a spring that fed our stream bubbled up from the ground. It couldn't have been a luckier find, for when I bent to wash the sweat from my face, I scooped up a palm of water and a green rock. It wasn't big—but good sized. Still, it glistened in the sun the color of a meadow filled with dark alfalfa. I shined the rock, and it sparkled like nothing I'd ever seen. I'd heard of a few miners lucking into some ruby rocks and maybe one or two into the green stones, but I never imagined finding one. I searched for the better part of the week around that spring—never found another. That was the truth. The lie come when I let the Bartons believe there was a vein of emerald, and only I knew where it was. This one would guarantee the safety of my family.

"But the Bartons don't know that. And the possibility of a vein of gems is what's kept the Bartons at bay. They're like hungry wolves, biding their time. Stalking. They can wait for the right moment to attack."

"Thomas will be back," Raney said as she dried the youngin's face with a rag.

I patted the youngin on the shoulder. She winced, like a skittish cat. "Old Joshua won't let nothin' happen to you."

The edges of her mouth curled upward, and a smile parted her lips.

"You got a name, little'n?"

No answer. Just a few coos and squeals.

I'd heard about folks like this girl. People down toward Cumberland say they're crazy. Most can't talk, or if they do, they was hard to make much sense. Some pitch fits and act like wild animals. But when I looked in this baby's eyes, crazy ain't what I saw.

I saw a person locked up in a prison with no way to escape—a soul banging on the shell of a body, pleading for a crack to slip through.

Raney pulled the girl's blond hair into a clump on the back of her head. "Hand me that doily over there."

I reached over the table and snatched a crocheted circle from the corner of the table.

Raney pressed it around the girl's hair and pinned it tight to her head. "There. How's that?"

The girl giggled as her chunky fingers felt up her neck and onto the hair. She squeezed the bun and then wrapped her arms around Raney's neck.

"Aw. Ain't you the sweetest." Raney's eyes watered up.

Truth be known, I fought tears back too. "Purty," I mumbled. "She looks right purty all spruced up." There was something different about this little girl. Something besides her state.

Guess that's when I made another decision. Another choice. I wasn't about to let that innocent child fall into Barton's hands. Didn't matter if they owned the Company Store or not—if they was money mongers or mine owners. I wasn't gonna let another child fall because of the Bartons. Thomas would have to show me proof of her being connected to him.

The Bartons might own the mines and the Company Store, but they didn't own me. They'd let this little one slip out, and since Barton never answered my question, whether the child was his or not, guess that meant she'd be stayin' with us for a spell.

Raney sent me to the barn to pull down the basket that held Anna's things. I didn't ask why, but I figured Raney had decided to share some things with the child. Raney pulled out a dress she'd stitched for Anna and seamed it up to fit the girl. I was surprised Raney would let loose of Anna's things, but I reckon the child touched her. The day was warm, and a sweet breeze blew down from the mountain, so the morning dew burned off the grass quickly. Raney toted that child everywhere she went on the farm. As the sun worked its way over the summit, Raney had the child stirring soup on the stove.

"The youngin needs a name, Joshua. We can't keep callin' her *girl*." Raney let the child straddle her lap. Her head rested against Raney's chest.

I knew in an instant that was a mistake. Raney missed Anna as much as me, and five years in the past was still not enough time to blot out the pain of her loss. Plastering a name on this child meant coming to know her. And I wasn't sure Raney or me could manage that. Still, Raney was right. We couldn't keep calling her *girl*.

"What do you call a child who has nothin'?" Raney asked. "Ain't you got no thoughts on this, Joshua?"

I swallowed hard, then pushed out the words. "Well, no, Raney. I got nothing here." I held up both hands and shrugged. "All that comes to my mind is addin' and subtractin'. Aught plus aught equals aught. Nothing." If Raney insisted on giving the girl a name, it should be something that represented her truthfully.

"Aught," I said.

Raney tilted her head, her brow furrowed. "What?" She rested her hand on her hip.

"Aughtie. She ain't got a thing to her name. Aught plus aught equals . . ."

"I get what you are sayin'. But it's naught. Naught plus naught equals naught." Raney laughed. "Still, Aughtie sounds about right. I like it, despite you getting it wrong."

I took in a breath and blew it out. Now we were left to figure out what was next. What or how would we manage this mess we'd stepped in?

Barton would be back. A body would never know when he'd sneak around. Just he'd come one way or the other. Whether this youngin was his or not, the Bartons was notorious for pursuing what they wanted.

Once a body or a thing was a possession, it was like a toy—like a mountain lion playin' with its prey. It's their greedy nature. That if-I-can't-have-it-neither-can-you attitude. I expected a fight. The fire under this mess would catch up and commence to burn. I'd have to figure out how to put out the flames.

SIX

I PUSHED MY curly hair out of my face and pressed it flat to my head with my hat. The band, cold with sweat, reeked a foul odor. I needed to scrub it with Raney's lye. The sun peeked over the ridge, leaving a dark line of mountains on the horizon, and I took in a breath of the morning air. My work waited. I picked up my sickle leaned against the barn, then headed to the lower field on the far side of the barn. Rye stood hip deep, and it would take me the better part of the day to hack even a portion of it down and rake it.

Funny how hard work beats good sense into a man. I'd laid awake most of the night concocting ways to draw revenge on Barton, knowing it wasn't the sort of thoughts I needed to entertain. Still, loss and anger planted the seeds. Memories forced my muscles to press hard against the sickle. I drew the tool back and swung with a strength that could only come from anger.

Truth was, I wanted Barton dead. Every time I swung that sickle, I imagined it was him I was cuttin' down. The memory of that day seeped to the surface. I had walked away from the mines a few days earlier. Raney'd sent Anna into the field to gather flowers from a stand of daisies to celebrate. And it was me that let her.

"Anna." Raney let out a bloodcurdling scream. "Look out!"

Barton and his posse come roaring across the field.

The memories darted in and out. Each one throwing a punch to my gut.

"Noooo!" oozed from my lips as I had watched Barton knock Anna off her feet and the four men behind him trample her.

"You run my baby down. What's wrong with you?" I shouted.

Like flashes of lightning in a storm, pictures of that day flooded back.

I might have thought it was an accident—but one horse and rider tripped up. Maybe they couldn't see her in that rye. But once they'd hit the child, there was no hesitation. No stopping. No remorse. There had been no question they'd hit something.

I took off across the field, but the men drew me tight into their circle. "You got a debt to pay."

"You run down my girl?" I screamed. "Get outa my way." I tried to break between the horses. My chest banged against the side of the animals. Raney run into the field screaming. I drew back and kicked at Barton's horse. "My daughter?"

"There ain't no gettin' anywhere but up the mountain." They'd tied my hands, lashed me to the saddle, then slapped the horse. The last thing I remember was the wind being knocked outa me bouncing on that horse.

When my eyes opened, I was on the ground, and there stood old lady Barton. She lifted her foot and stabbed the heel of her shoe into my chest.

"Why didn't you just kill me?" I asked.

"You can't pay if you're dead. And Momma Barton insists all accounts are settled before you walk away," Ima Barton growled.

I'd walked away from the mines days before and my debt was paid.

Thomas drew back and hit me in the face. "There was things that come up after you left. More debt."

"More debt my foot. My account was paid." I spit blood from my mouth. "You run my girl down in the field. You've killed my child."

There had been no remorse from Ima or her sons. They'd just wanted me to pay the Company Store.

Don't know why I'd thought they cared. That was the way of the mines. The mountain folk worked relentless hours and was paid in scrip—coins pressed with the name *Barton Mines*. The tokens were only good at the Company Store. Men never saw a real penny of their hard-earned money. The Bartons dished the tokens out and raked 'em right back in. When the coal was sold, the Bartons banked the money. When I wanted out of the mines, all that mattered was that Ima got the money I owed her. If that wasn't enough, she wanted the rest of my money—even if that meant killing an innocent child.

I shook my head tryin' to rid myself of the memory. Despite the years that passed since Anna died, I still couldn't shake the picture of her being caught under those horses' feet.

There was a stand of rye to be cut, and the pondering fueled my anger. With this frustration on my side, I'd get the bulk of the rye took down before nightfall.

"Joshua," Raney hollered. "Come quick. It's the girl. Something's wrong."

I dropped the sickle and bolted toward the porch. Bellows of screams steeped out of the house. I stomped on the first step and leaped to the porch.

Raney squatted on one side of the porch, hand out like she was tryin' to coax a kitten to her. Aughtie lay balled up against the corner of the house. Shrill screams poured from the child. She shook, and a foamy drool dribbled from her mouth.

"I can't touch her. When I try, she starts slappin' and kickin'!" Raney shouted. "What if she's got rabies like some wild animal?" Raney tried to talk to the child, but Aughtie's eyes were squeezed tight.

I stood there helpless. "Get a blanket. Maybe I can cover her and pick her up."

Raney grabbed a blanket and tossed it over Aughtie while I reached down and scooped her into my arms. Her little body was stiff, yet she shook like it was the middle of winter. Raney spread a second quilt on the bed. "Put her there, on her back."

I couldn't figure out what Raney had planned, but before I knew it, she'd pulled the edges of that quilt around Aughtie and stuffed them tight. Aughtie's arms wrapped snug inside the quilt, like a butterfly in its cocoon. It was just minutes before her body relaxed and her screams stopped.

"It worked when Anna was a baby. Nothing better than swaddling." Raney crossed her arms and stared at the girl.

"What do we do, Raney?" I asked. "There ain't a doubt this child is sick."

"I don't know, Joshua. You know Barton ain't gonna sit by idle if he thinks you know about the girl."

"Well, that's the thing that's naggin' at me. See, Barton come down that mountain by hisself looking for this girl. It's like he's hiding something."

I pressed my hand against Aughtie's forehead and brushed her hair to the side. "Something's off here, Raney. If this youngin meant anything to Barton, wouldn't he have a whole army looking for her? As it stands, it was just him. Odd, don't you think?"

"It is peculiar. Still, Barton ain't stupid. He's gonna put two and two together."

"That's my thought too. It ain't a matter of if Barton will come back, but when. I guess we take things a day at a time. The child is sick. She needs cared for, so we do that. We care for her until Thomas proves otherwise."

The water in the coffeepot rumbled as it come to a boil. I pulled the hook away from the fire and dropped the coffee, wrapped in cheesecloth, into the pot. Raney sat slumped on a stool, her arm laid across Aughtie's chest. The night hours had passed slow as we watched to see if Aughtie would have another spell. I leaned against the wall of the cabin and pushed open the window. A whistle echoed down the rugged wagon path, and I peered out to see who was coming.

"Barton?" Raney asked as she jolted upright.

I squinted to focus into the sun. "No, no . . . looks like Clive Simpson. Clive and Manny."

"What's the schoolteacher doin' coming here?" Raney pulled the girl onto her lap and commenced to rock her.

"He's running for mayor. Maybe he's rustlin' up votes. Try to keep her quiet. The more folks know she's here, the more danger they're in, and the worse it is for us."

I headed out to the barn by the south fence. I wrapped my fingers around the brim of my hat and waved toward Clive. "Down here."

Manny veered the wagon away from the house and headed to me. He stopped the horse nose to nose with me.

I slid my arm around her neck and patted her. "What brings you two down here? Closest youngin is the next farm down."

Clive tipped his hat. "Naw, not looking for students." He climbed from the wagon and shook my hand. He looked to be in his late twenties, but his hair harbored streaks of gray by his ears. Him and Cleda Mae was married a few years back, and he'd managed to pick a plot of land to make his home. Like the miners, he'd fallen to the Bartons' ruse of a good life in the mines. It didn't take long for him to learn the pennies he was paid wasn't enough. As the schoolteacher in Ruben's Mill, the mining school, he oversaw a one-room shack with a chalkboard and slates for the youngins. The Bartons only paid him to teach so they could prove there was a teacher for the miners' children. The school was as poor as Clive, but he managed to share four books among his students. I'd heard he was interested in runnin' for mayor in Hiltons. The man had a firm handshake. Not like most of the politicians in the country. He'd be a good mayor if he could withstand the corruption from Barton Mountain.

"I wanted to talk with you, Joshua. Manny here come along for the company."

"Talk away. I'm all ears." I teased and wiggled my ears, then climbed into his wagon and leaned back on my elbows. "Go ahead. Get with it."

"You're the only one I've met to have done it." Clive pulled the reins tight around the wagon's brake and walked around next to me. He slid up on the wagon bed by me.

"Done what?"

"You're the only one to beat the company. Get out from under the Bartons and the Company Store—not to mention live to tell about it."

"You got my attention, Teacher. Go on." I wondered what Clive had up his sleeve. It had to be serious for him even to mention me getting out from under Ima Barton and her boys. That was something folks in these parts didn't talk about.

The Bartons had ears all over the mountain, and folks had to watch their p's and q's. If word got back to the mines that a body had said something against the hand that fed them, they could just as easy wind up face down in the Cumberland River.

Clive smiled a weak smile and scanned the farm.

"You lookin' over your shoulder for a reason, Clive?"

"I'm tired of making the forty-mile trip to the Gap when I need supplies. The scrip they pay me for teachin' ain't good nowhere but their store. And the only real money I have is what my wife brings in sellin' canned goods. A body can't buy supplies in Cumberland Gap with scrip. And Manny here told me you unloaded some buckshot at Thomas. I thought you might just be the man to help."

I dropped my legs outa the wagon and jumped to the ground. "What's your point, Clive?" I walked toward the barn door, and the two of them followed.

"My point is, I used to own my land. Now it's got Barton's name all over it 'cause I ain't paid enough teachin' in the mines to make it without borrowing against it. Ima Barton pays me in scrip just like she pays the miners, and I ain't a miner. I'm in hock to my belt buckle to the Company Store, and what used to be mine . . . ain't anymore."

"And what do you want from me?" I asked.

"Help. You broke free of the Bartons. We need your help," Manny said as he spit and wiped his mouth.

I offered him a pinch of tobacco from my bag. Did I dare trust him? He might be the ears that Barton sent to spy. "Like I said, what's your point?"

Clive leaned against the barn. "Joshua, if you could do anything for the people on this mountain, what would you do?"

"Put a bullet in Barton's back instead of buckshot by his feet?" Manny grumbled.

I picked up the sickle by the barn door. Taking a small whetstone from a shelf, I scraped it over the blade to sharpen the edge. The long neck of the tool wrapped in a curve from the end of the handle. Drawin' back, I made a slice at the air. The sharp blade almost hummed a tune as it slashed through the breeze.

"What would you do, Joshua?"

I stopped and leaned against the sickle. "What I want to do and what I can do is two different animals."

I swung my sickle, took a step, and swiped again. Clive dropped his head and started toward his wagon. He threw me a backward wave. It'd been nothing but making one hard choice after the next these past few days. What more could come?

I give him a few feet before I said anything, then I huffed out a breath. "Clive," I hollered.

He stopped and turned. "Just so you know, I wouldn't put a bullet in him. I'd take down that Company Store."

Seven

A couple of days passed, and Aughtie seemed to recover from her bein' sick. It was strange because a few hours after she had that fit, the youngin was fine. It was like nothing had happened. It took me the better part of three days to lay a portion of that rye field and rake it. The cuttings needed to be baled and put in the barn. That would make Raney's flour and help me with bartering when I went for supplies. Life seemed . . . normal.

I scooped several piles of rye into bales, shapin' and tyin' them with twine. When Raney was frying up the last of the bacon, I knew I'd be making that same forty-mile trek over the Gap for supplies that Clive had talked about. I scanned the rye I'd cut. There'd be enough to barter with in town. I laid my sickle against a pile of rye and stopped at a bucket of water hanging on the barn to wash up. The sun was straight overhead, and if I worked much longer, Raney would send me to the river to bathe. I made my way to the house.

"Guess you better gather up your canned goods and whatever else you got for me to barter with. I'll plan a trip to Cumberland in a day or two."

Raney kissed my head. She reached around Aughtie and put the fork in her little hand. "Hold tight, little one. Scoop and then bite. We ain't gonna eat with our fingers." She guided the small bite of beans to the girl's mouth.

I could see the joy on Raney's face working with Aughtie. I also saw her growing attached to the youngin. An attachment that shouldn't happen. "You should keep your distance, Raney. The girl's not ours."

"She's not our blood, but she became our responsibility when she followed you home from the field."

"She didn't follow me home. Let's make that clear. She saw our cabin, and she saw you outside." I stopped myself from sayin' something I'd regret. Laying blame wouldn't fix nothing.

I could see Raney's thinking, and I hated it when she was right. If I'd left the girl alone, never approached her in the field, none of this would have happened. I'd opened a can of worms that couldn't be sealed back.

A thunderhead topped the mountain, and its rumble echoed through the valley. A breeze blew through the cabin windows, flipping the curtains on their pole. I lifted my nose into the breeze, and the smell of rain filled my lungs. For a moment I closed my eyes and took in the freshness of a sweet shower. Pictures of lilac and honeysuckle come to mind. I breathed in the moment, knowing that a welcome downpour meant me working faster than I could on my own. I'd only baled half the early rye I'd cut, and if the rain laid in, it would be a week before it'd dry enough to bale . . . a week for the critters to snack and that much less for me to use for barter—that much less money in my pocket.

"I can't bale fast enough on my own, Raney, and there's a storm settling over the summit. You're gonna have to help me."

"I can't, Joshua. This girl can't be left alone."

I stepped onto the porch and raised my nose a second time. The breeze carried the fresh scent of a cleansed earth and a dampness I couldn't ignore. There wouldn't be much time before it came, and once again Raney was right. Aughtie couldn't be left alone. Not after that fit she fell into earlier. The child hadn't said a word, so we couldn't count on her hollerin' if something was to happen. We still didn't know if she could talk or if she was just holdin' her voice. I pressed my head into my palms and wiped my eyes.

"Bring her. She looks to learn some. We can let her rake or scoop."

Raney dropped her dish towel onto the table and gave me a hard stare. I knew what she was thinkin'. Anna had been in the field, and now I was telling her to take Aughtie there too.

"We'll keep the girl between us and not let her wander."

Raney thought a minute, and then she knelt at Aughtie's side. "Baby girl, you wanna go help Mr. Joshua in the rye field? You'll have to stay right by me and Mr. Josh. That alright?"

Aughtie clapped her pudgy hands together and let out a piercing squeal. She hopped from the chair and grabbed my hand. In her own way, she wanted to help. Raney gave me one of them looks that said *you best be on the guard.* I understood her reluctance, but if I was gonna have anything to barter with, we had to bale what rye was cut. The rest of the stand could go a few more days before cutting.

"What if Barton shows up?" Raney asked.

I rubbed my chin and sighed. "Well, I guess we come clean, won't we?"

Raney never answered, which told me what she didn't want to say—she agreed.

Raney wiped Aughtie's face and took her by the hand. "Come on, gal. I'll run with you to the rye field."

I watched as the two run and played across the field. I once saw a boy like Aughtie in Cumberland. His daddy had him in a homemade cage in their wagon, and the boy screamed and shook the cage. Folks was scared of him. Looked to me like nary a soul ever made an effort to teach him anything. I've never understood what there was to fear from a youngin like Aughtie. Course, I hadn't experienced a child with this sort of sickness, but the girl seemed fine outside of that one fit she had no control over. She was slow, didn't have no book smarts, and she hardly uttered a word, but I reckon it didn't mean she couldn't. I figured time would tell. She mostly spoke with nods and shrugs. But in the few days we'd had Aughtie, Raney had found ways to teach her so much, like eatin' with a fork and not like an animal. There was a sweetness about the girl. An unconditional sweetness you couldn't help but let grow on you when she wrapped them pudgy arms around your neck and squeezed.

I caught up to the two of them, and Raney had already showed Aughtie how to rake and scoop. Even though she wasn't much help, it entertained her. I scraped and shaped the bales while Raney tied twine around them. Baling was hard work when a man took his time, but it was brutal when he was in a rush.

The wind picked up just as we rounded the last row. There'd be no more baling. Raney took Aughtie and headed back to the house, while I drove the wagonload of rye into the barn and covered it. The air grew heavy with sweat as I made a run for the house.

Sheets of rain blew across the field, pushing me like a hand on my back. The roar of the wash falling from the sky would deafen a person. I stomped onto the porch, knockin' the water off my clothes with my hat. It was good to see the rain. It had been dry a couple of weeks.

"Raney," I shouted, "can you bring me . . ." And when I looked up, there stood Clive and Manny. Raney was stooped with her arms around Aughtie.

Eight

"What did you tell them, Raney?" It was obvious she had to tell them some story behind Aughtie.

"Just that we found the girl, and Barton come lookin' for a child. I told the truth," she said.

"Is what it is. It'll be fine." Though, I wondered if it would.

I tipped my hat to the men. "I see you've met Aughtie."

"We did. What was you thinking, Joshua?" Manny's voice was gruff.

I opened the door and motioned them into the house. "Raney, will you fix us something hot to drink? I'm chilled from the rain."

Aughtie sat on the hearth, tinkerin' with a doll that had belonged to Anna. I touched my pocket and felt Anna's coin. That doll would mean as much to Raney as this coin meant to me.

"What are you doin' back here today anyway?" I asked, hoping to change the conversation.

"Manny and me brought strawberries for Raney and Cleda Mae to make preserves come the weekend."

I could feel the eyes of judgment on me. "It ain't what it looks like. The child was wandering the back fields for days before I could catch up to her. I don't know about you, Clive, but I ain't one to let a half-naked, sick youngin wander without tryin' to find her folks."

Clive set the basket of strawberries on the table, then took one and popped it into his mouth.

"Why didn't you give her to Barton when he come hunting her?" Clive asked.

I liked Clive, but his cocky youthfulness grated at me. "Given that Barton run down my girl and killed her, and Manny's daughter died 'cause he couldn't get cash against his pay to take his youngin to a doctor—because of Barton. Why would I give a helpless youngin over to a monster?"

Clive's eyes scanned the ground. His lips moved like he had something to say.

I shoved my hand into my trousers. "Well? I'm waitin' for your answer."

"You're right. I wouldn't give an innocent child over to him either. Not without trying to figure what was going on." Clive stuck out his hand, his eyes wide open and clear. "No hard feelin's? I was just thinking that you keeping this child from Barton would only bring down his wrath."

"Might still bring Barton's wrath down on the valley, but this youngin ain't well. She was a mess, starvin'. I kept quiet to Thomas until I could figure out what was going on." I took Clive's hand and shook. "No hard feelin's." I could tell Clive didn't mean no harm. So I told them everything about how I'd found the girl and how Barton come in search of a child.

It felt good to spill the truth. I'd carried that lie for days battling whether I'd done right by the girl. I guess it was the first time Preacher Riley's sermon about the truth setting you free really had any meaning. Keeping this child had done a number on my conscience, so pouring out the truth gave me a taste of peace.

"Ain't none of my business"—Manny took the hot cup of coffee and blew away the steam—"but I don't blame Joshua. We've both lost youngins at the hands of Thomas Barton. I wouldn't give her up either."

I started to pace. "Alright, first off, we don't know if she does belong to Thomas. Just that he was lookin' for a child. And just so you know, I didn't go in search of this girl. She'd been out by Anna's grave for days. Manny, you remember. I tried to show you the child the other day. She'd vanished."

Manny slurped his coffee and grinned. "I do, and I thought you was losin' your mind."

"It just tickles me to the core that you had the gumption to shoot at Thomas." Clive stifled a laugh. Manny slapped his knee and let out a guffaw.

"Truth is, I tried to get him to shoot Thomas in the back," Manny said as he nudged me.

"I couldn't shoot a man. Shot at the ground to give him a start," I said.

"Seems Josh here is a better man than me," Manny butted in. "I'd have done worse. I'd have used a rifle and a bullet. Them Bartons don't care about nothin' but their coal—their blood money."

"Why didn't you tell me about her the other day when I was here?" Clive asked.

"I reckon it was a matter of protection. Protection for you and the girl. The fewer people who knew she was here, the less chance they'd be harmed. You know the Bartons. I got no need to explain."

I knew his next question. It was the same one I'd been asking since Aughtie come to our house. "Before you ask, I don't know what I'm gonna do. I know that to find this little girl half-starved and purt near naked in my rye field ain't right. The child could have died." I walked to the window and looked to the north to be sure no one was coming off the mountain.

"Think about it, Clive. Put two and two together and I bet you come up with the same answer. The girl is a secret. And she isn't just a secret. She's Thomas Barton's secret, so we figure for him to come looking for the girl by hisself proved Ima Barton . . ."

"Ole Momma . . . don't know she exists." Clive finished my sentence. "If she knew, there'd be hell to pay for somebody who didn't keep her informed. But the real question is, what would Ima do with the child?"

"I've seen some mean women in my time, and the truth is, I'd rather fight a bobcat than Ima Barton. She fights conniving-like. Sneaky and deceitful-like. I'm livin' proof of how she treats her miners." Manny shook his head. "But it sounds like you might have Thomas over a barrel."

"Her and John Barton come to the mountain dragging two little boys. And when they lucked into that vein of coal, two seemingly nice people went sour," I said.

"They opened up that mine and commenced to drag the mountain folk along under the pretense they'd be cared for and paid well. Nobody knew what was to come." Manny went to pacin'. His face grew red, and he was breathing right heavy. I could see his anger grow.

"It was a lie. A big lie. And all the people in these parts took hold hook, line, and sinker. I was as foolish as the next man to bite. The day the lower end of that mine caved in, I saw what happened. I see the things the Bartons are doin' to the miners every day when I load up to go to the mines.

I know how deceitful they are and how they twist anything to their advantage. Thing is, Ima knows that I know things. Her and her boys would just as soon I was dead. That's why she wouldn't lend me money against my pay to take Mary to Cumberland. That's how the Bartons killed my girl." Manny sat hard in the rocker. He crossed his arms over his chest and huffed.

"I remember, Manny. I walked out when the deceit become too much. Thomas and me had a partin' of the ways after that explosion. He'd not listened when I tried to tell him the things I saw."

Manny's hands shook. "I told him there were men in that mine the day they blew it, but he was following Ima's instructions—even if it meant takin' the life of his own daddy. He did what Ima told him. As far as I'm concerned, Thomas Barton become a killer that day, taking sixteen men to their grave."

I walked to the window and watched the sheets of rain flush across the rye. Manny was right. There was no talking to Ima Barton. Her boys knew how to work a mine, and John's death, though regretful, didn't seem to faze her. She took hold and run that mine like a slave driver. No mercy. Only thing she cared about was that the quota was met for the railroad and her palm was greased with the cash.

I was about to do a lot of assuming, but I saw no other way to unravel this mess but to start at the root. "All them memories will rush back once we start opening the floodgates, but little Aughtie here is what is important. The girl has a momma—somewhere."

"We need to find out who that girl's momma is," Clive said. "You'd think folks would be talking if a youngin was missing."

"I've been ponderin' that. We agree—Ima Barton doesn't know. So the way I see it, the cards is stacked in our favor. Thomas is hidin' something from his momma. As much as little Aughtie here has creeped into our hearts, we'd have to give her up if we found her momma. It wouldn't be right if we didn't. That's a chance we take—that she'd go back into the hands of who let her outa their sight." I picked Aughtie up and hugged her.

Raney sobbed out a no-o-o.

"She ain't our youngin, Raney." My voice grew stern. I knew this would be hard, but even Raney understood that the girl belonged to her own momma. It was all I could do to hold back my anger toward Barton. Every time I looked at Aughtie, the stake of hate just dug deeper, but I reckon that coin droppin' at my side was the good Lord's way of reminding me that hate would only eat away my soul. It seemed a battle bigger than Barton raged inside me—one I'd have to sort through.

"I'll be if I'm givin' this youngin up without a fight," I said. "And that means finding out this child's story and why she was wandering alone for the better of a week out by Anna's grave. For Pete's sake, the child was eatin' dirt, Clive. If it comes to tattling on Barton, then the truth comes out, and that would please me."

"Sounds right. So where do we start?" Manny set his cup on the table. "I'm in."

I pulled my hat off and tossed it in the corner. My insides got the jitters. Could I trust Clive or Manny? What if one of them is Momma Barton's ears?

"As I see it"—I leaned against the hearth and scratched the itch on my back—"we start with the mayor wannabe here, visiting all the homesteaders. We work under Clive's desire to be a politician. Every family we visit, we look for anything that looks outa the ordinary. Young women who might have come into some unexpected belongings—a necklace, ring, nicer clothes. These people are poor. They ain't gonna have expensive trinkets."

Clive chugged the rest of his coffee. "Got anything stronger? I'm gonna need it." A smile tipped the edges of his lips as I opened the cabinet and brought out the hooch.

"My guess is this woman is as big a secret as the girl." I poured Clive's cup full of whiskey.

"Barton might be payin' the child's momma to be quiet. It won't be obvious," I said. We would have to do a lot of supposing to get to the truth. Supposing is always dangerous.

I knelt next to Aughtie. "Little girl, I wish you could tell me who your momma was." I brushed my fingers through her hair.

She held Anna's doll tight in her arms, rocking to and fro.

What thoughts was locked up inside her head? I picked the youngin up and sat with her on the chair. She pressed the doll against my cheek as if to kiss me. Raney took her from me and swayed with her, hummin' a song she used to sing to Anna.

To our surprise, Aughtie commenced to hum, and then it happened.

She spoke.

Nine

Summer rains in the mountains could choke a toad. The rain pelted the house as the wash run off the tin roof like a waterfall. I wasn't sure I'd heard quite right. I stuck my finger in my ear and ground it around.

"Child, tell Missy Raney what you said." Raney tried to coax the girl into repeating her words, but all she'd do was giggle.

"Come on, Aughtie. What did you say, sweetie?" Raney asked.

The girl tinkered with the doll.

I brushed her hair from her eyes, then held up a slice of apple to coax the youngin. It'd worked once. I'd try again. "I sure wish you'd tell me who your momma is."

Her eyes lifted, and a tiny drop of drool trickled down her chin. She took a deep breath, and her shoulders relaxed. Maybe the girl was just unsure about us. Afraid. I tickled her chin and asked again. "Honey, who's your momma? Can you tell Mr. Josh?"

"Momma Joo." Her words were hesitant and slurred, but I could make them out.

Clive sounded out names. "Judy, Justine. Who else on the mountain has a Joo name?"

Aughtie lifted her hand into the air and waved. "Momma Joonnnnn."

"Are you sayin' Momma June?"

Aughtie kicked her feet and let out a yelp that would have scared a dog. She ran to the window and waved her chubby hand real wild-like. "Momma Joonnnnn."

I wheeled around to Manny. "June! June who? You're in the mines. You know the miners and their wives. Who's June?"

It was amazin' the youngin spoke, and I had to wonder if it was a sign from the good Lord that looking for the girl's momma was the right decision. Maybe it was the first step to making things right over my Anna.

Clive paced around the table while Manny picked out names. "Well, there's three or four I can think of. June Carson. That's Jack's girl. Too young, barely six. June Mason, Olivia and Tyson Mason's girl. She's too young too, only about five." He grabbed the back of his neck with one hand and crossed the other over his chest, grasping his shoulder. "June Rayburn, but she's older. Probably late twenties, early thirties, but I think she's gone from the mountain. Ain't sure."

"That'd be about right. She's closer to Thomas's age," I said.

"Aughtie looks to be about six, so she could be Rayburn's girl."

"That's her." I slapped my leg. "She's the one."

"I agree. Call it a gut feelin'. Something just says this is her," Manny said.

"You've heard what assumin' does, right?" Clive pointed his finger at me.

"I have, but we have to start somewhere—a hint, a thought. Anything is better than nothin'. Besides, everything we're talkin' about is built on a gut feeling," I said.

Raney sat next to Aughtie as she waved at Mater out the window. "I wasn't too keen on searching for her momma, but when I seen her so excited . . . We have to find her mother. It'll break my heart to give her back, but . . ."

"Well, let's not get ahead of things. A step at a time, and we start with findin' June," Clive said.

We needed to find this woman. I've never been one to mess in other people's affairs, and I didn't set out to do that this go-round, but it seemed like we had no choice. Not if we were gonna find this child's momma.

It made no sense that Barton was the only one searchin' for this youngin. Where was her mother? Why wasn't others on the mountain launchin' an all-out search? Was it because she was a sick child? Things just wasn't adding up. What did add up was something underhanded here, and this girl played a big part in it. Thomas knew, but Ima didn't.

I ain't never been a man to look at fate and consider it my destiny. But when I saw Aughtie, something had to be done. I just didn't expect it would be the sky openin' up like this.

It was time. Time for the tyranny to end, and I knew that I needed to end it. "Folks are tight lipped, afraid to talk about the Bartons for fear the Bartons will come after them—like they did me. We're going to need something to loosen their lips. Raney, gather up all you can that I can use to barter with. You two comin'?" I asked.

"Wouldn't miss it. They'll expect me back to work in the mines, but I can serve as your eyes and ears there." Manny tapped Clive on the back. "You need a ride home?"

"I reckon I do. I'll gather Cleda Mae and bring her here to stay with Raney. Manny, can you talk your son into watchin' over our farm chores while Cleda Mae is with Raney?" Clive tipped his hat. "I'm in too."

Raney stepped in front of the door. "Now just hold up there a minute. Exactly what do you plan to do?"

I pulled her close and kissed her head. "The most important thing is this child." I picked Aughtie up and rested her on my hip. "Somehow, I think all this is linked—Thomas, this girl, and the Company Store. Maybe this will all work together and kill two birds with one stone. Aughtie and the miners."

"The girl is the first." Raney pushed her finger into the flesh of my chest. "That clear?"

"Clear as a sunny day over the meadow."

"Ain't nothin' like a good reason to clean up a manure pile." Clive smiled.

"Let's go grab a shovel."

It only took a bit for Manny and Clive to run home and return, dripping like the wash that ain't been rung yet, with Cleda Mae in tow. Wasn't no time but the present to leave. So I heaved a breath and waded through the slush of mud to the barn. Rain pelted me like buckshot. Inside the barn, me and Clive stuffed Raney's canned pickles and green beans under the buckboard seat and tied down the tarp that covered the bales of rye.

Manny added corn. The wagon was stuffed. The day was slipping past. It was time to leave.

"I hate this trip to Cumberland. The road gets worse every year." I pulled the rope tight across the tarp.

Clive crawled into the wagon.

"Clive, did you forget something?" I smiled a wiry smile.

"Not that I know of."

I pointed to the horses in the stall. Clive crawled outa the wagon and opened the stall. "Don't you say a word."

Manny mounted his horse. "I'll keep my ears open for anything out of the ordinary. If I stay gone much longer, they'll suspect something. You'll be back end of the week?"

"If all goes well." I nodded.

"I'll meet up with you then. Until then, I'm your eyes and ears on the inside." Manny shook my hand. "I wish I could travel with you."

"Just keep things under your hat. Barton can't know what's goin' on. And . . ." I paused.

"And what?"

"Keep an eye on the women, will you?"

"Consider it done." With that, Manny headed up the trail toward the mines.

Clive wrestled with the horses, doin' his best to hitch them. The man was a schoolteacher, not a farmer. Best I could do was stifle my laugh as I watched. We'd grabbed saddles in case the wagon got hung in the mud along the mountain pass. Leastways we could get somewhere if there was a problem.

Raney come running after me. I saw her foot pull out of her shoe as it stuck in the mud. She shouted at me to wait. "Joshua, you best be careful."

I slipped the harness over the horse and fit the bit into his mouth. Raney grabbed the wagon traces, and I hooked them to the pole.

"You will be careful, won't you?" Raney asked.

I glanced across ole Rufus, my horse, and patted his rump. I said nothing.

"Joshua Morgan, I done lost a daughter. I can't lose the only man I've ever loved. Them Bartons are ruthless. They nearly killed you once." Her voice quivered, and the lines between her brows told me she was set on worrying. Raney hadn't showed any real carin' for me since . . . since Anna died.

"Where's the girl?"

"She's playing on the porch. You're not taking that child off this farm." Her tone changed to downright hostile.

I walked around the wagon and clasped my hand around her cheek. My thumb gently brushed her brow. Raney was a pretty woman. Her eyes, the color of the sky, sent chills over me every time I gazed into them. Even when she was soakin' wet, she made me glad I was the one fortunate enough to call her my own. I'd do whatever I needed to do to protect her—to protect this homestead, and now Aughtie.

I'd let her down once. Never again.

"You know there ain't nothin' in this world that means any more to me than you." I kissed her nose and walked around the wagon. "I live and breathe you."

"As sweet as them words are, they're tellin' me you got more in mind than I'm gonna be happy about."

"Never could fool a smart woman, now could I?" I smiled.

"Stop wallowing around the hog pen. Where are you goin'?"

"I'll make a trip to Cumberland. We need supplies."

Her face dropped, and the color washed away.

Clive gave Raney a friendly hug. "Don't you worry. I won't let him do something he'd regret. Cleda Mae is here if you need her."

"Lordy mercy. You're going to the mines, ain't you?"

"We might happen by the mining camp. Maybe try to barter at the store there too. And while I'm there, I'll nose around."

"Aughtie comes first. You said she would." Raney fought back the tears. I could see the fear in her eyes. She knew what the fallout would be for me going back to the Company Store.

"She will be first, Raney. If I can get ahold of that ledger Ima has, it lists all the miners and their families. We can see if June Rayburn is still on the mountain."

Aughtie sloshed through the mud from the house to the wagon, her smile like a ray of sunshine peekin' through a light misty rain. I lifted her to my hip and headed into the barn. "Grab me that hammer," I said as we passed by the tools.

Aughtie snagged it off the wall. I sat her on the rickety worktable and pulled down a metal box from the shelf. Opening the lid, I pulled out the rock, lined deep with emerald. I took the hammer, broke off a piece, wrapped it in my handkerchief, and stuffed it in my boot.

"Can you put that rock back?" I handed it to the girl.

Aughtie dropped the rock in the box and slid it back on the shelf.

Ima Barton never wanted to lose a miner, even if it meant makin' up new debt that wasn't real. That's what she did to me, but a sliver of that same gem bought me freedom from the Bartons. I could only hope it would still work to our advantage.

Getting into that store and layin' hands on that ledger would help us find the Rayburns. If things went south, the gem might set us free.

"Please, Joshua, don't do this. Don't go back there. You remember what Ima said." Raney clasped her fingers tight around my arm. "Remember what they did last time?"

I remembered Ima's remark as she took the sliver of emerald I offered her.

"Raney, if you're referring to being hog-tied and toted up the mountain, I won't never forget that." I took her by both arms. Ima'd taken my emerald chip and wrote *PAID* across her ledger. But she didn't like it, and she made it clear that I wasn't never welcome back up the mountain. Still, there was things worth more than my sorry hide. "They killed our baby. You saw it with your own eyes. And now you see that little girl—that sick little girl with no smarts, no learning, and half-starved. We can't let them kill another youngin."

I couldn't bring Anna back from the dead, but maybe I could save Aughtie. Maybe we could kill two birds with one stone and help the miners too. "Raney, them Bartons can't keep hurting people. It's evil. Think of Aughtie?"

"And you've appointed yourself God Almighty as their savior?"

"Not *their* savior—Aughtie's. If the miners are helped along the way, then everyone wins. But I need the miners to help her and protect us." I tried to help Raney understand why I needed to go back to the mountain.

"And what am I supposed to do if they kill you?" Her fear steeped out like steam from a boiling kettle. "How does that help Aughtie? I want this fixed, but not at the risk of losing you."

I pressed my hands around her face. "This ain't about bein' anybody's savior. It's about finding Aughtie's momma and figuring if this child really belongs to Barton without getting him or us killed."

She leaned into my chest. "I can't lose you too." She sobbed.

"You won't. I'm too stubborn. Good Lord wouldn't have me anyway." I gently kissed her. "Raney, you're a strong woman. Stronger than I could ever be. This will work out for all of us."

Raney straightened my suspenders and squeezed my chin. "Get your backside back here quick. Understood?"

"The sooner, the better," I said.

"And if you find June?"

"We'll bring her here." I winked.

"You're sure this is about Aughtie and not them miners?" Raney asked.

"I'm sure."

Those were hard words to say because my gut instinct was to go after the Bartons, but the truth was, little Aughtie needed to come first. Anything else was gravy on the biscuit. That youngin deserved to have her momma. She deserved to be clean and have food to eat. Aughtie needed help and lots of it.

This was about saving the one child that we could save. It would take some doin', but I knew this was my mission.

Clive finished hitchin' up the horses, and I prayed they could pull a loaded wagon through the sticky mire of a rain-soaked mountain. I tapped the horses. "Hup now, horses. Hup." The animals groaned as their muscles tightened and their necks extended. The wagon creaked and commenced to roll, never slowing when it hit the thick muck. Clive took hold of the buckboard seat and pulled hisself into the wagon.

"Ain't no turning back," Clive said.

"Nope."

TEN

I RESISTED THE urge to take one last look over my shoulder. Wasn't likely I'd turn to salt, but it felt like it'd be an omen.

"Think we'll find Taylor Rayburn or the girl's mother?" Clive asked like he wasn't sure he wanted to hear the answer.

"Dunno."

"Did you know Rayburn?" Clive tapped his fingers on his knees.

"Yep. From the mines. Taylor was a good man, the best I remember. Always stood up for the men—bucked the system if need be. I knew he had a daughter, but she was young. Or so I thought. Never saw her. Rayburn said she was smart as a whip and wanted to be a teacher in Cumberland someday. His wife died from the fever. I heard he broke free from the mines a few years later. Don't know how he managed it, let alone staying outa the way of the Bartons. His place was on the back of the mountain. Right under their noses."

"That ain't much to go on, Josh." Clive tapped his fingers, then his foot. "Reckon the good Lord will be with us?"

"Hope so. How many more questions you plan on askin'?" I pressed my hand on his knee to stop his wiggling.

Clive glanced toward me. "One."

"What is it?" I grumbled.

"You worried?"

I frowned. "You?"

He nodded.

"Well then, I reckon you're in good company." I let a grin cross my lips.

A few hours of good rain, and it didn't look to end in the next bit. The rain turned to a gentle drizzle. The breeze off the summit chilled me.

Despite that, I was warm. The kind of warm a body feels when you know you're doing the right thing. Finding this girl's momma was the right thing. I only hoped she was nothing to Barton.

The mountain path was just wide enough for the wagon, and when we come up on a group of burrows, we shimmied over to the safe side of the narrow path and waited till the animals shuffled past.

Miners, faces black with ground-in coal dust, followed the burrows and nodded as they passed.

"Josh. How be ya?" Willie Jones stopped and reached out to tap my shoulder as our wagon passed. His black coal-stained hand left its mark on my clean white shirt. He coughed hard and spit. It wouldn't be long for him. Willie'd either die from the coal in his lungs or starve when Ima put him and his family out when he couldn't work no more.

The Bartons spent a good amount of time hauling rock from the base of the mountain. They'd drop it in piles along the steepest parts of the mountain pathway. It gave the pack animals something to steady their feet on when the weather was bad. I'd seen men try to steady the beasts loaded down with coal, and when the animal's footing gave, burrow, coal, and miner would all end up tumblin' to their deaths. Worse yet, if them men happened to be tied together by ropes for support, then they'd all be dragged off the slopes. I could still hear the screams of beast and man tangling together. The worst part . . . the silence after.

Our horses leaned into their harness and took the slope slowly until they came upon the rocks. Ain't a man alive could convince me animals ain't smart. For when those horses hit the rocks, they'd ease up and rest, knowin' they could take out again without as much effort.

Halfway up the mountain, the timbers overhead popped. The echo of Willie's coughin' behind us and the trees crackin' made a music that only a miner could understand.

The heavy rains had brought down trees, loosening the dirt on the side of the mountain. The sound of breaking trees meant the worst was to come. I tapped Rufus. "Hup there, Rufus. Come on, horses—lets us get around this bend."

The horses sensed the danger and picked up the pace.

The mountain has its own voice. It talks to a man if he's willing to listen. I'd always likened it to the pastor's sermon on the Holy Spirit speaking in groans. It ain't always words that a body hears. It's the breath of the mountain itself.

It was that same way when I was underground in the mines. When the mountain was tired of being poked and prodded, it'd take things into its own hands. When it did, somebody usually died.

The rain was steady by now, and the wind had quieted. There wasn't a sound . . . not a cricket, not a bird, nothin'. I sat up straight. My heart went to racing. I knew this silence. I knew the mountain's warning when she grew quiet. "Clive," I said.

"Yeah."

"Get out."

"What?"

"Get out now! Get out and push the wagon."

I leaped out of the wagon, pulled the reins to the side, and slapped the horses hard. "Hiyah! Go, horses."

Clive's feet hit the ground, and he raced behind the wagon, buried his shoulder against the buckboard, and heaved. "What's wrong?" he shouted.

"Push!" I hollered. Hours of heavy rainwater had loosed dirt and rock on the side of the mountain. The earth was soaked to a mush. When the ground went to rumbling, I knew she was about to open up and vomit. "Get around the bend."

We shoved the wagon, helping the horses pull the load around the steep curve. Behind us, the miners hollered and took to runnin'. My feet slipped, and I felt for the rock pathway. Trees above me cracked and swayed, and an explosion roared through the trees. The mountain turned loose and let everything she had pour down the slope.

The men behind us did their best to get ahead of the slide that was comin'. Mud, trees, and rock rolled down the mountain, breaking trees, pourin' like thick cake batter out of a bowl.

"Clive, push!" I shouted.

He screamed as he weighed against the wagon.

"Puussshhh!" The horses hit the next run of rock, and the wagon rolled faster. I prayed the mudslide would hit the road and roll across instead of taking the mountain path down—otherwise it would kill everything in its way. The wagon rounded the bend, and my feet flew out from under me. I went to my knees, hangin' tight to the step board.

Clive reached out to help me.

"No!" I screamed. "Keep moving." The mud hit the path and grabbed my legs like a calf being lassoed. It sucked me into the roll, spinning me around and then spitting me over the edge of the slope. I landed hard on a rock ledge, and when I looked up, mud, trees, and rocks spewed over the edge of the slope like a waterfall. I pressed my body against the side of the mountain. Snuggled against the wall on the only ledge along the ridge, I prayed the slide would continue to spray over me and not break the ledge.

"I reckon You ain't done with me yet, huh, Lord? It's only by Your grace I'm here." Sweat beaded on my forehead, only to be washed away by the rain.

I shoulda been dead, shoulda been dropped onto a tree below like a piece of bacon stabbed on a skewer. The Lord favored me. That was all there was to it. Luck and the good Lord. Maybe there was a reason He kept His protecting hand over me.

Though it was just minutes, it felt like hours until the rush of mud stopped. I wiped the splatters of clay paste off my face and shook my hands clean.

"Joshua!" Clive screamed over the edge of mountain. "Joshua?"

"Down here." The taste of dirt filled my mouth. I spit, trying to clear the nastiness off my tongue. "You alright? The wagon alright?"

Clive broke into a hee-haw. "You just washed over the mountain in a river of mud, and you're asking about the wagon? I'll get a rope." I heard him talkin' that I was both crazy and lucky.

My hat lay at my feet like a faithful hound. I picked it up and slapped it against my legs. Clay flipped off in clots. I pressed it down on my head. When the mud dried, I'd have to pry it off. Until then I leaned against the side of the ridge and took in a breath. My heart slowed and my body ached, but I was alive. Alive for a reason.

"Clive! Can you see the miners behind us?" I shouted. "Do you see Willie?"

Silence. I despised silence like this. Waitin' to hear something. "Clive!"

Dirt dropped from above me, and Clive, Willie, and the miners jutted their heads over the embankment.

"They're all good." The mountain gave us some mercy by dropping that mud over the ledge instead of down the road.

"What you worried about us for? You're the one over the side of the mountain." Willie busted into laughter. "Reckon you might need a little help?"

"Help and a bath. And it ain't even Saturday," I spouted.

"Hold on, Joshua," Clive shouted. "We'll tie some rope and make a seat. Rope's too slick from the mud for you to climb."

Hold on. That was the best he could come up with whilst I stood prayin' the sliver of ledge I stood on didn't give way? I shook my head. "Hurry!"

Up through the branches, clear blue sky peeked through the mud-soaked trees. The storm had passed. We was all lucky, and I couldn't help thinkin' the good Lord had gone and confirmed our mission.

A rope with two loops tied in it dropped from above. "Step in the loops. They oughta tighten on your feet, and then hold on."

I stared at the loops and wondered if this was any safer than a slick rope. Then I stepped in and wrapped the ropes around my arms.

"Alright. I'm ready."

The men pulled, and the loops snugged tight around my boots. They hauled me up and over the cliff to safety. Before I knew it, the miners grabbed me by the arms and dragged me under a rush of clean water pourin' off a ledge. They went to hee-hawin' and making fun.

"Ain't you a sight?" Willie grabbed my shoulder and slapped it. "Good to see you alive. Yep, yep. Good to see you alive."

I realized right then the bonds I'd made with the miners, working by their side, was tight. Surely to goodness, me and Clive would help Aughtie and these men too.

Eleven

"Lordy, lordy. I thought you was a goner." Clive grabbed me in a bear hug. "I promised Raney I'd get you home safe. But that was from Ima, not a mudslide. Seems I've been spared sharin' bad news. Besides, we got to talk to them miners. If you was to come up dead, that might not happen." Clive grinned a wide smile and patted my shoulder.

"Gotta say, I thought I was a goner myself." I sat on the pathway, elbows resting on my knees while the fear settled in. Fear is a funny thing. A body gets in a fix, and you grow determined to save yourself. After the trouble is done and you got a second to settle, that's when the reality of fear hits you in the gut.

It reminded me of being down in that mine—that horrible hole. I hated mining even though it fed my family. I despised feeling like a fresh-served meal for Mother Earth. We'd chisel through rock, then shore up the overhead with timbers. But Lord knew the earth could crack them timbers like toothpicks.

"You alright?" Clive asked.

I stood to tryin' to pull myself together. "Well, let me see, here. I was caught in a mudslide, knocked off a cliff, and pulled to safety by some contraption that looked anything but safe. Then tossed under a heavy wash of water. None of which I shoulda survived. Am I alright?"

Clive took to laughin'.

My hands commenced to shake. Memories of me and Bill Astin gnawing away at a slate shelf underground come to mind. The clap of the pick against the shelf sounded like the thump of Raney's knuckles on a ripe melon. You'd strike that slate, and it'd be so hard it'd jar your guts. Bill would draw back and whack that wall, then cuss. Draw back, whack, and cuss, as if his cussin' would loosen that slate. He'd lifted that pick to make one more jab at the rock when the floor started to shake. Before I could shout, "Daisy, hold your drawers," that rock wall had let go of the ceiling and dropped. We was all tethered together by a rope, and when Bill dropped with the rock, it yanked me to my tail. And that took the man behind me to his stomach and the one behind him to his knees.

But that's how them holes in the earth was. Didn't always matter how you tried to prop up the ceiling—you never knew what laid behind the next crack. It might offer you a vein of black gold, or it might be your invitation to hell. Your guess was as good as the next man's.

I shook the memories and gathered my wits about me.

Clive punched my shoulder. "Nervous?" He pointed at my shaking hands.

"More like aftershock." I leaned against the side of the mountain and cackled. It seemed better than crying. That stream of water the boys tossed me under gave me a chance to scrub till I saw pink skin appear from under the mud coating, but it chilled me, and my teeth chattered.

Clive pulled a dry shirt out of his bag and tossed it to me.

"I'm beginning to wonder if this trip is worth the hazard. What if old man Rayburn is dead? If Barton is hiding Aughtie's momma, we ain't likely to find much without him to tell us," Clive said.

I furrowed my brow, stunned at the man's smarts. "That's a mighty big assumption." I cocked my head and rested my hands on my hips. All that bottled-up fear let loose. "Reckon Rayburn's dead? Reckon I got a youngin in my house that needs to be with her mother?" There was a pile of ifs to be pondered. If Rayburn was dead, findin' his daughter would be harder. And knowing if June was Aughtie's momma would still be a mystery. If, if, if. The whole mess of thoughts muddled together into a muddy soup.

Clive come up next to me. "Hold up, here. You're getting worked up over nothin'." He walked the horses back to the wagon and hitched them.

I wondered exactly what Clive rated as nothing.

"Simmer down. Rest a minute." Clive patted the horse on the rear and then sat next to me. He lifted his arm and hung it over my shoulder. "You're alright, my friend." He slapped my back. "Yes, sir. You're fine."

"The fear from the slide got under my skin. I'm just cold from that soakin'. I'm sorry." I'd snapped, but my hands kept on shakin' like a newborn pup in a snow pile. "I don't miss this hellhole. Too many memories."

Once I caught my breath enough to stand, we mounted that wagon and finished the last leg into the mining camp. I couldn't help but say a prayer of thanks that the good Lord spared me. Funny how things come back on you when you've faced death. In the midst of being washed over that ledge, the picture I had in my mind was that sweet little girl nuzzled up against Raney's chest. I could see that child sleepin' peaceful in the arms of a woman who could and would love her. In just a few days, that girl had wormed her way into our hearts. When I looked harder, I could see contentment on the face of the woman I loved. Raney was my world. And I kept telling myself I was doing this all for her—for her and Aughtie. But there was more. There was the miners. It would be hard to keep my focus away from them.

The path snaked into a filthy excuse of a camp, and we stopped to light a lantern. A small meadow, leveled of trees and filled with stumps and dead branches, squatted on the shoulder of the mountain. One-room shacks leaned to the left or right, depending on which way the wind blew, and smoke twirled and twisted toward the sky, mixing with the misty fog that had settled in. The air was rank, a combined smell of soot, mud, sweat, and smoke.

It was quiet—even the youngins that played in the puddles seemed to have no voices. Women stopped their chores and stared as we passed by. Though clean, their skin carried a black tint from the coal dust that hovered in the air. A man swiped the sweat from his forehead, leavin' a smudge across his skin. You couldn't get clean living in the camps—living on top of the devil's ceiling.

Clive stepped off the wagon, and it rolled to a stop. He walked up to the miner and shook his hand. The dirt and soot was a harsh reminder of what I'd escaped, and I was more than grateful I'd not signed my land over to the Bartons. Hard memories seeped to the surface.

"I'm lookin' for Taylor Rayburn. You know where I can find him?" Clive asked.

The man shrugged. He wasn't the first to not answer. It wasn't a stretch to know any man who talked about Rayburn might be the next target of the Bartons. Ima kept the miners runnin' scared. The more afraid they were of her and the boys, the more she kept them under her thumb.

"Thanks. I'll keep hunting. It's real important I find him. If you see him, tell him Clive is looking for him."

The man nodded and went back to work. Clive spoke with several of the men, but they clammed up tight. He climbed back onto the wagon.

"We keep trying." I patted his back. "We keep trying."

"Mister, that rye for sale?" A woman smacked the side of the wagon, dug into a makeshift pocket on her apron, and pulled out a token. "I'd buy it. Rye bread would be good." She poked the token at me.

I took it from her fingers and rolled it in mine. *Barton Mines 5 cents.*

It broke my heart to see these families had given up their land to live in . . . in . . . *this.* Nasty, barely the necessities to feed their family. My anger boiled that the Bartons could hold these miners and their families hostage like this.

I handed the reins to Clive while I reached around, loosened one end of the tarp, and kicked a bale onto the ground.

I stretched my hand out and motioned the woman over. "The rye is a gift."

The woman's face lit as she ran behind the wagon, shoutin' for her friends to come and partake of her feast.

My nose flared, and my fists balled. It was a shame they had so little. I climbed off the wagon, knees still weak from my fall. I tapped her shoulder to draw her attention.

"Thank you, mister. Thank you."

"My pleasure." I nudged her, and she glanced up. "Here. Keep this."

She stared at me in disbelief. Her hand eased upward. I slipped the token into her palm and closed her fingers around it. I held her hand tight for a minute. "You know anything about Taylor Rayburn or his girl June?"

"I heard June moved to Cumberland. Ain't seen her in years. I ain't see Rayburn either. You sure you don't want this token?" She pulled her hand away.

"Positive."

It was seconds before a crowd of women pulled that rye bale apart and stuffed it into their aprons. It was like watching ants crawl over a bite of apple. They were hungry, and Ima Barton and her Company Store was to blame.

Rage built inside me, and it became clear, as I watched them women push and shove for a morsel of food, that I had a mission. I'd do what it took to end this torture. No matter what.

I looked over the women, searching for Rayburn. I'd been gone from the mines for five years. There were new people from the north face. Some from as far as Pennington Gap. Ima had to keep finding new blood because when the mountain grew hungry, it'd eat a few dozen men in one bite.

That was part of the ruse Ima Barton told. "Come to Barton Mountain. We'll buy your homestead, and you can live on the mountain for free, work the mines, and buy what you need from the store. Momma Barton will take care of you." And unwitting folks, good people, would sign their *X* on the line. Their lack of education and lust for an easy life caused them to sell their soul to the Bartons. Their innocence prevented them from understandin' what they'd done.

It only took a matter of weeks for them to realize the promise wasn't true. They'd been suckered. Their hard-earned homes were sold for pennies and their lives taken hostage—indebted to a woman who ruled the mountain with an iron fist.

Clive eyed the people as we passed in the wagon. He pulled his coat over his mouth and nose to filter some of the stench. "Sad," he said. "These folks have been here so long, they don't smell the filth."

"Black dust paints itself over your senses and numbs you," I said. And it did. Between the smell of soot and the constant darkness of the mines, a body was lucky to keep their head in line. I searched the crowd of women and children. Stained clothes, black streaks on their faces—the mines marked their prey.

"I don't see old man Rayburn. Do you?"

"Naw. He's probably moved out of the mines. Old Lady Barton won't let outsiders stay in the camps. It's matter of findin' someone who might know where Rayburn is now." I nodded at Clive, then stood up in the wagon. "Keep lookin'."

From behind us, I heard the slapping of hooves on the muddy path, and when I glanced over my shoulder, it was just the trouble I was hoping to avoid.

"Joshua Morgan. What you want up here? You ain't welcome here." It was Thomas Barton.

I halted the horses. My eyes met Barton's, and we stared, both knowing there was a secret between us—a child he was searching for.

"You got gall comin' up here. What do you want?" Barton kept a good distance between us.

I reckon he feared I might shoot at him again. "I come to sell fresh rye to the store. Thought the people up here might like some fresh grain."

"Like they'd buy from the likes of you."

"I think they might if the people are hungry enough, and since that mudslide washed over the path a mile back, I'm guessing you'll be needing it until that gets cleared."

Barton eased his horse next to the wagon and leaned against the saddle horn. "What do you really want, Joshua?"

I pointed my finger at him and whispered, "Lookin' for answers. You willing to give me some?" I chuckled. I could see him squirm.

Barton was smart. He knew I was hinting at his coming round looking for the girl. It was obvious he was hiding something, and I planned to figure it out.

Barton backed his horse away and slapped the reins against the animal. "This ain't over, Joshua."

"I didn't much suspect it was. Why are you so upset that I'm bringin' fresh grain up here? We're just tryin' to help . . ."

"You best watch your back." Thomas pointed his finger my direction.

"That a threat? A threat right here in front of all these people?"

Barton glanced around to see folks staring. I kicked off another bale of rye. And then another. The people rushed toward the bales, grabbing all they could carry.

"Look a there," I said. "Looks like the store could use some fresh grain."

Barton kicked his horse and dashed past. I could see the rage in his eyes and the frustration of having his hands tied. Maybe he had a feeling for how I felt that day they hog-tied me. Either way, Thomas had too much to lose, too much to hide to pick a fight with me today. He knew when I figured it out, it would be the stick of dynamite I needed to blow this mountain apart.

TWELVE

ME AND CLIVE pulled the wagon alongside the shack of a building called the Company Store. I stepped down from the buckboard and pulled the basket of canned vegetables from under the seat. "These might make good bribing tools when you talk to these women here."

"I reckon I'm a little nervous," Clive said.

Odd how things took a turn, for my fear had ended, and Clive's worries had just begun. We were takin' a big risk comin' into the mining camps, much less facing down Thomas Barton. He was none too happy when he'd left, and the possibility of his comin' back with his thugs set us both on edge. Clive's eyes grew to the size of saucers as he scanned the area for Barton's men. His hands trembled when he tied the horses to the post.

I eased next to him. "Clive, we're like a squirrel sittin' stiff as a board, hoping the snake passing by don't notice. Being nervous is alright, but you can't let the snake see the weakness. You hear me?"

He nodded.

"You're runnin' for mayor. Talk to these people while I'm in the store. Pull yourself together and go show that snake you ain't backing down."

Clive twisted his head and shrugged his shoulders. "Yep, I'm alright."

"You sure?" I nudged.

Clive knelt to tie his boot, and I toed his arm with my boot to get his attention. "You understand me? Clive?" My voice grew firm. I'd grown to trust Clive, but his nerves was gonna get us both killed. I had to snap him out of this, help him catch his nerve.

"Yeah. I understand." But he still didn't move.

"Get your head on straight." I gritted my teeth, and the muscles in my jaw tightened. "Now ain't the time to turn chicken."

Clive crawled to his feet, his voice a snide whisper. "We're on the same side here, Joshua."

"You got your nerve back?"

Clive stared for a second and realized I'd poked him into reacting. A weak smile stretched across his face. "I'll talk to the miners."

"You're a good man, Clive. I don't want you dead, no more than you want to be dead. Make them some good politician promises." I patted his shoulder as I passed. "We're here for Aughtie. Remember that." I took a deep breath, remindin' myself of the same, only to choke on the dust-filled air. I coughed, then retched. Remnants of the mines would always hide in my lungs. It was a stiff reminder of what was at stake.

"What's your aim once you get in there?" Clive asked as he handed me a basket of canned beans.

"I aim to try and get a look at that ledger of Ima's. See if I can catch a glimpse of where Rayburn might be living. If he's still living, that is."

My boots, thick with mud, stuck to the planks of the porch, leaving a perfectly formed print. Course mine was just one of many. I scanned the long porch and thought about how those boot prints belonged to souls held in chains by the slave driver inside. A slanted board with a brush attached sat next to the door. Caked with clay mud, it had scraped its share of muck from the bottom of boots. I slammed my foot against the board and then dragged the sole of my boot over it. Mud curled like peeled tater skins. I brushed the clots of clay off the porch with the toe of my boot, then pushed open the screen door and walked in. The door creaked and slammed shut.

Necessities lined the shelves. Food, seed, and fabric for stitching clothes. Empty jars for canning. Pots and pans. The store was stocked like the kitchen of a wealthy man. Anything the miners wanted lay in wait if they had enough in their paycheck to buy it. I pulled down a pair of trousers and a shirt, eyed their sizes, and tossed them on the counter.

There she was. Ima sat with her back to the door, her chair groaning from her weight. "Ma'am." I tipped my muddy hat.

The door opened behind me, and Manny walked in. I nodded. "Manny."

"Well, look what the dog dragged in. Joshua Morgan." Manny reached his hand and winked. "Good to see you."

I took his hand and shook, then nodded again. Manny went to perusing the shelves.

The counter was lit with brass lanterns, and the smell of kerosene and coal dust formed a mixture in the air I could taste.

"This oughta pay for a change of clothes." I pulled out my pouch and sprinkled two tiny green flecks, smaller than peas, on the counter.

A chair squeaked as Ima scooted from behind a tin-topped desk. A ledger book lay open on the counter. A knife balanced on the end of the table, with pencil shavings piled high. She glanced over her glasses and sneered.

Ima cleared her throat, and without looking up said, "Have a rough trip up the mountain? You look like you was dragged through the mud." She snickered under her breath. "Some of the men said there was a slide." She peered over her glasses. "Looks like you mighta found it."

Ima was tryin' to play coy with me, but I knew she had an eye on that emerald bit.

"I got rye in the wagon. Thought you might could use some fresh grain up here."

Ima laid her pencil to the side and put her palms down on the table. She leaned onto her hands and stood. Her head sucked into her shoulders like a chicken hiding from a wringin'. She clicked her claws against the tin tabletop, drew a deep breath, and hissed it out real slow. The legs of her chair squalled against the plank floor as she pushed it away. Manny's eye squinted at the screech of the chair legs. He took a step back as the old woman stomped two steps to the counter.

"Joshua Morgan." Ima pushed her glasses high on her nose and picked up the emerald fleck. She rolled the gem between her thumb and forefinger, then laid it gingerly back on the counter.

"I see you still got no need for my supplies. A man that totes around gems wants for nothing. So what're you doing here?"

She pushed the stones toward me.

"I told you. Rain's been good this year. Crops are plenty. Thought I'd be neighborly and offer you some fresh grain." I reached to pick up the emerald, and she slapped her bony fingers over it. Her greed always won out no matter how Ima tried to play the game.

I was countin' on that speck of a stone to keep me alive.

Ima leaned over the counter. "You got guts comin' back up on this mountain. I told you not to come back here."

"Well, I didn't pay you no mind when I worked the hole, and I pay you less now. You want the rye or not? I can head on west toward the Gap. Just thought I'd be neighborly."

"Threats don't set well with me." She pressed closer to my face. Her breath reeked of onions, and her skin looked dry and scaly, like a dead trout.

But I didn't dare take a step back. "I don't make threats. You want the grain or not? Looks like your people are hungry."

Her nose flared, and one side of her lip lifted into a snide grin. She raised the fingers that caged the gems and walked to the window. I followed behind her.

She eyeballed my load. "Seventy dollars in scrip."

I burst into laughter. "Scrip ain't worth the metal it's printed on. Eighty in cash. Not a penny less."

By now the people had gathered around the wagon. Clive wandered through the crowd, talking.

Ima squinted one eye. "There's more to this visit than your stab at kindness."

Thomas Barton kicked open the door. "We got no need for nothin' you got."

"Well, Thomas, we meet again. What, it's been two, three days?" I grinned right snide-like.

"You two been talkin'?" Ima's eyes turned toward Barton.

"No, not really." I followed Barton across the room. "I was just lending a hand to a man who'd lost something." I winked at Barton.

"Manny, what's your business here?" Thomas asked.

"Nothing special. I saw Joshua here and thought I'd thank him for comin' to my Mary's funeral. You remember my Mary, don't you? She died when you wouldn't extend me cash on my pay to take her to Cumberland to the doctor." Manny stepped away from the shelves of supplies and walked toward the counter.

I could see Manny's hackles risin' when Thomas stepped closer. I took

Manny's arm and twisted him toward me. "Me and Raney was happy to come. I'm sorry about Mary. Seems we both have lost precious daughters." I commenced walking Manny toward the door. "Clive's out there. You should talk to him. He's considering runnin' for mayor. He might help you and Hettie."

I opened the door and showed Manny out.

"Right kind of you to show a grievin' man some compassion," Manny said.

I walked back to the counter, eased around it to Ima's desk, and then twisted the ledger toward me. I scanned the page hoping to find Rayburn's name. It only took seconds for Ima to come across the room and slam the ledger shut.

"I reckon your place is on the other side of my counter." She pressed her finger into my chest and pushed me around to the other side. Ima sneered as she rested her elbows on the counter. "You got business here, Joshua, or is your business to just nose around?"

Thomas picked up the gem, but Ima snatched it away.

"I see you still like the feel of wealth in your fingers, Ms. Barton." I picked the stone from her fingers and held it to the light. The green of the emerald sparkled. I opened her fingers, laid the stones in her palm, then picked up the clothes and headed toward the door. "That should cover the change of clothes, and I take your answer on the rye is a no."

Ima tightened her grip on them stones like a youngin clutching the last piece of candy. Barton followed me out the door so close I could feel his breath against my neck. I motioned to Clive.

"Let's go, Clive. Loosen the horses. Bartons don't want to help their people."

Clive untied the horses, and the two of us climbed onto the seat.

"Store don't want your rye?" Clive asked.

"Nope. It don't. We'll take the west trek toward the Gap. Sell this in Cumberland."

Ima stepped onto the porch. "Clive, you planning to run for mayor?"

"Thinkin' on it."

Ima stepped off the porch and snatched Clive by the wrist. "I might be willin' to help finance your campaign."

"I may or may not consider takin' it, but not today." Clive pulled his wrist away from Ima. "I'm still pondering what to do."

Ima glared and pressed her hands against her hips, her lips squeezed so tight they turned purple.

I tapped the reins on the horses. They groaned and pressed against the yoke, jolting the wagon wheels free from the thick mud. As we passed by the end of the store, a tall, heavyset man tipped his hat. Angus Barton, the older of the two brothers. His stare was cold, and though I didn't flinch, I felt the evil creeping under my skin.

We didn't look back. Even while Ima stood ranting that we'd pay for coming back to the mountain. Instead, I kicked two more bales of rye onto the ground. The people went to grabbing all they could.

"That ought about do 'em."

Thirteen

I figured my stopping at the Company Store served to set Barton on edge about that girl. Thomas was a smart man. He'd figure I had the girl without me saying as much, and my going and waltzing right up to Momma Barton showed him I meant business. He should be runnin' scared. The bad thing about a scared man is they'll do anything to cover up their sins. That's all that seems to matter—cover the lies.

The next step was to try and find Rayburn. Hopefully, a nervous Thomas wouldn't be thinking straight, and he'd accidentally show us what we needed.

We took the western path that wound its way around the back side of Barton Mountain and across the Gap to Cumberland. The trip, outside of being long and slow, wasn't bad. The mountain peaks kissed the summer sunset as night fell. The rain had passed, and as far as we could see from the summit, the skies were clear blue, dripping streaks of honey yellow from the sky.

"Mighty purty trip across this ridge." Clive leaned back and propped his feet on the footboard.

"Yep, yep. Sure is. I swear it's the door to heaven." I leaned my face toward the warmth of the evening sun. "A man can't get no higher than this mountain. You have to wait for the good Lord to open the door and invite you into paradise."

Clive patted a tune on his leg with his palm. "Makes me wonder why God Almighty would let a witch like Ima live so close to His gates. Don't you wonder?"

I thought for a minute. "I reckon the Lord knows the best thing a body can do is keep his enemies close."

Clive tapped his foot and wiggled in his seat. I could tell he had something on his mind.

"Go ahead, Clive. Either say what's eatin' at you or sit still."

"I guess the first is, I sealed my fate with Ima, didn't I?"

"If you're referring to not takin' her help for your campaign . . . maybe. You covered by saying you was still ponderin'."

"How you suppose she'll take to me leavin' it open for her help?" Clive asked.

"Ima never likes wishy-washy, but that might just be what she's looking for in a mayor. Somebody who don't rightly commit. Works to her advantage."

"Reckon she'll fire me from teaching at the mining school?"

"Don't suppose, Clive. Like I said, Ima needs a politician in her pocket." I sighed.

"Think she'll try to kill me? She's been known to make people disappear what don't help her causes. And I certainly ain't helping her causes."

"She won't kill you." I bumped against Clive's shoulder. "She wants a pawn. Somebody she can use in the local government—someone to help her get more from the people. She's a vulture. Vultures need prey, and sometimes politicians help with their dirty work. Pull in a few surprise meals."

"That's comforting . . . I think." Clive stretched an arm over his head.

"You worry too much, my friend." I lifted myself off the wooden seat and stretched my legs. "Look, Clive, it's like this. A man can stand his ground and do what's right or tuck tail and run while chaos wreaks its havoc." I sat down and pulled my hat to shade my eyes from the setting sun. "I figure you chose to do the right thing. There's always a price to pay for doin' right."

"I guess."

"Ima pays off every politician within a hundred miles of these mines. She wants them on her side. All but the sheriff, that is. He don't give." I waved away a lightning bug. "Follow Ima and you let her trample the good out of everything in sight."

Clive went to laughing. "Did you see the look on her face when you tossed that rye out to them miners? Oh lordy. Thought she'd kill you on the spot."

"We put food in their mouths. Now if they could only leave the mountain to buy supplies. Ima only gives miners ten cents on the dollar if they want cash for pay. She's got them by the pockets with her scrip and her Company Store," I said.

Clive pulled the reins tight, and the horses come to a halt. "Reckon here is as good as any to bed down. What do you say?"

I scanned the mountainside and nodded. I climbed over the wagon bench and stretched my mat across the rye. The top bales were gone, leavin' a nice place to bed down. Raney had packed us some fried bacon, bread, and a few beans, so we lit a fire and warmed them in a tin plate. The bacon popped and crackled as it heated, giving off a smoked scent of fresh pork. My mouth watered, and my jaw ached from the scent. Clive held out his plate, and we split what we had.

When he went to take a bite, I called him on it. "Whoa. We give thanks first."

"Oh shoot. I'm sorry." Clive spit his bite of food onto the ground.

I grinned. "The good Lord gets His due." I bowed my head, and Clive followed suit. "Well, Sir. Here we are. Ain't rightly sure what You got in store, but it must be worth something 'cause You saved my sorry butt on that mountain today. I'm much obliged. I ask You to bless these morsels of food, and, Sir, I ask Your protection. You know the devil we face."

"Amen." Clive then sopped his bread in the beans.

Raney never let a soul down when it come to her cooking. Even cold, her beans was tender, but warmed, a body couldn't beat them. We sat eating as the darkness folded over us. The only noise was the flapping of Clive's jaw.

"Joshua, I was thinkin'. I know you well enough to know you ain't greedy. But ain't you worried Ima will grow tired of waiting on you to show her where them gems are and come for them?"

I just kept eating.

"I mean, Ima must think you have enough gems to keep you and Raney well off. But I ain't never seen no signs of you splurging."

"Ain't nothin' to splurge." I shrugged.

I couldn't tell Clive where I kept the stone, how much I had, or where I'd found it. I couldn't put him in danger. The longer it stayed buried, the longer its mystery would grow. I could use bits of the stone to buy Ima off. Ima was sly, and though she could move to have me killed in a split second, she also knew how to watch her back. She'd wait as long as it took.

"You have to trust me," I said.

He wiggled a bit, finished his beans, then took his canteen of water off the wagon and rinsed his plate. "I do, Joshua. And if I'm gonna make an effort to be a mayor, I have to learn to listen and take a man at his word." Clive pressed his hand into my shoulder. "I trust you, my friend."

We bedded down. I lay there for a spell before I sat up, crawled off the wagon, and loaded my gun and cocked it.

Clive raised up from his bed. "Something wrong?"

"You shoot much, Clive? You got any experience handlin' a weapon?"

I knew Clive. We was friends, but we'd never hunted together. He'd been my youngin's teacher. As much as I liked him, this was no time to find out he didn't know how to shoot.

"I hunt, and I can take a squirrel or a rabbit out if necessary."

"Good. Take this. Keep it close." I handed him the pistol.

He reached from under his blanket and took it.

"Best to be safer than sorry." I dropped another log on the fire and crawled onto the wagon. I straightened my blanket and laid my gun next to me. "Sleep with one eye open."

Fourteen

Four days later, with the trip to Cumberland behind us, me and Clive turned onto the pitted path to my homestead. The July heat didn't take long to bake the mud dry after the storms. Our wheels bumped and banged into holes and over dried clots, jarring my insides. The horses grunted as they tugged at the wagon to keep a steady pace.

"Just be glad the wagon's empty now." I reached and patted the horse's rear.

I'd dropped five bales of rye on Barton Mountain, and the rest we sold in Cumberland, so I had enough money to pay Clive for his company and for saving my hide in that mudslide.

It was a hard trip, and I was grateful to see home in the distance. A mudslide was a twofold mess. One, when the sludge poured like a river over the trails, and the other when it dried into hard clots, makin' travel rough. It meant more work for me, busting them big chunks of dried mud along the trail to the house so the wagon would pull better, but that was life on the homestead. Always work to do.

"I'd say it was a productive trip. Wouldn't you?" Clive swiped his forehead with his sleeve, then set his hat. We'd rehashed our visit to the mines several times. Talked over the folks we'd spoken with and things we'd discovered. The women told us June had moved, and that helped us know she had to be hiding somewhere. Goin' over things one more time wouldn't hurt—just to make sure we'd not missed anything. A body had to be sure things was in order where Ima was concerned.

"Maybe," I said. "We managed to stir up a hornet's nest. I just hate I couldn't find June's name before Ima slammed the ledger closed. If you consider that, then it wasn't so productive."

"Shoving them bales of rye on the ground got us better answers," Clive said.

"Who'd have thought to just ask the women while they picked up grain?" I laughed. "Raney always told me I tended to do things the hard way."

"But there was nothing real helpful. No one has seen June in ages, and we already knew Rayburn lives outside the south camps." Clive scratched his knees.

"It tells us June ain't been around though. It was that easy to know where not to look. Just ask a woman!" We chuckled. "Still, goin' in that store was smart. It set Ima on edge. She's wondering what's up my sleeve, and despite you turning down her money, you probably made her all the more determined to win you over. She needs the next mayor."

"Leastways we have an idea of where to look for Rayburn. And he's easy to get to, bein' outside the south mining camp. That's just a few miles from my place and far enough from the mines. Bartons don't tend to move far from home, and the south side is a good distance."

"I need to mull over the best way to the camp. We gotta look for Rayburn without stirrin' up too much dust. If we can find him, then maybe we can find June and settle if she's Aughtie's momma."

The bend toward home was in sight, and I remembered why I'd dreaded the trip to Cumberland. Two days over the mountain and two back. It was a long trip. I leaned my head back and took in the fresh air. A breeze carried the nutty scent of the late rye and clean river water. *Home.*

I couldn't remember the last time I was this anxious to see home—Raney. Aughtie. That little girl had already turned my heart soft, and as much as I'd like to call her my own, I knew she wasn't. It was a strange place to be. Torn between findin' the child's family and makin' her part of mine. There was only one right answer.

We rounded the bend, and I could see the house. A tree lay along the far side of the porch. "Dang sycamore. I've been tryin' to kill that tree for a year, and Raney wouldn't let me. She likes the shade. Now look. It nearly fell on the house. It only took the rain a short time to do what I've been trying to do for a year." I leaned back on the seat and dropped the reins.

The horses knew the way to the barn. Doves whistled their calls back and forth, and the river's song offered to lull us, but from the far side of the homestead, a faint noise worked toward us.

It was in the distance. I sat up straight and cupped my hand around my ear. Wasn't sure what it was, but I heard something.

"You hear that?" I asked Clive. I grabbed the reins and pulled the wagon to a halt so we could listen. "Can't make what it is, but I swear I heard something."

"Almost sounded like a cry. Somebody hollerin'."

I glanced toward the house again and eyed the property. There was hardly a twist of smoke coming from the chimney. By this time, Raney would have the fire roaring to cook.

There it was again. The cry echoed. Something wasn't right. Raney would usually be outside doin' her chores, and we'd left Cleda Mae with her and Aughtie.

"Where are the women?" Clive shouted as he come to his feet in the wagon. "I don't see the women."

Panic hit me square in the gut.

I stood in the wagon and shaded my eyes from the sun as I scanned the property again. "Barn looks okay. Shed? House?" My eyes scoured across every inch of the homestead.

Then I heard it again.

"Oh Lord. Somebody help me!" This time the voice echoed across the field. It wafted past us on the breeze. The echo was faint, but we could make it out.

"Cleda? That's Cleda Mae!" Clive leaped out of the wagon and tore across the field. I snapped the reins, pulling the horses off the trail. They kicked into a hard run over the field.

"Clive, get in." He grabbed the side of the wagon and pulled hisself in. I didn't think my heart took a beat.

The woods lined the rye field, and as we grew closer, a woman burst through the underbrush into the field, screamin'.

"There she is! Stop the wagon!" Clive jumped out and met Cleda.

She fell into his arms, screaming hysterically.

"Where's Raney?" I shouted.

"They're gone! I couldn't stop them," Cleda Mae cried.

"Who's gone?" I jumped out of the wagon, took her by the arm, and spun her around. "Cleda Mae, where's Raney and the girl?"

She managed to utter a few broken sentences between her sobs and screams.

"A man. Black hood. Snatched up Aughtie when she slipped out of the house."

Fear crawled into my throat. "Raney? Where's Raney?"

"She tried to grab Aughtie off his horse. The man kicked her backward, then knocked me down with his horse. Raney fell, went sailing down the side of hill. Before I could get my wits about me, she was on her feet tryin' to run after them.

"Where is she?" I shouted.

"They went this way." Cleda Mae took off up the side of the hill.

It was all I could do to follow her. *Let her lead you.*

I dropped the reins and followed Cleda Mae on foot. Each step she took, she shouted strings of words that hardly made a lick of sense. But I heard enough to know Raney was hurt and Aughtie was gone. It had to be Barton. He'd made his way back down the mountain to get that girl, and Raney got in his way.

My own string of foul words flew outa my mouth. "If this was Barton's doin', he's a dead man. An eye for an eye." My lungs burned for air as we run up the steep embankment.

"Aughtie didn't want to be cooped up no more, and she busted out across the fields. That's when he—" Cleda Mae tripped and fell to her knees. Me and Clive helped her up, and she went to flailing and slapping. "Let me go. We have to find Raney." She jerked away and high-stepped over dried brush and broken tree limbs. "Raney saw him start into the woods with Aughtie, and she went after her. This way!"

"Could you see who it was?" I huffed out the words as we climbed the steep hill.

Cleda Mae stopped dead. "I told you he had a hood over his head." She pointed to a clearing. "There. In that clearing."

"Raney, honey, where are you? Raney?" The only noise I heard was the huffin' and puffin' of the three of us.

"Over there," Cleda Mae screamed. "There's where she fell."

Panic surged through my bones. I made a beeline for the edge of the ravine. Without thinking, I jumped and slid down the embankment, grabbing at saplings and bushes to slow my fall. "Raney!" Nothing. I dug the heel of my boots into the bank to slow myself.

The palms of my hands scrubbed against rock and dirt, scraping my hands. My skin turned a fast red, like I'd grabbed a hot skillet. When I finally hit the bottom, I come to my feet, running. The only woman I'd ever loved was nowhere to be found. I felt like a hound hunting down a fox that just eluded me.

A small pool of blood and a shred of Raney's skirt tail lay next to a bush. The fabric was stained red, and a small amount was smeared toward a trail. But when I tried to follow it, nothing.

"Lord, You've saved me this week. Save Raney," I prayed under my breath. I wanted to be angry at the good Lord, but right now I didn't have time. Raney was first.

"Joshua, she there?" Clive hollered.

I darted from bush to tree, looking for any sign of her or Aughtie. "No. Law no. She ain't here. Just a puddle of blood."

"Stay there, Joshua. I'll get the horses. Stay there." Clive grabbed Cleda Mae by the arm and gave her a yank. "Come on. We're gonna need you at Joshua's cabin."

I dropped to my knees and buried my face in my hands. Rage boiled in my gut, and I knew what needed to be done.

I've never been a man that carried a grudge until Barton ran down Anna. Now my pushed-down anger and fear mixed together, and what was cooking from it was nothing short of revenge.

As Clive took Cleda Mae to the house and went for the horses, I knew I needed to get my thoughts straight—try and cipher which way Barton and Raney had gone. The anger in my gut was like a burnin' fire. My fingers wrapped around the torn and bloody material. Blue with tiny flowers on it. I'd saved a month's worth of wages to buy that skirt for her.

"Joshua, it ain't even my birthday," she'd said.

"Don't have to be no special occasion to give you something nice."

Raney had taken the skirt and walked to the bed. She'd laid it out nice, brushed the wrinkles away. Then I'd watched as she dropped the skirt she wore to the floor and replaced it with the new one. She was always a pretty thing, and she never acted like she deserved a gift. Still, I did my best to make her feel special.

I sat on the ground, knees bent with the torn fabric from the dress wrapped around my fingers. The rage inside me grew. Why would a good God let something happen to a good woman like Raney?

Tears squeezed from my eyes, and the words to a familiar hymn Raney sang came to mind. "Leanin'. Leanin'. Safe and secure from all alarms," I hummed.

It wasn't right. I'd tried to save my daughter, and I couldn't. I'd tried to be the safe haven for her and Raney. Protect them and care for them. Aughtie too. And all I'd managed to do was sentence them to death.

Leanin'. Leanin'. Leanin' on the everlastin' arms. For a minute my heart stopped, and I gasped. The pain of losing all three choked the air out of me. What good was leaning on the everlasting arms when they turned loose and let you fall?

FIFTEEN

I LISTENED TO Clive's and Cleda's footsteps leading away while I lay there next to that pool of blood. Cleda Mae was no good to us in the mess she was in. We'd managed to get her to show us the last direction she'd seen Raney, and that would help. Clive would leave Cleda Mae at the house before unhitching the horses from the wagon and bringing them here. He'd promised to be back soon, and I figured that'd be quick enough. I was learnin' to trust the young man. Besides, it gave me a minute to collect myself without a soul watching. On my back, I bent my knees and planted my feet on the rocky ground. My arm rested over my eyes. The midday sun baked me like a potato in a fire.

I used to love stretching out in the grass and letting the sun warm my bones. It's like the warmth draws what ails you right out of your body. Me and Raney would take a picnic basket and work our way up to a clearing near the pass. The river rushed over rocks bigger than ten men put together, and the roar of the water was so loud, we'd shout. But somehow we'd end up lazin' in the grass, my head resting in her lap.

This couldn't be happening to me. Not twice. I found myself heaving sobs, and the more my chest pitched up and down, the more my anger built. I'd not lose another loved one to the Bartons.

I couldn't say I had any regrets about bringing little Aughtie into our home. Something had to be done for that little girl. Between seein' a child in need and suffering my own loss, I didn't think about the fallout. I just never imagined all the possible consequences. I sobbed loud, hard cries, something I hadn't done enough since Anna's death.

The sun burned the tears off my face, and I rolled to my knees. Lying here doing nothing wouldn't help my family. Clive had demanded I wait and not go off on my own hunting Raney. He was right, even though every bone in me was screamin' to run and search. But there was still searching to be done right here. I scoured the ravine where Raney had fallen, climbing up and down the bank, trying to find anything that would lead me to her. Going any further from here on foot was dangerous. I needed my sure-footed horse. "Raney!" I shouted.

My call for Raney was answered with the whinny of Rufus, my horse, echoing in the pass.

"Joshua! I know you're around here somewhere. You hear me?" Clive hollered.

"Over here!" I dabbed the small drops of blood from my scraped-up palm with my handkerchief and then spread the piece of fabric on the ground. I rolled the torn bit of skirt into it and stuffed the mess in my pocket. It was just seconds before I heard Mater's howlin'. I had to give Clive credit. He'd done good to bring the hound. Mater rounded the trees, hiked his leg, then loped to me.

"Good boy." I took his head in my hands and rubbed his jowls. Slobber dripped down my fingers, stringin' the blood down my arm.

Clive come around a patch of laurel trees towing Rufus. He'd hung my rifle in its side holster and took a second one for hisself.

"I think I got everything." He eased the horses next to me. "Got both rifles, extra shot, the dog."

I run my hand up and over Rufus's head and then down his neck. He didn't look any more worn for travel.

"I know, Rufus. It's been a long day, but you gotta help me." I twisted the stirrup around and hooked the ball of my foot inside. The saddle squeaked as I pulled myself up.

"You did good, Clive." I straightened in my saddle. "I never thought to tell you to bring Mater."

"I got a good friend named Joshua who's taught me a little about bein' a homesteader." Clive smiled, trying to lighten the moment.

"Mater. Here. Come on, hound." The dog bolted from under some brush and slid to a halt next to Rufus. I pulled my handkerchief from my trouser pocket. "Up here, boy. Come on up here."

The dog raised to his hind legs and rested his bear-sized paws against my leg. I unrolled the material from Raney's dress and rubbed it against his nose.

That dog's nose punched deep into the bloody material. He'd always been a good huntin' hound. Rabbits, squirrels, groundhogs. Didn't matter. Ole Mater could flush them out of a briar patch.

His nose went to the ground, and that long tail pointed straight into the air. Mater circled the horses and the trees, then let out a howl. He hesitated, to be sure I was paying attention. Then he bolted through the trees.

I leaned forward in my saddle and pressed my knees into my horse's sides. The hound was on the trail. His howl resonated with the mournful wail in my heart. As we tore under tree limbs and around bushes, every thought I had was about Raney and Aughtie. Mater took up a bank, his feet diggin' into the soft dirt. We climbed off the horses and led them up the steep embankment.

Me and Clive followed Mater for good bit before the hound lost the scent, so we stopped to rest. We stood at the top of a ridge, eyes scannin' the beauty in the green of the treetops, in the soft whisper of the breeze. "Raney!" I shouted. Clive followed behind me shouting her name.

When there was no answer, we rested on a large boulder that jutted over the edge of the mountain. No doubt the summit was beautiful, but the thick undergrowth and rugged mountainside proved Mother Nature could clamp her teeth down when she wanted. *You don't want Raney. She ain't the one who stirred up trouble. She's innocent.*

"We don't know for sure this was the Bartons' doings. Grant you, it seems all too obvious." Clive pulled his hat from his head and swiped his brow. "I don't think we can just assume this was the Bartons. Mind you, I ain't on their side."

"I know." I swallowed hard. "It's all I can do to fight the urge to kill Thomas Barton. But you're right. We don't know for sure." But who else would steal a slow child?

I pushed my hat back on my head and leaned onto my elbows. Mater lay at our feet. I rubbed his back with the toe of my boot. I needed something to break the tension, and a smile come over me. "Mater got his name from raidin' Raney's tomato patch. Blasted dog would walk the rows of tomato vines and smell the tomatoes until he found hisself a yellow mater. Then he'd pick it right off the vine. We'd catch him holed up under the edge of the porch, having hisself a snack.

"Raney run him out of her garden a hundred times until she finally took after him with a broom. He made a beeline for the barn with a yellow tomato hanging from his jaw. She changed his name from Duke to Mater. Reckon I couldn't argue with her. It was fittin'."

Clive shook his head and grinned. "Let's find Raney."

I shoved that piece of Raney's skirt under Mater's nose again, hoping it'd stir something up in him. "Hunt, dog!" I shouted. "Hunt!"

He snorted, paced a couple of rounds by the horses, then went to howling and barking.

"Find Raney."

He lifted his head, jowls swinging, and eyed me like he suddenly realized who it was he was supposed to be finding. That nose hit the ground, and he was off. I pressed my hat tight against my head. Rufus reared and bolted into a run.

Clive hung tight on his horse, his arms and legs flapping with the rhythm of his horse's gallop. The horses' hooves echoed in my head as we ducked under low-hanging limbs.

Mater slid to a stop and took a stance like he was ready to fight. He lifted his head and let out a howl. Every hair on his neck stood on end—he'd found something.

"Here! Over here." I threw my leg over my saddle and hit the ground before Rufus come to a stop. Hanging on a briar bush was another bloody strip of Raney's dress. I held it up for Clive to see.

"Blood ain't dried yet. She can't be far." Clive shook his head.

"We gotta find her. She's hurt, and I swear, if this is Barton's doin', which I'm guessin' it is . . ."

"Stop it, Joshua. Just stop it. We ain't got time for revenge. We gotta find Raney and Aughtie. Revenge is the Lord's."

Revenge is the Lord's. Ha. That coming from a man who don't pray before he eats. Where was the good Lord when Anna was trampled to death? Nowhere I could see. I appreciated Clive's thoughts, trying to keep me focused on the task and all, but the Bartons made this battle personal a long time back.

I stuck the bloody material under Mater's nose. "Heaow, boy. Hunt. Hunt!"

The dog leaped through several bushes and tore across a creek.

Clive spurred his horse and took out while I threw my leg over Rufus and pulled myself into the saddle. "Hup, horse. Hup!" My insides jarred as the horse hit a hard run.

Mater tore up the side of a hill. The dirt was too loose for the horses, so we dropped off their backs again and tossed the reins into a bush. I whipped my rifle from the side holster and shoved it tight under my arm. Mater was a good distance ahead. His howls grew muffled, but I wasn't about to slow down.

Me and Clive went to our knees under low trees, fighting our way through thickets of honeysuckle and brambles. Clive slipped and rolled backward down the hill.

"You okay?" I hollered.

"Go. I'm fine. Just go. I'll catch up."

I didn't wait. I run like I was runnin' for the last piece of corn bread in the pan. Then the howling stopped.

"Mater! Yo, dog." Silence. Silence . . . then a faint whine.

"Raney," I screamed. "Raney!" I busted through the honeysuckle and fell flat on my face. When I crawled to my knees, the bile in my stomach rolled into my throat. "Oh lordy. No."

In front of me stood a giant oak tree, and there, arms stretched over her head, dress ripped to shreds, lay Raney. Her head tilted toward her chest, and I could see the blood drip from her mouth. I was torn between anger and sheer terror.

Her legs were bare and scraped up, her face bloody, and a gash cut down her arm.

I rushed to her side just as Clive made his way through the thicket. "Lord have mercy," he mumbled.

"Don't just stand there—help me."

Clive grabbed his knife and tossed it toward me as he ran out of the thicket.

I sawed through what was left of her skirt. The shreds had wound tight around her legs. Her ankles was swolled up, and her palms was scraped raw.

"Raney, can you hear me? Please hear me, baby."

Her eye was blackened, her lip split and pooched out. She struggled to open her eyes.

Once we got her skirt untangled from the thicket, I pulled her into my chest and held her tight. Clive tied a piece of her torn skirt around the cut on her arm.

"I got you, honey. I got you. What happened? Was it Barton?"

She rolled her head to one side and whispered, "A man with a hood over his head. Big man."

A big man? My mind went to sorting through men. Thomas wasn't no bigger than me. For a minute I was disappointed. I wanted the chance to beat the tar outa him, but it seemed I couldn't pin this act on him. But who?

"Raney, I need to pick you up."

She groaned when I slipped my arms under her and lifted. That one arm hung limp.

Every step I took gettin' her outa that ravine just made me madder. "I don't want to even know how you wound up here."

"Aughtie," Raney whispered. "Where's Aughtie?"

As harsh as it sounded, I needed to lay my worry for the youngin down and take care of my wife.

"We ain't found her, but we will," Clive said.

"Big man." Her eyes rolled, peering off to the distance.

"Hush, baby. We know," I said as I handed Raney off to Clive and lifted a branch for him to pass under. It took us both carrying her, passing her back and forth, to get back to the horses.

"Reckon who she means?" Clive said, ducking under a branch.

"I don't know."

Raney's moans grew, and I took her back so I could make that last push to the horses. Clive held out his arms, and I laid Raney, once more, into his. Her head rolled against his chest, and she cried out in pain.

I untangled the reins from a bush and climbed onto Rufus. "Hand her up."

Clive shifted Raney up into my lap.

I cradled her against my shoulder like I was burpin' a baby, and she winced in pain. "I'm sorry, baby. So sorry. We'll be home in a bit. Hang on. I promise I'll take care of you. Try to think of them beautiful flowers in our back field and how they stretch their heads up toward heaven when the sun hits them. You love that."

Clive took the lead, and we crept through the ravine and down the steep bank toward the field. I kept askin' Raney who did this, knowin' full well she couldn't answer me. She couldn't tell me it was Thomas.

Big man.

Who could she mean? I didn't know yet, but you best believe I'd figure it out, and then there'd be a price to pay.

Clive was quiet for the most part, but when we hit that field, he turned and studied me. I could see thoughts click in his head.

"I think I know who Raney's talkin' about. I'd have never thought it, except I walked into him at the Company Store."

I nudged Rufus ahead. "Spit it out! We ain't got time to fiddle around. Who in tarnation do you think it is?"

Clive halted his horse and climbed down. He toed the dirt with his boot. "Only really big man I can think of is Angus."

That was it. Angus Barton, Thomas's older brother. He was the size of two men put together. His belt barely held his trousers tight below his gut. My nose flared, and my jaw tightened. Angus Barton was known as a bully. Was Angus working with his brother?

I swallowed hard tryin' to keep my wits about me. "We gotta get Raney home and cleaned up. I can get Cleda Mae to help me patch her up if you get the doc."

"Will do." Clive straightened hisself in his saddle. "I'll be back." He dug his heels into his horse and took across the field toward the little town at the base of the mountain—the only town that'd managed to steer clear of Ima.

The house come into sight, and I nudged Rufus into a trot. Cleda Mae stood on the porch, wringing her hands. When I hollered, she come running.

"Raney, we got you." Cleda Mae primed the water pump, and when the water rushed out, I just laid Raney under it.

She howled like Mater, but it was the fastest way to wash her wounds. We stripped her naked, and I could see the bruises on her sides and back darkening. "She's been beat, ain't she?"

We covered her with a blanket and took her into the cabin.

"Lordy mercy, I ain't never seen the likes." Cleda Mae tore strips of cheesecloth and wrapped Raney's arm. The blood that had slowed to a trickle broke loose and poured. I pressed my shirttail against the cut to hold the bleeding. "It don't look like she was beat, Joshua. It looks like she fell. Look at the palms of her hands."

Cleda Mae was right. Raney's palms and fingers was scraped up like she'd tried to hold on to something and then slipped before she fell. But in my mind, in my rage, all I could see was a Barton beatin' the woman I loved.

"Look a here, bits and pieces of rock and twigs are pressed into her cuts. It was like she'd grabbed at the mountain as she slid." Cleda Mae lifted Raney's hands and twisted them palms up.

"You sure? I swear I think she was beat." I felt the panic in my gut grow as I looked over her wounds.

Cleda Mae gasped. "Oh lordy, Joshua, get your wits. I can't manage you and her."

"I'm so sorry, Raney. If you'd just have stayed home—let me go after the girl. Maybe you wouldn't have got hurt."

Raney lifted her hand to my cheek and brushed her knuckle over my lips. She whispered, "Ain't your fault." Her words were weak, and she winced as she struggled to speak. "Just do me one thing."

"What? Anything."

"Find Aughtie."

SIXTEEN

ON THE MOUNTAIN where we'd found Raney, I'd been torn whether to take her home myself or let Clive take her whilst I went after Aughtie. Ain't never had a harder decision. But the woman I loved was banged up . . . Only God knew what else that man did to her, with the way we found her. But Raney had nearly died trying to save the girl.

"Raney, honey, you have to wake up and talk to me." I gently tapped her cheeks.

Her eyes cracked, and through her pain she managed a weak smile.

"Who did this? Who took Aughtie? Did he beat you?"

Her words were faint and garbled, like she had a mouth full of berries. "He had on a black hood. I done told you. No!" Her voice sharp with pain and frustration.

"No what?" I prodded.

"I tripped and fell—now leave me be!" she cried.

Rage hit me like a river swelled with floodwaters. It had to be a Barton. Even if he hadn't beat her, he'd taken Aughtie and put my Raney in danger. Maybe he'd lured her into a place she'd fall down the mountains . . . just like his brother'd intentionally run down my girl. And he was wrong if he thought I'd stand back this time. I wanted to kill the lot of them for it.

"Clive should be back soon with the doc, but we gotta do something to slow this bleeding." Cleda Mae handed me another rag to press over the cut on Raney's arm.

I looked around the room and spied a wooden spoon. "Hand me that wood spoon, and tear me a new piece of cheesecloth."

Cleda Mae jumped to her feet and grabbed the spoon. She tore a new piece of cloth and handed it to me.

"We'll pull it around her arm and twist it tight with the spoon. Loosen it for a couple of seconds every little bit." It was a small wonder Raney hadn't died between the time it took me to find her and then the ride back. She shoulda been drained of all her life. I reckon the Lord wasn't ready for her to come home.

I opened the door, then stopped and turned toward Cleda Mae. "I need to know what happened. I can't find Aughtie if I don't know what happened and how or where to start to look."

"I've done told you what happened. Raney tried to grab Aughtie. The man kicked her. She took after him. When she grabbed that saddle, it flung her. Raney tried to run again but tripped and fell down that ravine. She wasn't beat up. She fell, just like she said. I don't know 'cause I wasn't there." Cleda's tone was growin' frustrated. "Where you gonna look for Aughtie?"

I scrubbed my face with my knuckles. "I don't know, but it looks the place we found Raney is the place to start. I ain't sure I can leave Raney."

"But Aughtie . . ." Cleda Mae shook her head.

"I know. I know. Aughtie. Find Aughtie."

I pointed at the spoon Cleda Mae held. "I saw Doc Starnes do that once in the mine when Levi Stokes got caught under one of them coal carts and tore a gash in his leg the size of my fist. Doc grabbed a hammer and a strip of his shirt to do the same thing. Funny how things like that come back to you when you least expect it.

"I'm gonna check to see if Clive and the doc are in sight."

I pulled my blood-soaked shirt over my head, tossed it in the corner, and pressed my fingers against Raney's face. Her skin was turning the color of ash after it cooled. "Raney."

She barely nodded.

I stepped onto the porch and shaded my eyes with my hand. Dust rose down the lane. It was Clive with the doc.

"They're here, Cleda Mae." My heart raced faster than a rabbit on the run. I leaped off the porch, pumped a bucket of water, then grabbed a shirt off the line and took it inside. By then Doc and Clive was at the house and I rushed to meet them.

"She's in there, Doc," I shouted.

He grabbed his bag and rushed inside. I trailed right behind him, but he put his hand in my face. "Stay out here. We need room to work." Doc gently nudged me back and closed the door.

He left me standin' on the porch. I rested my forehead against the door and fought back the tears.

Clive took me by the arm to try and calm me.

"Clive, I need her to talk to me. Find out which direction the man took Aughtie. I'm gonna kill Barton—Thomas or Angus, don't matter which is first."

Clive stepped in front of me. He yanked the clean shirt off my shoulder and shoved it in my chest. "Joshua, you are out of control. Raney fell down that ravine. That's what Cleda Mae said. That's what Raney said." He moved his head every way I moved mine. "Your rage ain't helping nobody."

I took in a deep breath and let it out, then leaned against the house and slid to my rear. I laid my head on my knees.

Clive eased next to me. "Take it easy. I understand your hate, but it's clouding your mind."

I nodded. Words could hardly come. "I have to find that youngin. I haven't forgot Aughtie."

"Of course you haven't forgot Aughtie. We'll find her," Clive said. "But Raney comes first. Then the girl."

Suddenly I was overcome with hopelessness. Sadness. *Oh, Lord, can't You help me? Just help me. Will You help an angry man?*

"First things first," I whispered, trying to convince myself Clive was right.

I buried my head in the bend of my arm. "I reckon I ain't as strong as I thought I was." Those words sank deep in my heart, and I knew I had to be strong. Clive was right. I had to be smart. Take things in order. I couldn't jump past all that just so I could kill the Barton brothers. Our minds can twist the truth in order to justify our sin. The hardest part is sayin' no.

The hours that passed felt like days, but the door finally opened, and

Cleda Mae motioned us in. I rushed to Raney's side. She was sleeping. Albeit restless. I leaned over and pressed my lips against her forehead.

"She gonna be alright, Doc?"

"I stitched her up. She's fortunate. I reckon the good Lord was watchin' over her." Doc scrubbed his hands in the basin. The water turned a crimson red. "She'll be weak for a spell. Lost a lot of blood. Feed her chicken livers. That'll build her blood back up. Time is what she needs."

"Was she beat, Doc?" I had to be sure.

"She's banged up, but it don't look like someone beat her. Woman took a hefty fall or two. She was able to tell me a little about it. She should come round in a week or so."

A sigh of relief hissed from my lungs.

Doc dried his hands and took his hat. "Cleda Mae knows what to do in the meantime. Keep her warm. Losing that kind of blood makes a body cold. Give her a swig of hooch to numb the pain." He opened the door. "I'll be back around to check on her." Doc tipped his hat and left.

I touched Raney's cheek. Her hand balled the material of my shirt.

"It wasn't Thomas. Don't do nothin' foolish," she said.

Her words were weak, but the strength in what she said was convicting.

"You rest, now. I promise we'll find Aughtie." I gingerly kissed her knuckles around the bandages.

Raney pulled me close. "A body oughta be thankful for their blessin's. I'm alive. That's a blessin'."

I was much obliged Raney was alive, even if it was by the skin of her teeth, but I was hard pressed to be thankful for much else.

I had stood at the wake of John Miller, a miner, and told his wife, "God uses the pain to draw us into his lap, and when He does, that's as good a reason as any to give thanks." Now here I was trying to do the same.

Problem was, right at this moment, my wise words weren't worth nothing. All I wanted to do was hunt down the animal who had done this to Raney and taken Aughtie.

"Joshua, we need water." Cleda Mae handed me a basin.

Clive took it from me. "I'll go. You stay here with Raney. But don't you start pushin' her for more answers. She needs rest, and the more you push, the harder it is on her."

Clive was young, but his youth didn't seem to mess with his clarity. It was me waiting to leap out of the thicket onto the prey, not him.

"Aughtie! Joshua, where's Aughtie?" Raney roused, talkin' outa her head.

I needed to find the child, but I couldn't bear leaving Raney.

Bitterness against the good Lord snuggled right up next to my anger for Barton. Why would God let bad things happen to the innocent? Worse yet, why would He make it so I'd have to make this choice? Stay here with Raney until she was back on her feet or leave her and go looking for Aughtie. It was a miserable choice. I couldn't choose between Raney and Aughtie.

"Joshua, you alright?" Clive settled a hand on my shoulder. No doubt he meant to calm me, but the words came to me through the raging fire in my veins.

I shot him an icy stare. His eyes widened, hands flying up in surrender.

Part of me could see that I was teeterin' on the edge. That little bit of my mind knew Clive wasn't the enemy. But the good Lord knows that the bigger part of me was like that mountainside with two days' rain up against it. I was about to slide into the ravine and gobble up anything in my path.

Raney rolled her head toward her shoulder. Her hand raised enough to motion me toward her.

I went to my knees next to her. "What, Raney?" I brushed strands of hair from her face.

"Find Aughtie."

Raney was forcing me to choose. Forcing me to feel guilty if I chose her over the girl. My frustration grew, and I felt like I could rip the bark off a pine tree.

A tear squeezed from the corner of her eye. My heart ached. I knew what she wanted me to do, but I couldn't. I couldn't pick the girl over my wife. My place was here. Or was it?

I leaned close. Her breath warmed my neck. I rubbed my hand down her bare leg, tryin' to not touch the bruises. "You know you mean the world to me."

Brushing back strands of sweat-dampened hair, I sang the hymn Raney loved. "What have I to dread? What have I to fear? Leanin' on the everlastin' arms." I gently sung into her ear. "Leanin'. Leanin'. Leanin' on the everlastin' arms." That little part of me said I should take heed to the words of the hymn myself. But the floodwaters had busted through.

There was nothing left for me but my tears. I pressed my face tight into her hair and cried. "Don't die, Raney. I can't live without you."

She sighed. Her body relaxed, and my stomach turned.

The happiest day of my life was when Eldon Marlow permitted me to marry his girl. From the time we were kids, I'd followed along behind her like a duck trailing after its momma. I'd race to the end of the holler every morning to meet her. Eldon would bring her to the edge of the trail in the wagon so we could walk to school. Every day I asked her the same question, "Can I carry your books?"

She'd answer the same. "I got strong arms."

I kissed her head and wondered if she remembered my response. "I reckon you ain't as strong as you think you are." But right about then, I knew she was stronger than I ever thought she was.

It was horrible, this woman weakened to this point. I breathed in the scent of her damp hair. Nothing at all like the lilac smell she'd get when she boiled flowers into tonic water. Raney's broken arm dropped to the side.

"Don't go, Raney. I shoulda never stirred the hornet's nest." I laid her flat and pressed my head against her chest. It was there. Faint, but there. The beat of her heart dug into my soul.

"Joshua." Cleda Mae eased me away. "She's gonna do alright. Go outside. Get some air. Let me finish cleanin' her up."

I glared at her, but she come right to my face. "Go. Outside. Now! Get your wits about you. What's done is done. She told you what she wanted. Now go find the girl!"

Clive took me by the shoulders and guided me to the door. "My little woman is small, but when she means business, she means business. Let's go. We got Raney down the mountain to the house. Got Doc. Cleda Mae will help clean her up. Let's leave her to it."

As much as I hated the thought, the time had come to decide. Raney or Aughtie? I needed to put my anger behind me. Cleda Mae was right. *Grow up.*

I was amazed how attached we'd gotten to that little girl in such a short time. There was something especially sweet about her. Something that needed protecting.

This deed could have only been done by the man who had something to gain—Thomas Barton. But there was the lie again, and I knew it. It was what I wanted to believe. Stronger than my deepest weakness. Them words come back to me again—*you ain't as strong as you think you are.*

SEVENTEEN

THERE WAS A time I was friends with Barton. A time when we had each other's backs. Those days in the ground, digging out that black gold. But when you lose trust in a man, when he's not as good as his word, then a great divide happens. A chasm that can't be crossed.

The morning after we got Raney home, Manny rode up to the barn and jumped off his horse. "Hettie sent me to check on Raney."

I raked a pile of hay into a stall. "How'd you know? We ain't said nothin'." I leaned my rake against the barn and stuck out my hand to welcome my friend.

"Word travels fast. Doc was by checkin' on Hettie after us losin' our Mary. He told us there was an accident. I'm guessing there is more to the story."

I nodded. "Somebody snatched up Aughtie while we was gone. Raney went after them. She fell down a ravine. I'll go after the girl once I know Raney'll be good. She's a strong woman, and though she's beat and banged up, she'll pull through. It's what Raney does." I dragged the toe of my boot in the dirt, biting my tongue to keep quiet.

"Let me guess. You think it was Barton?" Manny leaned against the barn next to me. "I remember the day Thomas turned sour. Don't you?" Manny nudged me. "I watched him pace the side of the mine shaft, burying his fingers deep into his hair and rubbing his head. Ole man Barton and fifteen men went into the mine carrying picks and pulling mules. A new vein had opened up."

I remembered the day Manny recalled. Mother Earth was not pleased the rodents had dug their way down. We could hear her rumble and growl beneath our feet. No question she wanted them men out, and she shook the ground to warn them. A horrible memory.

"'We gotta shut that hole down before somebody dies,' I'd told Thomas. But Thomas was determined to do what Ima told him. She signaled everything was good."

"Kills me to think back on that day. Draws my anger to the top." Manny went to bangin' his fists against the barn like he was pushing them memories back. I understood his frustration 'cause part of me wanted to do the same.

I could see it all in my mind. The ground had shaken for two days. It wasn't safe. I knew . . . Thomas knew . . . it wouldn't be long before the ground gobbled up them men, but Thomas set them sticks of dynamite despite his knowing the truth. "Blow the mountain when Momma says to blow it," Thomas had shouted at me.

I shook my head tryin' to forget the picture. I rested my arm on Manny's shoulder to comfort him.

Ima was so greedy that she'd been willing to risk her own husband's life for that fresh vein of black gold. She didn't care about the men or their families. I'd been walkin' the upper rim of the shaft as it trembled.

"You remember the mules?" Manny's voice was quiet, almost to a whisper. "The mules squalled as they slipped and stumbled outa the hole. Animals know. Those critters rarely made a noise until they sensed the danger. The men tried to get them mules to move, but they bore down and wouldn't go in that hole. Instead they bucked and run. Wish the men would've done the same."

We was quiet for a few minutes. Both rethinking that day. Manny offered me a pinch of snuff. I motioned him a no.

"Thomas set them dynamite sticks along the shaft's far side, then waited." My stomach tightened as the memory of that day dug in. "I pushed for John and them boys to pull out of that mine."

"Greed is the kiss of death. And Ima's the devil herself." Manny swiped his face with his handkerchief.

"No matter how we had tried to convince Thomas to walk away, he wouldn't. He paced and fretted, looking toward Momma Barton's place. She stood out on the overlook, arms crossed and hair pulled tight into a bun."

I'd squatted to the ground and drew in the dirt with my finger, writing the names of the men in that mine, hoping to convince Thomas. He had to make a choice. The same choice I was forced to make. Choose who lives and who dies.

Manny pressed into the barn wall, staring at the house like it might be hiding the mine. "When I saw he wasn't going to call them out, I slid down the bank to the shaft and hollered for them all to get out. But John shouted up, 'Not now. We got to this new vein. No need to blow the walls.'" Manny pushed the bottom of his boot against the barn.

"I started hard up that bank to tell Thomas to hold the fire—to try and change his mind. But just as I topped the hill, he lit the fuse. There was men in that hole. I rushed toward the crackling fuse, but it had done eat its way over the hill where I couldn't get to it and live to tell the tale. I fell to the ground and covered my head just as that dynamite blew. The ground rumbled, and I could feel it droppin' rock and dirt. Dust and boulders flew into the air. The boom echoed for eternity through the valley, and when I stood, I saw Thomas walk away." Manny squatted to the ground. "Barton stopped and shrugged, then disappeared over the hill. No remorse."

Me and Manny sat flat on the ground and propped ourselves against the rough barn wall. A man never forgets that sort of thing, and every time you talk about it, it's like reliving the moment. Sixteen men and one was Thomas's daddy. It was cold murder. When I'd looked up that hill where Ima stood, it galled me. She never moved, and when I went running toward her, hollerin', she turned and walked away. Just like Thomas.

"You know who has that girl, don't you? Your gut's done told you." Manny elbowed me.

The only person who could want Aughtie was this man who'd murdered not once but twice—the men in the mine and our daughters.

"I got an inklin'. But no proof." I stood and dusted the dirt from my trousers.

"Thomas Barton killed my girl too. When you decide to go after him, I'll be hot on your heels ready to plug him full of holes." Manny mounted his horse. "Only my ammunition won't be buckshot. My best to the missus. Let me know if me and Hettie can help."

I watched as Manny rode away. Nobody understood his pain more than me. I grabbed the rope on the barn door and pulled it closed. When the latch clicked, I realized I'd made my choice. It was what Raney wanted. Go get Aughtie.

"There'll be no turning back. Clive, you sure you wanna go? Sure you wanna involve yourself in a mess that you most likely can't scrape off your boots?"

"Yep."

"Then we agree. We find Aughtie."

"Yes, sir, we agree. That little girl is in danger."

"Truth is, I'm glad you're comin'. I need a voice of reason."

Clive chuckled, then muttered under his breath, "Like that's gonna help a stubborn man."

He was right. I was stubborn as a mule, and there wasn't nobody who could change my mind. The problem was, we had no idea where to start. Did we start back up the mountain to the mining camp or circle the base to the farmers? Should we make our way to Cumberland or work our way through Harlan?

I pulled the reins over Rufus's head. "Hard to know which way to start, but I think we start from where we found Raney. You agree? We know she made it that far trying to catch them." I could track a deer, but huntin' a child was a different sort of thing. I rubbed the fierce aching in my head.

Clive touched my arm. "Take a breath. We'll find her." His voice was calming. He'd have my back, and the thought eased my mind.

"We'll start where we know and follow the trail." I tightened the strings on my boots. The mountain was big, a lot of miles to cover, and the Bartons had their hands in everything from Kentucky to Tennessee. But it made sense to start at the last place we knew the masked man had been.

"Agreed." Clive pulled the strap tight on his saddle, then lifted hisself onto his horse.

I pushed my hand into my pocket, digging for my kerchief, and took a deep breath. "Whatdaya say we flip to see which way we go?"

"Works for me. I call heads." Clive wrung his hands.

"Fine. Once we get to the ravine where we found Raney, heads says we go north to Harlan. Tails, we go west toward Cumberland Gap." I blew the coin, balanced it on my thumbnail, then flipped it.

Clive snatched it out of the air and smacked it on the top of his hand. "Heads wins!"

"Backwoods of Harlan it is. Lot of wooded area with good places to hide. Seems right to start there." And we headed toward the Cumberland River.

It took the better part of an hour to get to the pass. Me and Clive said little. We just listened to the sounds of the mountain. A soft breeze whispered through the treetops, and the smell of lavender spoke tender words to my heart and reminded me of Raney. I already missed her, and worry was an understatement. She loved the smell of lavender. It was like the Lord was sendin' it to remind me of Raney. I realized how lucky I was to have her. It's easy for a man to forget what is important until he hits hard times. Raney loved that smell so much, she made little bags of it and stashed them everywhere. The thought had me praying that the good Lord would see fit to spare my wife. The problems with the Bartons weren't her fault. They were mine. I'd started this ball rollin'. It had to be me who dealt with this.

Wasn't long before the sound of the water overcame the sound of plodding horse hooves. And not long after that that we could see the river. The wash of the water skipped and twirled around the rocks. Cranes stood balanced on one leg, preening their feathers, while a deer and her fawn drank on the other side of the river.

"Somethin', ain't it?" Clive said. "Good Lord sure makes pretty sights. Look at these mountains."

Clive was right. The mountains had their beauty. I'd not took time over the last few weeks to notice the beauty of the summer. Cattails sprang up along the crevices in the riverbank, the water still cold enough to see trout leap into the air. I took in the mountain air and held it, like it was cleansing my lungs of the leftover muck from the mines—the very dirt that took the lives of the men slaving in the belly of the earth. I let out the air and took to coughing, expelling the remains of coal dust best I could. It was a reminder that we had a child to find.

We turned north and followed the river into the backwoods. It wasn't long before the path narrowed and the forest thickened. It was the middle of the day, but the trees hung heavy overhead, darkening the path. Me and Clive rode that grown-over way for a couple more hours before the trees thinned and opened into field.

Daisies dotted the deep-green grass, and the shadow of a hawk flashed across the field. The scent of the clean air filled our lungs, and we stopped in a patch of tall grass to let the horses rest.

"I don't know about you, but my backside's right sore." Clive threw his leg over his horse and dropped to the ground. He bent over, stretched his legs, and then went to rubbing his rear.

"I reckon being a teacher, you don't do much ridin'. Still, I agree—my rear could use a rest." I laughed.

That wind whispered again, catching my attention. I coulda swore I heard something or somebody.

I furrowed my brow, then cocked my head and closed my eyes. I needed to focus on the cry.

Clive was runnin' his mouth faster than a chipmunk after greens, going on about saddle sores.

"Hush. You hear that?" I snipped.

"Hear what?"

"Well, if you'd hush a minute, you might hear it."

Clive pressed his hand over his mouth.

"Hear it?" I asked.

He cupped his hand around his ear and nodded. "Which way is it coming from?"

It's hard in the mountains to catch the direction a sound rings. Noise catches on the wind and bounces from one hillside to the next. I cocked my head further, then lifted my nose toward the sky. *Come on. Speak so I can get a fix.*

The whine rode the whisper of the breeze, and I heard it. My eyes flew open, and I grabbed the reins and threw myself on Rufus. "Hup, horse. Take it slow, now. I need to listen."

Rufus whinnied, then stepped into the grass along the path. Clive come right behind me. The cry seemed to come from the far side of the field. We crossed the meadow, grass bending to the horse's footsteps. I dodged low-hanging tree limbs as we left the field and edged deeper into the woods. When the bank of the Cumberland River came into sight, I halted Rufus. He snorted and slapped his head from side to side, so I walked him to the water's edge.

Once again I closed my eyes to concentrate. Listen. A branch snapped, and I wheeled around.

"Joshua Morgan. What's you doin' up on company land? This is off limits."

A tall, broad, and solid-built man stepped out of the woods. He toted a rifle on his shoulder.

"Angus Barton. Ain't seen you in a spell."

Angus made two of his younger brother, Thomas. Angus, like his daddy before him, was built like a bear—both could scare anyone with just his looks. His shoulders were wide, and his scraggly beard hung to his chest.

He moseyed across the path and pressed his hand against Rufus. The horse jumped and kicked. "Whoa there," Angus said. "Mighty spirited horse."

I wanted to smart off and tell him Rufus had a good sense of character and knew when to kick or stand firm, but it seemed Angus had grown even bigger since I last saw him. Was he the masked man?

"Wanna sell this horse?" Angus run his hands down Rufus's leg and lifted his foot, eyeing his hooves.

"Naw. I reckon I'll keep him. He's good to plow, pull, and ride."

"So what's got you up on this side of the mountain?" Angus lifted Rufus's head and stepped around the horse.

He was proddin' me for information. What did this bully know about Aughtie and June Rayburn? Would he be willing to help a little girl, or was he likely to be as heartless as his younger brother? I was pretty sure he'd already stole her. What did he intend now? This was the bad thing about stepping in someone else's messes. Choices kept popping up, decisions as to whether we scrape the mess off our shoes or track it onto the porch. I scratched my head. Tell him or not?

Eighteen

I SPIT ON the side of the river, then swiped my mouth with my shoulder. My poker face was firm as I stared at the ground. The wind picked up the edge of my hat and loosened its grip on my head.

"I ask again"—Angus rested his rifle in the bend of his arm—"what brings you up on Barton land? Especially since you've been told not to come back."

"I'm lookin' for a person."

"Who might that person be?" Angus stepped closer.

"Ah, just a youngin that Raney and Clive here was workin' to educate." I wondered if Clive would flinch at my lie.

Angus pushed his hat to the back of his head. "Well, now. Thought we had ole Clive to do the educating? Didn't know your missus did that sorta thing." He stretched out his hand to Clive, but he didn't take hold.

"Yep. Well, there's a lot about my family you don't know and don't need to know. Clive here was good enough to help me search for the child."

"Looked like you and Clive were pretty buddy-buddy the other day at the store."

I felt the pressure of his size as he towered over me. He was trying to intimidate me. Scare me. I wasn't small, and backing down was not in my spirit.

"Raney helps him with this child, and he did help me lug that rye across the Gap. Like I said, Clive here is a nice young man. Running for mayor. Ain't you, son?" I hoped Clive would talk, but he seemed froze up.

If there is one thing I hate, it's being misleading. And here I was—misleading. I wasn't sure where I stood with the good Lord at this point. We had our things to sort through, but I ain't willing to count Him out neither. I could only hope that those everlastin' arms we had sung about in church would hold true when this ordeal was over. For now, I had to do what I had to do. Even if it meant shading the truth a bit. This wasn't like lyin' to be dishonest—it was to save a child.

"A youngin, heh?" Angus kicked a rock.

"Yep. Girl. Raney was worried when the child didn't show up."

From over my shoulder, I heard a whimper. Angus heard it too, because he shifted from foot to foot. I took the reins in my hand and stepped into the stirrup.

"Hold up. I'll go with you." Angus took out across the path just inside the trees and mounted his horse.

Now there is a time to wonder and a time to act. I was caught somewhere in the middle. I didn't trust Angus any more than I trusted his brother, but I'd done stepped into a mess for the sake of Aughtie. I'd follow through. That masked man had scooped her up and run with her. The child needed to be found—for her safety. And found for mine and Raney's sanity. If Angus was the masked man, he was putting on a good act. Right now that wasn't a detail to chicken pick at. Aughtie was most important. We'd nitpick later.

We turned them horses up the steep grade of the mountain path. The weak cry grew louder. At the top of the grade, a small pond lay to the far side of a grassy meadow. I threw my leg over Rufus and dropped to the ground, yankin' my rifle out of the holster. Angus and Clive followed.

"Aughtie, you up here, girl? It's Mr. Josh." It took all I had not to tear through the field like a wild man. My heart raced, and it was hard to breathe. I had to stay calm.

"You go that way." Angus pointed toward the pond. "I'll go this way."

It seemed odd he wanted to be so helpful, but I played out the game. Kept up the story for Aughtie. I took hold of the barrel of my rifle and swung it at the knee-high grass. "Aughtie. Where are you, honey?"

Angus walked the outside edge of the clearing, searching under bushes and trees. Just as I sidled up to the pond, I saw her hunkered down in the water, shivering.

I fell to my knees next to the water and pushed my hand toward her. *Lord, thank You.*

"Aughtie, come on. Come to Mr. Josh." She stood waist-deep in the water. Her clothes and hair were soaked, moss and pond muck on her face—like someone had dunked her. Tried to drown her. She coughed and spit water.

My nostrils flared and my hands shook. Never in my life had I fought back such anger that a body would hurt this youngin. I had to live the lie until Angus was gone.

I waded into the mucky pond. My arms reached toward the girl as I motioned for her, but she backed away. "Darlin', you know Mr. Josh ain't never laid a mean hand on you." I inched closer and spoke in a whisper. "I found Raney. Let's go see Miss Raney."

She lunged into my arms and wrapped her legs around my waist. "Raney, Raney."

I made my way to the pond's edge, and Angus stuck out his hand for me to grab hold.

"She alright?" Angus asked.

"Looks to be. Just scared. Lost."

Angus patted her back, and Aughtie squeezed harder into my neck. "No, no, no," she cried. The youngin slapped at his hand, squealin' like a stuck pig. Her words were muddled and hard to understand, but I got what she was saying. I held her tight. Clive picked up my rifle and stuffed it into the holster on my saddle.

"Angus, much obliged. I'll take the girl home now. We'll be off your land."

Angus eyed the child. "Didn't know you and Raney had any children. Not after little Anna." He followed awkwardly behind me, looking the child over.

I gritted my teeth. *Just be pleasant. Now ain't the time.* "Well, I don't spread my business over the mountain. But like I said, Raney helps Clive teach the child. You can see she ain't bright. Raney has a sweet way with her. I appreciate your help. We'll be leavin' now."

Clive nodded and reached out to rub Aughtie's head. "The youngin stays with us from time to time. Josh is right. Raney has a way with the child. We missed her this mornin'. Scared us to death."

Clive had just stepped into the mess with me.

Aughtie leaned into Clive. A sign to Angus that she was familiar with him. And so, another lie.

Angus stammered around tryin' to sound concerned, but my gut told me Aughtie was downright terrified of him. I had no way to prove he took her. He'd had plenty of time to kill her. Yet he hadn't. My head went places I didn't need it to go—I had no idea what he might have done to the child. And my gut was rarely wrong.

"Josh. Take Aughtie." She wrapped her arms around my neck and stuck to my chest like bees on a honeycomb.

"Baby girl, you spoke!" I was taken back that Aughtie finally said words. Not a coo or a giggle. But real words. "I knew you had them words in you." I squeezed her tight. "That's my girl." I couldn't have been prouder of the youngin, but the circumstances didn't allow for celebration.

Clive helped me climb onto Rufus, and I tipped my hat to Angus.

"We're going home. Take you back to your momma. You hold tight." What was one more lie at this point? It was what was necessary to keep this youngin safe and find her momma.

Guilt has a way of colorin' a body's look, and the color left Angus's face when I saddled up with Aughtie. That give me a right good hint he was the one that took her. Now was not the time to face him down. I needed more proof. The youngin had been through enough for one day, and I'd face him down eventually.

"We'll be off your land now. Thanks for your help. I'm sure this youngin's momma will be glad to see her." I tapped Rufus with my heel.

Angus opened his mouth like he was gonna say something, but then snapped it closed. He turned and made his way back to his horse, shuffling his feet, head down, and hands in his pockets.

Clive and me took a winding path across the pass, and when I felt we were far enough away from Angus, I stopped the horse. It took a minute to pry Aughtie loose from my neck, but I did so I could look her over.

Both arms and wrists bore the bruise prints of a tight-gripped person. She was skinned up from head to toe, like she'd tried to crawl away but got caught. But what bothered me most was all the pond muck on her face and hair. It dripped down her hair from the top of her head and strung in long strings from her nose. My heart didn't want to believe that someone tried to hold her under, but my mind made up the answer.

I snuggled her close to me. What crawled up from my stomach was a determination to make this right. Find Aughtie's momma.

I'd gotten Raney and Aughtie back, but this feud was just beginning.

About a mile from home, Aughtie went to wiggling and whining, pointing to a stand of trees at the edge of the clearing. Got so I thought she'd fall. So I stopped, set her off Rufus, and let her run. Dropping the reins over a branch, we followed the girl to the woods.

I couldn't believe my eyes. Just when I thought I'd had enough hard times for one day, I saw Aughtie kneel over a mound of sticks and pine needles. As I eased closer, I saw a muddy hand lying palm up. And when I took Aughtie by the shoulders and lifted her away, I could see the swollen face of a woman.

"Oh, honey, don't touch," I said as she wiggled to free herself.

The woman looked to be dead for a spell. Critters had already started to gnaw at her flesh. The stench was foul.

"Momma Joon. Momma Joon." Aughtie pulled away from me and grabbed the rotting hand.

I took Aughtie in my arms, lifted her onto my hip, and then stepped away. Was this June Rayburn? Clive pressed his hand over his mouth and gagged. For a minute I couldn't cipher my feelings. The disappointment of not having this girl's momma to hold over Barton's head was gone. Worse yet, the woman was dead, and Aughtie had tried to cover her.

"Momma. Mommmmaa." Aughtie stretched out her arms toward the body.

"Honey, is that Momma June?" Clive took Aughtie from me.

"Momma Jooonn." She leaned hard toward the woman. Tears dripped off her cheeks. "Wake up, Momma!"

My heart ached for the youngin as it become clear this was her mother. This body was June Rayburn.

I scratched my forehead with one hand. This was more than I could take in. The sadness for Aughtie—her momma gone. Or the anger for the destruction of three good women. Raney, Aughtie, and June. Never in my life had I ever felt this kind of wrath grow. Aughtie cried sobs that ripped away chunks of my heart. She wanted to hold her momma, but I couldn't let her. It took a while, but she finally settled, so we could figure out what to do.

"Miss Aughtie, you sit here on Rufus. Let Mr. Josh give your momma a proper burial. We're gonna gather some sticks and logs. Can you sit right here?"

"My help." She wiggled down and picked up a few little sticks.

There wasn't much to dig with and less to bury. June had been dead for some time. There was no movin' this swelled-up corpse now. Me and Clive decided the best thing was to build a fire over the body and let the flames do the burying. We could bury June's bones later.

"Leanin'. Leanin'. Safe and secure from all alarms." I quietly sang the words to that hymn and thought out loud, "Ain't no safe and secure for you. Rest in peace, June Rayburn."

We searched for enough broken tree limbs and dried-up pine brush to cover her best we could. Aughtie picked up small sticks and handed them to me. Every now and again, she'd lay on the ground and beg her momma to open her eyes. I knew the grief the youngin felt. I understood the pain, and if I could have changed it right that minute, I would have.

Clive found a number of good-sized rocks we could use to stack over her and hold a fire in place.

"Bye-bye, Momma Joon?" Aughtie cocked her head to one side.

I patted her chubby knee. She raised her hand to wave to her momma, and a small leather bag dangled by a string from her fingers.

"That's a pretty bag. Where'd you find that?" I tapped the bag, and it swung like a pendulum. Aughtie pulled it close to her chest and hugged it.

"Momma Joon's." Aughtie stuck her hand inside the bag and pulled out a tiny river rock. I figured it was something June had made her and filled with pebbles for Aughtie. Neither me or Clive saw where Aughtie found the bag, but it didn't matter. It wasn't like June needed it. Since it offered a bit of comfort to Aughtie, I left it to her.

"Say goodbye to Momma June. She is with the good Lord. You did good takin' care of her until we could put her to rest." I didn't know how I expected this little girl to take a moment to reflect and say goodbye . . . when I couldn't do it with Anna.

"What you reckon we do now?" Clive asked.

"Light the fire." And we did. It was hard to let Aughtie watch us rub sticks till we started the dried leaves to burn, but there was no place else for her to go. The white smoke from the dried leaves whipped and curled around the limbs as Clive blew hard breaths to catch the flame. The sun caught on something hangin' from a small branch that covered June's body.

As the flames took hold, I snagged a necklace with a broken locket. *Must have been broken in the struggle.* Pullin' Aughtie close, I dropped the necklace into her leather pouch. If anything, she had two things that belonged to her momma—a small leather purse and a broken necklace. Aughtie reached up and kissed my cheek.

We stood back to watch as the wood burned. As the heat grew intense, we moved further back, but Aughtie kept inchin' closer to her momma. The child didn't understand a lot of things, but she somehow understood this, and she intentionally stood there until the flames gulped her momma up.

Nineteen

I WAS NEVER as tired as I was after I got that youngin home. It ain't enough to have the devil worried out of you, but to run the mountain like me and Clive did, heart racing, juices pouring . . . it took me standing on the porch of the house staring into the hint of sunset for it all to hit me.

"Joshua, you alright?" Cleda Mae stepped onto the porch and handed me a cup of coffee. The tin, hot to the touch, was almost too much for a warm summer night, but there was just something about the woody smell of fresh coffee to calm a soul. "Today was a new day, and this has been a good start."

I swirled the cup under my nose and took in the scent. My mouth went to waterin', and I pressed the cup to my lips, gently blew, then took a sip of the balmy liquid. "That's good. Just what the doctor ordered. Thank you, Cleda Mae." I put my arm around her and gave her a hug. "And thank you for all you've done for Raney. I'm grateful."

"It's not the end. Don't you worry. I sent Clive home to bring us a change of clothes and some of our necessities. He will get Manny's boy to watch the farm whilst we stay here. You're takin' over that tack shed until Raney is back on her feet. We'll stay here at the house. I need to be here to do the nursing."

"You're runnin' me outa my own house?"

"Is what it is. You need help with Aughtie and Raney. I'm here. Tack shed for you."

I smiled. Clive did say Cleda Mae was small but mighty.

"Aughtie, no help." A soft but stern voice broke the quiet of the night. I turned, and there was Aughtie standing, back against the side of the house, lip pooched out and tapping her toe.

"Listen at you chatter." I brought her close to me and rubbed her back. "She's talkin' more."

"She started speakin' more after you got back from findin' her mama. I think she was scared to death before. Youngin's been through a lot. Fear stops anybody from doing things. Seems she decided we ain't so bad." Cleda Mae crossed her arms and smiled. "Amazin' what a little love can do. And Clive says she's not dumb, just slow. Things ain't right with her, but she can learn."

It felt good to know Aughtie trusted us enough to finally talk. That could change things for her. I glanced toward Aughtie and blew her a kiss.

Cleda Mae turned Aughtie toward the door. "Bedtime, gal."

The child huffed and stomped toward the door.

Cleda Mae grinned as she leaned toward the child. "I ain't sure where that attitude comes from, young lady, but you put it back in your pocket. Everybody needs help from time to time, and what makes you all grown up is realizin' when you need it." Cleda Mae tweaked Aughtie's cheek.

The youngin pooched out her lip again. I wondered if I was about to witness the meetin' of two bulls headbutting. I scooped Aughtie into my arms and gave her a hug. "Miss Cleda Mae is right. Everyone needs help from time to time, even Aughtie. Now, you go on inside and crawl in that nice pallet of blankets at the foot of Miss Raney's bed. She needs to know you are safe."

I set her down, and she grunted as she passed Cleda Mae.

"Hold up there, young lady. Take a few steps back and thank Miss Cleda Mae for helpin' you and Raney. If it wasn't for her, we wouldn't have found either of you."

Aughtie furrowed her brow but made a turn into Cleda Mae's arms.

"That's my girl." Cleda Mae pressed her hand into the youngin's hair. She kissed her forehead, and that was all it took for Aughtie to soften up. "Go on. I'll be there in just a minute to tuck you in."

I couldn't help but chuckle. It was obvious the youngin wasn't as bright as most children. The shape of her head, her eyes, and them pudgy hands and legs screamed that things wasn't just right. Still, she had a fire about her, a personality, and an opinion. And Cleda Mae might be right. The girl could have been afraid to talk. When I thought back to when I found her . . . I could hear her singin' in the field.

"I've seen one other child like her down in Cumberland. That child was worse off than Aughtie. But same sort of problem—things just wasn't right about him." Cleda Mae took my empty coffee cup. "More?" She motioned.

I nodded my head in agreement. Cleda Mae stepped inside and, in a few seconds, returned with a fresh fill.

"Child has smarts. They ain't book smarts, but you can tell she can make her way along. I think she knows more than she can tell us," I said. "Give her time. Despite her fire, the child has been through a lot. She ain't told us her real name yet."

"You reckon the child understands her momma is dead?" Cleda Mae asked.

"After what I saw today, yes. But time will tell how she handles it." I took a drink of coffee.

Cleda Mae bumped against me. "You need sleep. Time you head to the tack shed. Clive won't be back until tomorrow." I opened my mouth to disagree, but Cleda Mae's bony finger come within an inch of my nose. "Don't you argue. You hightail it down to the tack shed and get some rest. I made the bed earlier. We got the dinner bell if there's a problem. Besides, Doc said he'd be back late tonight. He'll need me to let him know how Raney is doin'."

I nodded, then peered once more inside the cabin. Raney was swelled up something awful, but there at her side was Aughtie, wetting a cloth and wringing it out. Blotting Raney's face. I pushed my hand into my pocket and felt the penny Anna had left. Maybe the good Lord sent me an angel to replace her.

I couldn't tell what the connection was with me and that youngin, but it was special. Though she might not be my child, it sure felt like it in my heart.

I stepped off the porch and stared into the night sky. Stars twinkled across the heavens, and I wondered, if only for a minute, if Anna was lookin' down. The only sound was the singing of crickets. There was something right easin' about their song. Something sweet-like.

"Joshua?" Cleda Mae stood on the porch, arm extended. "You might need this." She held up the coffee cup I'd left on the railing.

I tipped my hat and took it. Steam circled upward from my cup like a ghost floating out of the ground. Cleda Mae let the screen door ease closed, but its squeak would have woken a dead man.

You're alright. I talked to myself. *Maybe a little numb, lucky . . . scared.* I blew the steam off the hot liquid. *It's been a long day. Try and look at the blessin's in this. You got Raney and Aughtie back safe. You and Clive did good.*

"Did I?" I said out loud. Clive had said earlier that this wasn't my fault, but I couldn't help but feel the burden of my choices.

A summer breeze carried the call of a dove across the rye field. The huge oak behind the house swayed, like a child twisting in dance to an imaginary song. My legs were weak, and my hands shook. I'd need to cut up that fallen tree soon. I sighed. More work.

I lit the oil lamp outside of the tack shed, then opened the door and went in. The lamp cast a yellow haze over the room. It become clear how tired I was. I'd talked to myself all the way across the field. Maybe it was me uttering words I couldn't speak to anyone else. Maybe it was Anna speakin' to me from heaven. Maybe it was just the good Lord. Regardless, as I sat on the edge of the bed, my shoulders heaved and the tears ran like the hard summer rain. The day was over. My next job was just to wake up in the morning. As I closed my eyes, my last thought was, *Who was that masked man?*

My eyes hadn't hardly closed before she tugged my arm. "Tum on. Eat." Morning had come too quickly.

I rolled to my side and cracked open an eye.

Aughtie stood with her eye right against mine. "Tum. It's good."

I pulled my suspenders over my arms and rested them on my shoulders. When I dropped my feet over the edge of the bed, I stomped them right hard on the floor. "I'm comin' after you, gal!"

Aughtie squealed and took toward the house. It was a sweet sound. I only hoped Raney could hear the joy. I made my way to the outhouse, then washed up in the bucket by the porch. Cleda Mae and Clive stood waitin'. Aughtie rested on Clive's hip.

"I wondered if you was gonna get up. Sun beat you up by a couple of hours." Clive stuck out his free hand to shake mine. "I gotta say, you don't look no better. Guess rest don't fix ugly, does it?" He grinned right big, but I couldn't hold it over him. It was good to have friends who jumped in it with you and made you laugh.

The smell of fresh bacon seeped through the cabin door, and the scent of baked biscuits made my mouth water and my stomach turn at the same time.

"I'm obliged, Cleda Mae, but I ain't got the stomach to eat."

I paced the length of the porch, stopping long enough to glance inside and check on Raney.

"She ain't doin' real good, is she?" I gnawed on my thumbnail.

"Doc said she's got a hard row to hoe, but if I keep her wounds good and clean, he says she'll come around. Time, Joshua. She needs time. And she needs you to believe she will be fine."

"I know."

"No, I don't think you do know." Once again, that finger of Cleda Mae's shoved in my face. "When you walk in that house, you don't dwell on the sight of a banged-up woman. You look at the beauty in her. That's all you see, and you tell her that. Raney needs to know you're the strong husband she needs so she can let loose and rest—heal. Does that make sense?"

I shrugged.

Cleda Mae grabbed me by the arms and wheeled me around. "You ain't goin' inside that cabin until you convince me you've become the husband you need to be."

I looked at Clive, and he nodded. "Joshua, I'm afraid the little woman is right. You've been on the bottom since Anna died. It's time to rise to the top. Stop sulkin'. Start taking steps to be a man in charge of his family. Anna's death was an accident you couldn't prevent."

Those were hard words to take in, especially from a man young enough to be my son. But Clive was more than book smart, and he was right. It had been too long since I'd took hold of what I needed to do. I'd lost a daughter and nearly lost my wife. Time to step up.

I took a deep breath and pulled back my shoulders. Twistin' my head, the bones in my neck cracked. I huffed the air outa my lungs and took in another gulp of fresh air.

"Now, that's the man I remember. Look at that, Clive. He grew a good two inches." Cleda Mae patted my chest.

And I reckon she was right. When a man takes hold of his life and stands straight and tall, he grows a couple of inches. Felt good not bein' hunkered over.

I went inside the cabin, boots clicking on the hardwood floors. Cleda Mae followed and then handed me a plate with a crumbled biscuit, white gravy, and a bit of egg.

"Feed her tiny bites. Her jaw is sore."

I did, then gingerly wiped a drop of gravy from Raney's chin. I pulled a stool close to her bed, leaned over, and kissed her.

She frowned and whispered, "That hurts."

"What don't hurt?" I asked.

She pointed to her chin, and I kissed it gently. Then she pointed to her nose. And I kissed that. I leaned closer and tenderly touched her lips with mine. If my will was all it took to save her, my wife would be right as rain.

TWENTY

BETWEEN HELPING RANEY and doing chores, it made for a long day. She was sore and slow healing. I was tired. Cleda Mae went on and on to Raney about how good she was doin', nudging me to do the same.

"I'd say you pass for being a good husband. Don't you agree, Aughtie?" Cleda Mae laughed.

"Mr. Josh, alright." Aughtie clapped and giggled.

"You're silly," I quipped.

Raney managed a smile.

"I got no plans of keepin' things from you, so you need to know that me and Clive is going to find Taylor Rayburn. And you also need to know we found June. I know bad news is not what you want, but the truth is, me and Clive buried her in the woods. She'd been gone a spell by the looks of her."

Raney wadded her blouse into her palm. "Oh no. So when you started seein' Aughtie . . ."

"June was probably dead. The girl was wanderin' looking for people, and she found us."

"Rayburn'll want to know his girl is gone and that Aughtie is safe here," Raney said as she tried to raise up. "He'll want to take Aughtie."

"Maybe. If she was your grandchild, what would you do?" I asked.

Cleda Mae rubbed my back. Her sign of approval for what I'd said. Cleda Mae then helped ease Raney back to her pillow, and Raney was quiet for a minute.

Raney's face twisted in pain as she pressed her hand over my cheek. "It's hard."

"I know, but it's what's best."

"And it's what's right," Raney said as she relaxed. "Until then, we love her as much as we can."

"Until . . ." I cupped my hand over hers.

A tear seeped down Raney's cheek. "You find her grandpa. You hear me?" She sighed and closed her eyes.

"Raney!" I come to my feet. "Raney!"

"Joshua, she's tired. Let her rest. We're all tired, and night is here." Cleda Mae twisted me toward the door. "You and Clive got business to take care of." And she nudged me forward. "I'll take care of Raney and Aughtie. Go on, now."

Clive stood on the steps. Aughtie straddled his waist. Her head bobbled on his shoulder. His fingers gently tapped a rhythm on her back.

I rubbed her skinned-up legs, then grasped her chubby bare foot. "She's a sweet youngin, ain't she?"

Clive twisted from side to side, rocking the girl to sleep. "She is indeed. And though I know she ain't right bright, she's not dumb either. Youngin just has trouble with things stickin' in her head. She's able to learn some, just slower. So I'll keep working with her like any student."

"Now that she ain't afraid anymore, the youngin's started talkin'. It's hard for her to grab hold of her words—now she sounds like a younger child mouthing her words. If you listen, you can make 'em out." I watched as her hair floated with Clive's swaying motion. "Broke my heart to find her momma like that. Reckon she understands all this?" I walked to the porch steps.

Clive pressed his hand against her head. His fingers caught in her hair. "I'm bettin' she understands enough. She just ciphers differently. She knew where her momma was when she saw that spot. That says something."

"Let me take her." Cleda Mae slid her arms around the child's waist and took her from Clive. "I'll bed her down."

Cleda Mae pulled open the screen door and edged inside with Aughtie half-asleep on her shoulder. The child lifted her head and pressed her palm against her lips, blowing me a kiss. I took her hand and kissed it.

"Nite, little 'un." My heart melted. The child was doin' better with every day that passed. We'd done right by her.

"When I saw June in that pile of sticks and rocks, I wondered if Aughtie was the one who tried to cover her body." Clive leaned against the porch rail. "I don't know if I was angry, relieved, or what. I just know my heart broke for the youngin."

"It would be hard to tell if Aughtie tried to bury her momma or if the culprit did. One way or the other, the girl knew her momma was in that spot," I said.

"Last night I stood outside and stared at the stars after I'd packed the things Cleda Mae asked me to bring and loaded them in the wagon. They were something to look at. There was more than I could begin to count. Reminded me of when my momma used to tell me each star was the soul of one who passed. And the brightest ones were the newest."

Clive's thought was oddly comforting, and there had been nights I'd done the same. Stared into the heavens and wondered if one of them stars was Anna. None of this seemed fair. One child's life taken needlessly and another's changed by circumstances she had no control over. I'd never had such a battle in my soul. Seeing June dead just added another notch in the log.

"It ain't fair, Clive. None of this is fair." My hat dropped as I craned my neck to see the stars. We stood gazing over the field of rye that was waiting for me to finish its harvest. It was still growing and going to seed. Best to leave it and let it make a good late plant—ready to harvest in late fall.

"We need to find Rayburn. We got no way of knowing if he's searching for Aughtie. He'd surely be looking for her if he knew. I'm not sure we can be the ones to tell him about June." I rubbed my eyes.

"What? Who do you reckon oughta tell him it if it ain't us?" Clive snapped.

"I've pondered over this." I walked down the stairs. "I ain't found a solution that protects Aughtie. If we tell and Rayburn knows about the child, he'll probably come lookin' for her. It ain't that I don't want him to know, but I'm thinking of Raney. She's grown attached to the child. Is now the right time to take that from her too?"

Clive stood quiet. I could tell he was drawing his courage to say something.

"Go ahead," I said. "What's gnawin' at you?"

Clive shoved his hands into his pockets. "I'm just wondering if that's such a bad thing? The girl's granddaddy hunting her. Takin' her home."

This was my dilemma. What was best for Aughtie *and* Raney? It seemed every decision I made forced me to choose. One would suffer no matter what I decided.

"Look, Clive, I think Aughtie should be with her grandfather. Heck, I even said that to Raney a few minutes ago. If that was my grandbaby, I would want her with me. But there is so much we don't know here. So much we can't figure out. Like how are the Bartons tied to this child? If she belongs to their family, does Rayburn even know about her? The Bartons done tried to kill the child once." Frustrated, I slapped my leg with my hat.

"The truth is, this ain't all about Aughtie, now is it? It's about you gettin' even with Thomas. Now, I know the Bartons ain't model individuals, but you got an axe to grind with Thomas, and you ain't bein' objective."

I wanted to slap him, for he dredged up a frightful wave of anger in me. I felt my face grow hot.

"I know them ain't the words you wanted to hear, Joshua, but we need to keep the truth in mind. I'm with you on helpin' them miners. Lord knows the Bartons ain't kind, but for you, this fight hinges on you getting even with Barton for Anna's death." Clive inched closer. "You called me to be your voice of reason. And this is reason speakin'."

My nostrils flared, and I chewed on my tongue to keep from lightin' down Clive's throat. He was right to a certain extent. Regardless of how I felt, this was about being sure Aughtie was safe. Still I knew that in my heart, there was revenge.

I'd told myself so many lies that I couldn't tell what was real and what wasn't. I'd managed to convince myself that all the things I was doing was for the girl. I was finding out that the lies we tell ourselves ain't much different than the lies we tell others. A lie is still a lie, and when we use them to justify an end to the means, it never turns out good.

The thing about fibs is, they make us feel better about the things we've done that ain't right. A body can conjure up some real humdingers to keep their sins buried or their greed hid away. I thought back a couple of days when them words come back to me—*you ain't as strong as you think you are.* Lies make you weak. Don't matter how strong a person is. It tears down who you are. I knew the good Lord wasn't happy with me or these lies, but I was struggling, and He didn't seem to be offering me any reprieve. I needed to hunt to find the good I knew the Lord offered.

Clive hit the nail on the head. This was about Thomas and me. It was about hating the man that trampled my girl, and I wasn't sure how to put that to rest. My rearin' told me forgiveness. Right now, forgiveness wasn't an option.

"I want him dead, Clive."

"Uh-huh. But killin' him ain't gonna stop your grief." Clive commenced pacing the porch. "At least you and Raney could bury your girl. Imagine how old man Rayburn must feel, never knowin' what happened to his girl. Never knowing about his granddaughter."

I stood as still as a deer listening for the hunter, my thoughts reelin'. Every emotion in me crawled to the surface. Would the good Lord ever find anything worth a nickel in me, or was I too far down the road to hell to ever know?

"Nickel," I whispered, remembering Anna's coin.

"What?" Clive cocked his head, confused.

I pulled Anna's penny from my pocket and twirled it between my fingers. *There's always hope, Papa.* And that meant I'd have to find a way to talk to Raney about finally going after Barton.

Twenty-One

Morning in the mountains is always a sight. The air is fresh, and the morning dew dampens your face. I'd had the night to mull things over. I leaned against the window, ponderin' on what Clive had laid down. He made sense, even though I told myself otherwise. If anything, he went straight to my heart about Rayburn needing to bury June like me and Raney did with our girl. If I kept June's death to myself, I would be as cruel as the Bartons.

I wanted to bring God's wrath down on Thomas. I'd told myself that if Aughtie was his child, he didn't care about her, or he'd have manned up and claimed her. Truth was, Barton did come searching for the child. Maybe he really did care, and I'd believed my own lie.

An axe banged against wood, shaking me from my thoughts. Clive was at the side of the house, cuttin' up that downed tree, and the reality of a new day and the work that followed on the farm hit. "Might as well get some chores done. You plan on workin' anytime soon?" he said as he swung the axe over his head and down on the tree trunk.

I tipped my coffee cup and grinned. "You could help me finish layin' that field of rye for seed."

Cleda Mae made her way around the house to the clothesline, a basket balanced on her hip.

"Mornin', Cleda Mae." I smiled as she walked past.

"I've stewed since yesterday." She patted her foot in frustration.

I took in a deep breath and sighed, then waited for the questions to start. If a man waits long enough, a woman will pry until she gets the news she wants.

"You can't just up and tell Raney you found Aughtie's mama before you tell me. How can I help her through this mess, if you don't tell me ahead of time?"

"Truth is, Cleda Mae, it ain't good," Clive said. "We found June dead in a stand of woods at the foot of the lane."

Cleda Mae stood silent.

Clive took her basket of wet clothes and placed them on the tree stump. "We didn't tell you because we knew it would be hard to take in. You needed to take care of Raney," Clive said.

"I understand." She turned to walk away. I could see she was holding in that explosive temper, but after a few steps, she wheeled around on her heels.

Me and Clive readied ourself for the storm she was getting ready to unleash.

"You two do your ponderin'. You figure out the best thing to do and then remember this. Ain't nobody hurting that youngin." Cleda Mae's face was red as a pickled beet. "And next time, you tell me before you dump bad news on the woman I'm nursing back to health. Understood?"

"Understood," I said.

"And while you're at it, hang them wet clothes on the line. Be useful."

"Yes, ma'am." I smiled and took in a deep breath.

Clive shook his head and picked up the axe. I pulled a wet shirt out of the basket, shook the wrinkles, and then hung it over the clothesline. Then it hit me. Angus knew I took Aughtie home. He'd surely tell Thomas, and my first lie would come back to bite me.

Another trouble with lies is that a body must keep conjuring new ones to cover the old ones. I figured it wouldn't be long before Thomas knocked on my door again, questioning me about keeping Aughtie. I run everything through my mind—did my best to justify my doin's because I was trying to protect Aughtie.

Guilt knotted in my throat, and I could have sworn I saw Anna standing in the field shaking her head at me. I swallowed hard. Again, the truth bit me in the backside, and Clive's callin' me on it come back. *This ain't about Aughtie. It's about you takin' vengeance on Thomas.*

We'd worked in the rye field until dusk. Talked through all the possibilities of how to tell Rayburn about his girl. Now we needed to rest to let the thoughts cure. I let Clive walk ahead of me to the house, and I stood alone in the field where Barton run my girl down. I dropped to my knees.

Good Father, I'm struggling. Flounderin'. Wantin' to blame You when I know the truth. You ain't to blame. I'm like Adam in the Good Book. Deceived by my own doings. I know You can forgive me. My question is, are You willin' to forgive me for the mess I've made? Bein' able and bein' willing is two different things.

The struggle I felt against the good Lord run deep in my soul.

I crawled to my feet and dragged my rake behind me. Mater laid at the door of the tack shed. I leaned the rake against the shed. The hound rolled them dark eyes up at me and groaned. "I know, buddy. I know." I stepped over Mater and into the shed. Cleda Mae had thought ahead and filled two large buckets of water. Reckon she knew the stench of a sweaty man. I washed up and headed to the cabin to visit Raney.

When I opened the cabin door, Aughtie took toward me, squealing and laughing. Just in the short amount of time she'd been with us, Cleda Mae managed to tame some of the wild in the child. She was a loving youngin. I gave her a quick hug and walked to Raney. Cleda Mae had Raney up and sitting at the table. The swelling was going down, but now the black and yellow of the bruising had begun.

"How you doin'?" I pressed my hand against her cheek.

"Some better," she whispered.

I pulled my chair next to her, and we shared some stew. I'd take a spoonful, blow on it, then tip it into Raney's mouth. She'd swallow and smile, then grimace. It hurt. I wished I could take the pain on myself, where it rightly belonged.

"So since we're all here, I think we need to talk out what to do for missy here." I gestured to Aughtie.

Cleda Mae repositioned the spoon in Aughtie's hand and helped her scoop a bite of stew.

"Me and Joshua worked that field and talked all day tryin' to decide how to handle this the safest and best way. We'll talk to the miners again to try and locate Rayburn. But we'll wait a bit to go. The miners' shifts will change again. With everybody changing from above ground to under and the other way around, we won't be noticed in the crowd. We could talk to folks one by one," Clive said.

"Aughtie comes first?" Raney whispered.

"Yes." I rubbed her hand, reassuring her this was for the child.

I stood and paced the cabin, pulling my thoughts together. "Should I decide it's my place to tell Rayburn about June, figurin' what is safest for Aughtie is the key? Do I take the pastor and Aughtie along? Leave both here? What's best?"

Cleda Mae stopped in her tracks. She sat her pot on the iron stove. "So you two are going to tell Mr. Rayburn after all?"

"Now that Angus knows I have the girl, he'll tell Thomas. Thomas will know I lied about seein' Aughtie. Might be that Rayburn is the only one who can protect her."

Cleda Mae turned. "Lies always catch up to you."

"Cleda Mae, think about what Joshua is trying to say." Clive stepped close to his wife. "Everything we decide will be hard. This ain't all cut and dry."

I poured myself a cup of coffee. "I appreciate your honesty. I know lyin' ain't right, but in the beginning, it was to protect a little girl that was near naked and half-starved. Grant you, I have some malice in my heart toward Barton. But I didn't want Barton to carry off a youngin knowin' what he did to my child." I stood toe to toe with Cleda Mae. "I swear I only wanted to do what was best for Aughtie, but I need you and Clive to stand behind me. Help me. If Barton asks, tell him you picked her up runnin' loose in a field. That's partly true."

"It ain't no such thing. We never picked up a youngin. You did." Cleda Mae's voice climbed a notch.

"That's why I said it was partly true." I give her my best hound-dog eyes. "It's for the girl. Just till we get this figured out. Lyin' ain't what I want to do, but in this case, it's what's necessary to keep Aughtie safe."

Cleda Mae stared me straight in the eye and never uttered a word. After a minute she twisted around to her husband. "And you think this is the right thing for Aughtie?"

Clive shifted from foot to foot. "Sometimes a body does what is best for the greater good. Knowing what's right becomes a gamble. Puttin' Thomas off a bit longer buys us time to help Aughtie. It helps us figure out who the masked man was that grabbed Aughtie and make sure it don't happen again. I don't know if it was Thomas or Angus or someone else entirely, but we need time to put the pieces together. This is the greater good, Cleda Mae. Trust us."

It would be hard to do anything just right for Aughtie. She was the exception to the rule. The child was caught in the middle of a family that might very well want her dead. Clive wanted to run for mayor to try and help the miners. I wanted to help Aughtie as well as the miners. If we could make our way back to the mines under the ruse of Clive's running for mayor, it would give us a chance to hunt for Rayburn along the way. Talk to the miners again one by one. There was no way to know if he was still alive. The possibilities for Aughtie reminded me of a cup of fishing worms all tangled together. Pull one out, and the knot just gets tighter. We had to start somewhere, and we were all on edge. Everything Cleda Mae said was true, and her heart was in the right place, but even she knew we had no choice.

"Think greater good," Clive said.

I had to admit, I was pleased Clive come underneath me so quick. He'd calm Cleda Mae's worries.

"When this is said and done, we can put Aughtie in the best place and maybe make the Bartons take care of their men and their families. This ruse is only for a little while."

Cleda Mae sat on a stool by Raney. "I understand." She pulled Aughtie onto her lap.

"I ain't saying it's right. I'm saying, for the time bein', it's what's best. Eventually it'll all come to light, and hopefully, everybody wins." I patted Aughtie's head.

I had gone to my knees in the rye field and admitted my wrongs to the good Lord. I'd told Him my anger and my hate. I had to trust He would show me grace and help me do what was right. Either way I'd come to a peace about this. Raney always said a peace is a nod from the Lord. Sometimes He leaves us to our own devices. I was hoping this wasn't the case.

Aughtie slipped from Cleda Mae's lap, her eyes heavy, and that little hand twisted back and forth at the wrist as she waved at us. "Nighty night."

"I'm coming, little girl. Let's get you ready for bed." Cleda Mae wagged her finger at me. "You get Raney into bed, then head to the tack shed." She turned her finger at Clive and me. "This ain't easy, but I trust you."

And that was something. Cleda Mae trusted us. A step in the right direction.

"I guess it's back to the tack shed for me." I smiled as I helped Raney stand and walk to the bed. She eased onto the mattress.

"Joshua, you know Thomas already knows Aughtie is here, right?" Raney pressed her hand on my cheek.

"I do."

"Then do what you have to do for Aughtie. Cleda Mae means well."

That was all I needed to know as I made my way to the tack shed. Raney supported me, and I knew this journey was gonna have to be done differently—no going in guns blazing. It needed to be done quietly. Easy-like to protect the child. My heart was speaking. *Aughtie first, the miners second. Anna was the past.* Just then the good Lord helped me turn my girl loose.

This mess with Aughtie had started out as Barton's problem, and now it was mine. If our plan failed, I figured Thomas would kill me for sure. Live or die, I knew this was the best thing to do.

I knew what my heart was preaching at me, but my soul was burning with something else. Right now it was hard to put the fire out. Raney and I had been through the wringer, and the more I thought about Cleda Mae's telling me to step up, the more I realized I had the power to change things. I couldn't save my own girl, but here was a chance to save another. Redemption. I'd seen this as my chance to get even with Barton, but I'd have to change that. It wasn't about seeing Thomas dead. This was about protecting a little girl. Changin' my heart would be a hard row to hoe, but one I needed to dig. Anna was dead. Gone. I couldn't change that, but I could change things for Aughtie. Maybe this was the way the good Lord would show me peace. Giving over the hate and turnin' it into good. *A man lies to suit hisself. The goal is a change of heart.*

And I was determined to change. I knew it would be hard, and the human in me would slip up, but that little girl was the rock that would make me stand. *Lord, help me. I'm a weak man.*

I looked up at the stars. They were beautiful. I stopped at the door of the tack shed and ran my fingers over the top facing. Then I pulled Anna's coin from my pocket. I rolled it between my fingers, kissed it, and laid the coin on the doorframe.

Twenty-Two

I woke the next morning to Aughtie singing. "Reening. Reening. Reening on the eferlastin' arms." Her voice rang across the field.

I stood, stretched, and looked out the tack shed window. There was Aughtie, trying to throw a wet shirt over the line and singing at the top of her lungs. I couldn't help but laugh. Cleda Mae lifted her so she could spread the shirt across the line.

I was touched she sang the hymn she'd heard me sing. The one about the arms I had thought had let me down.

Watching Aughtie made me feel like the child had always been with us. The way she helped Cleda Mae. How she doted over Raney—brushing her hair away from her face, tucking the covers, always squeezing her hand. No wonder me and Raney attached to her so easy.

I walked to the porch and sat on the top step.

Aughtie ran to the porch, arms extended. "Josh!"

"Hey there, gal."

She crawled into my arms.

"You ready for breakfast?" I poked her tummy.

She covered her mouth and giggled. "Swing." Aughtie pointed toward the swing in the big tree by the house.

Me and Clive had been sawin' a day or so on the tree that fell on the other side of the house. At least here the swing was safe.

"No, breakfast," I teased.

I felt great compassion for this youngin. She wasn't a well child, but I reckon I tasted some of the good Lord's mercy over her. I supposed God gifted these little ones with a special love. The kind of love that convicts a man. And as she leaned against me, I knew the battle had to go on. She deserved justice. Raney earned it—June too. Barton needed to be held accountable. It bothered me. What had June done that she deserved to die? I guessed we'd never know, unless Aughtie . . . Could the youngin know something?

"Mornin', Clive." I tipped my hat as he walked onto the porch.

"Well, you are up early." Clive punched my arm. "Breakfast is ready, and you'll be happy to know Raney is feeding herself."

I stood, but my knees nearly gave way from the stiffness. We walked into the house, and Raney waved. "Looks like you've turned a corner," I said as I kissed her cheek.

She nodded. "I heard your boots on the porch this mornin'. You was here before the sun come up."

"I wanted to be closer to the house." Only Raney would recognize the click of my boots on the porch, but the truth was, I'd been worried that one of the Barton boys would show up.

Right in the middle of breakfast, Mater clawed his way from under the bed. He let out a bark and jolted me. I spit my coffee. Raney jumped.

Clive come to his feet. "Aw, Mater. You scared the devil outa me. Hush."

The hair on the dog's back stood as he dug at the door. Aughtie broke into a piercin' scream, and Cleda Mae grabbed her up.

"Aughtie, honey." I waved to her. "Come here to Mr. Josh. It's okay. Ole Mater scared us all."

Aughtie bolted across the room into my arms. Mater kept up his growling, so I sat Aughtie next to Raney. "Can you watch Miss Raney?"

She nodded.

Mater's yappin' wouldn't ease up. There was something or someone outside. "Hush up, dog!" I snatched my hat off the table and pulled my suspenders over my shoulders. Clive followed close behind me. Could it be the masked man returnin'?

"Quiet down, dog." I lifted my rifle from its rest, cocked it, and leaned it next to the door. Clive pulled his rifle from the shelf above the fireplace. The slats on the porch creaked, and the sound of boots to board clicked across the planks.

"Well now, Mater, looks like you might be right on this one." A shadow crossed past the plaid curtains of the window. I waited against the wall like a bobcat waiting for its prey.

The footsteps made their way around the porch and stopped at the door. A tap on the screen door slapped it against the frame.

I took hold of Mater's rope collar and pulled him to the side. He howled and snarled a warning. "Stay there, dog." The animal eased to his belly, but a low-pitched growl let me know he was cocked and ready.

I took a deep breath and pulled open the door real slow.

"Joshua? I come to check on Raney." Angus stood at the door, hat under his arm. Something didn't set right. I was not willing to trust anyone, much less a Barton.

"Angus?" My voice was quiet but stern.

"Just clearin' some bush on this side of the mountain. We found a spot to blow a new hole, and, well . . ."

"Well, what?"

"Well, I kept thinkin' about Raney and that girl. Just figured I'd be neighborly and make a visit. Since I was already on this side of the mountain and all."

I eyed Angus, my brow furrowed. Everything in me screamed not to trust him, but I played his game. My best guess was Angus was plenty smart enough to know I was playing along. We stood starin' eye to eye, exchangin' idle pleasantries. It was the bull two men spread when one traipsed on the other's ground. We were like two boys circling in the schoolyard, daring each other to take the first swing.

"Angus, it ain't that I don't appreciate your concern. But it's not like we're buddies either. I'm much obliged for your help on the mountain and this visit. But we're fine. You can head on home."

Angus leaned against the door. "That mean you ain't gonna invite me in for coffee?"

I busted into a laugh. "That's exactly what it means."

Angus smiled as he snugged his hat onto his head, then crammed his hand into his pocket. Aughtie slipped off the bed and stood behind me. I felt her hands quiver as she grasped my legs. She leaned to one side, peered around to see Angus, and then gasped.

"It's okay, honey. Angus here just wanted to see how you was doing."

"Hey there, young lady." Angus squatted and waved. His voice softened. "You feelin' better?"

Aughtie moved further behind me.

I felt like Mater as the hair on my neck stood. My thoughts went to the possibilities. What had Angus done to her on that mountain? I didn't trust him as far as I could pick him up and throw him.

Raney eased around the door. She stepped in front of me and leaned hard against me. "I'm comin' along. Aughtie's well. Clive and Cleda Mae brought her by for a visit. Would you like to say hello?"

Nothing shocked me more than for Raney to limp to the door, much less invite Angus to see Aughtie.

"I ain't sure that's such a good idea. Angus has probably got some work he needs to get to." I stepped into the doorway.

"No, Joshua. Let Angus see the child." And with that, Raney pulled the door open.

Aughtie had plastered herself to Cleda Mae like moss on a tree.

"Huh, youngin seems a mite scared of you. Must be your size. You're a big man to such a small child." Raney's knees gave, and I grabbed her. "We appreciate your kindness. Come again another time."

Angus stood speechless. I couldn't figure out why. I could have sworn I saw compassion . . . longing? . . . in his eyes for a moment. That couldn't be right. He nodded and stepped away. When he tried to speak, words hung in his throat.

"Miss Raney, I . . . I . . . appreciate gettin' to see you and the little one." Angus put his hat on his head and started down the stairs. He stopped. "Joshua, I'd like to know if the girl has an idea who did this. They need to be brought to justice." His voice was soft. Not what I expected from Angus. Maybe he was a sight more conniving than I'd given him credit for.

I took Raney's arm. "If she opens up, we'll see about lettin' you know."

"Raney know anything? Get a look at the man that did this?" Angus was asking good questions, but for me, his questions was odd. Even though it was right neighborly of him to come by, I wasn't about to give him one iota of information. Did he know something, or was he trying to hide behind kindness?

"Raney fell. She don't know nothin' else. Like I told you, I'm obliged by your concern. But let me ask you a question."

Angus drew a blank stare. "You got a question for me?" He rubbed his two-day stubble.

Clive took Raney inside, and I closed the door. I walked onto the steps and eyed Angus.

"Well, I reckon I can answer your question long as it's got nothin' to do with politics. I don't talk politics."

I imagined there wasn't no need for him to talk politics when his family owned the soul of every politician on the mountain. That was like the pot calling the kettle black.

"Where's that lowlife brother of yours?" My nose flared.

Angus dug the toe of his boot into the porch wood and dragged it in a line. I saw his jaw tighten at the mention of Thomas. He hesitated before he spoke. "Thomas done something I need to know about?"

"You mean outside of killin' my daughter and possibly stealing a child? I reckon that about covers your brother. And what about you, Angus? Why's that child so afraid of you? Did you do something to her on that mountain?" I sneered.

"I didn't do nothing to that youngin. I wouldn't hurt no child. Just what are you accusing me of?" Angus straightened his shoulders, and his fists balled. He rocked on his heels.

What surprised me was that Angus seemed taken back. Shocked at my question. Again, things just didn't add up, so I pressed him. "I'm saying, the child acts like you've done something to her. She wouldn't let you touch her on the mountain. That sorta leads me to think you mighta been up to something in them woods, and we come along in the nick of time."

"Things ain't what you think, Joshua." Angus took a step closer.

"And what do I think?" I snapped.

"You think Thomas had something to do with all this?"

"I'm sayin' something ain't right about either of you. Things don't add up, and you and your brother seem to be at the top of the suspect list."

I could feel Angus's breath against my face. Before I knew what happened, he slammed his fist against my shoulder, knocking me to my rear.

"Stay down, Joshua. I'd hate to kill you in front of your family. You answer my questions, and I might walk away and forget this happened."

I crawled to my knees and stood. "I don't stay down for a Barton. Spit out your questions, and let's see if we can end this." I jutted out my chest.

Angus took me by the shirt and yanked me up on my toes. "What makes you think Thomas has anything to do about this?"

I was ready to let Angus know what I thought, when Aughtie opened the door.

"Mr. Josh, tome in. Please?"

Clive took her by the arm.

Angus gave me a shake and turned me loose. "Well, I see the girl has a voice."

"Ain't nobody ever hinted she didn't have a voice." Clive snatched Aughtie into his arms and stepped back. "You need my help, Josh?"

"He don't need no help. Do you, Joshua?" Angus raised his hands.

"Take her inside." I motioned Clive into the house.

"I guess I got me some detective work to do, don't I." Angus pulled a cigar from his pocket and bit the end.

I'd said too much already. I stepped close to Angus, and my heart raced. "Get. Off. My. Land."

What I wanted to do was rare back and plant my fist in his jaw. He sneered and turned on his heels. "I didn't do nothin' to that youngin. That's the truth."

For a second I almost believed him.

"Angus! Hold on a second." I opened the door. "Wait here." I walked into the house, and pulled the box I'd kept in the barn off the top shelf in the kitchen. I dumped a rock the size of a small apple onto the table. With the butt of my knife, I chipped away at the wide band of green that run through the rock. A tiny sliver fell onto the table. I put away the stone and walked back outside.

I took Angus's hand and dropped the tiny sliver of gem into his palm, closin' his fingers around it. "I pay my debts, and I owe you for your help. You take that. We're paid in full—again! Now get off my land."

Angus stared at the tiny piece of emerald. "You do have a vein, don't you?"

"That's my payment for your help. Take it. I'm obliged, but I ain't obligated." I planted my feet apart and crossed my arms.

Angus rolled the sliver in his palm, eyeing that emerald fleck real good, then grinned and slipped the tiny piece of gem into his shirt pocket. He smirked and shoved his hat tight on his head. "We ain't finished."

I felt my knees weaken. In the few seconds it took Angus to decide what to do with the gem, it came back to me that this was the cause of my sin. The Company Store had been killin' me. I'd worked dawn to dusk and made worthless scrip. I couldn't feed my family, but when I fell upon that one rock with a green vein, I'd seen a way out of the mines.

I'd bought my way out, and it'd seemed right to tell Ima I knew where a whole vein was when she threatened me. It was a lie, but it kept her from killin' me. They kept watch from a distance, hoping to find my treasure. This was the lie that started it all.

"Joshua, if Thomas is behind hurting that youngin, I'll see to it he pays." Angus spit, then walked to his horse, mounted, and pulled the reins. He let out a laugh that swallowed that ounce of compassion I thought I'd seen earlier.

"Why don't I believe you?" I whispered.

My lie about that emerald started this mess. Maybe it could end it . . .

Twenty-Three

Raney was a couple of weeks before she really could sit very long or even walk alone to the outhouse. Meanwhile, I kept busy around the farm. I had no intention of leaving her until I felt sure she was alright.

The doc said she was doing good. "Give her another week and she should be managing on her own."

The timing fit our plan perfectly. The miners would be shiftin' again. Course that didn't mean it suited me. Every day I waited for Raney to heal, my anger festered like a boil too sore to touch. Each day that passed was another day we lost findin' Rayburn, but it was the right thing to do. To wait. Settle this right. I blamed myself, blamed Barton, the Company Store. I found myself blaming little Aughtie at times. If she hadn't come into our lives, none of this woulda happened. But I knew my struggles weren't her fault. It was my own doin'.

Manny come back and forth from the mines and updated us on finding Rayburn. He and Clive made several trips to the mines for Clive to talk about being mayor. They were building trust with the miners.

Ima watched like always, and I stayed behind. The less the Bartons saw of me, the less they'd suspect Clive.

Those days gnawed at my craw. I hardly slept, but time does heal, and Raney had made huge strides. She was doing well enough that Cleda Mae decided her and Clive could move into the tack shed, and I could stay with her now. To my surprise, Clive and Cleda Mae moved Aughtie with them. The three had grown close, and with Clive doin' some teaching, Aughtie was making progress.

I'd missed being in the same place as Raney, but Cleda Mae wouldn't leave her side until she was sure Raney was able to manage on her own. When I opened my eyes that first morning back in my own bed and saw Raney hobble to the stove and stoke the fire, I was beside myself.

Jumping up, I led her to the rocker by the fireplace, pulled a quilt from the bed, and tucked it around Raney's legs.

"Thank you, but I'm fine." Raney clasped her hand around mine. "I can move about," she reassured. "Open the curtains."

The sun was a welcome sight in the house. A sign of joy. Relief. I pulled the curtains open and let the yellow glow fill the room, then raised the windows. The morning breeze sailed through the house, pushing the musty stench out.

I walked to Raney. Her eyes, still a little swollen and black, was the flint that struck the flame in me. She was gettin' up to make coffee.

I knelt in front of Raney and laid my head in her lap. Her touch was tender as she scratched my shoulder with her nails.

"Three weeks ago, I thought you was a goner. And now look at you. Back to makin' coffee."

She inched her fingers into my hair. "Thank you."

"For what?"

"For findin' Aughtie. Saving her." It was hard for her to muster the words, but this was Raney's nature. Even in her pain, she cared. This was one reason I loved her so tight. She never thought about her own safety. Just Aughtie's.

"I saved you first." I grasped her fingers and kissed them gently. I pulled a stool toward Raney and sat. "You was my first choice. Not Aughtie. I had to choose. It was a terrible choice . . . waiting to find Aughtie. But you was my first concern."

Raney cocked her head, her eyes drooped with sadness. "I'm sorry you had to choose. But I can see there's something on your mind."

"I gotta ask these questions, Raney. We're gonna go find Rayburn. It's time to find him. But I can't go up there knowing only part of the story. You gotta tell me everything that happened to you. No matter what it was. I gotta know who did this."

Raney's eyes darted, then took on a stare. "I already told you. I don't know who took Aughtie, and for the last time, I fell. I've told you everything I remember, and honestly, I'm tired of repeatin' myself."

"You don't remember nothin'?" I pressed her. "You were close to him. Would you recognize him if you saw him again?" As soon as those words come from my mouth, my stomach tied in a knot.

"This is the last time I'll say it. The man had on a black hood. My mind was on Aughtie. Just Aughtie. So now might be a good time for you to walk outside and leave me alone. I'm tired of this conversation ringin' over and over."

Raney's tenderness turned sour, and I knew I'd pushed too far. Raney gave me no justification to take action against the man I hated, and that made me downright mad.

I'd pent up my anger against Thomas for years. It smoldered in me like twigs tryin' to catch and burn. When I saw Raney all busted up and bleeding, I was sure Barton had to be guilty. But I didn't have no proof.

I went to my knees and grasped Raney's hands. "I'm sorry. I just . . . I just . . ."

"You just want revenge. I'm all for fightin' this battle, but we fight it because good comes from it. Not out of revenge. Not out of hate. We fight *for* Aughtie, *for* the miners. Not against the accident that killed our daughter." Raney yanked her hands away. "I tried to blame you, Joshua. I tried to hate you for Anna's death. The Lord knew I was bitter toward Thomas, but when Aughtie come into our lives, the hard shell of hate in my heart cracked. I reckon the Lord finally convinced me that her death was an accident. I know there are all sorts of what-ifs and you shouldas, but the hard truth is, Anna was at the right place at the wrong time." Tears streamed down her cheeks. "Can't you accept that? Get on with your life?"

Raney had just said the words I needed to hear and accept. Anna's death was an accident. We both knew it, but neither of us could utter it before now. Raney was a far better person than me—letting go of her bitterness over Anna's dyin'. I knew it in my heart, but I struggled to forgive. I felt the good Lord nudge me, and I knew He was answerin' the prayer I'd prayed in the field. *Help me.* And He was, but instead of accepting His help, I bucked it.

When a parent loses a youngin, nothing explains the loss to satisfy their heart. You walk through guilt—the what if I'd done this or that—but guilt doesn't change the loss. When you don't find peace with the loss in guilt, then there's blame and anger, bitterness. I reckon Raney was right. I needed to let go. Nothing would change Anna's dyin', and nothing would truly bring me peace until I let go. It would take time for me to draw in the bitterness, and it wouldn't be easy.

"I'm sorry this man tried to steal Aughtie, hurt you . . . and who knows what else. He don't deserve forgiveness, just like Thomas don't." The words slipped out before I could stop them.

Her face hardened as she recognized my stubbornness.

"It's more than a fight for the miners." I scrambled to explain. "It's personal. Part of me sees the truth and part feels the relentless guilt for Anna's dyin'." I pressed my face into my palms. "I aim to catch the man who killed her, and when I do . . ."

"When you do, what then, Joshua? You'll kill him or get killed? What about me, then? What about Aughtie? What then?"

"I know, Raney. Believe me, I know." I looked her in the eyes. "I . . . me . . . Clive . . . we'll bring the person to justice that hurt Aughtie and killed June. It just draws such anger out of me. Such revenge." I opened the cabinet and pulled out a wooden box of shells, then took the extra rifle off the hook and filled my pockets with bullets.

"You didn't answer me, Joshua." Raney's voice quivered. "Haven't we been through enough? If you die, what do I have left?"

I turned right briskly and whispered. "Peace."

I stalked out of the house past Clive. All the pent-up rage, hurt, and confusion I'd held in for weeks finally blew like one of them holes on the mountain.

"Where you goin', Joshua?" Clive asked.

"Huntin'." I headed toward the barn.

"You need someone to help you?"

I put my hand on Clive's chest. "This is my battle, son. It ain't yours to shoulder." The emotion of the last three weeks washed over me. One second I was angry, the next broken and hurting.

"No. No. I'm goin'. Come hell or high water, I'm comin'."

"Go home, Clive." I brushed past him.

He didn't answer. Just headed to the barn to saddle the horses. "I promised to be the voice of reason, and I plan to do so."

Raney stood on the porch hunkered over and holding tight to Cleda Mae. "Joshua, wait."

I turned toward the porch. "How is a man supposed to work through these feelings? I can't win, no matter what I do. How should I act, grieve? Shouldn't I be angry? Someone tell me." I lifted my hands to the sky. *Lord, help me.*

I never put a color to my hurt, anger, and fear, but I'm good to say it was redder than blood. Hotter than the flames of hell. Smelling like powder about to blow. Louder than the roar of the river. I pushed my hand up my forehead into my hair. Raney's voice echoed in my head. Her sobs carried across the field like the howl of a wolf. All that hate rolled in my gut, and the only face I could see was Barton's . . . and that nudge from the good Lord was snuffed out.

I'd lost sight of what was good when I didn't get the answer I wanted from Raney—permission to kill Barton—and I sunk to Barton's level and named myself judge, jury, and executioner. And it felt good.

I headed toward the barn, and Aughtie trailed behind me. "Papa Josh!"

I stopped dead in my tracks. A chill run up my spine, and shame filled me. Her sweet voice poured cool reason all over my rage. If I went up the mountain to kill the Bartons, it wasn't just me who'd be swallowed by the blowback.

"Papa Josh!" She threw her arms around my legs and grinned at me.

The landslide of revenge didn't stop unless someone decided to stop settin' charges. Sometimes it took the innocence of a child to cut us to the quick, and Aughtie was like a sharp blade. My determination for vengeance was wrong, and the price for acting on it too high. It was the second time a child saved me.

Twenty-Four

That Aughtie was the one to end my rage was a sign to me. She was more than special. Me and Clive sat down in the barn and had a long talk. I gave him the apology he deserved, and he was kind in accepting that he understood all that was pent up in me. We agreed Raney was doing better enough that we'd continue our plan to find Rayburn—asking the miners as they shifted from hole to hole. We agreed to tell Rayburn about June and Aughtie. Then we'd find Thomas Barton and let him know we had the girl. It wasn't what I wanted, but it was the right thing to do. We couldn't lie no more.

"You watch your temper," Raney reminded me.

Aughtie wagged that fat little finger of hers just like Raney. "Watch temper!"

I couldn't help grinnin'. The child held the reins to my heart. She kissed her palm and waved.

Cleda Mae wiped a tear as she pulled close to Clive. "You be alright?"

He nodded and hugged her. I tossed our saddles in the back of the wagon, and we climbed in and started down the trail at about noon with a tight plan.

We'd traveled a number of miles, and just as we started up the mountain, I pulled the wagon to a halt and swiped the sweat from my forehead.

"Why are we stoppin' now?" Clive asked as his fingers tapped a tune on the buckboard.

"We need to take time to get our heads right. Rest a minute. Even with a solid plan, you know we can't just waltz into the Company Store and demand Ima Barton turn over Thomas. Never hurts to let things simmer to get clarity." I dropped my feet out of the wagon and went to looking for sticks to start a fire. Never hurts a body to take a deep breath before heading into the muck.

Clive's nerves were rising, and I couldn't think for his constant yapping.

"You remember, we ain't fer sure it was Thomas," Clive said. "I'll unhitch the horses."

"Good idea. Why don't you be useful and set them horses up to graze." I stacked some kindling, then pulled out my flint. In minutes a small fire burned. I held my tongue and poked at the fire, watching the embers float upward.

The sun bored down on the trail around the side of the mountain, and a soft summer breeze carried the scent of something more than wood burning. I lifted my nose into the air. "You smell that?"

Clive sniffed. "Yup. Smells like smoke. Probably the campfires from the mining camp carrying down the mountain."

"This smells . . . thick. Different. Like coal burnin'." This wasn't no campfire smoke. "Something's wrong! Listen. It's quiet. No sound. All of the birds has hushed." I cupped my hand around my ear and listened hard. "When the forest grows silent, something's up. Nature's smart. She knows when to tuck tail and run. Her noises don't just stop dead for no reason."

I twisted around. There was smoke rising from the ground ahead of us. We heard thunder. "You hear that? Thunder. Ain't a cloud in the sky."

Clive shaded his eyes. His horse reared and pulled loose from the tree where she grazed. He jumped to grab her reins. "Easy, girl." He patted her neck. "Simmer down. Ain't nothin' out here to spook you."

The thunder rumbled again, and the ground trembled. "Oh mercy!" I shouted.

"What's happenin'?" Clive kept ahold of his mare. "Whoa. Easy."

The ground shook again, and a crack the size of my arm formed a few feet beyond us. Steam seeped up. Then before you could shout *Johnny jump up*, a flame popped through the crack.

Rufus snorted. "Ho now. Easy." I tried to calm the horse.

Another orange flame shot through the ground. It was like hell was busting through the clay dirt. Smoke rose fast, and the trees crackled. The mountain would soon be ablaze.

Clive covered his nose with his arm. "The ground's on fire. I ain't never seen the likes."

"It ain't the ground. It's a vein of coal burning. There's an underground fire in the mines. We need to find the open hole. Start lookin'. They'll be men trying to get out. Cover your nose and mouth."

I'd only seen coal catch fire underground once before. When a body drops a lump of coal on the fire, it takes a spell for the rock to heat and then catch. But underground, things is different. It's hot, damp. The kind of damp that burns. Fumes are like oil. They catch easy—only takes a spark. A body can work years in that clammy mess and never have a problem, then one day Mother Nature burps and a spark catches. When things are just right and nature can't take no more, her belly commences to ache. She'll belch, flames will spit out of the ground, and that coal burns hot.

My mind went back to when me and Thomas was in the mines. "Joshua, break that coal outa that crevice over there," he'd said.

I'd cut away at the vein. It run along a deep slice in the wall. Every time I took a whack with my pick, a spark flew. Them shafts are deep, and there are times it smells like burning manure. It'll overtake a man. When that smell is present, it's like working in a puddle of kerosene. One spark lights the air on fire.

"Chip it off easy," Thomas had reminded me.

But there wasn't nothing easy about breakin' coal loose. I'd smashed my pick against the black strip, and a flame had shot out of the crevice.

I'd dropped to the floor and yanked Thomas down just as the flame reached into the darkness like fingers on a ghostly hand—grabbing at anything living. The walls blazed, and that dry coal lit up bright red.

"Let's get outa here," I'd hollered. We'd run like the devil outa that hole, and as we stood across the hill from it, we saw fire shoot out of the ground. Any place there was a crack, the flames billowed up. It'd burned for days before it died down.

That was when me and Thomas was friends and money didn't drive him. I'd had his back. Now all I wanted was his head.

Another burst of flame lapped at the sky, reminding me them miners needed help.

I let Rufus go and went to runnin' around the rocky path, pulling up limbs and trying to find the entrance to the mine.

Clive pushed away brush and trees, fanning the smoke from his face. We dropped to our knees and crawled on all fours. A sour smell filled the air. Sometimes the entrances were dug straight down and then at an angle. Other times they opened in the side of the hill, but the smoke made finding that opening nearly impossible. When we'd seen Angus, he'd mentioned they'd found a new place to blow open, so it would still be a hole, not a shaft yet.

Flames pooched through the earth, and Clive panicked. "Joshua, we gotta get outa here before we die."

"No! There's miners in that hole. They might not be able to cut through the smell and smoke. We gotta find the openin' and pull them outa the mine."

We snugged our handkerchiefs around our faces to try to sift some smoke from the air, when I heard Clive grunt. "You okay?" I shouted.

"Here! I found it. Over here."

I tightened my handkerchief around my face again and headed toward the sound of his voice.

"Here! Joshua. I got Manny."

Clive draped Manny's arm over his shoulder and stood. We grabbed him and pulled him out of the hole.

"Who else is in there?" I smacked his face. "Manny!"

His eyes rolled, and he coughed. "Elray Smith and . . . Thom . . ."

Clive run back and crawled through the hole until he found Elray. "I got him."

"Sit here, Manny. Let me help Clive."

I dropped into the hole and met Clive dragging Elray. We heaved him out of the ground. Clive's horse was slingin' her head, trying to find her way through the smoke, so I grabbed her reins and pulled her toward me. We threw Elray over her back and heaved Manny up behind him.

"Go on, horse!" I slapped the animal.

Rufus pranced in a panic as we snagged him. I climbed onto the horse's bare back and lent Clive an arm.

"Hup, horse, hup."

Rufus bolted like he'd been hit with lightning. The horse stumbled, but we found our way through the smoke.

We caught up to Manny, helped him down, and then lifted Elray onto the ground. His face was covered in soot, and his hands was cold. I smacked his cheeks.

"Elray. Come on, buddy. Get me some water out of the canteen."

Clive grabbed the water, and I lifted Elray's head. It rolled lifeless to one side.

"Elray?" Manny shouted. It was too late. The smoke had got him. Manny pulled Elray to his chest and screamed. It took him a minute to get his wits back before I could talk to him.

"What happened down in that hole?" I asked.

"We was headin' out from setting beams for the shaft. We just opened up the hole yesterday. Fumes hadn't cleared." Manny coughed hard and gasped for air. "I saw somebody toss a lit stick in the hole, and it blew. Oh lordy—Thomas. He's still in that hole!"

"Did you see who it was?"

"No, just caught a glimpse. Looked like someone with a hood on."

Manny kept smacking at Elray, pleadin' for him to wake up, but Elray was dead. Couldn't have told you if the stick of dynamite caused it or the smoke. But he was gone, and what I had was somebody else who'd seen the hooded man.

That made two dead on the mountain—June and Elray. Two hurt, Aughtie and Raney. And two aiming to find Barton.

Manny stood and then fell to his knees. He coughed up a black spit and gagged. "Thomas is in that hole on the other end." He gasped for good air.

For a minute I figured my problems was solved. Barton would just die in that hole. I went to pacing. "Are you sure?"

"Positive. I got to get him out." Manny's cough worsened as he gasped for air. He leaned over and vomited.

"The world's a better place without Barton," I snapped.

"That might be right, but any man with a conscience would listen to the good Lord's heed. Save who you can. Barton might be a killer, but I ain't. Leavin' him would make me as bad as him."

I understood 'cause that same conscience was eatin' at me.

Manny tried to lift hisself onto Clive's horse, but he was coughing so bad he could hardly stand. "I can check. I understand if you won't go."

"Aw, bull. Get down. You ain't in no shape to go back into that mess." I pulled him to the side. "Clive, saddle up your horse. I'll be back." And with that, I mounted, yanked the reins to one side, and kicked Rufus. "Come on, horse." The animal's back was wet with sweat, and I had to squeeze my knees hard to keep from sliding off.

The smoke grew thicker. A deer shot past me, its ears perked to a point. Squirrels, rabbits. They was all just trying to survive. As me and Rufus maneuvered our way through the smoke, a thought came back to me. Anna's sweet faith. *There's always hope.*

Here was my opportunity to just let Barton die. It wouldn't be my fault. It would be an accident in the mine. Still, I'd know it wasn't the truth. *Follow the truth or ignore it?*

I found my way to the opening of the mine, then takin' my canteen from around my shoulder, I doused my handkerchief and wrapped it around my face again. My eyes was burnin' so bad between the smoke and the tears, seeing was nearly impossible.

I made my way inside that hole, then dropped to my belly and tried to get below the heat and smoke. "Barton! You in here?" I hollered.

I heard a groan, and sure enough, it was Thomas. He was flat on the ground. I took his arm and pulled him up. "Come on. I can't move you on my own, and if it comes down to me or you . . . well, I win. So move!"

Barton wobbled to his knees, and we crawled till we could stand. For every two steps he took, I dragged him three. It was all I could do to lug Thomas out of the mine—and it was the last thing I wanted to do, but I did it anyhow.

Through it all, I wanted to be the better man. Needed to be worthy of Raney and that little girl that saved me.

TWENTY-FIVE

RUFUS WAS PANICKED—prancing in circles, snorting, and stumbling. Getting Barton on the horse's back was like threading a darnin' needle in the dark, but I managed and then clambered up behind. "Come on, Rufus, run!" The animal bolted and nearly dumped us both off, but I kept hold. I leaned Thomas against the horse's neck and grabbed around him to catch a breath. It was just minutes, but it felt like a lifetime before we reached the others.

Manny met us, hardly able to stand for his coughing. Clive pulled Thomas off the horse, slammed him to the ground, then went to pourin' water down his throat until he strangled and coughed. I grabbed the canteen of water for Manny.

My lungs ached like them flames was burning deep in my chest.

Thomas rolled to his side, sputtering. "Lawsy mercy. How'd that mine blow?" He swiped his mouth on his sleeve.

I stared at Barton. He was as much a victim as Manny and Elray. No matter how I tried to work a plan in my mind that would make Thomas the devil, I couldn't. There was no blaming him for this mess. He wasn't the hooded man that took Aughtie or the man Manny saw. Barton had been too far back in the mine.

There ain't nothin' worse than eating crow pie. Raney tried to tell me. In all his blabbering, Clive tried to make me understand that the culprit in all this might not be Thomas. I didn't want to believe it. All I'd wanted was for Thomas Barton to die for killing my girl. It was like a knife rammed my gut and sliced me clean to the heart. There was no revenge to be had. Thomas wasn't the one wearing the hood. He wasn't to blame.

I rested my head on my arm. Sweat drained down my neck. It was over, and I'd lost to the Bartons once again.

"Joshua." Thomas coughed and pulled hisself next to me. He raised to his knees and leaned over my back, his breath against my neck. "They ain't words enough to say thank you," he whispered.

I lifted my head and dumped him off my back.

Thomas lay on the ground groaning. "They ain't no words. I know you'd just as soon seen me dead."

"You reckon?" I snipped.

"But you risked your life to save me," Thomas said.

I sat starin'. Thomas was right. There was no words. I couldn't come up with one iota. I pointed to Manny. "See that man, Thomas? That's one you wouldn't help, and his girl died. *That* is the man who saved your sorry butt. I just did the legwork."

Manny toppled to one side and went floppin' like a fish out of water. I glanced over at him. Coal dust circled his mouth, and drool strung down his chin. Through the black of the coal soot, there was a hint of blue on his lips. When a person was dying, Raney used to say that the coldhearted death angel left his mark by suckin' the life out of a man's body and leaving his lips icy cold and blue.

"Manny!" I pulled him up against my chest. His eyes rolled back in his head. Thomas and Clive come next to us. "Manny, look at me." I couldn't do a thing but hold him in my arms whilst he shook. When his body stopped quivering, he opened his eyes and clasped his hands around mine.

"Fin . . . finish this. For . . . Mary. For . . . for . . . Aughtie." The life hissed out of Manny, and now four people that meant something to me . . . were dead.

My heart felt like it exploded as I shook Manny. "Don't you die!" I cried out. "Manny, don't you die. Manny, don't do this."

Drool slipped from his mouth, and his hand loosened from my shirt and dropped to his side. I held my friend in my arms, his body lifeless, and I couldn't fight back the tears. Would death not stop? I eased Manny's body to the ground.

My heart cried for Manny's family. Hettie and his youngins. What would they do now? It was for sure Ima had every ounce of money the man had earned tied up in scrip. And everybody knew Ima would keep every penny owed to Manny away from Hettie and her youngins. I pulled my knees up and rested my arms across them. Next thing I knew, Thomas was laid over Manny, sobbing.

Sobbing. I was never so perplexed as I was just then. Thomas Barton, ruthless and cold, crying over a man he'd wronged.

Clive come to his feet and lifted Barton off Manny. He sat next to Thomas. It was something I can't say I'd ever witnessed before. The two of them mourning together. I wasn't sure what to do. This was a side of Barton I'd never seen. A broken side.

Weak. I picked up a rock and flung it hard across the field. "Not Manny!" I shouted. "No!"

We tried to console one another. Mourn the losses and show gratitude for the hand of mercy that had saved us. I crossed Manny's arms and pressed his eyes shut. There was no trying to make things better. The only noise was the crackle of the flames and an occasional rumble below the ground.

"We can't wait no longer before these men start to stiffen. We need to get them home. Sun will be settin' soon," I said.

"I'll take Elray." Thomas stood and swiped his forehead on his sleeve. "Ain't no need in puttin' your life at risk. I'll take him and help Merrylin bury him. If you can take Manny . . . I wouldn't be welcome in his home."

"Do what?" I said. "You're gonna try and take Elray home with no horse? Alone?"

"We can lash a flat together. You can take my horse, Thomas." Clive stepped up.

Thomas knelt by Elray and wiped the soot away from his nose and mouth. "I don't need the horse. Just help me make a flat."

Clive gathered some heavy sticks, and we lashed them together with thick vines, then rolled Elray onto the flat.

"You can use my horse to pull him," Clive reminded Thomas.

"Much obliged. But it ain't necessary. I'll pull him."

"It's a steep climb up the mountain. You'll need that horse," I said.

Thomas come face to face with me. "I'll be fine. You've done enough.

And I won't forget. Besides, ain't nothin' more I can do to honor this man than to drag him myself."

Right then I could see something different in Thomas's eyes. He was a man that was changed. How and why was a mystery, but when a body's changed from the inside out, his eyes is clear. It's true the eyes are the window to the soul, for there was a clarity in Thomas's eyes and his soul looked . . . clean.

Thomas stretched the rope across his chest and leaned into it. The flat moved slowly. He got a few hundred feet before a loud explosion rang across the mountain.

"They blew the hole to put out the fire. Should be safe soon." Thomas tightened the rope around his chest. "Go home, Joshua. Go home to your wife. Take Manny home. I'll see to it Hettie is cared for . . . Merrylin too."

Thomas disappeared into the smoky fog. I stood speechless.

"Reckon what just happened here?" Clive brushed his face across his sleeve, spitting and sputtering to get the coal dust outa his mouth.

"I ain't rightly sure."

"Ain't never seen Thomas Barton cry."

"I ain't never known him to be nice unless it benefited him. Even when we was friends. He's usually meaner than a rattler." I slapped my hat against my trousers, knocking off the dirt. "Beats all I ever seen." I knelt next to Manny and patted his chest. "You are a good man—a good friend."

"I'll hitch Rufus to the wagon." Clive squeezed my shoulder.

I had time to sit there and mourn my friend. Time to tell him goodbye. Soon the smoke began to clear, and I could see no more flames was risin' outa the ground.

Clive pulled his horse close and rubbed her neck. We lifted Manny into the wagon and headed toward his home.

"Reckon that blast was big enough to collapse the whole tunnel? Ima ain't gonna be happy she lost a good vein of coal." Clive shook his head.

"I reckon she ain't. And she'll be worse if Thomas does what he says—take care of them widows."

"You think Thomas has found religion?"

I eyed Clive and didn't say a word, but I got what he meant. Thomas caring for the widows . . . seemed to be what the good Lord expected.

As we headed home, the stench of burnt coal and trees choked us, blinded us. I didn't think me or Clive could take in what we'd seen.

We was at Manny's home before the sun set. Clive sent Manny's boy to gather some of the farmers down by the river to help us bury Manny. It took the better part of the night to dig a grave and lay Manny to rest. I told Hettie we'd make room for her and her sons on the farm, not to worry. I figured with the help of the farmers, we could raise Hettie a small cabin down by our barn. We could pull Manny's farm and mine together and make a good place for Hettie—maybe Merrylin too. It seemed like a flood of disaster hit every day.

Me and Clive slept a spell in Manny's barn and left out for home later than I'd have hoped. It wasn't long before we rounded that bend once again to the house. I could see the sun wrap its arms around the afternoon and raise up over the field filled with red poppies dotted with white daisies. Cleda Mae sat in a rocker next to Raney, watching Aughtie chase butterflies.

"You ain't hardly said a word since we left Manny's," Clive said.

"Ain't nothin' to say."

"Well, that's a buncha hogwash." Clive huffed. "You was set to tear outa here yesterday mornin' like a bat outa hell. You was determined to kill Thomas despite what Raney or me said. Then the youngin talked you out of it, but you didn't go willingly. What's changed?"

I knew it was partly grief and partly that we were both worn out, so I tried to ignore him.

"I told you there wasn't no proof Thomas was involved in killing that woman or hurtin' Raney. Things didn't add up." His voice took a pitch higher, harping at me like an old madwoman. "Instead of figuring out who that hooded man was and following that to the responsible folks, you jumped the gun. Maybe if you'd listened, we'd have found that man before he could toss a dynamite stick in that hole."

"Alright! I understand. I jumped the gun. I was wrong. That what you wanna hear? What more do you want from me, Clive? I said I was wrong."

"I want you to let go of this anger so we can tend to matters." Clive took in a deep breath. "I gotta give you your due. I saw your change of heart when you went in that hole after the very man you wanted dead. That had to be hard."

I shook my head. Rufus come to a halt beneath the apple tree at the end of the lane. He nosed around on the ground until he found a soft red apple and dug in his teeth. "Go ahead, boy. You earned an apple."

"Ain't you gonna answer me? You coulda let an innocent man die." Clive kept on.

"But I didn't. I saved him instead. I reckon I call it mercy," I said.

"You sayin' you don't want him dead no more? What changed your mind?"

I shrugged. "You're like a dog with a bone. They ain't no turnin' loose."

"I wanna know why a man so hell bent on killin' another changed his mind." Clive pushed at me.

I took him by the collar and pulled him close. His rear come off the wagon seat.

"The good Lord's been gnawin' at my heart, and I'm trying hard to be a different man. Weeks ago I had my gun in my mouth ready to blow off my head when a coin fell off the door facing. It was Anna's. When she gave it to me, she told me that there was always hope. And she was right. If it helps you figure things any better, just call what I did mercy."

I let Clive go, then pulled my handkerchief from my pocket and blew my nose. "I've been fightin' with her words. Trying to make sense of her death. Blaming myself and Thomas. When the truth is, maybe her death was an accident. Thomas wasn't likely to see her in the weeds. He was just easy to blame. And I'm trying my best to accept it. And even if things was different, hating him don't make me worthy of Raney or Aughtie. 'Sides, Thomas looks to be a changed man." I shook my head.

Clive slid off the wagon seat and picked up an apple. He walked around Rufus and extended his hand. "Let's walk the rest of the way to the house. Rest, Rufus." And we did.

When Aughtie saw us, she come hightailin' it toward us, squealin' like she'd been given a nugget of gold. Her excitement warmed my heart.

It was time to stop lying to myself. Time to fix the mess I'd stepped in. "Truth ain't easy, Clive."

"No, it ain't. But it eventually eases the hardest pain."

Raney stood from the big pine rocker, and Cleda Mae watched her off the porch. She reached her arms around my neck and held me like she hadn't held me in years. I pressed my face into her hair.

I wasn't right sure when Clive and Cleda Mae left for the tack shed, but darkness was creeping in when they took Aughtie with them, stopping to swing her on the tree swing, and left me and Raney some privacy. I hadn't told Raney about the pain I felt, and she had no idea of the realization that had come to me while I was on that mountain. We'd never mourned together. Raney had done her cryin' alone, and I'd done mine with a gun barrel pressed in my mouth. Me and her walked down to the stone that marked Anna's grave. You could see the dirty streaks left from tears. Some was mine. Others belonged to Raney. We mourned our daughter together. It was five years coming.

Twenty-Six

We said a goodbye to our girl and walked toward the house. A breeze picked up, and the aroma of the mountains filled my senses—something between the flavor of pine trees and the musky smell of the woods. Lightning bugs flickered above our heads, and before I knew it, me and Raney was layin' face up starin' at the stars. Raney's hand went up, and a finger drew from one star to the next while I wondered which one was our girl looking down. Every star was a soul passed looking down on the world. I remembered.

After a good while, the lantern flickered, and we knew we needed to get back to the house. Raney stood real slow and dusted the weeds off her skirt. She wouldn't let me help her. Like always, she was independent despite her wounds. I scooped her up in my arms.

She laid her head against my neck and gently kissed my ear. "Don't you drop me. I'm sore enough without you addin' insult to injury."

I hugged her close to my chest, and we went back to the house.

Me and Raney didn't say too much. She somehow knew my heart without me sayin' anything, and when we crawled into bed, she rolled toward me instead of away.

"Something's different," she whispered. "You don't have to tell me now."

"I reckon now is as good a time as any."

I sat up and dropped my legs over the edge of the bed. The fire flickered, casting a tender shade of moon yellow across the room. Raney scooted close and laid her head on my shoulder.

"Manny died yesterday." I buried my face in my hands. Words come hard as I gasped to hold back the tears. "He was a good friend."

"What happened?"

"It was an underground explosion. Me and Clive pulled Manny and Elray outa the hole, but Manny insisted Thomas was still in the mine. I went in after him."

"You what?"

"I pulled Thomas out. Elray died right after we pulled him free. Manny a bit later. I reckon the fumes got the best of them. But Thomas . . . You were right. Thomas couldn't be involved with the hooded man. Manny said that man tossed a stick of dynamite into the hole. After that explosion, Thomas crawled out a changed man."

Raney rubbed my back. "That's enough for now."

"No, there's more. Me and you have been lying to ourselves." I brushed her hair away from her face. "We've told ourselves lie after lie to make the pain of losin' Anna bearable—to lay blame where there was no blame to lay." I swallowed hard. "On the mountain, when that explosion hit, it was like hell itself was breakin' through the earth.

"I tried to find some reason to let Barton die in that hole. It wouldn't be my fault. He'd just be another victim of the mine. But Anna kept speaking to my heart. So I went into that hole after Thomas."

"And you saved him?" Raney struggled to stand. She took me by the shoulders and twisted me toward her. "You saved Barton?"

I nodded.

She threw her arms around me and squeezed. "That was the right thing to do. You're a good man, Joshua."

I went on to tell her about his eyes. "You know how you look into a body's eyes, and you can tell things is different?"

"Like I looked into yours tonight. Yes." Raney smiled.

"Well, I could see clean through Thomas's soul. Raney, he was clean as he could be. I don't think there was an ounce of guilt in him. Barton was different. I don't know how, but he was different. When he laid across Manny and sobbed, I knew I'd wanted to kill an innocent man."

"But you didn't."

"No. I didn't. And to beat all, Thomas insisted he'd haul Elray home to Merrylin."

"That's when you figured out your lies?" Raney leaned against me.

"That's when it hit me. All the lies I'd believed that Thomas was a killer was wrong. The good Lord convicted me, and I faced my guilt."

"What's you gonna do now?"

"I ain't sure. But I reckon I try again to find old man Rayburn. Showin' him where we buried June and then . . ." My voice caught in my throat. I couldn't get a good breath for the pain seeping up.

"Aughtie," Raney said. "You're gonna ask about Aughtie?"

I choked on the words. All I could do was nod. Tears welled up in Raney's eyes as she took in a breath and heaved it out. "Then I'm comin' with you. This is as much my lie as it was yours."

We'd lost one youngin, and it didn't seem we'd ever fill the hole in our soul for the child. Then Aughtie come. It was like she was just dropped outa heaven into our lap. She wasn't ours to keep. Maybe she was sent to help me, and me and Raney heal. Either way, the lie to keep her was wrong. I needed to make this right. Who knew if Rayburn even knew his daughter had a youngin? Maybe he never had no dealings with his girl after she come up a momma. Wasn't no way to tell until I loaded the child up and took her to him.

"It's easier doin' wrong than it is doin' right." I coughed out the words.

Raney cupped my face in her hands. "It is. But right is always best. And it's time we both face that."

I reached into the wood bucket and grabbed a log, tossing it onto the fire. Embers floated up the chimney. A hint of smoke twirled around the cabin before the breeze from the window sucked it out. I lay back.

Raney wrapped her fingers through mine and then kissed my cheek. "Tomorrow is a new day. Tonight Aughtie is still here to love."

That was true. Tonight we could close our eyes and enjoy sweet dreams of this little girl who wasn't just right. A child whose mind didn't work the way most youngins her age worked. Aughtie was pure, honest, and loving. When I looked at her, I could see an inner peace that I longed to have. Despite the horrible things she'd been through. Despite she wasn't just right. She was at peace. If nothing else, she'd taught me that.

She wasn't mine to replace Anna. She wasn't mine to hide away. She wasn't a lie I needed to believe. Aughtie was a lost youngin who come into my life long enough to wake up my soul.

The log on the fire caught, and it went to crackling and spewing its song. The crickets outside chimed in with the rustle of the breeze in the trees, and it was like a whole choir singing a soft melody to lull me to sleep. The last thing I remember before my eyes closed was the taste of Raney's lips against mine. And there was peace.

Twenty-Seven

THERE WAS NEVER a morning that the old rooster missed a call, and today was no different. Ole Miser planted his feathered rear on the porch railing and let out a cock-a-doodle-doo that shook us outa sleep.

I come out of the bed and slammed open the window shutter. "Get from here. Idiot bird." Feathers went to flapping, and I grinned. "How's it feel? Bein' startled?" Miser landed on the ground by the washtub, shaking and fluffing his feathers to let me know he didn't appreciate payback. "Keep it up and you'll be the lean meat in Raney's dumplin's."

Raney made her way to the porch. I watched as she struggled to lift her arms and stretch. I wanted to help her work out the kinks, but Raney only wanted help if she asked.

"Waney!" The squeal of a sweet youngin rung across the field. Aughtie's talkin' kept improving. The more she come to trust us, the more she commenced to talk. Proved the child was smarter than you might suppose.

"There's my girl." Raney waddled down the steps and held out her arms. Aughtie plowed into her like a runaway calf. Raney grunted, but she managed to pick Aughtie up with one arm and squeeze her. You could see the pain, but Raney didn't seem to mind.

"Look at your pretty braids. Miss Cleda Mae dolled you up."

Aughtie leaned her head back and laughed. She was a happy child. I wasn't sure how, seein' all the youngin had been through. I once heard it said that the good Lord made up in other ways what a body was cheated. It seemed the good Lord gave Aughtie joy. Even in the bad.

"Mornin'." Clive come behind the house toting an armload of fresh-cut wood. "Here's your wood for the day, Miss Raney. And Cleda Mae said you was not to do nothing but sit in your rocker. She's gathering eggs."

Raney smiled and brushed Clive off. She inched Aughtie to the ground and straightened her dress. "Miss Raney needs to bathe. I feel like I've been rolled through a field of cow pies."

"I heard that." Cleda Mae shifted her basket to the opposite arm and slipped her free arm around Raney's waist. "I'll heat some warm water, and we'll wash your hair too. Reckon you must be up to it."

The two made their way into the cabin, Aughtie hot on their heels.

I sat on the porch steps and leaned my elbows on my knees. Clive sat next to me. "You alright?"

"Me and Raney come to terms last night. I told her everything about Manny and Thomas. I've done a lot of studyin'. And you was right."

"Am I believing what I hear? Joshua Morgan is admitting somebody else is right about something?"

I wheeled around and pointed my finger. "Boy, makin' light of me don't make this no easier."

"So what am I right about? I give you a lot of good advice yesterday." Clive went to laughing.

"You gave more than was asked for or needed. I was judging Thomas when I had no proof of his guilt. I done been through this making a mistake twice, and I got no intention of drudging through it a third time, so here's what me and Raney's come up with."

Clive rested his hat on his knee. "I'm waitin'."

"We're going to follow through and find old man Rayburn. And then . . ." My voice quivered.

"Lord have mercy. You're gonna take Aughtie to him, ain't you?" Clive come to his feet. "Is that what you're saying?" He brushed his hand through his hair. "Lordy mercy, I can't believe my ears. You've finally let go."

I nodded. My heart ached purt near as bad as it did the day I saw my girl die. "It's the right thing to do. Despite how much me and Raney have got attached to the youngin, she ain't ours to keep. I tried to convince myself she was abandoned, but truth is, she wasn't. She was lost after her momma was gone."

"Then I'm comin' with you. When you planning on leaving?"

"Raney's coming. Ain't no need for you to come."

"Oh no you don't. I ain't come this far in this battle to not stand by your side. Besides, part of this ordeal was about taking down the Company Store. Helping the miners. It was you that made it personal."

There was no need to fuss with Clive. I looked at him now as a son, and if a boy that wasn't my own could learn stubbornness from me, then he had. He'd proved to be a faithful friend and a moral compass. I reckoned the good Lord stuck him in my way.

Clive tipped his hat. "I'll hitch up the wagon." He started down the path to the barn.

Mater raised his head and cocked it to one side. His bum ear drooped, but the good one stood to a point. The dog owned this homestead, and when strangers come into his territory, he'd get right testy.

"Whatcha hear, boy?" That's when Mater scratched a hole in the dirt getting to his feet. He let out a howl that sent shivers up my spine. Down the lane come a man. A man wobbling in his saddle.

"Clive, hold up!" I hollered. I waved for him to come back, then pointed down the lane. Mater took down the lane growling and howling, and I took after him. Clive didn't take no time to catch up.

The man dropped forward around his horse's neck, and just as me and Clive got to him, he slipped off the saddle and into our arms.

"Thomas?" Clive smacked the man's face.

We threw his arms around our shoulders and walked him to the porch. There was black soot around his nose and mouth. His face was twisted and his lip bloody. Every time Clive patted Thomas's cheeks to wake him up, he'd open his eyes and they'd roll back in his head.

Raney come out of the cabin, her hair dripping water like a sieve, and Cleda Mae right behind.

"Oh my goodness." Cleda Mae slipped around Clive. "He needs water in him. Look how pasty he looks." She took Aughtie by the hand, keepin' her just far enough away from Thomas that she couldn't see the mess he was. "Baby, can you get some water in the bucket for me? And bring a cup."

Aughtie nodded and skedaddled to obey.

Raney pushed me to the side, pulled the tail of her skirt up, swiping at the soot. "Thomas. Open your eyes." Raney's voice was firm but tender.

He cracked open a slit, and then his mouth fell open.

"Oh no you don't. You ain't dyin' on my porch. No siree."

Aughtie set a bucket at the door with just enough water to cover the bottom. It was the best she could do.

Cleda Mae kissed Aughtie's hand. "Thank you, baby. Now go on and play with that old hound." She took the cup from Aughtie's hand and scraped up some of the water to pour into Thomas's mouth.

Aughtie leaned slowly around Cleda Mae, cautiously peering to see the man. She smiled. "Papa."

You could have blown us over with a feather. All of us stood starin' at Aughtie. She slipped around Cleda Mae and took the cup.

"Papa, you drink. Tome on—drink."

Barton's eyes cracked open, and Aughtie threw her arms around him. "Papa." She gently rubbed his face with her hand, her momma's bag dangling from her elbow.

"Let's let Miss Cleda Mae and Miss Raney take care of our friend." Clive picked Aughtie up and rested her on his hip.

"Mr. Tlive. Papa."

Clive walked her out to the elm and sat her in the swing.

My stomach turned. Cleda Mae nudged Raney out of the way so she could get some water in Thomas. I didn't think it was possible for anything else to hit me like a fist to the jaw, but there was no doubt—Aughtie knew Thomas. She called him Papa. I didn't know what was worse—the fact Aughtie called Thomas Papa or the twist of life that now sat in a chair in front of us. I had everything wrong about Thomas. He wasn't the hooded man, and now he wasn't out to kill Aughtie—she was *his* daughter. He really had been searching for her when he come to our cabin.

It took a bit, but the women kept at it until Thomas was sittin' upright.

"What in the Sam Hill happened to you?" I squawked.

Thomas held a cup filled with water. He turned it to his lips and sipped.

"I lugged Elray's body home, and before I got there, Momma had already put Merrylin and them youngins on their way."

"How did she even know about Elray dyin' in the mine?"

"Momma knows everything." Thomas shrugged.

Truer words couldn't have been said, for Ima had a hand in everybody's business. That's how she managed to keep control. And how she managed to own every miner that tried to work for a decent wage. Her eyes come from folks a body least expected. Wasn't many you could trust.

Since I'd broke free from her, buyin' my way out with that green gem, Ima pressed hard on the men in the mines. She made life harder than it already was. If them men worked to earn $1.00, Ima charged them $1.10 for their food in the Company Store. Then she'd hold their next paycheck hostage. She was greedy not just for money but for power, control. It was really no surprise she let her husband, John, die in the mine.

Thomas coughed and then gulped a few more swigs of water. It was clear he was tuckered out. There was questions about Aughtie we needed to know, but something else had happened. While I'd forgiven Thomas, I wasn't right sure I could trust him. There was little I could do about Aughtie knowin' her daddy, but I might be able to figure out how to make this situation a little better.

Clive left Aughtie to Cleda Mae and helped me move Thomas into the cabin.

"What happened?" Clive asked.

Thomas rested his head on the table. He took in a big breath and went to talking.

"Look, Joshua. I've done some terrible things to appease Momma. Like blowin' that mine years ago. And I know we ain't been friends for years, but there was a time we were best friends. Had each other's backs. Momma was the one who was the poison. Same thing happened when she caught wind of June."

Raney glanced up at me.

"June?" I asked.

"June Rayburn. I thought she was sweeter than berries. Grew to love her. And when I wanted to marry her, all Momma saw was a threat to the wealth in the mine. Her hands was squeezed so tight around her money that her knuckles were white."

"I'm sorry to hear that." Them was all the words I could find with Raney eyeing me.

"Momma wasn't about to let me marry anyone that was bright enough to take her money. And in her mind, June was able to do that, being a teacher and good with numbers. She was smart. And June worked in the store, so she knew Momma's books."

Clive spoke up. "June was the teacher? I took her place. Ima told me the teacher before left the mountain and went to Saltville to some highfalutin school."

"That wasn't true. June went to work in the store," Thomas said.

It didn't surprise me. For a minute I felt some give in my chest. I wasn't the only one who lied to suit his own needs. Maybe I didn't need to feel so harsh about my own.

"I took June. Set her up on the back side of the mountain, near White's Mill. I figured that was far enough away that Momma wouldn't look. Then . . ." Thomas hesitated. "Then I married her."

"What did Ima do?" Raney said as she knelt next to him and dabbed the blood from his lip.

"Nothin' for a spell, then by chance Angus followed me over the mountain. He snooped around till he found out me and June had married."

"Oh my." Raney pressed her hand over her mouth. "He told Ima?"

Thomas stared at the floor for a minute. "He did, and Momma sent him out like a wolf on a hunt."

It only took a second for us to figure out a boulder was about to roll down the mountain and land square on top of us. The door squeaked open, and Aughtie walked in.

Nary a one of us could say a word. Listenin' seemed to be the right thing to do. Aughtie caught a glance of Thomas. She cocked her head to one side.

"Papa! Momma Joon won't wake up." She crawled up in Thomas's lap, laid her head on his chest, and cried.

Twenty-Eight

"Sissy! Don't cry." Thomas wrapped his arms around Aughtie.

Her pudgy fingers drew the outline of his cheeks. She slipped her arms around his neck and squeezed.

"Lordy mercy, I was afraid you were dead." Thomas buried his face into the girl's hair and hugged her tight.

I wasn't sure what to say. All my lies had just come full circle and bit me in the tail. I glanced toward Raney and shrugged. She smiled that peaceful smile and pressed her finger against her lips.

"Thomas?" Raney stepped toward him and placed her hand on his back. "I need to talk to you, and I need you to listen with a good heart."

We couldn't deny that Aughtie knew Thomas and that he was thrilled to see his girl. He hadn't put all his suspicions together—the ones that told him me and Raney had his girl all along. When a man is caught up in his pain, he don't always put things together. I was proof of that. Still, I was preparin' for the worst when Barton did put things together. I trusted Raney and kept quiet. Getting past my history with Thomas was hard, and despite my efforts, I was still leery. Change didn't happen overnight.

She motioned me to scoot the stool close, and she eased next to Thomas. Aughtie straddled his waist.

Cleda Mae gently lifted her off his lap. "Papa is sore. Come sit with Miss Cleda." Cleda Mae smiled cautiously.

Raney cleared her throat. "A few weeks back, Joshua found this child wanderin' the lower field. It took him a spell before he coaxed her to come out. Poor child hardly had on any clothes. Her bloomers, one sock, and a torn nightshirt. She was covered in coal dust."

Thomas sat quiet, but the expression on his face said volumes.

"When Joshua found her, she was alone. Not a soul with her. She couldn't even tell us her name. She was hungry and nasty. Then you showed up."

"Was she here when I come lookin'?"

Raney shifted her weight on the stool and took in a deep breath. "She was, Thomas. But only a short time. We didn't know when you come huntin' if you was huntin' her as your own or if she was a pawn in a game. We was trying to protect a lost child we knew nothing about. It didn't seem right to hand her over to the first person who come around. The child couldn't speak for herself at the time." Raney waited for his response, but all he managed was a nod.

Thomas took Aughtie by the hand and twisted her from side to side, looking her over, head to toe. "She's well cared for. I'm obliged."

"Of course she is, Thomas. We've grown to love her."

"Was she bruised up?" he asked.

"Not at all. She was just hungry and dirty. We don't know how long she was wandering about without her momma."

"June? Sissy said June wouldn't wake up." The color left Thomas's face. "Where's June?"

I couldn't let Raney take the brunt of what was to come, and I stepped up. "A few weeks ago, a masked man scooped up the girl and took her." I proceeded to tell Thomas about the events. Us going to the Company Store, Raney goin' after Aughtie, me hunting her, finding her. It was a long, drawn-out story, but Thomas listened patiently.

"You said hooded man? The same one that tossed that lit stick in the mine?"

"Be my guess. While we was searchin' for Aughtie, we run upon Angus."

"My brother, Angus?"

"He asked some right odd questions, but stranger still, we heard whimpers from the pond just a few feet away. That's where we found Aughtie—in the pond."

"Angus tried to grab for her, but Aughtie dodged his tries like he was hot coals. We suspected something odd but couldn't be sure," Clive said.

I waited for him to come off that stool and fly into a rage. But he took Aughtie from Cleda Mae and held her tight.

"What about June?" Thomas snuggled Aughtie tight, tinkerin' with her long curls.

"Comin home that day, Aughtie went to squealin' and callin' for her momma. We stopped and let her off the horse. She led us back a few yards off the trail," Clive said.

"Oh no. She's dead." Thomas's voice shook, holding back emotion.

"We buried her where she was. There was no moving her body. She'd been there a spell." Clive went on. "Aughtie'd kept saying 'Momma June,' and we begin to piece things together. That led us to figure out June Rayburn might be her momma."

I leaned eye to eye with Thomas. "You and me ain't been on civil terms. I reckon it's time we stopped the anger and made peace. I could say an eye for an eye. You took my Anna, and I took your Aughtie. But that ain't right. Truth is, though Anna is gone, Aughtie is what we have in common, and this little one has changed us both."

Thomas's eyes never flitted. But I could see a look of puzzlement in them. He finally uttered a word. "How did I take Anna?"

Raney wrapped her arms around my shoulders. "Joshua, look at his eyes. He don't know what you are talkin' about. He's being truthful." And for the first time, what we'd come to believe was proven true. Thomas didn't know he'd run Anna down. It really was an accident.

And for the next bit, we reminded Thomas about the day he and his posse stormed the homestead.

"I didn't see her. Didn't feel her . . . I didn't know. Lordy. I'm sorry. Them was the days when Momma pushed us hard for every debt," Thomas whispered.

It seemed that for the next few hours we talked about our losses—two bitter enemies finally shared their pain. We wouldn't become best friends, but we began to see what we had in common. Years of anger and loss acted like mud sealing a crack.

After a spell, we walked to the stand of trees where June was buried. Clive whittled out June's name on a cross, and we planted it while the women made a grave cover of evergreen sprigs.

Thomas stood at the foot of June's grave, holding Aughtie's hand. In his gentleness with the youngin, I saw a different man. Strange in a way.

Nothing like the man Barton once was. Aughtie wiggled free of his hand and placed a flower on top.

"That's very nice, sweetie. Your momma will appreciate it." Cleda Mae nudged Aughtie toward Thomas. "Kiss Papa, and let's give him a few minutes alone with Momma."

The child kissed her papa and then skipped ahead of Cleda Mae and Raney toward the house.

Hearing Cleda Mae call Thomas Aughtie's papa was a gut punch. I felt a little jealous that Thomas could wrap his arms around his child—one I had hoped might become ours. My arms felt more than a little empty.

"Right ain't always easy." Clive bumped my shoulder.

No doubt my face said it all. But what could I say? So I shrugged. "Thomas, will you be alright?" It was hard pressed for me to let them words seep from my mouth after all the years of pain and hate I'd held toward him. This change I saw in Thomas was proof of hope.

Thomas Barton, my worst enemy, stretched out his arm and grasped my shoulder. I saw the line of his jaw clench tight. He took my hand and shook it. "This. Ends. Here. I'm tired of years of pain and anger. I'm tired of Momma. Tired of bein' a slave to her and these mines."

I nodded. "New start?"

"New start." Thomas stared at the burnt grass around June's grave.

I felt like Thomas was being truthful. He was shaken but not overtaken by grief. Every man grieves different. Like me, he'd lied to hisself for years, and it only put him in the same ugly hole. Neither of us was any better than the other. We were both wrong and too proud to look past our lies. Though I thought the resolution to our hate would have played out differently, what I saw here was Anna's words coming to life.

I made my way to Clive. "Never thought I'd see the day that two wrongs made a right."

Clive flung his knife blade, stickin' it in an oak tree. He grinned right big.

"You saying I was wrong?" I said.

"I'd say we have the ammunition we need to bring down Ima. Don't you?" Clive punched my arm and grinned. He pulled his knife from the tree trunk.

It took a minute before what Clive said hit me. Thomas said our feud ended here, but he hinted the real war was about to begin—his war with Ima? Would we fight her hold together?

Thomas walked from behind the trees, hands in his pockets and eyes locked on the trail. He stopped next to me and straightened his shoulders. "I owe you for savin' my life and Sissy's."

"Aughtie!" I corrected him before I realized what I'd done. "We didn't know what to call her, so we've been calling her Aughtie."

Thomas sighed. "Guess she's got another name now."

"I almost changed my mind on saving your sorry rear." I chuckled.

It was the first time I'd seen his lip curl in a real smile all day. "I got something I need to do, and I'm asking if you and Clive would be willing to help." Thomas dug a toe in the dirt.

"What's on your mind?" I asked.

"Momma is the root cause of everything on this mountain. Her and her greed for black gold and power. She killed my wife. She might not have done the deed, but the blood is on her hands, and I got a hunch you were right about something being strange about Angus. I bet you walked up on him about to do the same to my girl. Momma wanted June gone. She didn't know about Aughtie 'cause June kept her hid."

"Me and Clive figured if we take Ima down, the steel fist of the Company Store would end."

Thomas shook his head. "Seems to be right. You willin'?"

"Willing and able." Clive glanced at me. "Both of us."

I nodded in agreement.

Thomas's pace speeded up, and we let him move ahead, giving him time to take in June's death.

A thunderhead rolled over the top of the mountain, and I felt the rumble in my gut. My mind was telling me to believe Thomas, but my heart was sayin', *Careful, now*. I couldn't put my finger on the feeling, but something wasn't right. Was it that I still didn't trust him?

Twenty-Nine

Raney sat staring at the mountains. I eased next to her. "Been a long day, ain't it?" I slipped my fingers through hers.

"In all my years, I can't say that we've had more trouble dumped into a day. It's one thing after the next. Like a smoldering fire. Put out one coal and another takes hold." She rocked back in the chair.

"But we come through." I kissed her head.

"There was room in the barn for Thomas. Cleda Mae made him a right comfortable bed in the loft. Her and Clive took Aughtie with them to the tack house."

"Sissy," I corrected. "Thomas said her name is Sissy."

Raney eyed me. "What do we call her?"

"I guess Aughtie until Thomas decides to correct us. He said earlier he reckoned she had a new name." I tinkered with the sleeve of Raney's dress.

I could tell she was spent. And it didn't take a lot of brains to figure out what was comin'. "Right good supper you and Cleda Mae fixed up." I tried to lighten the mood.

"It ain't necessary for you to walk on eggs, Joshua. You know we got some talkin' to do."

I nodded in hopes she'd let it wait till morning.

"Let me start this awkward conversation. We've all had the rug yanked from under us today. Thomas, a man we both hated, looks to be our newest friend. Just having that happen was more than I could take in. But to find out . . ." Raney hesitated.

"I'd hoped in the back of my mind that my lies about Aughtie would turn to truths, and she'd be ours for real. That day Aughtie followed me home, I was in the barn with a loaded gun in my mouth, tryin' to get enough courage to pull the trigger."

Raney's mouth dropped open, and she took in a gasp of air. "You what?"

"I couldn't take the pain no more. I'd lost our girl by my own fault, and that caused me to lose you. There was nothing left. So I pushed that pistol in my mouth and tried with all my might to pull the trigger. Then this coin dropped off the door facing."

I went on to tell her about Anna's coin and how she'd given it to me.

Raney's eyes filled with tears, and her chin quivered.

"I can't say I'm all that surprised you'd think about takin' your life. There was times I heard the bottom of the river call my name. It almost took more courage than I could muster to not walk in the water and let it take me."

"Why didn't you tell me?" I asked.

"I can ask you the same. I couldn't bear to face you. And when that little girl followed you home, I thought my prayers was answered." She pushed her hair behind her ear. "On the outside, I was trying to do the right thing. Find Aughtie's momma. But on the inside, I was keepin' that youngin to myself."

Raney walked down the steps. She pointed to the stars popping out in the night sky. "Why didn't we trust each other enough to talk, Joshua?"

I brushed Raney's hair away from her face. "I don't know. I don't know. Maybe it's a growin' process."

My mind drifted back to the day we'd buried Anna. Raney had braided our daughter's hair and put tiny bows on the ends. Her dress was long enough to cover the cuts and bruises on her legs, and her arms, Raney covered them with a little sweater. We'd weaved daisies in her small fingers.

My eyes grew damp, and the hurt rose to the surface. The wails of loss that Raney let out that day won't never leave my head. The pastor covered Anna head to toe with a blanket, and we'd nailed that box shut. With every shovelful of dirt that'd hit her coffin, another part of my spirit split in two. My heart tore open, and all the love I'd ever felt dripped onto the ground. I lifted my fist toward the sky and cursed the day I'd heard the good Lord's name. I was lost from that moment on. A shell of a man, driven by guilt and held captive by the lies.

Raney slipped her arm through mine and brought me back to reality. When she laid her head against my arm, my numbness of loss leaked out, making room for the love I thought I'd lost. I pulled her close.

Raney straightened her skirt. She crossed her arms and gazed at the rising moon over the mountain. Dark outlines of clouds brushed the edges of the yellow ball that hung pasted at the edge of eternity. Crickets chirped out their calls. A hawk caught the last ray of sunshine and soared over the pass.

I hated to bother her pondering the night's beauty, but the words fell outa my mouth before I could stop them. "What will we do? Thomas is Aughtie's pa. We've lost again."

"We ain't lost, Joshua. We're found."

Mornin' come too soon. My nose woke me with the scent of freshly fried bacon and eggs. Aughtie was squealing and chasing the chickens from their nests, gathering what eggs them little pudgy fingers could find.

Raney had already put a spread out on the table. "Mornin', lazy."

I rubbed my eyes, straining to adjust to the morning sun. Thomas stood by the chicken coop, watching Aughtie, his hands buried deep in his pockets. I eyed him with a watchful eye, wanting to trust him but still not completely ready. He squatted down and held open his arms to her, and when she wrapped her arms around his neck, a sting of hurt hit my heart. The child knew Barton well, and she understood he loved her. The battle in my heart was trying to reconcile the old Barton to the new.

"Breakfast is ready. Y'all come on now." Cleda Mae hollered about the same time as Raney. The two chuckled. Cleda Mae placed a big plate of biscuits on the table. "Come on, boys. Eat up."

Thomas sat Aughtie on the bench next to Clive, then went to cuttin' her bacon and getting her plate ready. Cleda Mae pressed her hand over his.

"Thomas, she can feed herself. Give her a chance to show you. Them fingers work better than you think. And that mind . . . it might be slow on talkin' and such, but it's quick." Cleda Mae patted his hand.

He inched back, and Aughtie grabbed her fork. Thomas leaned down and quietly praised Aughtie.

It was something to see Thomas dote over Aughtie. There was so many questions. So much we . . . I needed to know. Thomas seemed to know about Aughtie, but at the same time, it was like he didn't know nothing about his girl.

I finally figured the best thing to do was ask. "Thomas, how'd you find out Aughtie was missing?"

He scraped his fork around the metal plate. "There wasn't much time to see June. Not and keep her safe. I'd slip and see her and Sissy a few times a month when I made rounds for Momma on the back of the mountain. When I made my last visit, the cabin was a shambles, and there was no sign of June or my girl. I saw signs that made me think there was a fight. Blood here and there. I suspected the worst, but I hoped for the best."

Guilt rushed through me like a cold winter wind. I should feel bad for Thomas, but something didn't sit right.

"June was a smart woman. I figured she could manage on her own, but Sissy bein' sick and all . . . I didn't know. I assumed the blood was hers," Thomas said as he brushed his hands through his hair.

I never dreamed I'd be sharing breakfast with a Barton again. Especially this one. I wondered if I could find forgiveness when I was still having trouble trusting Thomas. Maybe that's how forgiveness works—hard at first and growing easier with time.

Raney wiped her hands on her apron, and a smile stretched across her face. That smile was sweet to see. I knew what was to come would be dangerous and hard. But for now it was like we was all family, but not one of us was kin.

Clive stood and pressed his hat against his chest. "Let's give thanks for the food." When he finally reached amen, Aughtie clapped.

Thomas was quiet. He spent more of his breakfast watching Aughtie than putting food in his stomach.

"Thomas, you need your strength. Eat." Raney tapped her finger by his plate.

He nodded and buttered a biscuit.

"So how do we take down the Company Store?" Clive never was much on holdin' back his thoughts.

Cleda Mae elbowed his ribs.

He grunted. "Well, we need a different plan. Thomas changes things. I just like to have my ducks in a row."

"There's time," I said. "Thomas needs time to heal. We can't just rush in and expect Ima to be welcoming."

"Ain't never a good time to approach Momma." Thomas's voice was weak but determined. "Besides, I'd lay odds she already knows about my girl. Still, Joshua is right. I need a day or so to ponder how to work our way up the mountain without tippin' Momma off." He kissed Aughtie on the head, then took his biscuit and headed toward the door.

"Thomas!" Raney stood. "You need to . . ."

I stopped her midsentence and moved between the two. "Raney, let the man be. Give him the room he needs."

Aughtie gulped the last swig of milk in her cup, then huddled close. Her hand went to waving as her daddy opened the door. "Papa, no leave."

Thomas stopped on the porch, then wheeled around. I could see he had something on his mind.

"I oughta punch you for lyin' to me about my girl. But I'm grateful she's safe."

"Deckin' me ain't earnin' trust. Besides, I was doin' right by the child."

Thomas held out his arms. Aughtie raised a brow at Raney, as if asking for permission. I could tell it was hard for Raney to yield, but she stood Aughtie to the floor and gave her a nudge. The girl run to her daddy. Thomas grasped Aughtie around the waist and lifted her.

The hurt of loss ached in my bones, but the healing in doing the right thing made it bearable. Thomas carried Aughtie toward the barn, when I stopped him. "You hit me, you best sleep with one eye open. We clear?"

THIRTY

THE SUN COME up over the mountain, dragging along streaks of pink and orange. I stood on the porch looking over the field toward Anna's grave. It had been a few days since me and Raney had made what peace we could, and I was determined to keep it that way.

My eyes eased across the view to the barn. Thomas was stooped on one knee, showin' Aughtie something in a bucket. I figured he was helping her get feed ready for the chickens. I waved my cup toward Thomas to say hello.

"It kinda irks me that Aughtie took up with Thomas like she did," I said to Raney as she stepped onto the porch with me.

Raney wrapped her arm around my waist. "I think we're both a little jealous. We fell in love with that little girl. We knew better, but we did it anyway. Besides, Aughtie recognized him right off. He ain't new to her. A youngin will change you."

As usual, Raney was the voice of reason. I guess I was a mite jealous. I'd had the love of a little girl again for a short time.

"Reckon how long he'll stay in the barn?" Raney bumped my arm.

I kissed her forehead and took the new coffee she handed me. "Ain't sure. It ain't what I anticipated, but I think it's best to leave him be. He's sorting things out. I'm doing my best to take all this in. I've hated Thomas so long that I have a hard time dealing with this turnaround." I sipped the hot brew.

He'd been there several days, and though we didn't ask, he took on some chores to help out. He was up early, then later in the day, he'd walk and play with Aughtie.

I took in a deep breath and smelled the mornin' mixed with coffee. "You notice he's calling her Aughtie?"

"I noticed."

"Wonder why," I said.

"I don't know, Josh. But we said we'd follow his lead. And I reckon it don't matter. Maybe he's just being respectful of us not knowing her name. With Aughtie's understandin', it's probably easier to leave things like they are over messing with her."

I could tell Raney wanted to change the subject. "I need to talk to Thomas. Clive and me has been figuring a way to catch up to Angus."

Raney rested her hand on her hip. I could tell I was gonna get a talkin' to. "Joshua, you can't rush this. You said yourself, Thomas needs time. This is his family he's dealing with. Despite how warped it is, he's got to come to terms with how to deal with them."

Mater come out from under the porch howling. Raney slapped her leg and hollered at him. He tore down the lane, barking like he'd found some real catch.

"Speak of the devil. He may have just walked into our hands. Take on down to the barn and tell Thomas that Angus is coming up the lane. Tell him to get Aughtie in the barn and to stay there."

Raney shot off the porch like she was hit with lightning, and I stepped down and walked toward the devil on his horse.

Angus raised his hand and then tipped his hat. I watched as that hand come to rest on his leg. A whistle come from behind me. It was Clive.

"Wait up!" he hollered. I noticed he was toting his gun on his hip.

I returned the wave but waited until Clive caught up before walking further. "Well, lookee what the cat drug in," I said to Angus.

Angus brought his horse to a halt at my side.

"What brings you back?" I asked.

Angus threw his leg over his horse and slid out of the saddle. "Well, we got word you saved a couple of our men from that mine fire. Figured we owed you a passel of thanks." He took hold of my shoulder and patted. I wasn't sure whether to shake his hand or not.

"We was just passing by. Heard the explosion. We knew there was probably men in the hole."

"It was mighty brave of you to risk your own life to save someone else." Angus walked around his horse.

"Can't say we did much. Both of them died. They were my friends. I guess I thought you would have known that." I tried to keep a calm voice. I wanted to slap him seven ways from Sunday, but that wouldn't bear any fruit.

Angus dug the toe of his boot into the dirt. He didn't respond to my remark. "Uh. Momma is worried."

"Ima worried?" I chuckled.

"I'm gonna assume you mean that in a nice way. But yeah, she's worried. We think Thomas was in that mine. We ain't seen him since."

I glanced at Clive. "As a matter of fact"—I wheeled around to Angus—"Manny told us Thomas was in the mine. He insisted I go back for him. I had a real notion to leave his sorry butt there to die . . ."

"But . . ." Angus reached around his horse's neck and patted him.

"But my conscience got the best of me. I went back in. Found him choking on smoke. I pulled him out and left him beside the mine."

The barn door flew open, and Thomas come out like a bull right out of the corral. He walked straight to Angus, reared back, and plastered his fist in his brother's face. Angus grunted and hit the ground.

"You lookin' for me?" Thomas planted his boot on Angus's chest.

"You got something to hide, Thomas? Why else would you attack a man on a mission to say thank you?"

"I got nothin' to hide, but you . . . you have something to do with killing my wife?" Thomas slid his boot closer to Angus's throat. The pressure turned Angus's face a bluish color.

Angus grabbed Thomas's foot and twisted, taking Thomas to his knees. "What is wrong with you?" he squalled. "*Your* wife?"

"Why are you here, Angus? You got gall coming here," Thomas growled.

It only took a second before the brothers were throwing punches and rolling in the dirt. I couldn't make myself step in. It was like a perfect dream. Like how the good Lord turned them armies against theirselves to help King Jehosaphat.

Clive nudged me, and I begrudgingly helped separate the brothers. "Hey, not here. You wanna fight, take it somewhere else. Not here in front of the women and Aughtie."

"What are you doin' here, Angus?" Thomas yanked away from Clive and straightened his shirt.

"I could ask the same thing. Momma wouldn't take to you staying at the home of someone she calls an enemy."

"Oh, now I'm an enemy. No sweet thank-yous from Ima for saving her son," I said as I leaned against a tree to watch this brotherly love play out.

Thomas lunged at his brother again, and I snagged him by the arm. "I said not here."

"Where's the girl, Thomas? I wanna see that youngin you've been hidin'." Angus took several steps toward Thomas. He was cocked and ready to swing another punch.

"What do you know about a youngin?" Thomas spit at his brother's shoes.

"Momma might wanna meet her granddaughter," Angus shouted.

Raney stepped between the men. She held her arms out, pressing her fingers into their chests.

"I'm sayin' this one time, and then if I have to say it again, Cleda Mae is standing there with a rifle."

Cleda Mae pulled the rifle to her shoulder. "Stop this. Angus, get on your horse and get off our land."

Angus stared down at Raney. He huffed a long sigh. "You let your woman fight your battles, Josh?"

"Naw, she can hold her own. She fights her own battles." I crossed my arms, knowing full well Raney had things under control.

The rifle clicked as Cleda Mae cocked it. Thomas turned and headed back to the barn.

"Don't come back! You sorry . . ."

"Thomas, that's enough," Raney shouted. She wheeled around to Angus and pointed. "I'm waiting for you to crawl on that horse."

I figured it was time to step up beside Raney. She'd done all she could do. I pulled Angus's horse around, slapped the reins in his hand, and then pointed toward the lane. "That's the way back to the mines."

Angus mounted his horse. He glared at me and Clive and never said a word.

"I'm sure being the wonderful momma that Ima is, she'll be glad to know her son is alive. That explosion might have jerked some sense into him." I couldn't help but get in one last jab.

We watched till Angus was outa sight before I opened my mouth again. "Angus showing up here sayin' Ima's worried." I turned toward the barn. "The Bartons are watching. We need to talk to Thomas. I'm havin' to learn to trust Thomas. This ain't givin' me much reason to learn."

A sick feeling settled in the pit of my stomach. The kind that meant something bad was crawling round the corner but you couldn't quite see it well enough to plug it between the eyes.

Clive trailed behind me toward the barn. "You reckon Thomas is worried Angus knows Aughtie is his girl? Suppose Ima wants Thomas dead too?"

I stopped dead in my tracks. "Clive, go to the cabin and load all the guns. Stash some bullets around. While you're at it, get the women to the cabin. Raney can tag a deer in one shot, so she can defend herself. Seems like Cleda Mae can handle a rifle too. Just make sure they can get their hands on rifles if they need them."

Clive swallowed hard.

"When you finish, come to the barn."

It wasn't long before I saw Clive herdin' the women to the cabin. He toted Aughtie on his hip, and all the while she squealed and laughed. There was something to be said for that youngin. It was like her joy was the good Lord's way of protecting her from the things that was scary. Strange as it was, her laughter calmed me as I made my way to the barn.

Thomas met me at the door. "I knew it wouldn't be long before Momma would start lookin' for me. She would want to know what's going on. I reckon I owe you again."

"This ain't a matter of owing anybody. After that fight, it'll be a matter of stayin' alive. It starts with your trips to the mountain every day. I thought you was making rounds."

"I am making rounds on the back side of the mountain." Thomas wiped the blood from his mouth.

"Then why is Angus looking for you? Why did he say he'd *heard* we saved two miners yet had no idea they were dead? And then to say they hadn't seen you. How could that be if you've been going to the mines every day?" My trust waned.

"Joshua, I saw Angus yesterday. He smarted off to me, and I let it go. His showing up here was to rile me and trip you up. He's prodding to find out what you know about June. Momma and her clan haven't fit all the pieces together. Some of the women in the mining camps said you was lookin' for June. Between that and you comin' to the store, Momma's on edge. She questioned me about June. I told her June was in Cumberland last I heard. It surely don't surprise you that Momma would be plottin', now would it?"

"You saw Angus yesterday?" I asked.

"Yes. You can't fall into his trap. I'm tellin' you the truth. They're trying to figure out why someone is suddenly looking for June. And why I've been spending so much time on the back side of the mountain. Momma knows something is up. It don't take long for her to sniff out the scent once she gets wind. I reckon she's finally got wind." Thomas slapped his hat against his side. "I ain't lyin'!"

"Ima won't stop until she knows how much June has told about her ways. Not to mention Aughtie," I said. "Ima don't want her secrets known, much less told. She'll do what it takes to protect herself."

"If Momma thinks June has told me about her books, her greed will take hold. She won't stop till she knows I'm dead. Family don't mean nothing." Thomas commenced to pace. "She's got to protect what she has. For Momma, it's all about the power. And if she thinks I've figured out it was her that set June up to die, she won't quit till she's sure I ain't around to cause her no problems." He shook his head.

"Wait up here. You suspect Ima planned to kill June?" I asked.

"From the day she learned I loved June. I told you . . . Momma saw June as a threat. An intelligent woman who could pull the rug out from under her feet and take her fortune. June knew Momma's secrets. How she stole from the miners and how she makes problems disappear. She's only concerned about her wealth and her own hide. Don't you see?" Thomas pleaded.

I guess I wasn't surprised at how low Ima would stoop, but hearing it from her boy made me more determined to stop her. The more I thought about the injustices done to Elray's and Manny's families—to all the miners—the madder it made me. It didn't take much to remember how Ima came after me when I quit showin' up at the mines. A body can't walk away from the mines. Ima owns them. There's no choice. A body either works the mines or dies—one way or the other.

Thomas pushed a bale of hay off the stack and sat on it. "Ima may be my momma, but I'm tired of bein' her thug. I know she's behind June's death, and now she knows about Aughtie. What she don't know is how much or how little Aughtie knows."

Them was the words that scared me about Thomas. We'd mended a hole in our relationship, but there was still a lot of wire layin' on the ground. When he uttered them words "Ima is my momma," a chill crawled up my spine.

"Thomas, I see you're a victim too, but it's hard for a man to turn his back on his momma. I want to trust you. I do. But the fact Ima is your momma gives me just enough fear to keep me on edge." I walked toward the horse's stall and leaned on the door. "Help me trust you."

Thomas pointed to the house. Aughtie sat on Cleda Mae's lap, rocking. "That, Joshua. That is all the trust I can give you."

"Alright then. It is what it is. Ain't no way to know just what Angus knows. He's got a good poker face." I pushed my hat to the back of my head and swiped the sweat from my forehead. These mountains could hold the heat and draw a sweat right easy.

"We need a plan though. There's one thing for certain—we can't wait no longer. Angus is conniving, and sad to say, Momma is worse." Thomas kicked his heels against the bale.

A pinch of mistrust hung in my gut. It was easy for the devil to slip in and tell me more lies in hopes I'd believe them. This newfound trust would take a mighty amount of effort.

Thomas rested his arms on his legs. I could see he was torn.

"You still don't trust me, do you?" Thomas asked.

"I'm tryin', Thomas. You gotta have grace here."

"Reckon trust has to be earned." Thomas climbed off the hay. "I gotta be honest. I figured you'd point Angus to the barn. Can we agree we don't trust each other, then work from there? We got a common cause. Aughtie and the miners."

We eyed each other for a few seconds. "Beginnin' ain't never easy. But like I said before, new start."

Thomas walked to his horse and slipped his foot in the stirrup. "I reckon it's time I made a visit to Momma."

He was right, but that visit might just bring Ima's whole army down on our heads.

Thirty-One

By nightfall we'd done our best to secure the homestead. Despite hiding guns and bullets around the place, even after nailing the shutters on the house closed, I still had this burnin' in my gut. Ima was slick. For all I knew, Thomas was pulling the wool over my eyes. This battle raged inside me. *A body has to trust. But who was trustworthy?*

The women made supper, and we gathered around the outside table. Aughtie crawled on my lap and wrapped her arms around my neck. She pressed them sweet round cheeks against mine, then tenderly rubbed my hair with her chunky fingers. "Don't woo-ree. They's hope."

I nearly choked on my food. Had she heard us say that, or did she hear Anna like I did? I patted Aughtie's back and then pushed her locks away from her face. "There is hope. That's right."

Raney smiled as she picked apart a bite of chicken for Aughtie. "From the mouths of babes."

I sat Aughtie on the bench between me and Thomas. It was a child that separated us and a child that seemed to bring us together.

We was quiet sitting around the table for a spell. Eating tends to shut folks up, but when Aughtie stood on the bench and begin her singin', it was like the good Lord Hisself was pointing His finger.

"Jes-sus luvs me. I know . . . Bi-ble tells me so."

We were all took back, and we sat staring at Aughtie. We wasn't sure what to do—sing with her or praise her for her quickly expanding words. Cleda Mae went to clapping. "Very good, Aughtie. You remembered the words."

Then Aughtie took me and Thomas by the hand and raised them. "My famwee luv me too."

We were all quiet. Sometimes when you ain't right sure what to say, nothing is the best. The child called us both her family. If anything, it was a heart's nudge that I needed to work harder at trust.

"Aughtie knows where Anduss hides."

Everyone at the table looked up—none of us daring to interrupt her thought. "Roun' by da hole in the rock."

"Hole in the rock?" Clive twisted toward me. "Reckon she means Harmon's Cave?"

"There's holes all in these mountains thanks to the mining," I said.

Thomas handed Aughtie a carrot. "In a hole in the rock? Can my li'l Sissy remember anything else about that hole?"

She danced around, takin' a bite of her carrot and slobberin' out orange bits. "Watts of wa-der." Aughtie buried her fingers into her mashed potatoes.

Raney come off her seat and wrapped her arms around Aughtie, wiping her fingers on her apron. She sat her down and helped her wrap her fingers around a fork.

"You remember how Miss Cleda Mae showed you how to eat your food?"

Aughtie nodded.

"Harmon's Cave ain't far from here. River runs through it," I said.

"I told you he'd be watchin'." Thomas come up from the table. "That means Aughtie ain't safe here."

"Thomas might have a point," Clive said. "The women could go down to the Mabreys' farm. They got that cabin up in the woods. Might be a good place to hide."

Clive and Thomas went to making plans, and the more I thought about it, the more their watching irked me. I slammed my hands on the table. "We ain't runnin'. We ain't hidin'. We face this mess head-on. We clear?" There's a time when a man feels right backing down, and I'd backed down from the Bartons long enough. They'd done taken this child once, hurt Raney. Enough was enough. Hiding wasn't an option.

Raney come to her feet and wiped Aughtie's mouth. "Come on, sweet pea. Let's you, me, and Cleda Mae go crawdad huntin' down at the creek." The glare on her face let us all know we was outa line with our talk in front of Aughtie.

Clive took Cleda Mae by the sleeve.

She yanked her arm away, giving him the eye too. "Ain't none of you thinking about this youngin and what she hears. Not one of you!"

"I'm telling you both right now. We ain't tuckin' tail and runnin'. This won't never end unless we go at it head-on." I stood and rested my foot on the bench.

The rest of the evenin' we men paced the field, trying to figure what to do. Better yet . . . what not to do.

I sat up on the edge of the bed. The cabin was dark. Not even the moon shined through the shutters. Something felt wrong. I lifted my arms above my head and yawned. I took in a deep breath, and a familiar smell filled my lungs. Wood burning.

It took a minute for things to register, but when it did, I jumped outa the bed and rushed onto the porch. *Fire.* The pitch-black night was lit up with the orange glow of a fire.

"Raney, get up. Fire! The barn's on fire!"

I yanked my trousers on, shoved my feet into my boots, and then took off across the field. Clive met me halfway.

"Fire! The barn's on fire!" Clive shouted.

"Where's Cleda Mae and Aughtie?" Raney screamed.

Clive pointed toward a row of trees by the back field. Raney took across the field, Mater on her heels, howling and barking.

"Thomas. Did you see Thomas?" I shouted.

Clive shrugged, and we both made a beeline for the barn. Just as we got to the door, it flung open. Thomas landed on the ground at our feet, coughing and wheezing.

"The horses," I shouted. And me and Clive rushed into the barn to free the animals before the fire and smoke got to them.

Smoke bellowed from the barn in huge tornadoes. The dried rye stored in the barn went up fast and hot. There was little we could do but stand and watch the barn collapse to the ground. Clive managed to pull the plow out, and we were able to toss a few tools outside before the flames and smoke were too much.

"Was there any flames on the tack shed?" I walked a fast pace around the barn to see the tack shed. "Looks like it's alright so far."

Raney walked Cleda Mae and Aughtie toward the house. Aughtie's screams brought Thomas to his feet in a hurry. He rushed to Cleda Mae and took Aughtie. The women made their way to the cabin while me and Clive stood starin' at the barn. It wouldn't be long until the other homesteaders would get wind of the smoke, and they'd follow the lit-up night sky. Even if we doused the fire, the flames had done eat their bellies full of rye. The barn was gone.

"Angus's doing?" Clive asked.

"Got no proof, but that would be my guess, since he knows Thomas is stayin' in the barn." I slipped my arms through my suspenders and pulled them onto my shoulders.

The heat from the fire stretched halfway across the lower field. All we could do was keep moving further away from the fire. We could only hope the wind wouldn't kick up and spread the flames into the fields.

"At least everyone is safe. A barn can be rebuilt," I said.

"Ain't you angry?" Clive bent to tie his boots.

"Of course I'm angry, but at this point it don't do no good. Everyone is safe. Thomas is alive. I guess we're lucky the house didn't catch on fire too." It was strange. My first reaction would usually be anger. Blame someone else. Not this time. This time I was just grateful. Maybe my heart was changing. I was doing my best to be a better man. After that day I'd asked the good Lord to help me, I could feel His making a way into my heart to change me, but even He knew it was a hard row to hoe.

I could hear horses heading up the lane. I knew it wouldn't be long before the smoke roused others, and they'd be headed our way. Reckon the good Lord knew what He was talkin' about when He said, *Thou shalt love thy neighbor as thyself.*

As I thought, the homesteaders came and helped us turn under the burnin' wood so it would finish burning without the worry it would spread further. Melford Starnes and his sons had already started talkin' up gathering the men around to raise a new barn when the ground and ash cooled. The barn was gone, along with the rye stored up for barter.

As the farmers loaded up for their own homesteads, I tipped my hat as a show of gratitude.

Melford pulled his horse to a halt. "We'll be back, Joshua. Let them coals cool down. You need anything, holler."

"Well"—I turned to Clive and brushed ash out of my hair—"I suppose that's that."

We stood looking over the knee-high field of late rye. At least that was safe and I wouldn't be starting from scratch. I put my hand on Clive's shoulder and twisted him toward the house. "You gonna come get you a cup of coffee? Sun'll be up in an hour. No need trying to go back to bed." I hadn't much more than gotten the words out before that blasted rooster let out a crow. "Couldn't have asked for better timing from that rooster. Come on to the house."

Thomas sat on the ground a few feet away, arms wrapped around his knees.

"You alright?" I asked.

"Yes, I . . . I . . . just feel like this is my fault."

"Truth is, Thomas, I think it has to do with you too. You want me to lose my temper now or let it slide?" I nudged his boot with my shoe. "Come on to the house when you get your wits back."

And that was the truth. My barn burning had everything to do with Thomas, but right now I heard a soft whisper in my heart. *There's hope. I'm tryin' to do better, Lord.*

We stepped into the cabin, and Raney had already made a fresh pot of coffee. Cleda Mae had taken Aughtie from Thomas and calmed her down. The two were mashin' lard into flour for biscuits. Raney handed me and Clive a cup of coffee and then sent us to the porch. I reckon she knew we'd be rehashing the night, and Aughtie didn't need to relive it too.

Clive leaned against the porch rail. You could see the wheels spinnin' in his head. He slapped his leg and spoke up. "I got it."

"Got what?" I asked.

"I know how to get to Ima." Clive swiped his soot-covered face over his sleeve.

I prodded him into a rocker on the porch. "Make some sense."

"Mayor. You remember I was workin' on runnin' for mayor? You remember when we made that trip to the store and Ima offered to pay for my campaign?" The man was as excited as a youngin with a piece of hard candy.

"I do. What about it?" I tipped my cup and took a sip of coffee.

"That's our way in. Ima wants me on her side. What if I let her think I've changed my mind?"

"You told her no. I ain't sure she'll buy into you wanting her help."

"I didn't say no. I told her I needed to ponder." Clive stood and shoved his hands into his pockets. "I can convince Ima I've had a change of heart. I can go up on the mountain and tell her I could use some guidance from a wise businesswoman."

Fear flew through me, and I slung my head from side to side. "No. No. No."

"Why not!" Clive stopped dead in front of me. "Why not?"

I hated to snap at Clive, but he needed the truth. "Well, Clive, it's a matter of backbone."

"Backbone?" Clive come closer. His jaw twitched, and I could see his hackles standin'.

"Yes! You can't start out all keen and then back down. Your nature is to talk things out. It ain't to be firm."

"You're wrong. I can stand my ground. I can do this." Clive huffed. "I'm coming against you right this minute."

"Do what?"

I nearly jumped outa my skin when Thomas stepped onto the porch.

"What's all the hollering about? The whole mountain could hear the ruckus," Thomas said.

Clive glared at me, and I just shook my head. I leaned over the rail and spit. "Aw, law. Clive here has the bright idea he can go back to Ima and ask for her help in runnin' for mayor."

Thomas stretched. "I remember the day you come to the store."

"Joshua says I ain't got no backbone. Leastways not enough to pull this off."

"Momma always wanted a mayor or sheriff on her side. She might hold a little grudge, but if you show promise . . ."

"That's where you come in." Clive's voice climbed a couple of notches. "I figure you can help me convince her. Show me what to say to let her know I've rethought things. I could use a wise businesswoman on my side."

"I don't think Momma will listen to me." Thomas pointed to the barn. "That shows she's done waiting for me to shape up." He scratched his foot across the porch, pulled a flint from his pocket, and lit the lantern. I could see him runnin' Clive's idea through his mind.

"You ain't seriously considerin' this foolish plan, are you?" I said.

"Actually, it might just work," Thomas said. "Momma likes to feel like she has the upper hand. If she thought Clive was remorseful and saw the error of his ways, she'd be willing to dig her nails in. Callin' her a wise businesswoman might just be the right words."

"You hear that, Joshua? Thomas thinks I can do it." Clive jutted out his chest.

I wasn't the brightest candle in the church, but I was smart enough to know that Clive had two things going against him—his kind heart and his age. That kind heart made him wanna talk a body out of making a mistake, and his young inexperience wouldn't see Ima coming with the last nail for his coffin. She'd be able to manipulate him, twist his words, tie him into something he'd regret. I couldn't bear him falling into Ima's grip. Not only was he a good man, he meant something to me and Raney.

"I heard. I don't agree. But I heard." I wasn't at a place where I could trust Thomas. That's when he come eye to eye with me.

"He's got a good idea," Thomas said.

"I won't risk Clive's life." I shook my head.

Thomas gritted his teeth so hard I could hear the grinding. "Joshua, you saying no because it's Clive, or because it depends on me helping?"

My pent-up frustration built, pushing against the changes I knew I needed to make. This man in my face had cost me so much, but Thomas was right. It was him helping that galled me.

"Josh! Trust me." Thomas took me by the shoulders. "New starts now, remember."

Over Thomas's shoulder, I saw Clive nodding, reminding me that everything I'd thought Thomas had done, he hadn't. Despite my best effort, my chin quivered. "You better not let nothing happen to Clive. You understand me? He's got a wife and hopes for the future. He ain't like me." I turned and rested my knee on the porch rail. "Ain't nothing better happen to him. And there's hundreds of men workin' the mines."

Thomas smiled. He started off the porch, then stopped. "You've saved my life twice. You've earned my trust. Let me earn yours."

"Sun will be up soon. Ain't nothin' we can do but rest a little." I nodded.

Thomas pulled up a rocker. He rested his feet on the railing and pulled his hat over his eyes.

There I was, facin' Clive. I knew what was coming. He'd start trying to convince me. "Clive, don't start."

"Ain't nothin' to start on. Thomas thinks it's a good idea."

"And since when did you start believin' everything Thomas told you? And besides, have you forgot about Rayburn? Findin' June's daddy?

"No, I ain't forgot Rayburn or Aughtie's momma, and I ain't putting all my trust in Thomas, but he treats me like a man. I'm not a child."

I reckon I deserved that. The youth in Clive made him impulsive and easy prey. Still, he was a man, and he ain't my youngin. It was best I started treating him that way.

He headed toward the tack shed.

"Clive! Wait up," I hollered.

His hands were in his pockets, and his shoulders slumped like a whipped pup. He stopped, but he didn't turn. He just waited.

"You're right. I shouldn't treat you like a youngin. You're a married man. A teacher. Got a wife and a good head on your shoulders. It's just me and Raney care about you. We done lost one we loved to the Bartons. I ain't rightly sure either of us could bear to lose another. And remember, there's Aughtie and findin' Rayburn. We owe that to the child."

Clive turned and straightened his shoulders. He waved and then trailed on down the path to the tack house.

I watched as he closed the door. The light that shined under the door went out. It was like swallowin' a mouthful of rocks, but I needed to trust Clive could do this.

I turned to go into the cabin and heard the eerie hoot of a whip-poor-will. A cool breeze blew, and the lantern flickered. The smell of smoke still hovered in the air. Off to the side of the house, by the woods, I could have sworn I saw the outline of a man. I rubbed my eyes, and the image disappeared.

THIRTY-TWO

THOMAS FILLED CLIVE in on Ima's reasoning behind wanting someone with power on her side. She'd do what was necessary if she thought it would bring her more money. More power. More everything.

"Those miners are working by twos from before dawn to dark. They're going to work and coming home by the light of a lantern," Thomas explained. "They earn pennies a day, and they're paid in scrip. Momma's got the doctor from Cumberland in her pocket too."

Thomas stared at the floor, pondering his next response. "Momma has a ledger where she totals the men's pay and subtracts their provisions. She never let me see it, but I've caught a glance over her shoulder. More times than not, the men don't make enough to break even. They'll end up in debt to the store until next pay."

"No offense, but the woman is heartless." It made me mad just to think of what them miners and their families was still living through. Me getting free hadn't made a bit of difference.

"Listen, I ain't proud of the things I did." Thomas brushed his fingers through his hair. "I was young and tryin' to make my place in the family. June changed me—and then when she carried that youngin . . . They were all I wanted, but like the miners, I couldn't break away." Thomas come face to face with me. "You have to believe that, Joshua."

I just needed to keep quiet, but the words slipped out. "I believe you. Nobody knows better than me how Ima gets her claws into you." That wasn't what I wanted to say, but it seemed my heart spoke up this time.

Thomas went back to quizzing Clive. "You gotta convince her you're on her side. Talk to her about maybe addin' a tax to the miners. See if that don't raise her hackles. She'll start bribing you to double the tax and split the extra with you."

Listenin' to Thomas fill Clive's innocent young mind with all Ima's greed was too much. *Lord, don't let this change Clive.* I wanted to argue with them, demand this was wrong, but I closed my eyes and whispered a prayer that the good Lord would take hold of me. And He did. I walked away.

The same breeze that fueled the fire last night blew the flames away from the upper field. We were lucky the late rye was safe. There wasn't anything much prettier than rye weaving in the breeze. It was like watching the long hair of a pretty lady whip back and forth in the wind. The rye would be ready for the final cut soon. Fall was working its way around. Between me, Clive, and Raney, we'd done sickled the early rye and plowed it under. We'd picked at the remains of the early crop till we got enough seed for the summer planting. We'd learned to live without the mines. Learned to till the land, then buy and sell to the townspeople.

I found a big rock by the grainfield and crawled onto it. The heat from the burnt barn still radiated from the ground. My stomach turned at the loss. The barn could be rebuilt, but the loss was still real, and I was tired of loss. I wondered if I could let Clive go through with this stupid plan. *Lord, was I wrong to back down? Is healin' from this pain I've suffered gonna require me losing someone else?* Clive had grown on me, and me and Raney cared about him like he was part of us. *I'm struggling, Good Father, but I'm tryin' to trust.*

A little hand slipped around my neck. "Who's that behind me?" I grabbed her fingers and pretended to chew on them.

Aughtie broke into a hearty laugh. It was somethin' to listen to that laugh. I never thought I'd hear the giggle of a child again. I pulled her onto my lap and give her a squeeze, and a chill crawled up my spine. The kinda chill that comes when you feel like someone's watching. The shadows along the tree line moved with the breeze, and I caught a glimpse of something. I shook my head and give Aughtie another hug. My imagination. Sometimes a man's imagination gets the best of him. I was just on edge.

"Mr. Josh. You sad."

I pulled her onto my lap and rocked her. "Well, ain't you just sweet as apple pie. Mr. Josh is fine. Ain't no need for you to worry your pretty head."

"Aughtie saw the man too."

"What? You saw a man." My stomach turned.

Aughtie crawled off my lap and went to pickin' at clover.

"When did you see a man?"

But her mind was fixed on that clover, and there wasn't no getting her attention. That was the thing with Aughtie. Bits and pieces of information would seep to the surface. A body never got a full story. It was frustratin' as whiz, but this youngin's simple mind could only do so much.

I took her by the arm and coaxed her to walk with me. "Let's go see Miss Raney. She'll want to see that clover you picked." Fear covered me like a heavy quilt. I'd seen a figure in the dark the night before and brushed it off as a shadow. But now I wondered if I really did get a glimpse of a man. Chills run down my arms, and I felt staring eyes on our backs. Aughtie was lollygaggin', so I scooped her up and put her on my shoulders. "Wanna ride?"

She squealed and grabbed hold of my ears. I picked up the pace till I got to the house.

"Look who's getting' a ride," I said as I bounced Aughtie on my shoulders.

Raney waved. Aughtie giggled as I spun her off headfirst.

"Get yourself in that house and plop on that bed. It's past your nap time." Raney brushed the girl's hair and pulled it into a long tail down her back. "Go on, now. Git."

Aughtie grinned right big and went into the cabin.

"You look like you saw a ghost." Raney rubbed her knuckles across my cheek. "What's wrong?"

I didn't want to scare Raney, but I needed to tell her. We'd agreed—no more lies.

"Remember when me, Clive, and Thomas talked after the fire?"

"I do." Raney come close.

"When I turned to come back inside, I . . . I . . . saw someone. I ain't sure who it was, but I seen something out by the tree line. I brushed it off as my imagination."

"You what?"

"I glanced over by the side of the cabin by those back trees, and I coulda swore I saw . . . a . . ."

"Joshua Morgan, spit it out. Saw what?"

"A man." I took in a deep breath and brushed my hair outa my face. "I rubbed my eyes, and he was gone. I just figured it was a shadow."

"Lordy mercy. You don't reckon Ima's got that hooded man watchin' us?" She wrung her hands in her apron.

"Now, don't go getting your hackles up." I took her by the arm and pulled her close.

"That don't explain why you're white as a ghost right now." Raney looked me square in the eye.

I rubbed my scrappy beard. "I thought I saw movement back in them trees again. But I didn't worry until . . . well . . . You know how Aughtie just blurts out things but never can give you the whole story?"

She nodded.

"Aughtie saw the man too."

Raney took in enough air to choke a toad. "That means they're coming after her. That masked man and his thugs are coming after her. They're watchin' her. Watchin' us. When would she have seen a man?"

"The youngin don't understand lyin'. She's seen him. She was with Clive and Cleda Mae. Not here. Maybe she saw him through the tack shed window. I don't know when, but she saw him."

"She ain't safe, Joshua. That hooded man is watching our girl."

The words hadn't much more than slipped from Raney's lips before she slapped her hand over her mouth. Our girl—we couldn't help but think of Aughtie as our girl.

I took her by the shoulders and gently squeezed her arms. "I know what you mean. She'll always be ours in a special way."

Tears filled Raney's eyes. She buried her face in my chest and cried. "This ain't fair, Joshua."

There was nothing I could say to ease her hurt. It was my hurt too. "I need to get back to Clive and Thomas and put our plan into action. It's time. You listen good to me. Get Cleda Mae and Aughtie. Clive stashed bullets and a couple of guns around the cabin and about. You bolt that door once we're gone. Hear me?"

Raney reached around my neck and hugged me. "Time to stand our ground?"

"If that hooded man comes back and tries to take you or Aughtie or Cleda Mae, shoot him." I never imagined tellin' my wife to shoot a person, but that's where we were.

"It's time to go. We have to find Rayburn. Clive has to earn Ima's trust so we can find what June was holding over Ima's head. Then we bring Ima down." I gave her a kiss and sent her inside. "Raney. You don't go nowhere by yourself. If you go to the outhouse, you all go. Understand me?"

"Don't you worry about me. I can take care of myself."

"I'm countin' on that."

I headed back to the burnt barn. Thomas and Clive started gathering the wagon. It took me a minute to take in what was about to happen tomorrow. The last time I went up against Ima, I got my freedom, but it came with a price bigger than a rock with a gem. Truth is, I lost that battle when you consider the price.

There was a lot at stake here. Little Aughtie. Clive. Thomas. The miners and their families. A rush of sadness washed over me. I'd managed to free myself from Ima and the Company Store, but I'd turned my back on the men who'd stood by my side in the mines. The price I paid wasn't just losin' Anna. It was losing friends like Manny and Elray. We needed to get their families here and set them up a home. That wouldn't be near enough to make amends, but it would be a start. Breaking Ima's hold on them miners would be something too. Getting them men's wages paid in cash would allow them the freedom to leave the mountain when they chose. Find their worth. But more than that, it would assure Aughtie would be safe from Ima. But finding Rayburn was next.

My mind wandered to the simple things the miners missed because of Ima. Things like the feel of the sunlight on their face, a fresh loaf of bread, time with their families. They deserved to have these.

I looked up toward the mountain. Smoke still rose from the explosion days ago. I could see a line of men leading burros down one side of the pass. They were haulin' coal down to the wagons. The sun was dropping behind the bluff, and the echo of their work songs floated on the wind.

My mind slipped back to my time in the hole. The air so thick with the black dust that I could hardly breathe. I went to coughing. The memories was almost too much. Even though I was free of the mines, this battle with Ima and the Company Store was just beginning.

"Lordy mercy. A fight with Ima. What kind of manure have I sloshed through now?"

Thirty-Three

Night eased over the mountain, and the fresh scent of rain blew across the ridge. The leaves on them silver maples twisted bottom up—a sure sign rain was coming. But I wasn't worried. Summer rains on the bluff come and go faster than a jackrabbit runs. The clouds settled over the lane, and a thick white haze hovered low to the ground.

I noticed the light of a lantern down by June's grave, so I took my rifle and made my way toward the hazy yellow glow. Right around the bend I saw Thomas kneeling. His hands pressed against the dirt, balancing hisself.

"Thomas?" I spoke right soft so I didn't startle him.

He looked up and pressed his fingers against his lips to shush me. He pointed toward the pile of rocks that covered June's grave. I couldn't believe my eyes.

Aughtie was dancing around June's grave, singin' a soft melody that only she could understand. The youngin would dance a minute, then lay across the rocks and cry.

I reckon at that moment, a little girl broke through the rage and bitterness the years had harbored between me and Barton. Unlikely friends was what we were. Both of us broken, needing healin', and it took the innocence of a simple-minded child to start the process.

"When you found Aughtie, was she hurt?" Thomas asked. He picked up a stick tall enough to lean on as he walked.

"She was hungry. Thin. I got no way of knowin' how long she was by herself. But no, she didn't appear to be hurt."

"Was she scared?"

I thought back to the day I found her. "No. She come to me. She followed me home and took to Raney right off."

Thomas kept a close eye on Aughtie, making sure he didn't lose her in the evening mist. "When she was born, I wasn't there."

"I'm sure it couldn't be helped," I said.

"But the first time I laid eyes on her, I didn't see the oddities about her. I just saw a beautiful baby girl. It took June telling me she wasn't just right. She said people wouldn't accept a youngin like her. So we kept her hidden to protect her."

"That's the love of a daddy. Lookin' after their youngin's heart over what other folks see."

"I knew I had to keep them both hidden. If there was ever any hope of Momma allowing this child to be part of her family, it ended when she was born different than regular youngins. She has this sweet, innocent wisdom."

"I know. She's changed us all with it. That wisdom is convictin'. She was born with a pure heart," I said.

Thomas smiled. "Yeah, a pure heart." Thomas took her hand, and we walked to the house. "We'll find Rayburn, and June's killer too. I promise." Thomas scooped Aughtie up and hoisted her to his shoulders for a short jaunt.

Thomas trying to protect Aughtie eased my curiosity about why Rayburn wasn't part of Aughtie's life. But something still didn't sit just right. *I know, Lord. I need to trust You.*

Aughtie bounced up the steps to the porch and then crawled up on Raney's lap. The rain commenced falling—soft, easy. Me and Thomas just kept walking. There was no rushing. We just took in the summer rain. Remains of the ash from the barn bounced in the air as the rain covered it. I'd till that ash under the soil after harvest. Move the barn over by the north field, closer to the house. It would only happen with the help of the other homesteaders.

There was a time Thomas and I'd worked side by side in the mines. We'd laughed. Cussed. I remember when that stopped and the hate began. Now, through the pure heart of a child, we'd started to lay the past behind us. It was a hard change, sudden. And shaky, but it was a start.

Thomas said that trust was earned, and I reckon it was being earned with every step we took in the rain. It was like the drops of water was washin' us clean. Cutting through the pain and hurt that had followed us for years. There was a peace in that rain. "I reckon there's hope."

"I reckon so." Thomas nodded.

Hope. Just like Anna had said.

Cleda Mae and Clive had made a trip into town earlier in the day, and Cleda Mae borrowed a suit of clothes from the pastor for Clive. She stood on the porch, measuring and sewing the jacket to the perfect fit.

"Woo-wee, don't you look all gussied up," I joked.

"Ain't nothin' to joke over, Joshua Morgan. I ain't happy that you and Thomas is sending my husband into the devil's mouth." Cleda Mae jabbed a pin through the fabric. "Where you two been this evening? Besides not carryin' wood for the fire."

"We was down by—"

"Cleda Mae." Clive interrupted me. Clive laid a hand on his wife's shoulder. "This was my idea. And for what it's worth, Joshua fought us tooth and nail. This has to be done if we're to find Rayburn and the killer—if we're to help the miners. Now stop your bellyachin'." Clive twisted to find some comfort in the jacket.

Cleda Mae huffed and kept up her sewing.

"Clive is right, Miss Cleda Mae." Thomas shook the rainwater off his hat. "Joshua didn't want Clive to do this. I believe he called it . . . foolish."

"It ain't the best plan," I said. "But it does seem to be the only one right now. We know Ima has men watching the place. We can't take no chances. So you women stick together. Where one goes, you all go. There's strength in numbers."

Raney handed Aughtie to her daddy. He kissed her head as she wrapped her arms around his neck.

"Papa."

Raney made her way next to me and slipped her arm through mine.

"It ain't what I want either. But we have to do this to save Aughtie. Not to mention the miners and Thomas too," I added.

"Besides"—Clive scratched at the jacket collar—"Thomas has drilled me for two days. I can do this. I can convince Ima I'm on her side. Earn her trust."

The night breeze commenced to blow the rain onto the porch, so we made our way inside. Raney set out cups and filled them with coffee. "Ain't nothin' like a cup of hot coffee on a wet summer night. Cleda Mae had to tell the pastor why we needed a change of his clothes."

"What!" Thomas spit his coffee across the table. I went to laughing.

"Don't worry. She told him Clive was runnin' for mayor." Raney handed Thomas a rag to wipe up the coffee, then refilled his cup.

"I told the pastor we'd had some men prowling around. Pastor said he'd gather some men and the sheriff to keep watch while I was making political rounds." Clive continued pulling at the jacket until Cleda Mae smacked his hand.

I walked around the table and leaned against the fireplace. Raney's stew smelled right nice, and my stomach said it was time to eat. I pulled a bowl next to the pot and ladled in some soup.

Nudging Clive over, I sat down at the table and eyeballed him. "It's time we get things movin'. Clive will walk the women around the homestead and show them where he's stashed our guns. Raney, when the pastor gets here, you'll do the same for him. Cleda Mae, your job is Aughtie. If you women suspect there's someone here, go out the back and into the root cellar. We've stacked enough wood around it that it won't be seen. If it comes to it . . . shoot them." I hated barkin' orders to the women, but it was for their own safety. "Raney, I know you can drop a doe in one shot. So you make the bullets count. Hear me?"

She nodded yes.

"We have to have faith in one another. There's no time for whining. Only other thing I can say is, do some stout prayin'." I slipped my knife into the sheath on my boot.

It had been years since I'd done much praying. Most of that time, I spent blaming the good Lord for my own misgivings. I'd proved I was a lousy daddy and a terrible husband. It was time to pull myself up by the bootstraps and make things right.

The rain eased over the summit. We could see the flashes of lightning long past us. Each flash lit the side of the mountain, giving us quick glances at the mining villages. This mountain was filled with beauty that Mother Nature shed every fall and rebirthed every spring like a fresh drink of water. She was faithful every year. She was also selfish, and she never liked men diggin' around in her belly, stealing what belonged to her. For that, Mother Nature never let her mountain be forgiving. She'd taken lives. Gulped them up under the ruse of weather or landslides. Fires. It seemed for every bit of black gold the men took from her, Mother Nature took back.

Despite it all, there was nothing like these hills. Nothing like the fields that was hidden in their midst. When we was good to Mother Nature, she was good to us. Ima was never good to the life of the mountain. She stole and stole. And now it was time the taking stopped.

I walked back onto the porch and filled my lip with chaw. Raney kissed Aughtie and said good night. Cleda Mae and Clive walked her between them, lifting and swinging her every few steps while Thomas sat on the porch steps.

"Miss Raney, I'm much obliged at how you took my girl in. She's happy here. I can tell she feels safe," Thomas said.

Raney planted herself next to Thomas. "We shoulda told you about her when you come lookin'. We didn't know, Thomas."

"Aw, we could play this blamin' thing all night, and we'd only prove we was all wrong. It is what it is. What's important is you and Joshua, Miss Cleda Mae, and Clive have all taken good care of my daughter. I'm grateful." Thomas squeezed Raney's hand.

"She's nothin' but a bundle of love. Innocent. And that innocence makes her see things right clear. Things that we can't take in, Aughtie does."

Thomas laughed. "I wish you could have seen her down at her momma's grave. My heart broke when she kissed her hand and pressed it on them rocks that covered her momma."

Raney gave Thomas a little hug. "Truth is, Thomas, I hoped nobody would show up to claim Aughtie. I fell in love with her. But when she saw you, when she called you Papa, I knew she needed to be with you."

"I ain't sure how I'm gonna fair through this when we go up against

Momma." Thomas rested his arms on his knees. "She's onto me. She'd just as soon see me dead as to have me know her murderous secrets."

"Don't go thinkin' like that. This is gonna work out fine." Raney wrapped her shawl tight around her arms.

"I'm tryin' to ask you a favor." Thomas took Raney by the hand. "If I don't come through this, if Momma manages to kill me, I need to know you and Joshua will take Aughtie. Love her. Raise her."

Raney sat quiet for a spell before she spoke. "I ain't sure we're deserving of such a thing, but of course we will. We'll see Rayburn knows of her. Of course we'll take care of her. But you're comin' back. So no more bad thinking."

Thomas stood. He eyed the ground. "I'm sorry about Anna."

She took his hands and pulled them to her lips. "That's the thing about forgiveness. It's cleansing. We start new. We move ahead. You and Aughtie will be part of us. We're family."

Thomas nodded toward me. "Good night."

Raney waved as Thomas walked away.

Raney was almost right. We'd start new, but with what lay ahead, it didn't mean we'd be alright.

Thirty-Four

Thunder rumbled through the night, and them summer showers just kept coming. Lightning lit up the valley like it was daylight. I wasn't sure if I didn't sleep because of the storms or if it was worry. Despite how I tried to convince myself to sleep, I couldn't. It was hard to lie next to Raney knowing every move I made would keep her awake, and she didn't need to know my nerves was on edge.

I got up and meandered to the porch. The rain had slowed, but the flashes kept lighting the field. I focused on the tack house and wondered if Aughtie was sleeping through this. Cleda Mae and Clive was real accomodatin' to her, and she seemed to find comfort with them. They'd even made room for Thomas in the back of the shed after the fire. Everyone had a bed to rest on—if rest could be had.

Maybe it was that they were younger or that Clive and Cleda Mae spent so much time teaching Aughtie. Whatever the reason, she seemed happy with them.

Another flash of light lit the field, and I caught a glimpse of a horse and a rider facin' the tack shed. "I'll be!" I muttered. "I wasn't dreamin' the other night." I tore into the house and yanked my rifle off the wall.

I tossed another gun on the bed. Raney come outa the bed like she'd been bit by a snake. "What in heaven's name?"

"Get up. There's a man on a horse down by the tack shed. Watch my back."

I went out the door pulling my suspenders up and hollered when I got within earshot of the man. "Whatdaya want here? Who in the . . ." I hardly got the words out before he pulled that horse around and stormed toward me. I pulled my rifle to my shoulder and put my finger on the trigger. Pop! I let one round sail past him with no intentions of hitting him. "I won't miss the next time!" I shouted.

The man veered to my right, and just as I thought he was taking leave, he pulled that animal around again. This time I aimed at the ground in front of the horse, trying to force him to rear, but I couldn't compete with the rolls of thunder and lightning. The horse kept right on coming.

I rushed to load two more shots into the rifle, but before I could get them loaded, he darted past me and kicked me in the gut. My feet come off the ground, and I landed in the mud with a thud.

Another shot sounded. Raney stood on the porch, gun pulled. The man on the horse dropped over the horse's neck but took out across the field. Raney had tagged him enough to wound him.

The tack door flew open, and Thomas and Clive barreled into the night, headed toward me. Cleda Mae and Aughtie stood in the tack house doorway. It took a minute for me to get my breath back, but by the time the two made it to me, I'd crawled to my feet.

"What in tarnation?" Clive squalled.

Raney come running across the field screaming. "I think I hit him." She wiped mud off my face. "Are you alright?"

I coughed and grabbed my ribs. "I'm fine, Raney, and yeah, I think you tagged him."

"What was the shootin' all about?" Thomas squawked. "Who'd Raney hit?"

I held my hands up to shush him and Clive. "Let's go to the house. I'll tell you there. Bring Cleda Mae and Aughtie so they're safe with us." Once we were in the house, Raney lit a couple of lanterns.

"You alright?" Thomas asked.

"My heart jumped a few rocks, but I'm fine. I couldn't sleep. Between the storm and the worry about morning, I decided to walk out on the porch." I swiped my mouth on my shirtsleeve to get the mud off. "That lightning lit up the field, and I saw him."

"Who?" Clive stepped closer, and I held up my hand to keep him outa my face.

"I don't know who it was. But now I know I ain't seeing things. Same one as the other night. Just brushed it off as a shadow. Aughtie saw him too. I ain't sure where. But she did."

"Josh liked to have scared the tar outa me busting through the door and tossing a gun on the bed," Raney said as she handed me a wet rag to wipe my face.

"I tore down to the field. He was sittin' on his horse, staring at the tack shed. Horse was black. And I couldn't see his face. He had on a hood."

"The hooded man?" Raney gasped.

"Was he facin' the shed?" Thomas asked.

"Yep, and I hollered at him when I got within earshot. That's when he turned that horse and stormed me. I shot once to the side as a warning. But he kept coming. The second shot was in front of that horse. But with the thunder rollin', it didn't even faze the horse. I couldn't reload fast enough before he put his foot out and knocked me on my rear."

"He didn't aim to hurt you," Thomas said. "He coulda if he'd wanted to, but he didn't. He wants me. He, whoever *he* is, knows I'm here. I figure it's Angus."

Clive pulled a stool to the table to sit. His face was the color of the morning clouds. "Well, one thing's for sure. If Raney grazed him, we know what to look for at the Company Store."

Clive was right. If this was a thug of Ima's, then we'd be able to find him. "Where you reckon she hit him?"

I thought for a minute. "Ain't sure, but he leaned to the right side of that horse, so I'd guess she got him in the right arm or shoulder."

"That's good. It'll help. Boys, I don't know about you, but I believe we got ourselves a war. We oughta be loadin' up now and heading up the mountain by daybreak." Thomas eyed me. "You agree?"

I looked at Raney. She nodded her approval. "I reckon so."

"I'm ready," Clive chimed in.

"Then we leave at first light. The pastor and his men should be here then. This rain will make the pass a mess," I said.

"Don't worry about that. I know a better way in." Thomas rubbed his neck.

It hit me then and there that no matter how I looked at him, Thomas was still a Barton. It brought me some worry, but at the same time, it brought along some insight. Being a Barton meant he knew things the rest of us wasn't lucky enough to know. This might just be the ace we needed.

Raney doused me with a couple of buckets of water to wash the mud off. I was lucky to have an extra shirt and trousers.

She was quiet. Hardly uttered a word. I knew she was as worried about this mess as I was.

"Raney?" I took her in my arms. "I'm sorry about this. If I'd just have . . ."

She pressed her hand over my mouth. "You'd have what? Still been working in the mines? Still been miserable?"

I looked her straight in the eyes. "I'd still be a daddy and you'd still be a mother."

"We done talked this out. Ain't no need in laying blame no more, so stop. What matters is we make things right for Aughtie and the miners. If we manage that, then I believe there's hope."

Raney wiped her eyes. She finished loadin' up some biscuits and jelly in a cloth bag and filled a couple of water pouches. "How long you reckon you'll be gone?"

I scratched my head and then set my hat. "Well, it's gonna be a day's ride to the Company Store since the weather has muddied the paths. Though Thomas says he knows a different way. I don't know, Raney. A week or so. All depends."

She stood still, ponderin' my words. "If you ain't home in two weeks, I'll know you're . . ."

"Dead?"

"Yes." She tried to push back the tears.

"That's probably right. But then, don't put us in the ground too quick."

I tied my bag and then double-checked my gun and bullets. It took some time, but me and Raney walked the homestead, makin' sure guns was stashed so she could get to them from anywhere. We talked over the what-ifs and made our peace.

"The pastor will be here soon, and he's bringing the sheriff and a few men he can trust. Put one or two men in our back room. Bring Cleda Mae and Aughtie to the cabin. The pastor and the others can stay in the tack house." I kissed her forehead. "You should be safe."

"What about you?" Raney asked.

I patted my heart. "I got myself an angel watching over me. I'll take that penny with me for luck. We'll be fine. We have to believe that."

"I know. It's just . . . we've all been through so much. And Aughtie . . ."

I took her hand. "Life's gonna always put us through junk. It makes us strong."

"Well, we ain't as strong as we think we are," she mumbled.

"Yes we are. We got each other. We got friends. We got something to live for now. Something we didn't have before this mess. The mess has made us better."

"I reckon," she said.

There was a thumping on the porch. "There's Clive and Thomas." I brushed her hair away from her face. "We'll be fine."

Aughtie's bag swung from her wrist. The child had not let it outa sight since she'd found it by her momma. Cleda Mae's eyes were red from crying.

"Oh, honey." Raney started toward Cleda Mae, but she raised her hand to stop her. She motioned toward Aughtie.

The youngin was smiling despite herself.

Thomas took her in his arms and gave her a hug. "Now, you be a good girl for Miss Raney and Miss Cleda."

"Alright." Aughtie squeezed Thomas's cheeks between her palms. He stuck out his tongue, and she went to giggling.

"Papa needs to tell you something. Can you listen?"

Aughtie quieted and nodded.

"You know Papa loves you, right?" Her eyes never left his. "It means a lot to me to know you believe that."

Aughtie wrapped her arms around his neck.

"If something was to happen to Papa, you stay right here with Miss Raney and Mr. Josh."

"Otay."

Tears pooled in the corners of his eyes. It was like he already knew he wasn't coming back. Sometimes a man just knows things about his fate. The best we can hope for is that we're wrong about it.

The rain stopped, and a fresh breeze blew across the field. I hugged Raney. "Don't worry."

Clive crawled into the wagon, and I loaded up next to him. Thomas come alongside on his horse. I looked out over the field of rye, nearly ready to harvest. The rising sun colored the sky a golden color, like it was stealin' the color right off that rye. A hawk soared then caught a breeze and circled high above in search of its breakfast. It caught on the wind and soared up and over the trees. Home. This was home. We didn't have much, but we had these fields and these blue skies. We had the sun to warm us and the night to cool us. We had more than Ima would ever have. And I was . . . grateful.

"Thomas," I said.

"Yup." He kneed his horse into a walk.

"See that rye stand?"

"Yup."

"You got your work cut out for you when we get back."

From behind us, we heard a sweet voice callin'. "Tome back to Aughtie. Hear?"

Thirty-Five

I figured our trip to the mountain would serve to do two things.

One, it'd set Angus on edge. We wasn't for sure he was the hooded man, but he seemed to be the logical choice. His size and build pretty well matched, and he knew I had the girl and Thomas. For us to waltz right up to Momma Barton would show Angus we meant business and show Ima that Angus failed to rid her of Aughtie. He had to be running scared. A spooked man will slave to cover his tracks, and the consequences don't matter.

The second thing would be to make Ima Barton mad. She was that giant hornet's nest that hung in the top of the tree. And me and Clive was the youngins throwing rocks at it. The hornets needed to be stirred, and I reckon we were the ones to stir them to get truth outa the hive. We wouldn't be alone in bringing out the truth about June's death or how Ima messed over the miners. Thomas would take his stand against his own family. My hope was he wouldn't turn to chicken liver when we faced them.

Ima wouldn't think nothing of me and Clive traveling together, but she'd be wonderin' about our real reason for visiting the mountain. Just telling her she wasn't doing right by her miners wouldn't hold an ounce of water. I reached into my pocket and pulled out that nugget of emerald. I realized that gem was what had stood between me and Ima's wrath for five years. She wanted it, and she'd wait for it. After we confronted her, no amount of gems would prevent her wrath from comin' over me. She might not kill me today, but she'd not let go until I was dead. It was a chance I had to take. Aughtie needed to be able to live a life without fear. Thomas did too. And them miners needed to be treated fairly.

My life was nothing but a lie ever since I'd found that nugget. Every day I spent with little Aughtie proved that. It was easy to blame Thomas for the mess in my life, but I'd learned as long as we live, life will teach us from our choices. Last week I chose to start new with Thomas. It was hard, and my trust is still questionable, but I made the choice. Today, I chose to start new with me and with the good Lord.

Thomas led us up the south path then around the mountain toward the Gap. The trip, though slow, wasn't bad. The path wasn't as muddy as I expected. Thomas was right when he said not to worry about getting up the mountain. I don't recall knowin' this path was here. The south path wound its way around Barton Mountain and up the back side of the Cumberland Mountain. The peaks kissed the summer sunset as night fell, dripping streaks of honey yellow from the sky. A man could never beat the likes of a sunset over these mountains.

"Mighty purty trip across this ridge." Clive leaned back and propped his feet on the wagon.

"Sure is. I'd swear we're walkin' in heaven." I leaned my face toward the warmth of the evening sun. "A man can't get no higher than this mountain. Paradise is a finger's touch away." I lifted my hand and drew around a cloud with my finger. "We'll make camp here till mornin'." We sat staring at the coming sunset. Wasn't much any more beautiful.

Clive chortled, slapping his leg with his palm. "Reckon the Lord welcomes us up, but He don't open the door to heaven right away. Gotta keep Ima, the devil's demon, out."

Thomas turned and stared at Clive.

"Oh, I'm sorry, Thomas. I didn't . . ." Clive went to squirming.

I wondered if this would be when Thomas returned to his old ways.

"I've heard her called worse." He held up his hand, and we stopped the wagon. "I've been thinking as we made this journey." Thomas rested his arm on his saddle horn.

I could tell he was struggling to say what was on his mind.

"I'm standin' against my family. I was trying to figure out if there was anything that would make me change my mind. Was there any love, loyalty . . . anything to hold us together? Sad, but there ain't none. I never remember Momma being a real momma. I was never the chosen child 'cause I had a conscience. There was nothing I could do to please her. Even when I tried to do her biddin', it eat at me."

Clive patted Thomas's horse. "I'm sorry, Thomas."

"We was never loved. I didn't understand that until I met June."

I stood in the wagon to stretch my legs. "You gonna change your mind?"

Thomas let out a loud guffaw. "Not over my dead body. This ends so Aughtie can grow up happy."

"I reckon the Lord knows the best thing a body can do is keep his enemies close. This is your job, Clive. Get Ima close. Tempt her with a hope for unlimited power," I said.

Thomas reached over and slapped Clive's back. "Have you ever felt *this* important before?"

Clive tapped his foot and wiggled in his seat. His nerves was kicking up.

"What's eatin' at you?" I asked.

"Two things. I'm hoping I didn't seal my fate with Ima when I told her I was still pondering running for mayor."

Thomas pushed his hat back on his head. "Depends on what you offer her now. You got the possibility of a good amount of power in your hands. Momma will take that over money most any day. You'll have to sweet-talk her. Make her feel real special. Be confident." Thomas pulled his hat over his heart.

"What if she decides to kill me?"

"Body never knows what's on Momma's mind. But I ain't gonna let that happen." Thomas spit. "Trust me."

And there was them words again. The ones I struggled with—*Trust me.*

"Either way, I could end up dead." Clive pressed his hand against his cheek.

"We can all end up dead." I stepped off the wagon. "Look, Clive, we can stand our ground and do what's right or tuck tail. Choose the one you think best." I pulled my hat to shade my eyes from the setting sun. "I figure you chose to do the right thing. There's always a price to pay for doing right. The cost is worth it. Aughtie is worth it."

"She is worth it."

"Ima's used to payin' off every politician within a hundred miles. She wants them on her side. But once we get her in our pocket, then we can take a stand against her. Ima's gonna buck like a wild mule, but hopefully, we'll have her roped and tied." I waved away a lightning bug. "Course, you can stoop to the likes of her and let her trample the good out of everything in sight."

Clive rubbed his chin. "I've sat through two days of Thomas quizzing me. They ain't no more stooping to do."

Thomas climbed off his horse. "We can do this, then."

I pulled the reins snug and tied them to the brake. "Sun's goin' down. We need to set up camp before the light is gone."

I pulled out my mat from the buckboard while Clive unhooked the horses. Raney had packed fatback, biscuits, and a few beans, so we started a fire and warmed up the vittles. The fatback popped and crackled in the pan as it heated, giving off a smoked scent of fresh pork. My mouth watered. We split the food and sat down to eat.

I bowed my head and offered grace. "Well, Sir. Here we are. Ain't rightly sure what You got in store, but it must be worth something 'cause You've brought enemies to peace. I'm obliged. I ask You to bless these morsels of food. Sir, I ask for Your protection. You know the devil we face."

"Amen," Clive spouted as he sopped his bread in the beans.

After we ate, we bedded down. I lay there for an hour or so, then crawled to my knees and walked to the wagon. I pulled open the seat, got out my gun and six shells from the wooden box. Two went into the chamber and the other four into my pocket.

I pressed my hand through the handle and pushed the pump down, cocking it.

Clive raised up from his bed. "You expectin' a mountain lion?"

"Nope. Worse. Angus." I dropped another log onto the fire and pulled my blanket back.

"Get some rest. I'll take first watch," Thomas said as he rested against a tree and put his feet on a rock. "Let's hope tonight ain't the night for me to die."

Thirty-Six

Nary of us slept well. The ground ain't soft like a down mattress. I mighta dozed a bit. But Thomas was up long before the crack of dawn, stirring the fire and making coffee.

"You beat the chickens up this mornin'," I said.

"Yup. I've been doin' some thinking." Thomas poured me a hot cup of coffee. "I can't be with you when Clive visits Momma. She'll be on him like a fox on a rabbit."

"I know. We talked about this. Your job is to look for the injured man Raney shot. Startin' with your brother," I said.

"Momma is sly. She's biding her time. Waiting. She'll have told her men lookin' for me, and if any of them see me . . ."

"They won't, you hear me. They won't. You just have to keep your head low and your mouth shut. We know what we're up against with Ima."

Thomas sipped his coffee. "I just wanted to be sure you knew. Clive has to be convincing. And if I end up with Momma, I have to side with her for your safety. I have to convince her I hate you. You understand that, right? If she suspects . . ."

I gulped the last of my coffee. "I know. Clive knows. We have to hope Ima'll believe Clive. There's always hope. We're banking on that."

"Lord knows I've practiced Clive enough. I reckon he could convince a blind man he could see," Thomas said.

"Why's everybody talking around me? I'm layin' right here, hearing every word." Clive crawled outa the back of the wagon. He pulled out the pastor's set of clothes. "Once I get these fancy duds on, I'm ready to become a politician."

Thomas rolled his eyes. "Cocky don't suit you. What makes people like you, trust you, is that boyish innocence."

"He's right, Clive," I added.

"Just act like you know what you're doing. Momma can smell fake a mile away."

Clive gave him a thumbs-up and headed toward a trail of clear spring water running off the mountain. "Man has to be clean to be convincin'."

Thomas opened his mouth to say something else, and I shushed him. "Let him alone. He's getting up his nerve." I punched Thomas and motioned him toward the edge of the mountain path. A river of mountains jutted up from the ground like fingers on a hand, stretched across the horizon. The sun was just peering over the tops of the peaks. Clouds hung in the sky, still shadowed by night. Layers of purple, pink, and yellow painted the sky as the sun mixed their colors. We stared out over the pass.

"Ain't nothin' purtier, is there?" I asked.

Thomas nodded. "I figured we oughta look right good at the morning sun, seeing as this might be our last."

"Yep, it's a beautiful morning to die," I teased.

"I suppose I oughta thank you." Thomas rested his foot on a downed tree.

I stared straight at the mountains and how they rose and fell beneath the sunrise. "For what?"

"You saved my life and Aughtie's. Hope you forgive me for what's to come. I know the past colors the present, but I'm grateful." Thomas scraped his boot on the tree.

I wondered what he meant by *what is to come*. It felt like a warnin'.

"Regret is an ugly bedfellow. I don't like sleeping with it on my pillow. I . . . we . . . make an effort to get over the past. That's the best any man can do." I rubbed my arms to warm the chill of the morning.

The crickets' hymn died into the morning, and the birds picked up their songs. The sun pressed the night down, and its warmth crawled across the mountain like a warm quilt. "Like I said, ain't nothing purtier."

I walked to the edge of the mountain and looked down. The river rolled and twisted around the valley, cutting its way through rock and roaring so loud it echoed to the summit. "I wanna go fishin' when this is over."

Thomas had a right blank look on his face. "Fishin'?"

"Nothing like a good trout for supper."

A grin spread across Thomas's face.

I picked up a stone and tossed it over the ledge, then stared for a minute.

"Thomas, I . . ."

I turned to talk to him, and he was gone. "Thomas?" I walked back toward our camp. His horse was gone. Had he turned chicken? He was right. If Ima caught him anywhere near us, she'd never believe Clive. Thomas had left. He'd said his peace, and I reckon there was nothing left to do but get on with this.

"It's time, Clive. You ready?"

Clive straightened his shoulders, pulled up his trousers, and tightened the rope that held them. There was a look in his eyes I'd never seen, like his backbone got stronger. Clive's youthfulness seemed to take a turn, and I wasn't sure if that was good or bad. In front of me stood a confident man.

"I'm readier than I'll ever be."

And I believed him.

We cleaned up our camp and loaded the wagon. Clive mumbled to hisself as he worked. I figured he was practicin' his words for Ima.

The sun was bright in the sky, and morning was full. I lifted my eyes to the heavens and offered a few words. "Well, Sir, we're tryin' to make things right. I hope You'll oblige us with Your help."

Clive hooked up the horses, and we climbed into the wagon. He nodded and slapped the reins. "Hup, boys. Hup."

I leaned back on the buckboard bench and rested my feet on the front of the wagon. Thomas had a good start on us. All we could do was hope he could find the hooded man. The best I could hope was for Thomas to keep his word and that Clive could be convincing. We was heading to hunt down the devil.

We rolled into the mining camp after a spell. Miners was lined up by a table.

"Must be payday," I mumbled.

Clive stopped the wagon and stood up on the bench. "I'm Clive Simpson. Good to see you hardworkin' men. Most of you know me as the man who teaches your youngins to read and write. And you'd be right." He chuckled and glanced at me.

I eyed him, then nudged him to finish talking.

The miners watched as he stepped over the bench and into the wagon bed. Clive took off his hat and held it to his chest. "I've made a few stops in these parts talkin' up running for mayor. I'm here to solicit your votes for me as mayor on this mountain."

The miners were quiet. I wasn't sure if they were afraid to say anything or just didn't believe Clive, but their silence was awkward.

It took a minute, but the men gathered around the wagon as Clive spit out his promises for the miners if he became mayor. I could see his chest pooch out like a peacock. He was convincing me. One man slowly clapped. That was all Clive needed. He pranced around like a hell, fire, and damnation preacher, shoutin' promises and asking for votes. Them men cheered and waved. The teacher found his callin'.

He got so worked up that I didn't think he was gonna hush. Them miners gathered closer around him, asking question after question about how he'd get them a doctor that wouldn't cost them a week's wage. He went to makin' promises he could never keep. The crowd was getting rowdy.

"Clive," I said.

He kept on talking.

"Clive!"

"What?"

"These people take you at your word. You gotta remember they ain't used to seein' anyone from off the mountain. They're like sheep. Don't lead them to their death."

Clive hushed midsentence. He stared dead into my eyes, and the color left his face.

"We're here to help them, not get them killed."

He thanked the miners, then stepped on the bench and sat. "I got carried away?"

"A little." I elbowed him as I guided the horses through the crowd of men. "This can't move too fast. We can't rush in here and wreak havoc. Ima'll never believe us. A man needs the courage to push through. But he needs gumption to do it right. Today, you got gumption."

"I just wanna do this right."

"Yep, you did it right." I smiled and nodded.

The wagon bumped and bounced over dirt clods. We wasn't far from the Company Store. "You ready for another round?" I asked. "'Cause this mess depends on you from here on out. The store's just around the bend."

Clive's color was coming back to his face, and his nerves was showing. We rounded the bend, and I couldn't believe my eyes. I pulled the horses to a halt and punched Clive. "Now might be the time to start your convincing, and it wouldn't be wasted."

There in the middle of the wagon path stood Angus. I pulled next to him. "Angus." I tipped my hat.

"Well, well. What brings you two up on the mountain? You know you ain't welcome here."

"Last I saw you, that wasn't the case. You over your tiff with your brother? Or have you forgot your offer to help us if we needed it?" Me and Clive stepped off the wagon.

"Ain't you all fancied up?" Angus walked around Clive, eyein' his suit.

This was it. How would Clive manage? I felt the sweat beading on my brow. Angus stopped toe to toe with Clive. "Where's that youngin?"

I took in a deep breath and waited.

"Little Aughtie? On her way to Saltville. There's an orphanage there. Purt near broke my wife's heart. Not to mention Miss Raney. We'd got right attached to the girl." Clive pushed his hand deep into his pocket. "Orphanage seemed best for the youngin. I'd helped her as much as I could. You know her mind ain't just right. But she's a sweet youngin. Right pleasant. There's a doctor who might help her. But it's neighborly of you to ask about her."

Angus stared at Clive and then me. He drawed back and spit. "Like I said, what brings you up here?"

Clive glanced at me, then pointed. "Well, Joshua here convinced me I should follow up on that thought about runnin' for mayor."

Angus busted into a belly laugh. "Mayor?"

"Yes, sir. I've worked right hard the last few weeks gathering folks to support me down in the valley. I've come to take Ima up on her offer to help me. Make peace. She's a wise woman on business. I could use her guidance."

"Her guidance? You want Momma's guidance?"

Clive stepped forward. "I don't reckon I stuttered. Did you not understand me?"

It was all I could do to keep from laughing out loud. It looked like Clive had found the gumption he needed.

Angus took a step back, unsure how to respond.

"Now, I'd be much obliged to have a visit with Miss Ima. Where might I find her?"

"She's at the store. I can't promise how she'll take to you. Momma tends to hold a grudge."

"I believe she'll hear me out." Clive wheeled around and nudged me to the wagon. "Angus says Miss Ima is at the store. Let's pay her a visit. What do ya say?"

I noticed outa the corner of my eye that Angus mounted his horse and vanished. I didn't know what to say except "Alright." Clive had done good. He'd convinced Angus and me. I nodded and climbed into the wagon. When we was outa earshot, I finally let out that lungful of air I took in.

Clive leaned over the edge of the wagon and gagged. "Don't you say a word."

"Ain't nothing to say." I patted his back. "Ain't nothing to say."

Thirty-Seven

I never dreamed we'd see Angus right outa the pen, but Clive had stepped up. I was right proud, like a momma bear over her cub. We made the bend and headed on up the rugged wagon path to the store.

I gave Clive a few minutes before I nudged him to talk. "You alright?"

"I reckon I just proved myself." Clive stretched his arms over his head.

"I guess you did." I cracked a smile. "You went to preachin' a sermon to them miners. Must be them fancy pastor's duds. And woo-wee, you stood toe to toe with Angus. Made me right proud."

Clive grinned. "I suppose I did get wound up."

"Well, keep in mind, you got Ima next. She ain't the pushover Angus is."

Rufus snorted, slingin' his head from side to side. He was an old horse, but over the years he'd gleaned wisdom, so when he went to hesitating to pull the wagon, snorting, and carrying on, riling the other horses, that was enough for me to figure something was in the air, and it wasn't honeysuckle.

"What's with Rufus?" Clive asked.

I pushed my hat back and rubbed my forehead. "He's like a hound. Smells trouble in the air."

"Well, that's just fine. Whatta we do now?" Clive huffed.

"Move ahead like there ain't a thing wrong. You'll be fine, Clive. You did this once. You can do it again."

He took in a breath while I kept at Rufus to move. "Hup, boy. Let's go. Hup now." The horse flipped his ears, letting me know he wasn't happy, but he was obedient.

The store come into sight, and there on the porch stood Ima. "I reckon the horse has a good nose," I said.

It wasn't hard to know it was her. She wasn't much taller than my chest, and as wide as she was tall. She stood and leaned against her double barrel.

Ima raised her shotgun. "Stop right there. You ain't welcome here. Turn around and find your way back to your dinky little farm."

Clive stood and waved. "Now, Miss Ima, put your gun down. I come in peace."

She let out a cackle that echoed down the pathway. "You come in peace?" She could hardly talk for her laughing.

"Ima!" Clive shouted. "Put the blamed gun down and hear me out. Last I looked, you was still somewhat reasonable."

She quieted her laughing and hollered back. "Whatta you want?"

Clive climbed out of the wagon. He reached into his coat pocket and pulled out the papers that showed he was running for mayor. He was using his head now. He lifted his hands into the air and let that paper flap in the wind.

"I wanna offer you an apology." He slowly walked toward the store.

"An apology?" she growled.

"Yes, ma'am. I got to thinking about you saying I oughta run for mayor. Sometimes I'm a little slow and a lot stubborn. I had to think that through, so I went into Cumberland and threw my hat in. Got me a few folks willing to help."

"Well, well. Pretty boy thinks he can be mayor," Ima snapped.

Clive edged closer. I pulled the wagon right to his heels, hoping Ima wouldn't open fire.

"This boy *can* be mayor. Now, put the gun down, Ima. Hear me out. I come seekin' your wisdom as a good businesswoman."

That was all it took for Ima to ease her gun down. "Businesswoman?"

Clive waved the document in the air. "I don't know a person better qualified to guide me on the financial affairs of the mountain people."

"What are you getting at?"

"Miss Ima, you're good with money. Good with business. You know the affairs of this mountain. I figured if I was gonna do this, I should learn from the best. And the more I thought about what you said, the more I thought I would be a good mayor." Clive handed Ima the document from the courthouse in Cumberland.

"What makes you think you'd be a good mayor?" Ima squawked.

"I'd be good 'cause . . . well . . . you thought I'd be a good mayor. I'm willing to listen to those with wisdom. I'm a hard worker. I know who to partner with."

I wanted to jump outa the wagon and pat the boy on the back. He'd pulled an ace outa the stack.

A smile raised on Ima's mouth.

"Ima, you need a man down in Cumberland that can help you get more for your coal. Somebody who can take on them merchants. Show them the value in your coal."

"My coal is worth more. I got plans of chargin' more."

"Don't blame you at all. Seems fair to ask for more. Besides, I could use some good wisdom from someone who understands coal business. Down in Cumberland they got that coal yard. They're selling that black gold to folks to warm their houses. That's what I call a need, Ima. A real need."

Once again Clive surprised me.

"I'm here because I believe we'd make a good team." Clive looked Ima in the eye and didn't budge. After a minute, he turned and stepped off the porch.

"Let's go, Joshua. Looks like Miss Ima is passin' on a good opportunity."

My mouth dropped open. Clive had issued a challenge.

Ima waited until Clive pulled hisself into the wagon before she tapped the butt of that rifle on the porch. Her heels clicked against the planks as she come to the wagon.

"We can't talk out here. I'm willin' to hear you out."

A smile stretched across Clive's face as he climbed out of the wagon. "Wait here, Joshua." He extended his arm, and Ima took hold.

In all my days, I'd never seen Ima so taken. Clive had tossed the fishin' line and nabbed her hook, line, and sinker. She looked like a hungry dog, mouth open, tongue hanging, and slobber dripping. Clive had won her over.

"You willing to help a man get into the mayor's seat?" he asked.

Ima eyed him. Her mouth twisted to one side, and her brow wrinkled. I could see her lips pucker while she sized Clive up. Ima never *just* trusted anybody. She was pondering her prey.

The claws on her fingers walked across Clive's sleeve like a spider. She took hold and squeezed her nails tight into his arm. Clive patted her hand without a flinch. My heart jumped clean outa my chest. I waited for the gates of hell to open and swallow him.

Ima glared. Her eyes met his, but Clive never blinked. He held a tight hand, refusing to let go as she tried to pull away.

"Well?" he asked.

Ima twisted her hand. "I reckon I could teach you a few things about the coal business."

Clive loosened his grip, and she yanked away from his arm. She curled her finger, motionin' him to follow her inside.

I tied the reins on the brake and jumped outa the wagon.

Ima turned and pointed. "Not you. You stay right where you stand."

I tipped my hat and crawled back into the wagon.

Clive pushed open the door to the store. "Ima, that ain't no way to treat the man that's helped me get this far." He laughed a hard laugh, and chills climbed my back.

"Alright. But you keep your distance, Joshua. I don't trust you."

I wanted to laugh. Ima was telling the truth. As much as I wanted to jump down her throat, I kept my mouth shut. Clive had to do this on his own. He'd surprised me. It was like watchin' your youngin take their first steps. Your gut wants to reach out and balance 'em, but you know they gotta learn on their own. Clive had took his first steps. All I could do was hope he didn't trip and fall.

After a bit, I hopped outa the wagon and made my way to the porch. I leaned against the wall outside the store, arms crossed and mouth shut while Clive turned into a man I didn't know. I could hear him through the screen door, and the man could talk. I pushed my back against the wall and squatted to the porch to rest.

I couldn't count the times I'd had to shut him up. That paid off in his favor, 'cause Clive was like a dog with a bone. Every remark Ima made, Clive come back on her. Listening to the two of them banter was like listening to a couple of peacocks holler as they danced around the pen. Ima didn't like being wrong, and Clive wasn't gonna let her be right. Every negative Ima spit out about Clive being mayor, Clive replaced with a positive.

I stood and peered through the screen door.

"I reckon you got the chops to be a mayor." Ima eased around the counter. "Sit down. Let me pour you a whiskey." Ima cracked two metal cups on the table and pulled out her whiskey bottle.

Clive held out his hand. "I ain't no drinker, Miss Ima. My poison is hot coffee."

She leaned down and looked him in the eye.

"The hotter the better." He pushed her hand holdin' that bottle to one side. "You got my poison?"

I didn't reckon I knew a person alive that ever turned down anything Ima offered, be it money or whiskey. A body could see she wasn't used to being told no in any fashion. She poured herself a stiff shot and then walked to the potbelly stove and lifted a tin coffeepot with the tail of her apron. She poured Clive a full cup, then stood over him, waiting to see him take a swig.

Clive touched that tin cup with one finger, then yanked it away. He licked his finger. "Now that's a hot cup of coffee." He licked four of his fingers and rubbed them with his thumb. "It smells like heaven. You brew a mean cup of coffee." Clive took hold of that hot cup and took a big swig. I waited to see if his face would turn red, but he swallowed that hot coffee like it was water.

Ima slapped him on the back and let out that horrible cackle. "Let's talk turkey. See what I can do for you."

That was the moment I knew I could take a breath and live another hour. Clive broke through Ima's hard shell. He'd charmed and challenged her. Told her no. Even set some ground rules. It was something to behold. I'd watched Clive slide out of his teacher britches and climb into a set of trousers I never thought I'd see him wear. I guess what I feared was, would he be able to climb out when this was over?

The legs on Clive's chair finally squealed as he pushed away from the table. I caught a glimpse of Angus creeping past. Piqued my curiosity as to what he was lookin' to see. I watched through the screen door as Clive stood and stuck out his hand to Ima. Her skin looked like a wadded-up poke, wrinkled and stiff, and when she reached out to shake his hand, there seemed to be enough loose skin to fit two more women in her body. Them mean thoughts run through my mind like a rushing creek.

Clive mighta made his way into the store to share a cup of coffee with her, but Ima couldn't be trusted. She was a master at manipulation. Something told me we wasn't outa the hot water yet. He took a few steps away, then turned. "Miss Ima, I meant to ask you your thoughts on taxin' the miners."

Ima cocked her head. "Taxin' the miners?"

"I wondered if that was something you thought needed to be done."

She eased around the edge of the counter and stood right against Clive. "Well now, them men done buy all they need from me. Ain't right sure taxin' them would be any good."

Clive bent over and whispered in her ear. "You might collect that tax and keep a little for your work. Think on it." He made his way to the screen door and pushed it open. "I'll be back in a few days."

Ima nodded.

"You think on that tax."

She smiled.

I'd made my way to the wagon before they come outa the door. I untied the reins and waited.

Clive had planted the seed . . . set the trap.

Thirty-Eight

We rumbled our way back down the mountain. We was beginning to wonder if we'd failed completely since there was no sign of Rayburn or Thomas. I wasn't sure if I should be worried about him or lose what little trust I had in him. Thoughts of that hooded man still ate at me.

Clive didn't open his mouth for a while. The silence was awkward before I couldn't stand it no more. "You need to vomit?"

His stare broke, and he glanced at me. "Ain't gonna ever live that down, am I?"

"Nope." I bumped his shoulder. "You was something else with Ima. I was scared you'd turn chicken."

Clive tapped his heels on the wagon. "I wondered the same."

"I ain't never heard the likes of anyone outtalkin' Ima. But you talked circles around her. I believe you got yourself a new friend."

"My skin still crawls after touching her hand. A body could feel the meanness in her." Clive shivered.

"You did a fine job. The hardest step was to get under Ima's skin. You might just be an itch she can't scratch. We ain't outa the woods yet though. This was just the start."

For the next few minutes, I listened as Clive unloaded. The man had done right good. We talked about June and just what she might have known about Ima that would topple her. What was in it for June that would have made Ima want her dead? These was things we might never know—things that died with June.

We rounded the trail and hit the green grass of a mountain field. The bumps of the wagon trail eased, and the ride across the field smoothed out.

Clive leaned back and drew in a breath. "You reckon we can stop? These clothes is mighty fancy, and I'd like to get back into my work clothes."

I pulled the wagon to a halt and unhooked Rufus. He scrubbed his head against my arm, and I give him a rub. My hand left sweaty outlines on his skin. "You need a rest, fella?" I dropped the yoke, and Rufus stepped over. A small creek run across the field, and he moseyed his way to the fresh water.

"This might be as good a place as any to stop for the night. Don't you think, Clive?"

He didn't answer.

"Might be a good place to bed down."

Clive had only walked to the edge of the forest to switch out his clothes and maybe relieve hisself. He shouldn't be gone any longer than a tadpole.

"Clive?" I hollered. Nothing. "Clive! Where in tarnation did you go?"

I whistled at Rufus. He raised his head from lapping water, then went back to drinking. I whistled again, and he lumbered toward me. "Take your time. Fool horse." Things wasn't right.

My heart speeded up. "Clive?" I hollered again.

I hooked my fingers through the reins that dragged along the ground. "Come on, boy. Let's loop you up." I folded a loop into the reins and dropped it over the brake, then pulled up the yoke. My hand slipped under the wagon bench, and takin' hold of my rifle, I popped open the chamber to be sure it was loaded.

"Clive, you relievin' yourself? I know how a man has to concentrate at times to do his business." The only noise I heard was the coo of a few doves sitting in the grass.

I shouted again. "I'm comin' to look for you."

Rufus shook his head and neighed. I stepped into the darkened woods, easing through vines and downed branches. Where in tarnation could Clive be?

I pulled back a pile of low-hanging vines, and there he was, face to face with Angus, Clive just beyond and standing in a small clearing just a ways into the woods.

"What's goin' on here, Angus?" I rested my rifle on my shoulder. "There a problem?"

Angus shoved his hands into his trouser pockets, then twisted his toe in the dirt. He looked like a scared rabbit.

"Things ain't what you think, Josh." Angus's voice was soft. Not his usual tough tone. I'd heard that from him once before, and it didn't end well. "I've been followin' you down the mountain, lookin' for the right time to talk. Hopin' you'd stop and rest. There's things you need to know."

There were several times coming down the mountain I'd felt like there was someone watching, but I'd passed it off as just worry. I figured Thomas was riding alongside us, outa sight. Keeping watch. It was Angus all along.

"What are you talkin' about?" I eased closer, not trusting him. Once a body gets burned, it's hard to put your hand back on a hot stove. Angus flip-flopped like a fish outa water. One minute he was showing kindness, the next he'd turn like a wildcat.

"Angus says Thomas ain't telling us the truth. You need to hear him out." Clive took a step back. "He says there's more to June's death than Thomas is letting on."

There was the hitch in my giddyup. Brother against brother, and we was left to decide who was right and who was wrong. I wasn't surprised that there was more to it. The problem was who to believe. Whose words made the most sense.

"I'm listenin'."

Angus squatted to the ground and fingered a stone. It was obvious something weighed on him, but I wasn't willing to offer a lot of pity.

"You're gonna find this hard to believe, and I reckon you got every reason not to believe me, but I'm givin' you the truth." Angus went on messing with the stone. I watched as his lips moved without a sound coming outa his mouth. He was searching for the right words.

"Spit it out. Just so you know, I have a hard time believin' any Barton," I snapped.

"Hear him out, Josh," Clive interrupted.

I wasn't sure what Clive saw in Angus that I didn't. Maybe he'd said something before I'd found them—something that gave Clive reason to want to listen.

It was hard to weigh out our odds here. Thomas seemin' to be a changed man—being Aughtie's daddy. Angus seemin' broken when he saw Aughtie at the house but then turned hard-nosed and mean. How was a body supposed to figure out what the truth was?

"June was married to me, but Thomas forced her away. It was me that fathered that youngin." Angus just blurted it out. He got up and began to pace.

I bent at the waist and broke into a hard laugh. It wasn't hard to see through that lie. "You want me to believe that you and June was married, had a youngin, with her bein' married to Thomas? Try again, Angus. That don't even make no sense."

Angus walked toward me. He pointed his finger at my face. "She wasn't never married to Thomas. Thomas wants to take Momma down. He's always been Momma's favored, and he's tired of being second in line." Angus's voice rose a notch. "I'm tellin' you. It ain't what you think. June knew how Momma was drainin' the miners. She had all the proof. Thing was, she could do the same to Thomas. She knew Thomas wanted Momma gone so the mines would be his. Thomas would do anything to get her proof to protect his own hide. June wanted safety for Aughtie, her, and me." Angus grew desperate. "Josh, Thomas is settin' you up for a fall! He knows you'll not stop until you find the truth. He can't afford that."

That took me back a bit. My doubts climbed. Could Angus be telling the truth?

"Thomas wants to see Ima fall so the miners can be free of the Company Store. That's what he said." I shook my head in disbelief.

Angus ripped his hat off his head and slung it to the ground. At that moment me and Clive was lookin' at a desperate man. There was a lot of things I couldn't trust, but my gut was usually right. It was telling me Angus had some truth to be heard.

"Look, I know this seems twisted, but the way I stay alive is to do Momma's grunt work. She'd kill us in a heartbeat if we crossed her. She ain't the ideal momma. I just tried to protect June. If I tried to stop him from killin' Momma, he'd kill June." Angus dropped to his knees. "I just want my girl. I want what's left of the woman I love so I can leave here. Take Aughtie and leave here!"

Clive walked to Angus and knelt next to him. "Why fight Thomas?"

"I didn't set out to fight Thomas." Angus hit the ground with his fist.

"Thomas killed June to keep her quiet. Despite his wantin' Momma gone, protecting his own hide was most important."

Things started to come around for me. Those little things about Thomas that just didn't sit right began to fit together. Was Thomas lying?

"You're gonna have to explain, Angus. Give us something here." Clive looked at me and shrugged.

Angus grabbed a small fallen branch and flung it. He yelled hard and long. "When June told me she was carrying my youngin, I planned to take her and leave the mountain, head north to West Virginia. Thomas always loved June, but she chose me. That made Thomas mad. But when he found out June had the proof written down to end Momma, Thomas tried to take it all." Angus threw his arms up in frustration.

"Thomas caught up with me and June as we were ready to leave the mountain. He held a gun to my head, ready to kill me. He wanted June as his own."

I listened as Angus spilled his guts.

"June had everything written in a letter. She bargained herself so Thomas wouldn't kill me."

"What did June have on Thomas?" I asked.

"She knew Thomas would take her proof of Ima skimming more money off the top of the miner's pay and leak that to the miners. He could step back and let the miners' rage finish off Ima. They'd riot and kill her. June told Thomas she'd go with him, but she'd go to the sheriff if he harmed me. She had written proof on Ima and Thomas. She went with Thomas to keep him from killing me."

I couldn't have been more stunned at the twist in this story. "Thomas said he married June and hid her to protect her from Ima. Why should I believe you?" I asked.

"Thomas took June and hid her away. In his own sick way, hiding June let him claim her as his own."

"Thomas would have June as his trophy, and he'd gain the mines when the miners killed Ima. He'd be free and clear." Things came together.

"Exactly. Momma wanted June dead to protect herself. Instead, Thomas hid June and told Momma June was gone so he could use June's information against Ima when the time was right," Angus said.

It was startin' to make sense.

"How's Aughtie know Thomas as papa? Explain that!" Clive said.

Angus was growin' impatient. He took in a deep breath and sighed. "Thomas was the only one she saw. He was probably good to her. To the child, Thomas is the only one she ever knew. I never saw June again after Thomas took her. I never saw my child. Thomas threatened to kill June if I come lookin' for her. The first time I saw Aughtie was that day with Raney."

Angus was a huge man, and seeing him fall apart and panicked spoke volumes. His explanations didn't answer all my questions, but I could see where a man who was trying to save his wife could be pushed to do things he might not normally do.

"What's in this for you?" It didn't make sense that Angus would benefit from telling us the truth—if it was the truth. The more I run things through my mind, tryin' to see the truth, the more I saw the light. Angus had been truly moved when he saw Aughtie. There was no hiding his emotion, his gentleness as he tried to see her. But Thomas . . . his actions gave me pause.

"Clive, how did Thomas react when we told him about June?" I wondered if things measured up right or if it was just me bein' overprotective.

"He acted shocked. But . . ." Clive scratched his chin.

"But then he didn't seem upset like a man who lost his wife. Did he?" I knew every man reacted differently to the loss of a loved one, and though Thomas seemed shocked, he didn't seem distraught over June. Maybe that was what was gnawin' at me from the git-go. Maybe that was why I spent so much time trying to convince myself to trust Thomas. He looked sad on the outside, but there wasn't nothing underneath.

I could see Angus growing frustrated that I struggled to believe him. He stood and bolted toward me.

I drew my rifle. "Stop right there."

He stopped in his tracks. "You have to listen to me. I know my actions don't match up, but they will if you'll listen. I can prove I was June's husband."

What proof could he possibly have that would sway me? "Proof?"

"Solid proof!" Angus shouted. "June wore a locket. It was broke when

Thomas ripped it off her neck the day he took her. I gave her that locket. Here's the other half." He stuck his hand in his pocket and pulled out the face of the locket, wrapped in a piece of paper.

And there it was—some truth I could sink my teeth into. I'd found half that locket the day we set fire to June's remains and dropped it in her bag—the one Aughtie carried on her arm.

The brush beside me rustled, and out stepped a tall, bearded man. His clothes was tattered, and he looked rough for the wear. He carried two rifles, one across each shoulder.

"Angus! What's the commotion?" The man shoved his finger in his jaw and pressed his tobacco onto the ground. He walked up to me and spit. "My son-in-law done something to you?"

"Son-in-law?" I stammered.

The man walked to Angus and handed him his hat. Angus dusted his hat on his trousers and slipped it on his head.

I couldn't believe my eyes. Taylor Rayburn. The one man we'd not been able to find stood in front of me.

"Josh. It's been a spell." He inched closer to Angus and patted his shoulder. "It's alright, son. Tell them."

I felt the bottom drop outa my stomach. What more could Angus tell?

"Momma thinks Aughtie has June's letter with the proof. She's comin' after Aughtie."

Thirty-Nine

It was such a twisted tale that even I wasn't sure I believed it. Rayburn managed to calm Angus down and help him get his wits about him. We agreed to make camp for the night and make a plan. Stopping was not what I wanted, especially since Thomas knew Aughtie was on the homestead with the women. I could only hope that the sheriff and the pastor had made it to the homestead with a few men to help ward off the masked man if he returned.

I was still tryin' to take in Angus's words. It was beyond me why Ima wanted Aughtie dead. This youngin was slow. Things wasn't right with her. Why would Ima think this sort of child would have June's letter of proof? Still, Ima was on her way, and we had to figure out how to keep the youngin safe. There was still no sign of Thomas, and my gut was telling me that the trust he was pleadin' for was done gone.

Rayburn sat whittling for a good amount of time before he spoke up. "I heard you was trying to find me to tell me about June." He wiped his knife against his trousers and began to whittle again. "Right kind of you."

"It's been years. Didn't know if you was even still alive." I handed him a cup of coffee, then sat close to the fire.

"Ima's mean. It was me that caught her doctorin' her books. I saw her when I was loading shelves of flour in the store. She slammed that ledger shut in a hurry, but I saw enough to know. I just went about my business. But when I got home—"

"You told June, and she figured out the mess," I interrupted.

"I killed my daughter." Rayburn tossed his knife blade down in the dirt. His anger boiled. I watched as he gathered the wherewithal to continue.

There was no good words to say. By his looks, he'd been living a rough life trying to stay outa Ima's way.

"Rayburn, where are you living these days? How'd you know we would be here?"

"I stay in an old run-down mine shack. Ain't much, but it keeps the weather out. I didn't know you'd be here. I met up with Angus yesterday and told him I'd meet him here today. Wasn't expectin' you." He took a swig of coffee, then grabbed his knife.

"When did you walk away from the mines?" I asked.

"A few weeks after June decided to confront Ima. She'd planned on bringin' the sheriff up the mountain in hopes to get Ima arrested. But Ima suspected something was up when June kept making notes. Angus had married June a couple of months before. They snuck off. She come up pregnant, and well . . ." Rayburn's voice quivered.

I understood the pain Rayburn felt. I'd felt it myself. It wasn't the way of life for your youngin to die before you. I'd worked alongside Taylor Rayburn in the mines, but it had been years. I was young when he showed me the ropes. We'd lost touch when he was moved around. People get misplaced in the mines. At least now I knew what had happened to him.

Rayburn was still. I could tell he was thinkin', ponderin'.

"You wanna know what I want?" Rayburn asked.

What was I to say? No, I didn't wanna know. There wasn't much guessing to what his desire was. "What do you want?"

"I want Ima Barton and Thomas."

Morning in the mountains always comes with a freshness. The colors in the sky are different every day. Makes a man wonder how the good Lord mixes His paints to form new shades of pink and lavender. The birds chatter, and the deer feed along the tree line. The call of the river sings new words to a man's heart, and when you least expect it, a tender breeze fills your senses with honeysuckle. Every day is unique.

Squirrels leaped limb to limb, gathering their morning meal, and for a few minutes I took it in.

I rolled my blanket and dusted the leaves away before I tossed it in the wagon. The sun's fingers parted the limbs of the trees as I looked across the horizon.

Angus and Rayburn spent a good amount of time the night before filling us in on Ima. Things from openin' the bags of flour and emptying a good amount out, then selling them to the miners as full, to skimming their wages. I found myself pitying the Bartons for their hunger for money and power and missin' the joy in life.

"I got one more question." I leaned against the wagon while Rayburn tossed in his blanket.

"What's one more question?"

"It's been several years. Why didn't you go after June? You had Angus to help. Why didn't you both go after June?"

Rayburn eyed the ground, his fingers clicked on the side of the wagon. I could tell I'd hit a nerve.

"People say Angus is crazy, but he ain't. Thomas is the crazy one. He's mad. If he makes a threat, he don't think a thing about carryin' it out. He vowed he'd kill June if either of us tried to find her. June went willingly with him to protect Angus. We know now she was protectin' her baby too. When we got wind he'd come to you looking for a youngin, we knew June must have found an out for herself. She'd found a way to escape him. We was hoping she'd show up. Now I live with myself knowing she's dead." He kicked a rock and went to checking the wagon.

Clive knelt by the river's edge, rinsing the cups and coffeepot. Rayburn had doused the fire, but a few small branches still burned red. He went to set that yoke on the wagon for the horses while I walked them there. Clive went to singin'. I furrowed my brow, and a grin come across my face.

"What in tarnation is that howling?" Rayburn squinted and cocked his head. "Lordy mercy, I believe it's makin' my ears bleed."

I busted into laughter. Rayburn was right. Singing wasn't Clive's strong suit, but it was one of the things that brought him happiness. He was either humming, whistling, or singing all the time though. If I had my druthers, I'd druther him whistle.

"I'm sure the good Lord is smiling over Clive's singin'—sorta!" I said. We hadn't had a good laugh in a spell. Raney always said laughter wakes up the joy in a person. I reckon, for a minute, I felt the burden to take Ima down lift, and a tinge of joy sneak in. We were still a half-day's ride from home, and I would be glad to see that the women were safe.

I bent to help Rayburn lift the yoke on the wagon, when a flock of pheasants flushed from the tall grass by the water. Two deer shot out of the brush like something was after them.

"What the . . ." Rayburn cussed.

Clive glanced up as the pheasants landed by the water but quickly went back to his singin'.

I shook my head, then rolled my shoulders to crack the bones and loosen up. A horse whinnied, and when we looked through the morning dusk, the outline of a rider on a horse bolted from the forest. Clive, ankle deep in the riverwash, slowly stood. Rayburn dropped the yoke and made a beeline around the wagon. The hooded rider dashed past us with a bloodcurdling scream and nearly knocked Rayburn down.

"Clive, watch out!" I shouted.

But it was too late. The rider swung his rifle and hit Clive in the face, sending him careening into the water. In one swift move, the rider pulled his horse around, cocked his rifle, and shot. Clive's body bounced from the blow of the bullet.

"No!" I screamed as I grabbed my rifle from the wagon. "No!" I cocked the gun and pulled off a shot but missed.

Rayburn went after him, tryin' to catch the edge of the saddle, but he was a finger's shot away. There was nothing we could do. The hooded man rushed in, attacked, and escaped . . . again. His luck couldn't keep holding out.

I rushed toward the river. Clive lay face down, half in the water, half out. A trail of red mixed with the blue of the river water formed in an eddy between rocks. The only thing on my mind was saving the man who'd become like family.

"Clive!" I shouted. Me and Rayburn rolled him over and pulled him from the wash. A hole two fingers wide opened on the front and back of his shoulder, blood spurtin' hard and fast. Rayburn rushed to the smoking ash of the fire and pulled a stick still hot with embers. He run back.

"Don't you die, Clive. Don't you dare die." I pressed my hand over the hole in the front of his shoulder. "Looks like the bullet went clean through."

Clive groaned, and his head rolled to one side.

My mind went to Manny. I'd held him the same way, and he'd died in my arms. Not again. "Open your eyes! Now!" My shoutin' at him did no good. It didn't rouse him, didn't stop the bleeding. It did nothing.

"Rip off his shirt so I can get to the hole," Rayburn said. He cupped his hand and scooped up enough water to rinse the wound. "Hold him." Rayburn held up the burning stick. "Clive, son, I'm sorry." And with that Rayburn rammed the hot stick into the hole, sealin' the bleeding.

Clive screamed in pain as the scent of burnt flesh filled the air. There is something different about the scent of human flesh when it burns. It ain't savory like a rabbit or a squirrel. It's a horrible stench. I remembered the day we'd burned June's body. The smell turned your stomach.

Rayburn tore Clive's shirt into strips and wadded a few into a ball to stick in the wound. I tied some longer ones around his shoulder and chest to hold the patch in place. We lifted Clive and carried him to the wagon. Clive's teeth chattered, partially from the wound and partially from the cold river water. I covered him with my blanket.

"You'll be fine." I tried to encourage him, but panic was all I felt. "We need to get him back to the farm. We're still a good half day away!"

Rayburn come around the edge of the wagon and took me by the shirt. "You listen to me. I know this young man means something to you, but you're getting tore up ain't helpin' him. Settle down." Rayburn's voice was stern. He gave me a shake and then turned me loose. "Help me hitch up the horses."

I tucked the blanket around Clive. The thought of losin' him was more than I could take. I shook my head, trying to clear my mind.

"Where's Angus?" I shouted. "I thought he was the hooded man. Is he? Was this Angus?"

Rayburn kept workin' to hitch the horses while I pulled the rest of the rifles from under the wagon bench and laid them in the back.

"Where. Is. Angus? For that fact, where is Thomas?" I felt myself slippin' back into hate. "Thomas promised he'd be close to help protect us.

He's nowhere to be found. Angus gave me a sob story, and now he's gone. I should've never trusted either of them. Both of them are liars."

"Joshua. Stop it! It ain't what you think." Rayburn gritted his teeth. "Angus ain't the man you think. He left early this morning to find Thomas. He's trying to stop him. Thomas betrayed you. He suckered you."

That was the second time I'd heard those words. *It ain't what you think.* What was I supposed to think?

"What?" I hushed. Angus had left ahead of us to stop Thomas? He was going ahead to protect us?

I sat hard on the back of the wagon and took in a breath. "Who is this hooded man?" Then it hit me. We was only a half-day's ride from home. Why was this masked man so close to my home, to the women—to Aughtie? My stomach turned. "We need to get home. Things ain't addin' up."

I hopped off the wagon, taking one last look at Clive. He lay on his side, his mouth hung open. The bleeding had stopped, but the man was hurt bad.

"You hold on. Don't do something stupid, like die." I whispered. That was all I could think of to say.

Clive opened his eyes and pointed at me. "Any sign of Thomas?" He groaned.

I shrugged.

"Joshua, we've been had, ain't we?"

FORTY

CLIVE SAT UP in the wagon bed. I sat next to him as we bumped over rocks and holes. He groaned with every jolt.

Rayburn took us down the south pass that run by the river to the gorge. The sun belted down on us when we come close to the gorge.

"Pull by the edge of the water and let me wet Clive's bandages," I said.

Rayburn eased the wagon to a halt, and we lifted Clive to the edge of the wagon. Rayburn made Clive a sling to support his arm.

We dampened the bandages in the icy river water, grateful the bumpy ride did not start Clive bleedin' again, and rewrapped his wounds. Clive wasn't his talkative self, but he was coming around. He was able to sit up and talk some.

"Mercy, this river always had a bite. Makes for good fishin', Clive. Reckon you can catch us a trout next trip," Rayburn teased.

We let the horses drink and gnaw a bit on some grass before we scooted Clive to the back of the wagon.

"Won't be much longer before we're home. Just think of that nice down bed in the tack shed," I said. Once we had him settled, me and Taylor walked outa earshot of Clive.

"He's lucky," Taylor said.

"You saved him with that hot stick." I glanced back at Clive.

"We'll do our best to get him home. Hopefully, we won't meet any more hardship."

"We gotta do better than our best." I tucked my shirttail in my trousers. "Best be movin' on."

Taylor nodded, and we headed toward the wagon. The roar of the river shouted its story as it rumbled its way along the gorge. Rocks jutted up from the water, forced it to push harder to make its way by. Eddies and swirls tried to draw an unsuspectin' man into its grip. I stared at the rush of the water. Even the river had its lies. Water that looked shallow wasn't. The clear water showed the river bottom, tellin' a soul it was safe. But step in and it'd swallow you alive and hold you tight to the bottom until it sucked the air from your lungs. I wondered if there was any truth anywhere in the world.

Taylor started the horses, but we didn't get far before he pulled them to a stop.

"What's a matter?" I asked.

He held his finger to his lips, shushin' me. He cupped one hand around his ear. "Horses. Several."

I grabbed the rifles and shoved one next to Clive. We couldn't get the wagon pulled into the edge of the woods before the horses busted through the cover of the trees, a shirtless Angus in the lead. Blood drained down his chest.

"They got Aughtie!" Angus pulled his gun and twisted in his saddle. He fired.

My stomach knotted. We was this close to home—had they gotten Aughtie?

Taylor grabbed his rifle, squatted behind the bench, and took aim.

"Can you keep that gun close to your side?" I hollered.

Clive nodded and slid down into the back of the wagon, slipping his arm from the sling and doin' his best to fight through the pain.

Angus wheeled around to take a second shot, when I saw Thomas take aim at him.

"Angus!" I hollered. The shot rang out, hitting Angus and taking him off his horse. I heard the air blow outa his chest when he hit the ground. I couldn't believe I'd just witnessed Thomas shoot his own brother.

Thomas held up his hand to halt the riders behind him. Out of the woods, bringin' up the rear, was Ima, her dress hiked up and laid over her saddle. A rifle hung by her leg in its sheath. Behind her, the hooded man. Ima eased her horse next to Thomas. The masked man held Aughtie tight against his chest. Her pudgy hands was tied, and a red bandanna was pulled tight in her mouth.

"Lord have mercy," I shouted. "Thomas, what are you doin'?"

Aughtie wiggled in the man's saddle. She managed to throw her leg over the horse, slipping from the masked man's grip. She fell to the ground. I lunged from the wagon toward her.

"Hold it right there," Ima squawked. Her rifle went up, and I slid to a halt.

I wanted to give Thomas the benefit of the doubt. Maybe he was playing a part. Maybe he was using Aughtie as bait. But he said nothing.

Aughtie rushed to me. I grabbed her and held tight. "Don't worry, baby girl. Ole Josh has got you." I loosened her hands, and she wallered out of the ropes.

Thomas came off that horse and bolted toward me, but I held that youngin tight.

"I thought you loved Aughtie? I thought you wanted trust. I thought . . ."

Thomas grabbed Aughtie by the waist and tugged. "You thought what, Joshua? That you're a sucker . . . or worse, that I didn't *know* I run down your girl. Or that it was me that set that barn on fire. You didn't know, did you, Joshua? I killed the snitch, June."

His words stung. I felt a justified anger grow in me. Thomas had convinced me and Raney he'd not seen Anna that day. I swallowed hard. Another lie. "There won't be no more lyin', Lord," I whispered. I remembered all of them times I'd heard the pastor preach about an eye for an eye, and it seemed the devil had come to collect his dues. I was never so sorry about the wrongs I'd done than now.

Thomas yanked hard, but Aughtie was stuck to my chest. A muffled scream seeped outa her mouth. I wondered what ever possessed me to offer Thomas an inkling of trust. There was a time I wanted to be judge and jury, but I was tryin' to do better. Right now, judging Thomas sounded good.

"I. Trusted. You!" I gritted my teeth and held tight to Aughtie.

The hooded man made a lunge toward Aughtie, and another shot rang out. Rayburn took him down.

I couldn't believe it. Thomas had turned on me. Worse yet, he'd turned on Clive, who had still believed Thomas would show up to help.

I tried to push Thomas away with one arm and hold Aughtie tight with the other. Thomas lifted his foot and kicked me in the chest, takin' me to my stomach. I lost my hold on the youngin, and Thomas took the chance to grab her.

Angus crawled to his knees and tried to get to me, but he couldn't. Blood poured down his shoulders and over his chest.

Taylor come outa that wagon and busted Thomas in the head with the butt of his rifle, sendin' him to the ground with a thud. "Barton, you killed my girl! An eye for an eye."

Aughtie broke free. She run hard to me. I stood, grabbed Aughtie, and tossed her in the back of the wagon with Clive. Her little leather bag smacked me in the face.

"You killed my girl. Murderer." The anger in Rayburn's voice rose as he stood over Thomas. "You and your momma are heartless. Mindless killers."

"Here now! That's enough." Ima pulled her rifle and shot into the air. "I'm done pussyfootin' around. Step away from my boy."

Rayburn went to laughing. "Ima Barton, that rifle is as big as you." He barreled straight toward her, cockin' his own rifle. "Come on. Shoot me. I got nothing to lose. You done took all I ever earned in the mines. You took my girl. Let me see what a coward you are."

The pain in my ribs took me to my knees. "Rayburn. Stop. Don't be a fool."

I've heard it said that a man that carries vengeance in his heart carries stupid alongside hisself—after all, I was proof. You don't think clear, and fear turns to a hard rage. Taylor was in a rage.

He shoved the butt of his rifle under his arm and pulled the trigger. Ima's horse reared, bumping her and causing her to fall. Never in all my days had I witnessed such rage in a man. I wasn't sure if Rayburn was brave or if he just didn't care if he died, but he stomped toward Ima and planted his rifle barrel right in the center of her forehead. His foot pressed against her arm, keepin' her from grabbing her rifle that lay inches away.

Aughtie crawled from the wagon and commenced to run toward Ima.

The youngin grabbed Ima's rifle and come toward me. As she passed by Thomas, he'd come around enough to snag her by the dress. The child wheeled around, and the rifle went off, hittin' Thomas in the gut.

"Kill that youngin, son," Ima hollered. "She ain't right, and you can't care for a mishap. Kill her. She's got everything."

Thomas raised up, hardly able to stand. He pulled his knife from his boot, and as he drew back to throw it at Aughtie, a third round went off. I turned, and Clive sat balanced against the side of the wagon. His shot took Thomas down. This time Thomas didn't stand.

I glanced at Rayburn. He'd not moved. That rifle barrel was buried firm in Ima's forehead. I could hear him daring Ima to give him reason to pull the trigger. There was nothing I could do. Rayburn would make his own decision.

I managed to get to my feet and limp my way to Angus. "Ain't we the likes?" I laughed. "Ain't neither of us worth a hoot. Both of us is liars, and bad ones at that." I knelt beside him, and a grimace crossed his face. "Peas in a pod, huh?"

Aughtie run to my side and slid her little arm around my neck. I looked at Angus and saw he was dying. There was never a good time to give a dying man news, be it good or bad, but Angus deserved to meet Aughtie. Rayburn had Ima under control, and Thomas and the hooded man were dead. It was a bad time, but this would be the *only* time.

"Angus?" I lifted him into my lap and pulled Aughtie next us.

She hesitated.

"Trust me, baby," I said.

Aughtie's eyes met mine, and she eased closer. Angus opened his eyes. Blood seeped from the sides of his mouth, and his breathin' was hard.

"Angus, this here is Aughtie. This is your girl. She's a pretty thing, ain't she?"

Angus lifted his hand toward her.

I didn't know why—other than the good Lord blessed a youngin like Aughtie with a compassion like no other—but the child leaned over Angus and opened June's purse that she'd carried on her arm since we'd buried June. She dug around, pulled out the necklace, and wrapped it around Angus's hand. Aughtie slipped behind me, still fearful of Angus.

A tear dripped down Angus's cheek. It took all I had to lift him to his knees. If I could get him to the wagon, maybe we could get him home.

Clive crawled out of the wagon and tried help, but he didn't have enough strength.

Rayburn loosened his rope belt and yanked Ima up to tie her hands, his rifle snug under his arm. Ima wiggled enough to get a grip on his rifle to lift it. Before Rayburn could jerk it away, she pulled the trigger. The gun fired and knocked Angus face forward into the dirt. Rayburn slammed Ima to the ground and tied her. He took her by the ankle and pulled her close to her horse, then lifted her onto the saddle, stomach first. She was kickin' and screamin', but he snagged a second rope from the side of the saddle and finished a snug hog-tie on Ima. Once he had her snugged, he pulled her off the horse and dropped her face first on the ground.

"Now lay there!" he shouted. Rayburn took a few steps, then turned around. He drew back and kicked Ima in the side. "That was for killin' my daughter." He kicked again. "And that was for killin' my son-in-law."

Ima spit blood, then screamed at the top of her lungs. "You got no idea what that child has. You got no idea!"

I went to my knees and pulled Aughtie close. Her sobs were piercing. All I could do was hold her. The man she knew as her daddy lay dead on one side. On the other, her blood father breathed out his last breath.

I sat on the dirt and held the youngin. Clive rolled Angus to his back and unwrapped the necklace from his hand. He took Aughtie's arm and lifted the leather bag, then dropped the necklace into the small opening. He pulled it closed.

Ima shouted and cussed until she wore out her voice. Rayburn finally took the rag that had been around Aughtie's mouth and stuffed it tight in Ima's mouth. We sat on the ground for a good amount of time before Rayburn came close.

"Why don't you let Clive sit with Aughtie?" Rayburn helped me stand. "See if you can muster the strength to help me load these brothers in the wagon."

My ribs ached, but I just had to work through it. We lifted Thomas and Angus into the wagon, then Rayburn slung Ima over a shoulder and carried her to the wagon like she was a side of beef.

"Hard to believe evil weighs this heavy. I know just where to put her." And with that, he let out a grunt and laid Ima between her dead sons. "Give her time to say goodbye."

We walked across the field to where the hooded man lay. Reachin' down, I pulled his hood off. Just when I thought there could be no more surprises, the man lying on the ground was Ima's dead husband, John Barton. Back from the grave.

Forty-One

"I'll be . . ." I bumped Rayburn and pointed. "How in tarnation could this be John Barton? He died in the mines."

I couldn't believe my eyes. Ima's dead husband. Alive . . . no, dead. I'd not seen John since the day he went down in that hole with them men. There was no funeral 'cause them men was all buried in that mineshaft. But somehow John got outa that hole—or maybe never went in. This knot was just growin' tighter, and instead of answers, we was just gettin' more questions. Impossible questions.

We dragged him to the wagon and lifted him on top of Thomas.

"I ain't sure how you pulled this off, or what the purpose was for letting folks think John was dead, but I reckon you have to live with that," I said to Ima. "You're a sick soul, and your greed has ruined you."

Ima rolled to one side and sneered. She worked that rag outa her mouth and cussed a string of words even the miners wouldn't speak.

"John was workin' that vein of emerald."

"What?" I stopped in my tracks. "The emerald I found?"

She wiggled, growled, and cussed some more. "John found that vein. You just found a rock. We kept it a secret to keep prospectors out."

Rayburn spoke up. "You blew that mine on purpose. You killed them men so John could disappear and mine a vein of emerald?"

Ima cackled like a witch. "You thought you had me, Joshua. You didn't have nothin'. A single rock that John probably dropped. He'd been working that vein for months before you come along with a stone."

"That's why you stayed away from my family."

"I didn't need you. That little lie of yours kept us both in the clear." Ima grunted.

"Why Aughtie? Why do you want to kill an innocent child?"

Ima hesitated, then spoke. "She's got June's notes."

I couldn't bear looking at her another second. Rayburn secured her in the wagon. Made sure she was tight with her dead family, and then we helped Clive onto the wagon bench.

I gathered the horses and tied them to the back of the wagon, except one for me and Aughtie.

"Let's go home, little girl." I took Aughtie by the hand and started past Ima.

The little girl stopped in front of Ima and stared, then walked past.

The road home felt like an eternity. There wasn't much to say. We was all just trying to take in everythin'. I couldn't begin to imagine what had happened on the homestead with John takin' Aughtie. He would've had a fight with Raney. The sheriff. Cleda Mae. I feared they were all dead.

I brought my horse around to Rayburn's side of the wagon. "I'm sorry about June. You're a better man than me, keeping hold of your feelings like you did. I know you wanted Ima dead."

Rayburn nodded.

I couldn't change years of hate and anger overnight. I couldn't take back the lies I'd told, even the ones I told to try and protect my family or Aughtie.

I looked up at the sun passing over the ridge. "Rayburn, we *can* start fresh though, can't we?"

He pulled the wagon to a stop and then got out. "I reckon we done started. This mess is over. Didn't end like we hoped, but it's over."

And that's what we do on the mountain. Live, face hardships, and live again.

I handed Aughtie down, and Rayburn rested her on his hip while I dismounted. Again, timing ain't never been my friend, but this was the right time. Rayburn stood Aughtie next to me, and I took her hand.

"Aughtie, I want you to meet Momma June's daddy. This is your papaw, Taylor."

She eyed him for a minute, then wrapped her arms around him. Her fingers folded tight together. He leaned down and patted her back.

"Momma Joon tell Aughtie." And that was all it took for a stiff-hearted

Taylor Rayburn to drop to his knees and sob in a child's arms. He'd lost his daughter but found this little light. Like Raney told me once—*We ain't lost. We're found.*

Aughtie brushed her fingers through his scraggly hair and did her best to console him. After a bit, he stood and lifted her to me.

I waved him away. "I think she'll sit fine between you and Clive."

Rayburn managed a rough smile, then sat Aughtie on the bench next to him. We headed for home. After a while Clive pulled Aughtie's feet onto his lap with his good arm, and Rayburn eased her head onto his knee while she napped.

It was a long day when we finally rolled onto the homestead. Cleda Mae spotted us comin' around the bend, and she went to calling the sheriff. Aughtie's head popped up, and both women went to screamin'. Rayburn set the youngin off the wagon and let her run to them. It was something to see both Raney and Cleda Mae on their knees, shouting and crying. Rejoicing that the child was home. Put me in mind of the return of that prodigal child in the Good Book. I wondered what happened, how John managed to steal Aughtie. But the truth was, right that minute it didn't matter. Everyone on the homestead was alive. Within minutes the sheriff and his men surrounded the wagon.

"You found the child," the sheriff said. "Masked man stole her outa her bed during the night."

And that was enough of an answer. I didn't need no more.

Rayburn took time to give the sheriff the story as some of his men unloaded Angus next to June's grave. It seemed fittin' that he find peace with the woman he loved. A few of the sheriff's men offered to bury him.

I helped Clive up on my horse and walked him to the cabin, leavin' Ima and the dead behind. Cleda Mae met us, and the pastor helped her get Clive into the house. Aughtie did her best to help. Raney stood on the end of the porch, arms crossed, head gently shakin' side to side. I reached out my hand, and she slid her arms tenderly around me.

Her hair smelled like roses, and her skin was soft like a feather. "You're a day early. Didn't expect you till tomorrow."

I smiled at her humor, then kissed her.

She could see Aughtie had met her grandfather, and that was good. Some of the homesteaders had cleared the burnt wood from the barn and readied the ground to rebuild. It would take a few weeks, but we'd raise the barn with their help. The sheriff took Ima straight to jail, and he'd assured us Thomas and John would be buried.

Once Clive was bandaged up, we sat on the porch as night come over the rye field. Aughtie snuggled on the floor next to Rayburn. Not a one of us could think of a thing to say. Every word that could be spoken, had been.

Aughtie pulled her momma's bag from her wrist and opened it up. She dumped the contents on the porch.

"Lordy mercy." Rayburn gasped. He pushed away a few river pebbles to uncover a handful of emeralds. The necklace Angus had given June lay in a knotted mess, along with a small envelope of folded papers. I picked up the envelope and opened it. All the evidence June had against Ima and a map of the emerald mine. Everything Ima wanted. Funny how things worked out—that an honest dead woman could take down an empire. But June did.

It all seemed so cut and dry. Unbelievable. I figured I'd feel some sort of success, joy even. Instead, I felt like something was missing. Unfinished. Everything was laid out for the takin'. But it wasn't ours to take.

What started to save Aughtie and take down the Company Store ended worse than we could have imagined. Still, the pieces come together as best they could in the end.

Ain't good for a man to want somebody dead, and I'd wanted that for years. I'd wanted Thomas Barton dead, wanted him to pay the price for my girl's dying. What I got was two dead Bartons—one by the hand of an innocent man, the other by the hand of greed. Clive would have never killed a soul, but my driving at him, my pushin' under the ruse of takin' down the Company Store, nearly got him killed and made him a killer.

There was no love lost with Thomas's death. Nothing except I'd had the tables turned on me, and I sure felt the sting of what a lie can do when you're on the receivin' end. Seems the only thing that comes from a lie is consequence. Lord knows I'd had my share of that. Still, it gave the Lord good cause to change me—and He did.

I had that little girl to thank for helpin' that along. Her sweet innocence, her compassion, all twisted into one, showed me what my lies had done. That child only saw the good in folks, and her sweet way of looking at things laid a passel of guilt on me.

Raney had done told the sheriff all she knew from beginnin' to end—she'd even showed him June's grave. I figured I shoulda felt good. We'd managed to take down the Bartons, but the victory was bittersweet. Death was never the ending we wanted.

Ima would stand trial, not for the wrongs she'd done to the miners but for killing Angus and sixteen miners. Yet I still had this nagging feelin' something wasn't right. Something wasn't done.

"Clive, you doing alright, son?" I asked as I handed him a cup of coffee.

"I was lucky. Doc said it would take me a spell to get back on my feet, but I'll heal. I reckon the fact that you can see right through me is true." He rubbed his shoulder and laughed.

"It's a price you shoulda never paid," I said.

"I'm sure Cleda Mae will have me back on my feet soon."

"We'd like you to stay in the tack house as long as you want. We like havin' you around."

Clive smiled.

I glanced at Taylor. "We'll make room for you too. You're welcome to call this home. I'm thinking all this land needs is men to work it. We can raise you a place in a few days if you're willing to stay."

Rayburn shook his head. "That's kind of you. I'll think on it. I need to see my girl's grave. Figure out what June would want me to do. A man's heart gets yanked out at the loss of his child, then stuffed back in his chest by another. I reckon mine's been jerked around about as much as it can take. My chest aches."

"Well, we're here to help. I'll walk you down to June's grave at first light," I said. Rayburn shrugged.

"Everything you need to bed down is in the back room of the shed. You get some rest."

Rayburn took a lantern and headed toward the tack shed. He gave

Aughtie a gentle pinch on the cheek and threw us a backward wave. Cleda Mae heaved Aughtie onto her back, and her and Clive followed behind. Cleda Mae bounced Aughtie as they walked—the child's giggles never grew old.

"Looks like it's just us." Raney pulled my shirt up and rubbed the bruises over my ribs. She shook her head. "This went south, didn't it?"

"It did."

Raney slipped my arm over her shoulder. I could tell by the sigh she let out that she had somethin' on her mind.

"I gotta ask you a question. Something I wondered if you'd thought of."

"What's that?"

"You realize with Thomas and Angus dead and Ima in jail . . . there ain't nobody to run the mines."

"Yeah. I know."

"Something needs to be done. The sheriff will help. So will the pastor."

"Tomorrow," I said. "Tonight we rest in each other's arms."

FORTY-TWO

THERE WAS NO rest for me through the night. We'd taken the ones who'd caused the pain away, but we hadn't fixed a thing. That horde of miners still needed work. Still needed their wages. Still needed someone to guide them through the day-to-day work process. The more I paced the floor through the night, the longer it seemed to drag. I finally found some rest in the rocker.

What had I done? I was so busy trying to find a way to take out the Bartons, so busy convincin' myself my little white lies was truth, that they dug their claws into my soul and become real. I never once thought about them miners like I claimed or that they might pay a price for their freedom. There was always a price.

"What do I do, Raney? I was so blinded by vengeance. I never saw this comin." I stood.

Raney raised up from the bed, dropped her feet over, and walked to me. "Lean against the table and get your balance. I know your ribs hurt."

I could see her workin' things around in her head, searching for the right words. "I'd not thought about it till I heard Ima mumble under her breath, 'Who's gonna mind the store?'"

"Whatta we do?" I asked.

"I ain't sure. Them men can't be left to tend on their own. It'll be like a pack of dogs catching the smell of a coon. They'll hunt till they find a catch." Raney shrugged. "Seems you best be thinking of a way to keep chaos from happening."

Raney made me see what a mess I'd made outa things. But then, that's what a good woman does. She loves you despite yourself and helps you see the error of your ways. I put my arm around her, and we watched as the sun inched over the peaks.

"Rayburn's coming up the path with the wagon. He's up early. I'm gonna walk him down to June's grave. We can talk." I hobbled across the room and looked out the window. The sun just peeked over the ridge, trying to divide the night from morning. When my eyes focused, I realized Clive was with him.

"That idiot. Clive's in that wagon. The boy oughta be layin' down."

"Seems you oughta practice what you preach. I'll raise a boil on the coffee."

She went to stoking the fire under the coffeepot. "It'll be hot by the time you boys get back from June's grave."

I took my hat from the table. Pushing my hair back, I planted it tight on my head. Raney opened the door, and I made my way outside.

"Mornin', boys. Surprised to see you up, Clive. I figured you'd be doin' what the doc told you. Resting." They waved.

"Aahh. What's he know? He's got the same cure for anything that ails you. Lay down and rest."

Rayburn laughed. "Man's got a point. Besides, you ain't exactly a fox on a hunt. Good thing I brought the wagon. Reckon I was smart enough to know there was two cripples needin' some help."

I lifted myself into the wagon. The pain shot through me like a bullet. I groaned and scooted further back. "Shew, lawsy. Thomas broke a few of my ribs when he kicked me."

"Aw, them's just growing pains," Rayburn said.

"Growing pains?"

"Yep, every breath you take keeps growing harder and harder." Rayburn chuckled under his breath.

"You can keep your humor tucked in your pocket," I said.

Rayburn clicked his lips. Rufus stepped against the yoke and pulled. I wondered when to mention the miners—before or after we took Taylor to June's grave. There didn't seem to be a right time.

Clive pointed toward the stand of trees where June and Angus were buried, and Taylor halted the wagon.

"You want me to come with you?" I asked.

Rayburn stepped outa the wagon. "Naw. I'll be fine."

I lifted my hand and pointed toward the pile of stones we'd used to cover June's grave. "They're both there."

"Much obliged." Rayburn tipped his hat.

We watched as he ducked under the overhanging tree limbs and walked to the piled-up rocks. I'd reminded Taylor why we couldn't move June on the ride over. That didn't ease his heartbreak. Me and Clive sat quiet and waited. I'd told Rayburn to take what time he needed to say goodbye to his girl. It was only minutes before we heard him talkin' to her. He'd mumble for a minute, and then we'd hear him cuss. Then we'd hear the sniffles of a brokenhearted man. I couldn't hear all he'd spoke to June, but I did catch the words "Sorry I couldn't save you."

I understood those words. I'd lost count of the times I'd said them over Anna's grave. I was sorry, but I couldn't change what was already done.

I leaned toward Clive and whispered, "You know, Raney brought up a truth this morning—something nary one of us took into account."

Clive rested his elbows on his knees. "Ain't sure how much more truth I can take."

"She said they ain't nobody to run the mines now. Clive, she was right. Them men will go hog wild when they find out Ima's in jail. Folks will get hurt."

"What do we do?" The color left Clive's face.

I scratched under my hat. "Reckon we need to head back up that mountain again."

"Seems like we've made that trip before." Clive sighed.

Rayburn worked his way back to the wagon, his eyes as red as his nose.

"Taylor, I'm right sorry for your loss," I said.

"She was gone six years ago. I don't mourn the loss of her leavin'. Leastways she was alive when she left. This I mourn." Rayburn pointed at the graves, then stepped into the wagon. "One minute a man has a family. The next he's got nothing but the shirt on his back."

Taylor was right. I pulled my shirt collar tight, grateful I still had Raney.

Rayburn looked spent. He rested his elbows on his knees. "I'm much obliged for what you did for my daughter. I ain't seen her in six years.

Didn't think I'd ever see her again, much less like this." He leaned against the wagon bench.

My heart ached for Taylor. When you lose a youngin, no matter their age, it just don't seem like the natural way of things.

"I'm sorry about June. Raney always tells me that the good Lord provides good amidst the terrible. Best I can say . . . the good for you is meetin' that sweet granddaughter."

He nodded but said nothing.

Clive spoke up. "Aughtie is a right sweet youngin. And she picks up on things real quick. She'll be a fine young lady one day."

"She reminds me of her momma. Bold. Fearless," Rayburn said.

And I could see he was right. Aughtie was both those things.

Through it all, nothin' really made much sense with the Bartons. They were twisted in every sort of way. Still, I hated it for Rayburn. Seeing his love for his girl told me it was right for Aughtie to go with him. That was all the confirmation we needed.

"Well, boys, Raney has some fresh coffee fixin'. My guess is there's scrambled eggs and biscuits and gravy, if Aughtie has a say in it."

Clive laughed. "The youngin loves her biscuits and gravy."

We headed back to the cabin, ole Rufus yanking the wagon over dirt clods and bouncing us like a rock rolling down a hill. Me and Clive joked a bit before I noticed his hand trembling.

"You alright?" I asked.

"Yea. I just get a little shaky from time to time. I guess it'll take a spell to get over it."

"I was scared you was gonna die, Clive."

"Me too. But lookee! Here I am." He busted out laughing.

"This whole thing was too easy. Tied up like a bow on a package," Rayburn said. "How lucky could we have all been to end the Bartons in one swift kick?"

"Well, that's just it, Taylor. Something didn't fit just right. I got a feelin' things is unfinished." Clive shifted in the back of the wagon.

I could tell he was pondering something. The wagon bumped, and he groaned.

Rayburn sat quiet for a bit, then butted in. "We all agree things ain't kosher. So whatta we do now? The Bartons is gone. What's next?"

"I reckon we make our way back to the mines. Raney said the pastor would come to help keep things calm, and the sheriff said he'd bring some men to help. Them miners need to know what's happened. We tell them the truth. No more lies. We tell them everything. From Ima skimming their pay to the emeralds. We. Make. Things. Right," I said.

"Lord, help us."

"There's only one solution I can see. It's like I said before—them men are like sheep. They need somebody to keep things in order." I wiggled in the seat, trying to find a comfortable position to catch a good breath. "Best I remember, you was a right good foreman when we worked the mines together. You might be the right choice."

Rayburn hauled off and spit. He rested his feet on the wagon footboard. "Aahh law."

"Think about it. Those men know you. They've trusted you, and they won't have forgotten your leading."

Clive leaned up and poked his head between us. "Joshua's right, Mr. Rayburn. Them miners do know you."

Rayburn cussed. "Them men is gonna wanna be paid. How do we do that?"

Clive jumped in. "I know. Ima showed me her safe. I saw where she kept the keys. She was right proud to show off all her cash when we were talking about me running for mayor."

"Mayor? Clive, we need to visit the sheriff and get you named as an administrator. Serve as an overseer in the mines. Ima ain't gonna see the light of day, and someone has to manage the store," I said.

"We head to the sheriff today and get him to go with us. Help us establish authority in the mines. Trick is beating the news to the top of the mountain." Rayburn smacked the reins.

The three of us come to an agreement. What we tore down in a matter of days, we'd start to rebuild overnight. The women wouldn't be happy that we'd be making our way back up the mountain injured, but we had no choice. This time they'd come along.

We pulled up to the house, and the smell of fried bacon wafted past my nose. My stomach growled.

"Come on, boys. Breakfast is ready." Raney waved us to the table. "Joshua, do us the pleasure and say grace."

I swallered hard. Praying these days was getting easier. I looked around the table and trusted the good Lord would listen to this liar now changed. All I could think to say was, "Lord, help us."

Rayburn sent one of Manny's boys to fetch the sheriff and the pastor, and it wasn't long before they sat on the porch holding Raney's fresh coffee in hand. The pastor and the sheriff heard us out as we told them about the plan to return to the mines. Between us all, we'd figured how to manage the miners.

"You'll need me along," the pastor said. "If they get outa hand, they might listen to a man of the cloth."

"Agreed," I said.

"Joshua, I'm gonna get a couple of the men I brought along to stay a few more days to watch over the homestead."

"Much obliged, Pastor." I tipped my hat.

Raney pressed her hands around my arm. "I ain't sure you're up for another trip up the mountain."

I kissed her forehead. "I'll be fine. Besides, you're coming too."

"What if them miners don't believe what's happened?"

"A body never knows what a man will believe. Besides, we got Clive. They know he's runnin' for mayor. They'll believe him. The pastor will be there." The words jabbed at my gut. Nobody knew better than me what a man could believe. Lord knew I'd been pretty convincing to the miners.

Raney stared at the floor.

I could tell she was thinking. "What's on your heart?"

"Aughtie. Are we doin' right by Aughtie?" A tear raised in her eye.

I knew we'd face this conversation at some point. There was no doubt I'd dreaded it too.

"Best I can see, Rayburn is the girl's only relative. He's a good man."

Raney took hold of my hands. "I don't know if I can say goodbye to her."

"It's gonna be hard, but you know it ain't right for us to keep her away from her papaw. Besides, I think she's gained two more grandparents."

"Lord have mercy, my heart feels like it's gonna rip outa my chest." Raney pulled my hands close.

"You'll see her, and Taylor's gonna need help with her when he's at work in the mines."

If Aughtie had done anything, she'd brought me and Raney back together. She'd helped a lost and angry man find peace and given him a chance at forgiveness. That put me back in the hands of the good Lord. I looked back from whence I'd come. From that day in the barn when my dead daughter saved my life, I could see how what I'd lost had been restored. The pastor said the good Lord was right good about forgivin' and then never remembering what bad we'd done. Reckon he knew I needed to forget.

We loaded up and headed down the lane. I was determined. The nightmare would end today.

Forty-Three

We stopped at June's grave so Aughtie could say her goodbyes. It seemed only right that the child see the graves of both her parents. Raney run her fingers gently over the youngin's shoulders.

Despite how my ribs hurt, I climbed off my horse and knelt in front of Aughtie. "If I was to give you somethin' real special, you reckon you could take good care of it and not lose it?"

A grin stretched across her face. "I tan, Mr. Josh."

"It's real important. Means the world to me and Miss Raney. But I think she'd want you to have it too."

Aughtie's deep-blue eyes searched my soul. She clasped her hands together and tapped her foot impatiently.

"You won't lose it?"

"Noooo!" She shook her head wildly from side to side.

I pushed my hand into my pocket and pulled out the coin I'd retrieved from the door facing in the tack shed.

Raney's hands covered her mouth, and she squinted out tears.

"Aughtie, this here is a coin given to me by my little girl."

Aughtie cocked her head and grinned. "Ann-wa."

My heart sank. The youngin listened more than we gave her credit. "That's right. Anna. She died."

"My papa hurt her like he hurt me?"

Raney dropped to her knees too. "Aughtie, sometimes things happen. Your daddy cared about you."

The sweet smile never left Aughtie's face. "Papa not luv me."

You could have blowed me over with a feather at the realization of just how Thomas had hoodwinked us all. Right that minute I felt cheated that

Clive was the one who took the shot at Thomas. How could Thomas want to hurt this child?

I put my arms around her and hugged her. “Open your hand.”

She rolled them pudgy fingers open, and I put the coin in her palm, then closed her hand into a fist. “Don’t lose it.”

Tears dropped off Raney’s cheeks.

“Aughtie, honey, what makes you so special?” I asked.

She laid her cheek against mine. “I sor-give.”

In two words a weak-minded youngin taught me the lesson of a lifetime. What made her so special was forgiveness. I looked around, and Cleda Mae stood in disbelief, her hands over her mouth. She slipped her arm through Clive’s and rested her head on his shoulder.

“You do forgive, don’t you? Ole Josh has a lot to learn from such a smart youngin.” I pressed my finger against her nose. “Now, go hug your papaw. You’re gonna stay with him.”

Aughtie grabbed Taylor’s hand. “Papawww Rayyy.”

Rayburn leaned toward her and patted her back.

“Good land!” Clive said. “It ain’t like we ain’t comin’ home. Let’s get goin’.”

My chest ached to let that little girl go, but Aughtie’s wisdom and tenderness made it easier.

We headed up the mountain.

It took us a few hours to get up the mountain. The miners was already in and out of the mines, loading coal to take down to the train. News had not reached the mines about Ima. It seemed the good Lord was merciful.

“Taylor, you ready to be a shepherd?” I asked.

He hauled off and spit. Clive pulled the wagon to a halt, and Rayburn stood up on the bench. “I’m getting too old for this, but I reckon I can take ’em.”

I put my fingers in my mouth and whistled right loud to catch their attention.

“Rest them mules, boys. Meetin’ up at the store. Stop your work,” Rayburn hollered.

There was a long silence, and I wondered if they'd pay Rayburn any attention.

But he whistled right loud and squalled again, "Let's go! Now!"

The men went to waving to acknowledge him.

"Pass it round, boys. Get everybody up to the store. Stop everything. Every miner needs to be at the store. Important business." Rayburn climbed down and took his horse by the reins. "I'll walk from here. Reckon I can still manage." He nodded.

In that instant I saw Taylor push his hurt and loss behind him. It's the way of the mountain. Things happen. We muddle through, then move ahead. He'd been gone from the mines for a while, but when he stepped down from that wagon, he meant business and he'd moved on.

It felt right for Rayburn to run the mines. He was always a tough cuss, honest but fair. It was a matter of convincin' the miners.

We made our way slowly to the store. Rayburn gathered the men as we went.

"Clive, you sure you know how to get into Ima's safe? Them men need to be paid in cash today."

"Lordy mercy. Ima couldn't pass up the chance to brag about her money. I know where the keys and ledgers are."

My stomach was in knots. These last few months had taken their toll. I'd gone from bein' eat up with guilt to seekin' out the courage to tell the truth. We halted the horses in front of the store and climbed down from the wagon. All of us come together on the porch.

"Pastor, you best be praying for us." Clive limped toward the screen door.

"What about Ima's thugs?" the pastor asked.

"That's our job." The sheriff motioned his men over.

"I don't figure they're gonna be a problem, especially when Rayburn tells them they're getting paid," I said.

Me and Clive inched into the store. No lanterns were lit, and no sign of Ima's henchmen. I run my fingers over the fireplace and found the two flints. I lit the lanterns and opened up the shutters. A yellow glow filled the room, and the sunshine warmed things. It seemed what I'd said to Thomas ended up being the truth here. *A new start.* I eyed the shelves of goods. Flour, sugar, fabric. Ima had it all. She shorted the food, then charged the miners twice its worth. It would be wonderful seeing the women on the mountain come to the store and buy goods fairly.

"Joshua, come here," Clive said. "You need to see this."

Clive pushed open the door to a room. There was more money in that room than I'd seen in a lifetime. I'd figured Ima would have the good sense to have a safe, so it made sense now, seeing as the keys she held so tight to was for this room. It seemed right cocky to me, but then when a body didn't think the rules applied to them, there ain't no need for safes.

"Look at this," Clive said.

I walked to Ima's desk, where Clive had unrolled a leather holder. Inside was strings with wedding bands tied to them.

"Mercy me, she never thought nothing about takin a man's wedding band."

"Ima never thought about nothing but herself," Clive said. "Look a here." He pulled a small pouch open and dumped the contents on the table. Two small emerald slivers dropped onto the leather holder. "This belongs to you."

"Ain't mine. I paid my debt. Belongs to the store . . ." I glanced out the window. "It belongs to them."

It took us a spell to get Ima's ledgers laid out on the counter. Rayburn and the sheriff explained to the miners about Thomas and Angus. And when they told them Ima was in jail, a loud cheer went up. The sheriff laid out how things would run. Rayburn would run the mines. Clive and Cleda Mae would manage the store and pay. The judge named Clive the administrator, and though the mines still belonged to Ima on paper, she'd never be free from jail until she died. By birthright, the mines now belonged to Aughtie, but Clive would manage things. A group of men would be chosen to start repairs on the cabins in the mine camps so that everyone had good places to live. The mines would close until things was cleaned up and folks could live decent. They'd keep gettin' paid. Once things was in order, the mines would continue, and men would be paid fairly, by the hour and in cash.

You would have thought Clive had already been named mayor by the cheers.

Clive decided to pay each miner according to the years he'd worked and then add some. He and Rayburn would work together to set a fair wage for the men as time passed. For now, them miners needed money.

Outside you could hear cheers keep risin' up as Rayburn welcomed them to a new way. When the pastor opened the door for the first miner to walk in, it sounded like a thunderstorm of hollerin'.

Rayburn stood at the door with the first miner. "Joshua, this here is Ellis Johnson. He's been minin' for ten years." Rayburn took Ellis's hand and shook it. "Thanks for your hard work."

Clive motioned Ellis over. He run his finger through Ima's ledger, verified the years he'd worked, and counted out his money. Finally, Clive checked the ledger for a ring. "I see Ima took your weddin' band." Clive counted down the string and removed a wedding band with a string and paper tied to it. *Ellis Johnson.* He broke the string and laid the ring in Johnson's hand.

"We're paying you in cash." Clive counted several bills in his hand. "Every payday you'll get cash you can spend anywhere."

Ellis stood stunned. "Cash? Real money?"

"Yes, sir. Now see Joshua about your debt to the Company Store."

Ellis walked over to me and laid the cash on the ledger. "I reckon I'll owe it all." His voice quivered.

I pushed the money back toward him. "Put that in your pocket. That's yours. And here's your name in the debt ledger. *Ellis Johnson.* That's you, right?"

Ellis nodded.

"Put your mark next to your name."

Ellis took the pencil and scratched an *X* next to his name. I took the pencil and touching the lead to my tongue, then to the paper, I wrote P-A-I-D. "Paid. That work for you?"

The man stood speechless for a minute before he choked out a few words. A body would have thought the good Lord healed him of an illness. "Paid?"

"Yes, sir. Paid in full."

Ellis stood staring. He didn't know what to make of the debt bein' erased. It reminded me of the pastor's sermon about one man payin' a debt for everyone. Debt free.

"Take your money and go home today. Rest. We're closin' work on the mines for the next month. Show up this time next month and be ready to dig black gold."

Ellis slowly wadded the money into his soot-covered hands. He let out a whoop, then grabbed me by the arm and shook it. It felt like all those broke ribs I had, crumbled.

"Thank you. Much obliged." Tears clouded his eyes, and the look of freedom shined through.

I looked at Clive and Rayburn. "This is what forgiveness feels like."

Rayburn gave vouchers to every miner to help them get lumber to shore up their homes. This was a time of celebration. The miners and their families deserved a rest. And so it went on all afternoon until every miner was paid and every debt marked off. I never imagined this day would come. The day we took over the Company Store. I'd never felt such peace.

It didn't come down the way we expected, but it came down right.

All them lies I'd told myself through the years was redeemed. I reckon the good Lord felt I was worth forgivin'—that there might be hope for me yet. Now, if the good Lord would have me, I'd do my best to be a better man.

We sat on the porch after all the miners were paid and listened to the screams of disbelieving wives and the shouts of hardworking men. It was a sweet music. The sun eased between the holler, and a soft breeze cleared out the Bartons' nastiness.

Just as the last of the sunset glowed over the trees, the sheriff rode up. "Gentlemen." He tipped his hat.

"Sheriff." The pastor returned the pleasure.

"Looks like you boys did a right good thing here." The sheriff crossed his arms and smiled.

Clive stood. "We made things right, Sheriff. And you put a murderer behind bars. I'd reckon that could be called a good thing."

I felt my skin crawl as the sheriff climbed off his horse. "Sheriff, Ima ain't got you in her pocket, does she?"

He hesitated before he answered. "Don't reckon. We'll be checking in on you boys to be sure them mines is running fair."

"Sheriff, one last question." I moved closer to his horse. "What about Ima's portion of this wealth? Shouldn't we leave a small stash for her?"

The sheriff slapped his leg and roared. "Get a little box and put a lump of coal in it. Mark her name on it. That oughta do her. She don't need wealth where she's going."

I took his hand and shook. The sheriff mounted his horse and tipped his hat. As I watched him and his men ride down the path, I felt like we'd done some good. Anna might be right proud of her papa.

A raven soared overhead. His caw echoed across the mountain. If I believed what the granny women said, that crow was a bad omen. I swallowed hard. Things looked good. They wasn't perfect, but they was good. All we could do was trust there wasn't a lie waitin' to be uncovered.

Epilogue

Three Years Later—Barton Mountain, 1902

I STOOD AT the edge of the mountain pass, staring across a deep-blue sky dotted with wisps of white. A flock of ducks caught the high mountain breeze and soared over the peaks. It was a surprise this mountain would ever find peace, much less rest in the midst of hard work, but we had.

With the Bartons gone, the mountain seemed to take in a breath and exhale a sigh of relief. Mother Nature herself began to show us mercy. The better we was to her, the more generous she was to us. Raney come over the ridge, Aughtie in tow. They'd been buyin' a few necessities at the Company Store.

"Ain't you growin'? You're almost as tall as Miss Raney."

Aughtie giggled.

Raney reached up and kissed my cheek. "What ya staring at?"

"The valley. I come here to listen to the mountain speak. She does have a peaceful voice, doesn't she?"

"She?" Raney asked.

"Mother Nature." I nodded.

"Come look." I eased Raney and Aughtie to the edge of the ridge and pointed. "There. That's the homestead. You see the cabin?"

"Oh look, Aughtie. You see the cabin?"

Aughtie went to clapping.

"I should come to this peak more often. It's beautiful. Peaceful." Raney slipped her arms around my waist.

"Sun's going down. You should head back to the store. Rayburn will be there. Aughtie can ride home with him." I kissed Aughtie and tickled her chin. "Walk faster, young lady. Papaw is waitin' at the store."

Raney rested her hand on my cheek. "Don't be too long." She took Aughtie's hand and headed down the path to the store.

I turned and looked over the mountains that rolled through the clouds. Livin' here was a little like livin' in heaven. As the sun gently disappeared over the far mountain, it left me with shades of orange, lavender, and wisps of pink. I'd lost a lot over the last few years. The good Lord never promised us easy, and there's always a consequence for sin, but when we do right by Him, He does right by us. I reckon He'd given me a second chance, and I was doin' my best to make it count.

My consequence was I'd never have my girl back, but I'd found my wife. Our family would always miss Anna, but we'd gained Taylor, Aughtie, Clive, Cleda Mae, and her baby on the way. It wasn't perfect, but it was close.

My eyes closed, and I took in a good breath. These people had been through a lot, but we worked together to make things as right as could be. Hettie and Merrylin would never have their men back. Rayburn would never have his daughter again. A consequence.

Three years back Clive and Rayburn hadn't stopped until they'd talked to every miner and made things right that day. I gathered a group of men to make repairs on cabins. Ima proved she didn't care for those who made her rich just by the camps where miners lived. Clive and Rayburn managed to get the railroad to work their tracks up the mountain—something that changed the mountain forever.

Me and Raney remained in the valley for the most part. We took in widows and invited some of the men to help till and harvest the rye, then we bartered with one another. Clive and Cleda Mae moved up to the store to make sure folks had what they needed. And there was no debt ledger. Clive kept fair books, and Cleda Mae kept the store stocked fairly. The miners paid for what they needed with money.

The hardest thing was giving Aughtie to her papaw. Taylor Rayburn was a good man, and he wanted to raise Aughtie. He took a small spread on the homestead and made him and Aughtie a home. Rayburn would bring her to Raney while he worked the mines and get her when he was done. Though we didn't have her as our own, we could love her.

I reckon the consequence for all my lies was living without Anna. When Rayburn would take Aughtie, there was times me and Raney both shed a tear or two. But we was blessed to be a small part of her life.

I walked to the store just as the sun closed its eyes, and there on the porch was Rayburn and Aughtie.

"I figured you'd be on the train home by now. 'Bout your bedtime, ain't it?"

Aughtie shined them pretty teeth at me.

"Ahhh, she wouldn't go till you got back. Said she had something for you." Rayburn nudged Aughtie toward me. "Go on—give it to him."

Aughtie extended her hands, and in them was her tiny leather bag. "For youuu, Mr. Josh."

I kneeled and took the bag.

"Open later," she squawked, and she took Rayburn's hand. "Wet's go, Papawww Ray."

He shook his head and headed for the train. Raney pressed her fingers against her lips and blew Aughtie a kiss. We watched until the darkness closed in around them. Once we were satisfied things were good, we'd catch the last train down the mountain.

Raney had stew simmerin' and hot coffee, so we sat down to eat. I offered grace, and as Raney poured the stew into my bowl, I untied the string from the bag and dumped the contents on the table. Raney took in a gasp, and I felt the tears rise. That coin of Anna's rolled and spun, then stopped at my fingers.

I don't know if the good Lord allows Anna to sneak down to us from time to time, but He never lets us forget.

There always is hope. Ain't there?

Author's Note

It was important to me to write a novel that included mentally challenged children. Society looks at these children and often turns a blind eye. As a parent of a son with a mental disability, I know it to be true that individuals can be less than kind. My desire, by adding Aughtie into this story, is to show that just because there is a physical or mental issue doesn't mean these children are incapable of being wonderfully productive adults. Or that they are unable to learn, work, and make decisions.

I encourage you to take time, when you meet a child or adult with disabilities, to get to know them. God gifts these children and adults with an incredible ability to love unconditionally. Their eyes see a gentle and unjudging side of people that most of us "abled" folks ignore. In knowing them, you will learn what true compassion means.

This novel is meant to honor those individuals who walk through life on that different path.

One final thought. It was once said to me by a child of nine, "God wouldn't have given that boy to anyone else because He knew your shoulders were wide enough to carry the weight." That remark changed my life. In this world, there is room for everyone.

In these children, there is a fire and a hunger for life—one we all need to taste.

Cindy K. Sproles

Acknowledgments

My gratitude and thanks begin with the folks at Kregel Publications. They loved me, helped me, and prayed with me. I am grateful to Janyre Tromp and her team of editors who have worked tirelessly and given their best to make this work happen. To Dori Harrell, an amazing editor who "gets" Appalachian and from whom I've learned so much due to her edits. Thank you, Dori.

To my agent, Bob Hostetler, for his kindness and work to make me a successful author. I am grateful. Not only does he make me laugh, encourage me, and challenge me, but he prays fervently for me. Thank you, Bob.

To my friends Lori Marett and Larry Leech, whose input on this book was greatly appreciated. Your time and guidance is valued.

To my husband, Tim, lovingly referred to as the Prince, who stands behind me, supporting me fully, and to my sons and their wives, who encourage me continually. But also, to Chase, my firstborn, who has taught me what it means to overcome and who has shown me what true love, forgiveness, and kindness mean. You are the epitome of an overcomer.

Thank you to my friends who support me on a daily basis, encourage me, and believe in me, and to those readers who faithfully follow my work. I am grateful.

And in the most honored place, the God who is the master of creativity. Oh God, You have blessed me. Gifted me and heard my requests as an aspiring writer to allow me the gift of writing. I offer You my praise and thanksgiving. May it be a glory to You, oh Lord.